The Single Undead Moms Club

MOLLY HARPER

Pocket Books

New York   London   Toronto   Sydney   New Delhi

Pocket Books
An Imprint of Simon & Schuster, Inc.
1230 Avenue of the Americas
New York, NY 10020

This book is a work of fiction. Any references to historical
events, real people, or real places are used fictitiously. Other
names, characters, places, and events are products of the author's
imagination, and any resemblance to actual events or places or
persons, living or dead, is entirely coincidental.

First Pocket Books paperback edition November 2015

POCKET and colophon are registered trademarks of
Simon & Schuster, Inc.

For information about special discounts for bulk purchases,
please contact Simon & Schuster Special Sales at 1-866-506-1949
or business@simonandschuster.com.

The Simon & Schuster Speakers Bureau can bring authors to
your live event. For more information or to book an event,
contact the Simon & Schuster Speakers Bureau at 1-866-248-3049
or visit our website at www.simonspeakers.com.

Interior design by Leydiana Rodríguez

Manufactured in the United States of America

10 9 8 7 6 5 4 3 2 1

ISBN 978-1-4767-9439-6
ISBN 978-1-4767-9443-3 (ebook)

For Carter and Darcy,
for every time someone asked me when I was
going to write a book about my hilarious kids.

Acknowledgments

As usual, I couldn't get through writing a manuscript without the support of my loving family and ever-patient editorial support. Many thanks to my partner in snark, Jeanette Battista, who held my hand through early-chapter freak-outs. Thank you to Stephany Evans and Abby Zidle, for letting me try something a little outside of my norm.

Thank you to Darcy and Carter for being an inspiration for brilliantly sarcastic children everywhere. Some people may not understand where you learned to talk like that, but I know that you're everything Yaya said I deserve and more. To Judy Harper, who taught me everything I know about fierce motherhood and snarking your way through back-to-school nights. (Just once, she would have loved to hear *Molly's a joy to have in class* without it being followed by *but . . .*) To the employees and my fellow parent-teacher organization members at my kids' school, who are absolutely nothing like the people described herein, thank you for your understanding and patience. To my mother-in-law, Nancy, and my father-in-law, Russell, who are nothing like Libby's in-laws. Basically, ninety percent of the people in my life are pretty nice.

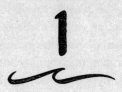

Becoming a vampire parent is like going through the infant phase with your firstborn all over again. You will be just as unsure of yourself, just as frightened. And at some point, someone will probably throw up on you when you least expect it.

—*My Mommy Has Fangs: A Guide to Post-Vampiric Parenting*

If you have your choice about how to be turned into a vampire, I strongly suggest that you do not post an ad on the supernatural version of Craigslist offering cash to any creature of the night willing to bite you.

I swear, I had my reasons. Really good ones.

Still, waking up in a paper-thin balsa-wood coffin three feet below the surface of the Half-Moon Hollow Little League Field wasn't exactly the result of a solid plan.

I remember my very first moment as a vampire with shocking clarity. I was dead, without thought or breath or being, and then, suddenly, I wasn't. Or I *was*, if you have more philosophical leanings.

And in that first moment of existential limbo, I panicked, thrashing out, crying as my knees and elbows smacked against the wooden walls. I was trapped. I could feel the weight of the earth pressing down on the lid of the coffin, pinning me in, separating me from the world—separating me from my son. I sucked in air by the mouthful, hyperventilating. What if I couldn't break through to the surface? What if I got stuck down here? I forced myself to suck in a deep breath and hold it, to make the most of what air I had in this little box.

Nothing. No distress. No pressure against my throat or lungs. No need to draw another breath. Because I didn't need to breathe. I was a freaking vampire. The undead. Nosferatu. A nightwalker. The other members of the PTA were going to be shocked. And then scandalized. And then shocked again.

I'd dreamed of this moment for months, ever since I'd come up with my insane "transition" plan. And yet it was so close to my very worst nightmare, taking the literal dirt nap, that I was almost afraid to move. What if I'd miscalculated? What if it was safer for Danny if I stayed here underground? What if, after all my scheming and planning, it was better if I was dead?

It would be easy enough for people to believe. Everybody in Half-Moon Hollow knew about poor Libby Stratton, suburban Half-Moon Hollow's cautionary tale of twisted probability. In two years, I'd gone from softball widow and mother of a busy toddler to actual widow and cancer patient.

Six months after losing my husband, Rob, in a car accident, I started feeling nauseated and dizzy at random. I woke up in the middle of the night drenched in sweat. I bruised easily and fell asleep before I could even give Danny his bath in the evenings. I thought it was stress—I'd just lost my husband, after all. There were bound to be physiological repercussions.

When my doctor said the words "acute lymphocytic leukemia," I kept expecting her to follow it with "just kidding." I kept expecting there to be a second test that said it was just anemia or fibromyalgia or something. But the doctor was not kidding, and I was not lucky enough to be dangerously anemic.

At the ripe old age of thirty, I was dying of cancer. My blood was turning on itself. For months, I went through a constantly shifting combination of chemo, radiation therapy, and drug cocktails as the doctors tried to figure out my atypically belligerent case. (Frankly, I was surprised my vampire sire could tolerate more than a few swallows of my toxic plasma.) All while I watched my mother-in-law, Marge, take over my role as mother to Danny. I was too wiped out for bedtime stories and Sunday-morning waffles. I wasn't strong enough to walk up the bleachers at his T-ball games. I was like a ghost, watching my life go on without me.

And a few months before my underground nap, Dr. Channing informed me that nothing we'd done had made a dent in my insistent little cancer cells. Nothing. And my chances of making a dent were not great. Dr. Channing very gently suggested I might want to think about long-term plans for my son.

For a long, awkward moment, I just stared at my oncologist, dumbfounded. What mother didn't have long-term plans for her children? What mother doesn't secretly squirrel away money in college funds and mentally budget for teenage orthodontics? And then I realized Dr. Channing was referring to plans for who would raise Danny after I was gone.

How could I make plans for someone else to raise my baby? My sweet Danny, my funny almost-six-year-old towhead with my eyes, his father's stubborn little chin, and the permanent expression of someone building castles in his head. He was already an incurable smartass and an amateur cryptozoologist. You never knew what was going to come out of his mouth, but when you heard it, you'd have to bite your lip to keep from laughing while you reminded him about showing respect for adults. He had the weirdest habit of picking up on the most uncomfortable aspect of any conversation and asking about it. And I wouldn't have changed a thing about him. He was creative and loud and quirky, and I adored him completely.

I knew it seemed selfish to go to such extreme measures to stay with him when Danny's grandparents were more than willing to take him in after I passed. Hell, they were already setting up a bedroom for Danny in their house. I trusted Marge, for the most part. She was a pain in my ass on occasion, but she loved "her boys" unconditionally. Under the pestering and fretting, there was an undeniable element of affection. Les, on the other hand, was the primary reason for my seeking out a vampire's help.

Les had raised Rob to be the epitome of a man's man—sports, hunting, never expressing a serious emotion, you get the idea. With Rob gone, Les seemed to think he could start over with Danny. I could see the gleam in my father-in-law's eyes when he watched Danny play. He saw my son as a clean slate on which he could rewrite Rob's life, instead of a bright, imaginative kid with a personality all his own, who was far more interested in telling pretend epic adventures with his LEGO people than hunting or fishing. If Danny lived with his grandparents, Les would have spent Danny's childhood systematically reprogramming my son until he was a mini-Rob.

The idea of letting go before Danny was grown up, of not seeing him graduate from high school, greet his bride at the altar, welcome his own children into the world, was simply not acceptable. And yes, for purely selfish reasons, I wasn't ready to die. The thought of passing into the unknown, of no longer existing, terrified me. So I made a desperate choice. More time, at any cost.

Once the idea was born, it took an alarmingly short time to make the arrangements. I found a willing vampire online, arranged payment, and within weeks, my anonymous sire told me where to meet him. I'd arranged to be buried, so I'd be tucked out of the way, far from prying motel maids or innocent bystanders who didn't deserve to be munched on by a semicomatose newborn vampire. I'd heard of people being turned into vampires for more ridiculous reasons—bad debts, vanity, trying to avoid jury duty. And I knew that I'd gone about it in a sneaky, underhanded manner. But I promised myself it would be worth it if it meant I got to stay with my son.

Lying in my coffin, I took another unnecessary

breath, forcing myself to focus. I closed my eyes, flexing my fingers. I could feel. I felt every cell in my hand, every nerve firing as my fingers bent and stretched. I had to do this. I *would* do this. I'd survived the meds, the treatments, the failure of both. I could learn to live as a vampire. I could learn control. I could be strong. And that all started with throwing one damned punch. I could do this.

Breathing deep, I clenched my fist and shoved it with all of my might through the flimsy wood surface and into the claylike earth above.

"Owwww!" I yelled, shaking my stinging knuckles.

Apparently, vampires had the exact same ability to feel pain as humans.

Ow.

I braced myself for another swing. The coffin lid splintered away, dirt sprinkling down onto my face like confetti from hell. I sputtered as clumps of dirt clogged my nose and mouth. I shoved my other hand up through the cheap coffin lid and tried to make a hole big enough to allow me to sit up. There was no room for me to maneuver. How did vampires who woke up in real coffins handle this?

But I was thirsty, so thirsty that the idea of spending one more minute without drinking was enough to make me thrust my arm through the earth above my head and stretch until I reached the surface. I threw up an arm, smashing at the lid with my fist, sputtering dirt.

Air. Sweet, warm night air, fragrant with fresh-cut grass. I didn't need to breathe it, but that didn't mean I didn't appreciate the sudden influx of oxygen into the little tunnel I'd clawed. I didn't hear anyone above-ground, which meant I'd timed my rising just about right. Everyone had left the ball field for the night, which was good, because I did not want to emerge from the mud like a cicada, only to realize I was being watched by a bunch of Little Leaguers. That was the sort of thing that got around the beauty-parlor circuit.

Grunting, I punched up with the other fist, leveling my shoulders against the falling dirt and sitting up. It took a few tries, but eventually, my head broke through the surface.

I forced myself to push up on shaking legs and crawl to solid ground. I coughed, spitting out the grave dirt and wiping at my eyes. I flopped onto my back, the damp blades of bluegrass tickling my skin.

"Ugh, that was like childbirth, only in reverse." I groaned, wiping at my mouth with the sleeve of my shirt.

I opened my eyes to a brand-new world. Brilliant stars in a beautiful mess of constellation patterns I'd never been able to make out before sparkled against a black velvet sky. I could make out every bump and pore on the man in the moon. I could hear every cricket's chirp, the motor of every car within a mile radius. The chemical garbage smell of the concession stand, sickly sweet soda syrup and greasy hot dog water, was so strong I gagged. That would be a downside I would worry about later.

And still, I was dying of thirst. My online sire had agreed to leave me in a shallow grave with synthetic blood waiting in a Coleman cooler by the nearby

Marchand Memorial Fountain. The blood-drinking aspect of vampirism had been the main obstacle in talking myself into this whole plan. I didn't want to feed off people, period. The very idea of drinking directly from the source made me a little ill. I would become the vampire version of a vegan: bottled synthetic only, thank you very much.

I hopped to my feet, thrilling at the ease with which I was able to spring up from the ground. After months of having little to no energy, hobbling around like an old woman, it was a lovely change of pace.

"It will take a couple of days to get used to that."

At the sound of the strange feminine voice, I dropped into a defensive stance. A sharp sensation ripped through my mouth, making me wince even as I bared my new fangs and hissed like an angry cat.

Ow. Badass, but ow.

Near the tree line stood a brunette in a pretty purple print dress and a rakish-looking man in faded jeans and a T-shirt that read "What Happens in Possum Trot Stays in Possum Trot."

The brunette looked vaguely familiar, but my brain was running too fast for me to recognize my own mother, much less a passing acquaintance. They were both pale, with dark circles under their eyes, and considering that it was eleven-thirty on a Tuesday night and they were strolling around all casual-like in a remote, badly lit location, I could only conclude that they were also vampires.

The brunette smiled, strolling over to shake my hand, while the man lingered near the trees. The woman handed me a warm bottle of Faux Type O, Extra Iron. "I'm Jane Jameson-Nightengale, representative of the local office of the World Council for the Equal Treatment of the Undead. I was a couple of years ahead of you at Half-Moon Hollow High, so you probably don't remember me. And this is my associate, Dick Cheney, also a Council representative."

The man offered me an awkward little wave. I nodded, tamping down the instinctual zip of panic up my spine. I'd known that at some point, I was probably going to attract the wrath of the Council, the governing body for vampires since they'd burst from the coffin a decade or so before. In the early days, when humans were lashing out against the existence of creatures that had existed under our collective nose for centuries without posing a direct threat to us, the Council stood as a protective force against the people who were staking and burning vampires by the dozens. Now they kept vampires in line by any means necessary. And despite the fact that I remembered Jane as the nice girl who used to tutor kids in my grade in literature and now owned a funky occult bookshop downtown, I doubted my first meeting with them was going to involve a Welcome Wagon basket.

But surely they would understand, right? I could make them understand, if I just explained about being sick and my son and—

Wait a second.

"I'm sorry, did you say Dick Cheney?" I asked, my words muddled by my fangs. I drew my bottom lip across the sharp edge of my left canine. My mouth filled with the coppery tang of my own blood, and I hissed. "Ouch. How do you make these things go back in?"

"Just give it a minute," Jane said, nodding toward the bottle. "The blood will help. And yes, I did say Dick Cheney. You can hear Dick's tragic name-related backstory some other time. Because right now, you are in a pant-load of trouble, sweetie."

"How so?" I asked, my voice the very bell-like tone of innocence. Hoping to quell the burning in my throat, I took a long, deep pull from the bottle of Faux Type O. It was . . . not terrible. Sort of saccharine, like diet soda. You knew you weren't getting the real thing, but it slaked your thirst temporarily. I could live on this, I supposed. I could drink fake blood every day if it meant I could be with Danny.

"Dumb is not your color, Mrs. Stratton," the unfortunately named Dick Cheney chided. He was a handsome man, in a sly, can't-take-me-home-to-Mama kind of way. His expression was guilty, somehow, and apologetic. And given his choice of outfits, I got the impression he didn't take his position on the Council too seriously. How had someone like him been appointed to oversee all vampire dealings in western Kentucky?

"Please don't call me that." I sighed. "Please call me Libby."

"Libby, then," he said, his tone gentle. "Would you care to explain to us why you thought it was a good idea to advertise online for a 'sire for hire,' agree to meet a complete stranger at the Lucky Clover Motel, and let him turn you and bury you in a public park?"

I grimaced, feeling grateful that Dick had omitted the details. Thanks to the magic of modern pharmaceuticals, the mechanics of being turned were a little hazy for me. And yes, I did see now that this was a tactical error in terms of personal safety.

"We know about your illness, Libby," Jane added. "Even if we hadn't run a background check on you, you've been on my mama's church prayer list for months. Plus, I've been reading your unusually loud thoughts for the last couple of minutes, and your story checks out, along with your not awesome but not megalomaniacal intentions."

I turned to Dick. "She read my mind?"

He shrugged. "It's a thing. Try not to picture people naked around her."

Jane ignored us both. "Look, it's not that I don't sympathize. I do. But there's a reason we don't do bite-for-hire transactions. Money takes the deliberation out of the equation. It's the equivalent of undead prostitution, which is a creepy thing even to say, much less do." She looked to her companion, who had stayed silent during this diatribe. "A little help here?"

Dick shrugged and actually patted me on top of the head. "I can't fuss at her. Look at her. She's all brand-new and scared, like a little vampire kitten with big, sad cartoon eyes. Don't you just want to hug her?"

"That's sweet, but please don't hug me," I told him, shaking my head.

"Don't hug her." Jane sighed. "Dick, we're supposed to be chastising her or giving her stern guidance or something. Stern guidance does not involve hugs."

Dick mumbled something about "feeling sorry for Jamie."

"So what was your plan?" Jane asked. "You get bitten, and a couple of days later, you let your son walk into your house to be alone all day, waiting for you to wake up? No preparation, just pray you can keep your thirst under control?"

"I had a plan," I insisted. "Danny's on a camping trip with his grandparents until Sunday, an end-of-the-summer thing before he starts school. I told my in-laws I needed time to recover after a treatment, which they were more than willing to believe. And since they told me they would have him home by four, that means I have until at least eight-thirty before they drop him off, because they're always late bringing him back. I figured I would have some time to get over the bloodthirst before he comes home. I have a babysitter all lined up to stay with Danny during the day while I'm asleep. I've already set up a contract with Beeline to deliver blood to my house starting this week. I took a calculated risk."

Jane harrumphed as if she was not all that impressed with my plans and/or backup plans. "If this was the result of your calculations, you suck at math."

"OK, so it was a crappy plan, but I was frantic. I'm sorry. And don't be too hard on my sire, whoever he may be," I added reluctantly. "He lived up to his end of the deal, at least. And he didn't hurt me. He shouldn't suffer because he helped me. Besides, I'm not really sure how to contact him."

"Oh, trust me, I've spoken to your sire. And he's not going to contact you, period. If his judgment is this piss-poor, he doesn't have the right to guide you through your transition."

"I really hadn't planned on contacting him anyway."

"You say that because you don't really understand the sire-childe relationship," Dick told me, sounding more severe than he had during this whole disaster of a conversation. "You're going to need guidance. And if your sire was anywhere around, you would instinctually look to him."

"Even if he is an enormous asshat," Jane added.

This made me smile, for some perverse reason. But given the irritated expression on Dick's otherwise winsome face, I decided to ignore that and resolve the issues I could handle at the moment.

"So what happens now? Are you going to turn me in to CPS?" I asked. "Report me for potentially exposing my son to inappropriate displays of vampirism?"

"And set back vampire parents' rights ten years because you took the half-assed route to being undead?" Jane said. "No, thanks. The courts are just now getting to the point where they give vampire parents fair consideration in custody cases. If you screw this up—if your story gets out about how you paid some random vamp to turn you so you could keep your son and you end up hurting him, or if you screw up and your in-laws, who as I understand it are already preparing for Danny to live with them full-time, end up taking custody of him anyway—it will be a public-relations nightmare I don't even want to think about."

If I'd been capable of blushing, my cheeks would have flushed with guilt. I hadn't thought of the effects my actions would have on other vampire parents. I would be the first to admit that I'd had tunnel vision, only concerned about myself, my son. I forgot how quickly the media hopped on sensational stories about vampires behaving badly, anything to recapture the initial panic of the Great Coming Out. The idea that my actions might result in some other mother losing her children made my stomach twist with guilt.

"I'm sorry. I didn't want to cause trouble for anyone else. I'll admit that I was shortsighted. I apologize for that," I said carefully. "And I know that a sincere apology is not followed by a 'but,' but I was desperate, and this seemed like the only option."

"Well, you apologized," Dick said drily. "Which puts you ahead of about fifty percent of our population."

"What does this mean for me? A fine? Vampire jail?"

"No. We are going to take a very *personal* interest in your transition, Libby," Jane said brightly. "You are going to go through Council bloodthirst boot camp. You will prove that you are in complete control of your thirst. And after that, we will monitor you every second until we are convinced that you will not cause a huge embarrassing news cycle for vampires everywhere. And then we will back off and let you live your unlife in a reasonably unsupervised fashion."

"Sounds fair," I conceded.

"I still kind of want to hug you," Dick told me, patting my head again.

"You seem nice, but—" I shook my head. "Resist the urge."

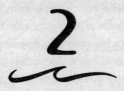

With your new nocturnal hours, two A.M. feedings won't seem like such a burden. Morning carpool, however, will remain just as dangerous.

—*My Mommy Has Fangs: A Guide to Post-Vampiric Parenting*

I didn't expect to just wake up, hop out of my coffin, and walk back into my life. I knew there was going to be an adjustment period. Still, it felt very weird to walk up my own dark front-porch steps, without any need of a light, to an empty house.

Even with Rob gone, the house had always been filled with noise and color. Danny, a classic only child, always managed to keep himself entertained, singing his original silly songs (usually set to "Old MacDonald") and staging broad-scale action-figure battles that spread to several rooms of the house. But now the windows were dark and quiet. There was no bellowing cry of "MOM!" followed by the patter of sneaker-clad feet as I walked through the door.

I dropped my keys onto the little foyer table I'd refurbished years before when Rob's parents built the house for us. As soon as Les and Marge heard that their son was thinking of proposing, they had built this sensible three-bedroom ranch on the edge of their property, claiming it was a good investment. I supposed it might have been profitable if they'd planned on renting it to someone, but they hadn't. Rob just moved in a month before the wedding, no discussion, no debate. He started moving our wedding gifts into the new house. And who was I to argue with it? What kind of idiot turns down a new home? That I didn't get to choose the fixtures or décor for . . . because Marge decorated it just like her house . . . so Rob wouldn't have to feel like he'd left his childhood home. Hindsight would come back to bite me on the ass much later on that one.

Bit by bit, I'd reclaimed the house over the years, "losing" a dried flower arrangement here, dropping/destroying a porcelain angel figurine there. I blamed Danny for several of the angel figurines when Marge asked about them, which might have affected me, karmically speaking. Now it was a comfortable, if slightly shabby-chic, little country house. The sturdy, denim-covered, Danny-proof living-room furniture was centered around a big faux-stone fireplace with a gas flame. The adjacent bookshelves were covered in my paperbacks and framed family photos, mostly of Danny with me and his grandparents. My word-of-the-day calendar sat next to my laptop on the old whitewashed rustic dining-room table I used as a desk. An old blue-and-yellow patchwork quilt I'd purchased at an estate sale was thrown over the back of a cane rocker in the corner. Danny's trucks lay abandoned on the blue rag rug that protected our hardwood laminate floors.

With my new vampire vision, I could see the thin layer of dust on the mantel, the lint bunnies under the couch. My housekeeping skills, which had never been *Better Homes and Gardens* level, had definitely fallen by the wayside since I'd gotten sick. Marge had tried, well, *insisted on* helping out at first, but it had made me so uncomfortable, her clucking her tongue as she helped "organize" my Tupperware cabinet, my closet, my *mail*, that I eventually told her I was back up to dusting my own baseboards.

It was a lie, but it bought me peace of mind.

I opened the front closet and saw that the packing boxes I'd put there a few days ago were still neatly stacked under our winter coats. I'd been organizing what I could, little by little, for months and stashing it in a storage unit near the county line. Each trip out there took so much out of me that I had to sleep the rest of the day, but I was ready to move. I'd even scoped out a few rentals I could afford. We had Rob's insurance and death benefits we could depend on until Danny was eighteen, along with the income from my bookkeeping business. So while we weren't rolling in money, we were comfortable.

Not to mention, I could move all of my own furniture one-handed now.

Once my in-laws found out not only that they were *not* going to get custody of their grandson after I died but that I was a vampire, I doubted very much that they would continue to let me live in their house rent-free. It was time for me to move on anyway. Maybe I should have moved to an apartment after Rob died, but Danny had just lost his father. I didn't want to traumatize him with even more changes. Plus, my in-laws kept saying what a comfort it was to have Danny so close, which tugged at my guilt strings. And then I was diagnosed, and I wasn't capable of moving a laundry basket, much less a household.

I had so much to do before Danny got home, a whole checklist of chores I'd worked up before going "underground." Not to mention, it was two A.M., and I felt like it was the middle of the afternoon. I could probably burn through the whole list tonight: finish packing, find a new apartment, file for my undead identification card online, do this week's payroll for my clients, *and* conquer my bloodthirst. OK, it was a little ambitious, but really, that's how much energy I had running through my undead nerve endings.

Jane walked casually up the steps behind me, as if she wasn't watching my every movement. It seemed that my supervision was going to begin immediately and run round-the-clock. I supposed I deserved that. The drive from the park had served as some sort of reboot on my brain, and I had come to understand exactly how badly this situation could have turned out if my local Council officials weren't reasonably compassionate people.

The vampires' governing body, known for its tendency to solve problems in a swift, ruthless, and untraceable fashion, could have decided that I'd gone too far in my sire-for-hire quest for immortality, no matter how noble my reasons. They could have decided to stake me the minute I rose, toss my ashes back into my little grave, and claim no knowledge of my ever having been turned. They could have locked me up in any one of the rumored underground facilities where "problematic" vampires were incarcerated. Or, worse, they could have made me move to Arkansas.

I'd taken a huge risk becoming a vampire in this way, but I couldn't keep relying on reckless optimism and the kindness of bureaucrats. Now that my initial desperation had passed, I would not waste my immortality on rash decisions and my own (clearly flawed) judgment. I promised myself that I would be a model undead citizen, more considerate, more patient, more rational.

And that lasted all of five minutes before I walked past the long, narrow mirror that hung over the foyer table and caught sight of a beautiful willowy blonde. I stopped in my tracks, realizing that I was, in fact, looking at my own reflection. I promptly burst into tears, the big honking sobs you only saw on the Oprah network.

I hadn't looked this pretty in *years*.

My skin, dry and sallow just a few days before, had taken on the pearlescent perfection of a fairy-tale princess's. My eyelashes were thicker and darker, fringing my blue-green eyes and giving them a wider, wicked appearance, like I knew a secret and was going to use it to my advantage. The hair I'd lost during treatments was now full, thick, and lustrous, glimmering golden even in the harsh fluorescent lights. Over the last few months, it had become so brittle I'd been almost pathologically afraid of touching it. But now I could run my fingers through it like I was the star of my own personal shampoo commercial.

When I'd gotten sick, I'd told myself it was stupid to fuss about my appearance when I had so much more important stuff to worry about. But it had been a blow to know I was losing my looks on top of everything else. I'd never thought much about being pretty B.C. (before cancer). I wasn't going to play modest. I'd always known I had a certain backwoods-girl-gone-good appeal. But now? I was the very best imagined version of myself, the girl who mentally dated Tom Hiddleston and accepted an imaginary Oscar.

"It's a bit of a shock, huh?" Jane asked. I gingerly touched my fingers to my cheek, as if I was worried that touching my own face would somehow ruin an illusion. Her smile was wry, almost fond, as she placed a hand on my shoulder. "The first time I saw myself in the mirror, I thought of it as the bookworm's jackpot, all of those little problems the women's magazines promise to solve for us fixed in one big swoop."

"I don't know what you're talking about." Dick snorted as he hauled an enormous Coleman cooler through my foyer. "I was a prime specimen of manhood even before I was turned. Nothing about me changed, not one bit."

"Except his modesty," Jane told me, her tone dry as sand. She pulled my hair back from my face and into a sort of half-updo. "I know the extreme makeover takes a bit of getting used to, but when you think about it, it makes sense. Predators have to attract prey to survive. And how could we could draw in a . . . well, I don't like to use the word 'victim.' Let's say 'blood source'— with bacne and a unibrow?"

"I've been avoiding mirrors," I confessed. "For months, I've looked away from the mirror because I couldn't stand seeing that sick person looking back at me. This angry, bitter, frantic woman who was wearing my face. I didn't even think about how I would look afterward. I was just looking for more time. To get this, on top of everything else . . . I'll never be able to pay this back."

Jane smiled at me, an honest, genuine smile that instantly set my nerves at ease. She squeezed my hand, and I felt Dick pat me on the shoulder. "I hate to step on your moment, but it's not about payback, Buttercup," he said. "It's about making the most of the time you have now and adding something to the world instead of just taking."

I mouthed *Buttercup?* to Jane, who shrugged. "Dick likes nicknames."

"I know you disagree with how I went about it, Mrs. Nightengale, but believe me when I say becoming a vampire was the only solution for me. And I will work hard to learn everything you have to teach me."

"I'm glad you said that," Jane told me. "Because we don't have a lot of time."

I'd been wrong. Turned out the Council did give a gift basket, full of samples of different synthetic bloods,

SPF 500 sunscreen, iron supplements, Razor Wire fang floss, and a contact sheet for every vampire-friendly blood bank in the area.

Unfortunately, Jane's idea of "training" me involved treating me like a recalcitrant cat. She fed me a steady diet of bottled blood hourly. I would work on my client accounts between feedings, to distract myself from my thirst and so my business wouldn't suffer. At random times, Jane would wave a bag of donor blood under my nose. I was shocked by how good it smelled, like fresh-baked warm bread and toasted marshmallows and every good thing you could imagine wanting to eat all rolled into one. Despite being so full I was sloshing, my mouth still watered, and my fangs dropped so quickly it was almost painful. And every time they did, Jane would shoot me in the face with a spray bottle full of cold water.

"Aaah!" I cried. "Damn it, Jane!"

"It's like aversion therapy," she said with shrug, shooting me in the face again.

"Are you trying to keep me from craving human blood or climbing on the couch?" I grumbled, wiping at my face "And ow, ow, ow, why is it burning?" I swiped at my cheeks, wincing at the stinging sensation rolling across my skin. And then my palms started to burn. "What the hell, Jane?!"

"It's a point-zero-zero-one percent solution of colloidal silver. Vampires are highly allergic to silver. To humans, it's perfectly harmless. In fact, you find it in a lot of health-food stores. But to vampires, depending on the concentration, it can be a minor annoyance, like a sunburn that takes a few minutes to heal—or it can melt your face off and kill you. Trust me, I know."

"God, you can be scary," I told her.

"Really?" Jane asked. "Thanks! I've been working on being diabolical. I only got appointed to the Council because the last lady who had my job screwed up big-time, and I think the bureaucracy was trying to give me some sort of ironic punishment, like Sisyphus but with more paperwork. I worry sometimes that people don't take me seriously as head of the Council. And it's dangerous when other vampires don't take you seriously as head of the Council."

I stared at her.

"Not the point," she conceded.

I discovered there was a whole range of synthetic bloods beyond Faux Type O. It was a little like coffee—there was the cheap stuff and the expensive stuff, the stuff you only pulled out when company was coming over. Until we were sure how I would react around humans, neither one of us was willing to risk my trying donor blood. I promised myself it would be a treat, like rewarding myself with a box of Vosges exotic truffles at the end of tax season—only this was a treat I was deadly afraid of and probably wouldn't indulge in for several years.

My first sunrise found me falling into the deepest slumber I'd ever experienced. And for the first time in months, I didn't worry about whether I'd wake up. I was amazed at how quickly the sun pulled me into unconsciousness. I'd no sooner slid under the yellow log-cabin quilt on my bed than I tumbled into oblivion.

I discovered that the undead dream. Instead of the blank slate I expected during my dead sleep, I had a very active subconscious. I saw myself stretched across the scratchy polyester bedspread of the Lucky Clover Motel, ignoring the potential parasites that lurked in the bedding as I waited for my sire to arrive. I'd taken a healthy dose of over-the-counter sleeping pills to stave off the pain of turning, so my impressions of him were pretty hazy. I could remember parts of his face but not the whole. I remembered high, sculpted cheekbones and deep, bittersweet-chocolate eyes fringed with long lashes. A smile that was warm, even a little naughty. As I faded in and out, he stroked his cool hands down my face and told me everything was going to turn out like it should, that I was safe and would always be safe. He kissed me, long and deep, cradling me against his chest like I was something precious. And then he bit my wrists, letting the blood drain from me while he dripped his own into my mouth. I latched on to that arm, clutching it to my mouth as I swallowed huge mouthfuls of his thick, slightly sweet blood.

I was dying, not in the slow slide I'd taken over the last few months but plummeting off the cliff into the unknown. My pulse echoed in my ears, beat by beat. I couldn't draw breath. The man held me close, whispering that death was always difficult, but when I woke, I would be like him. And I would be strong and beautiful and fierce. And he would be there, taking pleasure in every new step I took.

When I woke at sunset, it wasn't the blood but this man's kiss I tasted on my lips. I could smell him, that expensive scent of amber, and feel his cool hands on my skin. I was left wanting with a bone-deep ache. For the first time in my life, I understood the word "yearning," beyond mocking it in romance novels. Because for the first time, I felt like I was being denied something beautiful, something that was *mine*. Unfortunately, I was also pretty sure my brain had concocted that thing from a mix of sedatives and oxygen deprivation.

I wasn't a fairy-tale sort of girl. I'd never been able to afford that sort of whimsy. There was no dream prince. There was no true love's kiss. At the end of the story, the newly married princess went home to her husband's castle to deal with dental bills, laundry arguments, and a dowager queen unwilling to give up her throne.

Sometimes I felt like I was too harsh with Rob, or at least his memory. Weren't widows supposed to put their dead husbands up on a pedestal? Wasn't I supposed to have some sort of little shrine on my nightstand devoted to him, with a big eight-by-ten photo and votive candles? It wasn't that I disliked Rob. In fact, I liked him very much in the beginning. He wasn't a bad husband. He just wasn't a good one.

By the end, we were more roommates than anything else. Rob had a lot of hobbies—hunting, fishing, softball, basketball with his friends. When we were first married, I appreciated the space. Marriage was difficult for me. I was used to having quiet time for myself.

When we were first married, I bucked Stratton

family tradition and continued working at a local accounting firm, Freegate and Swanson. But after Danny was born, I liked working from home, so I opened my own business. (To be honest, I poached a bunch of clients from Freegate and Swanson when I left. It wasn't my fault that my bosses had so little faith in my "work-from-home mom" scheme that they didn't make me sign a noncompete clause.) So my world slowly shrank down to Danny, Rob, e-mails from clients, and other moms. The freedom allowed me to make my own hours. I could stay home with Danny when he was sick. I could do a monthly payroll statement at two in the morning, which was sometimes the only time I had to think without a toddler crying in my ear or a baseball game blaring on the TV.

It was fortunate that I could tailor my schedule this way, because I was raising Danny alone long before Rob was gone. I was the one who got up with Danny in the middle of the night when he was throwing up. I was the one who went to parent-teacher conferences, doctor appointments, the meeting with the Sunday-school teacher when Danny walked out of the "Adam and Eve" lesson and told the congregation that they spent the whole morning talking about naked people. I thought that as Rob matured a little bit, got a little more comfortable with Danny, he would dial in, get more involved. He always said he would spend more time with "his boy" when Danny was old enough to throw a ball, shoot a gun, do something interesting. Until then, the dirty diapers, the two A.M. feedings, the teething cries—they were my problem.

I felt so disconnected from everything—except Danny. It was like a cocoon around my heart had opened up. I found my happiness in my son, his sweet, funny little soul, his crazy imagination. I found solace in volunteering at his school, taking him to story time at the library, making his Halloween costumes. I knew that one day he would grow up, marry, have a family of his own. But for the time being, I was enjoying motherhood and hoped that he would choose a spouse more wisely than his mother had. And when Rob died, I didn't really mourn him so much as the life we could have had, the husband he could have been.

I did not discuss these singularly depressing thoughts, since Jane was a pretty talented mind-reader and probably already knew. Also, she kept mentioning how much she disliked my "unethical, shameless jackass" of a sire. Every night. I considered this a bad sign, since Jane seemed to have a pretty high tolerance for sketchy people. Jane herself had been mistaken for a deer by a drunk hunter, gotten shot, and been turned by a passing vampire to keep her from dying. All that, and she still found my story a little scandalous.

Jane clearly thought of Dick Cheney as like a brother, and I was pretty sure that before being turned, I would have hidden in the ladies' room to avoid Dick at a rest stop.

But as I got to know him during his numerous visits to check on Jane and monitor my progress, I saw that despite the shifty exterior, Dick truly cared about Jane, and because Jane cared about my progress, so did Dick. They had history. Not only was Dick the best childhood friend of Jane's husband, but on Jane's first night out as a vampire, Dick was the one who stopped the disastrous parking-lot fight that almost got Jane's skull crushed. Dick was also married to Jane's friend and business partner, Andrea, and occasionally worked at Jane's bookshop to keep an eye on "his girls." Jane said these sorts of multilevel entanglements were common in vampire relationships.

"Just wait until you meet Gabriel, Zeb, and the rest of the bunch," she said as we sipped a particularly iron-rich Maxwell House International Coffee Café New Orleans blend of blood and caffeine. "You'll see how enmeshed we really are."

For some reason, that warmed my still heart. Despite my bumpy start, Jane was going to introduce me to her family. And given the way she talked about them all, with that fond, exasperated tone only a mother could understand, I knew how important they were to her. Maybe I would be able to find a community among vampires that I'd never had as a human. Oh, sure, I had acquaintances, women I knew from church and the PTA, but I didn't have a lot of close friends. Or any close friends, really. I told myself it was because I didn't have time, but I suspected that I simply wasn't good at making them. My childhood hadn't exactly prepared me for sister-friends.

I was a classic adult child of a single parent. I never met my dad. Mom never said much about him, other than to tell me that they hadn't had a lot of time together but he'd been the love of her life. I appreciated that she never threw him in my face as I was growing up. She never blamed me for her expulsion from one of the Hollow's nicer subdivisions to the Garden Vista trailer park. She never accused me of ruining her life. She just didn't share that life with me. We were more like roommates, moving in circles around each other, carefully avoiding long conversations or anything that might make the other uncomfortable.

My father was just another topic Mom didn't discuss. I didn't think about it much until we studied genetics in high school, and I had to leave half of my personal Punnett square blank. I didn't know what color my father's hair or eyes were. I didn't know what color his parents' hair or eyes were, so I had no idea whether my deep-set blue-green eyes came from his side of the family. I was pretty certain the blond hair and fair skin came from my mom's side. But since her parents kicked her out when she announced that she was pregnant and then moved from the Hollow to "get away from the shame," I hadn't had much of a chance to study their genetic traits.

My father, like so much of my childhood, was an equation I'd had to figure out on my own, and when the answer didn't come, I'd set it aside for consideration some other day. There were times when I felt rootless, like not knowing more about my parents meant I lacked an identity. But I tried to turn the problem on its side and see that lack of detail as setting me free from the constraints of someone else's expectations. The only limitations put on me were the ones I put there. Oddly enough, I seemed to have put a lot of them on myself without even realizing it, but that was an epiphany I wouldn't have until much later in life.

I realized that my life story sounded pretty pitiful, a lonely waif child left to languish in a single-wide. But I didn't feel sorry for myself. I knew what some of the other kids in my neighborhood were going through. By comparison, I had it relatively easy. I didn't get smacked around. I didn't have a fully functioning meth lab in my bathroom. Mom may not have been a font of praise and maternal wisdom, but she worked hard to provide what she could for me. I learned how to do things on my own, how to take care of myself, and that's more than a lot of my classmates graduated from high school knowing.

And then she was gone, leaving me alone. While I was used to being alone, I wasn't used to *feeling* alone. Without the only family I knew, I was adrift, ripe for the picking, when I met Rob a year or so later, at the Qwik Mart, of all places. He was looking for flowers to buy his mom for her birthday and asked me what kind he should get. I told him not to buy his mother gas-station flowers. (That should have been a clue, really.) Rob was a few grades ahead of me, so I didn't really know him. And I hadn't been into extracurriculars or school dances, so he didn't recognize me.

I'd thought I was lucky to catch Rob's attention. I'd never dated before. Between homework and a part-time job that helped keep up with our bills, I didn't have time. And I was so afraid of ending up like my mother that I practically hid from boys when they tried to speak to me. To end up with a man who not only wanted to marry me but also had a ready-made family looking for a daughter seemed too good to be true.

Which, of course, it was. But again, I was a late bloomer when it came to epiphanies.

For now, I was just grateful to have more time with my son. Everything else? It was just another equation, a problem to solve. I would keep chipping away until I figured it out.

When she wasn't making vague threats to my un-named sire and his tender parts or trying to get me to attend meetings of the Newly Emerged Vampires Support Group, Jane was torturing me with assigned reading. Since I'd rushed into my decision, Jane was enforcing a strict course of study of vampire history, politics, and personal safety. Jane happened to own Specialty Books, a charming little shop downtown, so she had a wealth of instructional materials to school me on my new culture, including *50 Ways to Add Variety to Your Undead Diet*; *From Caesar to Kennedy: Vampires and Their Clandestine Political Influence throughout History*; and *Love Bites: A Female Vampire's Guide to Less Destructive Relationships*.

At the top of the stack was a slick paperback with a pale, cheerful woman holding a cherubic toddler on the cover. It was called *My Mommy Has Fangs: A Guide to Post-Vampiric Parenting*.

"I was a librarian when I was human," Jane explained while I stared at the book with disdain. "Helping books find the people who need them is sort of my thing."

"I would be insulted by the parenting book, but I feel like I don't have much of a leg to stand on, in terms of dignity."

"That's true. But the first thing I want you to read is this," she said, dropping a book titled *The Guide for the Newly Undead, Second Edition* on top of the stack. "This is your new Bible. Everything you need to know about being a vampire, all of the random questions you come up with at five A.M. and don't want to bother anyone with, it's all in here. It's the cornerstone product at my shop. And it's a second edition, so it has a feeding plan for once you get settled into your diet and a list of reliable online vampire vendors, both of which are pretty darn handy."

I flipped through the stack of books, wondering how I was going to read or remember any of this information. I don't think I'd studied this much for the CPA exam. "I was never good with homework," I muttered.

"I've seen your desk, sweetie. I don't believe that for a second," she said, putting my laptop in my hands. "Now, by tomorrow night, I want a five-page essay on the structure of the World Council for the Equal Treatment of the Undead and how it governs local vampires like yourself. The main focus of your essay should be how to stay off the Council's radar."

"You're kidding. You do realize that I have to run a business from home while my child sleeps, right? A business that I need to keep running if I want to feed said child?" I laughed. But Jane did not smile. "You're not kidding."

"No, I am not," she said, dropping the *Guide for the*

Newly Undead in my lap. "Double-spaced, one-inch margins. You can find the time. You're a multitasker."

I stared down at my textbook. Despite the fact that I'd ruthlessly retrained my potty mouth after Danny and tried to replace the foul words with more intellectual terms from my word-of-the-day calendar, I let loose a "sonofabitch."

Jane's assigned reading list was illuminating and sort of horrifying. I was in junior high when a vampire tax consultant named Arnie Frink flung vampires out of the coffin onto an unsuspecting human public. Arnie sued his employer for the right to work overnight in his office, claiming to have porphyria, a potentially fatal allergy to sunlight. His tax firm denied his assertion that allergies, even if they did make his skin blister like bubble wrap, were a legitimate reason to let him have unsupervised access to the copy machine. And when the court sided with the firm, Arnie threw aside his layers of protective clothes, and, while his skin sizzled like bacon, declared in open court that he was a vampire, with a medical condition subject to the Americans with Disabilities Act, and they were stomping all over his rights.

After enduring several lengthy appeals and extensive testing by mental-health professionals, Arnie won his lawsuit and got a respectable financial settlement, evening hours, and his fifteen minutes in the media spotlight. And an entire planet full of people flipped the hell out. Humans burned, staked, and dragged vampires out into the sun without giving the undead any chance to defend themselves or prove that they weren't murderous monsters. And if the deaths could reasonably be explained away as accidents, the authorities took on a stubborn "see no evil, hear no evil, believe total bullshit" policy.

The World Council, an elected group of ancient vampires, realized the stubbornness trend wasn't going away and came forward, asking the world's governments to recognize them as nonmythical beings who should not be set on fire simply for existing.

After the United Nations officially condemned vampire hate crimes, the international vampire community eventually agreed that it was more convenient to live out in the open anyway. Bottled blood might have been less exciting, but it eliminated the need to dispose of bodies and explain away heavy-duty foil over their windows.

And in exchange for providing census information and agreements not to launch supernatural war against humanity, the Council was allowed to establish smaller regional offices in each state in every country. Selected local Council members were charged with supervising newer vampires to make sure they didn't attract negative attention from the human community, presiding over squabbles within vampire circles, and investigating "accidents" that befell their constituents.

Unlike my classmates, whose mothers rushed to shut off the news when they felt the Coming Out reports got too scary, I was unsupervised and therefore glued to my TV screen. And honestly, as scary and sensationalist as some of those reports were, I didn't have a problem with vampires. In my teen years, I followed the government-imposed curfews but only because I didn't particularly want to be arrested. As an adult, after the curfews had been abolished, I didn't let a potential encounter with the undead affect my schedule. I figured that if a vampire was going to make a snack of me, he or she would have done it already. I doubted they would have waited until they were living out in the open to chow down on my neck. So I didn't let it bother me. I was a woman. I was already hyperalert while walking around in dark environments.

And really, I hadn't run into that many vampires over the course of my lifetime. They didn't frequent trailer parks or PTA meetings. Sure, I'd visited Specialty Books on a few occasions (because it was the only store in the Hollow that carried my favorite urban fantasy novels), but I'd only dealt with Jane's manager, Andrea. It took me three visits before I realized that she wasn't just a super-pale, incredibly attractive human woman. So really, I didn't have moral quandaries about changing my life status.

But now it felt like I was having a small panic attack every few minutes. My fangs kept dropping at inopportune moments. I misjudged my strength and reduced a coffee mug to porcelain rubble when I tried to pick it up, and I was sure I would crush Danny's skull just as easily if I hugged him.

What was I going to do when he was older? How strange and sad was it going to be when we were the same age? Or, worse yet, when he was physically older than me? I was going to outlive him, unless he decided he wanted to be turned. Oh, no, what would I do if Danny wanted to become a vampire?

I would ground him. Forever.

My future seemed more uncertain now than when I'd been diagnosed. And one evening, I had a particularly exhausting night, overslept, and didn't wake up until ten P.M., which, if Danny had been home, would have been well after his bedtime. This sparked a whole existential "What good am I?" shame spiral that made Dick none too subtly skulk out of the house to safer, less weepy pastures.

"What if I can't do this?" I wailed as Jane looked on with an amused expression. "What if I've completely screwed up? What if I can't be around my own son and this was all for nothing? What kind of idiot am I? How am I going to take care of him? He's a child. He belongs to the day. He needs someone who can take him to the park and the beach and other places where the sun is. What did I think was going to happen? That he would just adjust to my schedule and become nocturnal? How selfish was I, doing this to him? And all I'm left with is eternity, watching my boy grow up without me—"

Yet again, Jane raised the spray bottle and shot me in the face with it.

"Damn it, Jane!"

"Well, it's better than slapping you!" she exclaimed.

"I don't see how that could possibly be true," I told her.

"You are a mother who didn't want to let her little boy grow up without her. That is not selfish. You may have gone about this in an absolutely batshit-insane way, but your heart was in the right place. I say this as someone who, by the universe's divine wisdom, did not have children, because I'm not sure I could keep small humans alive. You are a fantastic mother. You put Danny's needs first, always. Everything else is just logistics and clever scheduling. You will figure it out." Jane put her arm around me. "Did you freak out like this when you were pregnant?"

"No," I said, shaking my head. "I was weirdly calm."

"Well, then you're due for a good meltdown," she said. "You'll get through this. Every vampire I know has a moment of doubt after they're turned. 'What if I can't handle this?' 'What if my personality changes completely?' 'What if I massacre a whole village?' And those are all legitimate concerns. If you didn't worry about that sort of thing, I would be concerned about your sense of decency. You know, you might feel a little better about this if you attended a meeting of the Newly Emerged Vampires. They talk about this sort of thing all the time. You might feel less alone."

"I'm not much of a joiner," I told her. "I never have been. But . . . other than that, I'm not sure who I am. For years, I was Rob Stratton's wife. And then I was Danny's mom. But eventually, he's going to grow up, and I will be . . . not obsolete but less vital in his life. And I don't know what I'm going to do with myself after that."

"I can see that," Jane said. "I'm going through the same thing with Jamie, obviously on a much smaller scale, since I didn't raise him from birth. But with him leaving for college, the house seems so empty. I didn't realize how much he was distracting me from the calm that descended over our house in the last year or two. I mean, when I first became a vampire, it was total chaos. It seemed like someone new was trying to kill me every year or so. And I got used to it. Chaos became my lifestyle. Gathering my friends together, figuring out how to get ahead of the crisis, eventually getting my ass handed to me in some capacity. And without that, I kind of worry that Gabriel and I are going to turn into my parents. After my dad retired, it got kind of ugly around the house. Mama was used to having the house to herself all day, and suddenly Daddy was there, giving her suggestions about how she could improve her housekeeping skills. We're lucky it didn't turn into some backwoods episode of *Dr. Phil*. And that was only because my sister intercepted Mama's application tape."

"Well, you'll always have young idiot vampires like me to boss around, and you work for one of the most terrifying organizations in the world, which has to be just lousy with infighting and potential archenemies," I told her.

She grinned. "Thanks, that actually makes me feel better."

"No problem."

"But this conversation isn't about me, it's about you and your quarter-life crisis. You need to sit back and think about all the time you have left and then consider how you want to spend it. Because, unlike how it is for most people, time is something we have in unlimited supply. Look, it's all manageable," she told me. "OK, sure, the first night I was turned, I tried to attack my best friend. But I'd shrugged off my sire and didn't have any guidance. I didn't even try to dull my thirst. You're preparing. And preparing is half the battle."

Jane walked up behind me and placed a firm, cool hand on my shoulder. "You're going to be OK," she told me, her voice so quiet that even my superhuman ears strained to hear it. "You're going to be strong. You're going to welcome your little boy home, listen to his stories, put him in a bath, and tuck him in for bed. You are more than your thirst. You are a mother first, and then a vampire." Jane jerked her head toward the door. "Come on."

"What?" I huffed as she led me out onto the front porch.

"I've been so focused on keeping you contained for our conditioning that I've denied you an important rite for any newborn vampire," she said, slipping out of her wedge sandals. I followed her, already barefoot, onto the grass.

"You're looking at the world with brand-new eyes," she said. "You can feel every blade of grass against the soles of your feet. Listen to the wind rustling through every leaf on every tree. Listen to the heartbeats of the animals in the woods. Look up at the sky."

"Trust me, Jane. I've done the 'new senses' appreciation bit. I haven't stared at the craters in the moon so hard since I tried that special brownie for the chemo side effects."

"Can you just let me have a surrogate-sire moment here?" she grumbled.

"Sorry."

"Now, I want you to bend your knees, dig your toes down in the grass."

I bent, prepared for some sort of tai chi meditation technique that would help me stop having such a histrionic reaction to every damn thing. "OK."

"Now, jump," Jane told me.

"What?"

"Jump."

Frowning, I pushed up from the ground with my feet . . . and jetted fifteen feet into the air. I shrieked, flailing all the way down to the ground. I landed on my ass with a hard *thunk*.

"What the hell was that?" I cried, splayed out on the grass.

"Vampire vertical leap," Jane said. "Go on, have some fun."

"You're not going to tag me or put some sort of tether on me?" I asked.

"Do you plan on running away?"

"No."

"OK, then, go run."

Unsure of whether this was some sort of trick, I bent at the knees again and leaped. I was a bit more prepared for the sudden change in altitude and landed with some grace about ten feet away from Jane. She gave me an amused little wave and sat on my porch step.

I leaped again, taking off at a full run for the swing set I'd built for Danny when he was three. I ran straight up his slide, jumped nimbly onto the top bar, and with perfect balance walked across the length without stepping on a single swing bolt. I stopped at the end and, praying that my vampire bones would heal quickly if necessary, jumped off the swing set with a flip and a twist.

Landing on both feet and raising both arms in a gymnast's "I stuck it" gesture, I laughed aloud. I hadn't felt like walking the length of the driveway in months, much less running laps around my yard for the pure joy of being able to move so freely. I jumped. I flipped. I did a back handspring that ended in a disastrous face-plant, but without emergency-room bills to worry about, it didn't bother me to watch the bones in my wrist reset on their own. After almost an hour, I jogged back up the porch steps to join Jane, who handed me a mug of warmed blood.

"Feel better now?" she asked.

"That was pretty awesome," I conceded.

"No more freak-outs?"

"No more freak-outs," I promised.

"Good. Now, get your stuff together, because your in-laws' truck is coming down the road."

A few seconds later, Les and Marge's F-250 pulled up in the driveway. Danny was home. He was about to run out of that truck smelling like woodsmoke and bug repellent, and the first thing he was going to do was throw himself at me and tell me all about his weekend. The panic welled up inside me like lava. Oh, God, what if I couldn't do this? What if I hurt him? What if—

"Did you just tire me out so I wouldn't have the energy to bite anybody? Like you'd do with a puppy?" I asked Jane.

"I regret nothing," she told me, shaking her head.

The truck door flew open, and my son came barreling across the lawn, a short fireball of crackling blond energy. And even at his insane first-grader's speed, my vampire eyesight could track every movement he made as if it was a freeze frame. And he was the most beautiful thing I'd ever seen. Even in the moonlight, I could see every wavy blond hair on his head, every golden eyelash. I could see every tiny freckle on his sun-kissed skin. And my eyes, my own blue-green eyes, looking back at me, expectant and absolutely sure of my love.

My Danny.

Deep in my soul, beyond my consciousness and my heart, I knew with absolute, concrete certainty that I would never be able to hurt my son. And that little bit of fear, at least, melted away into nothing as he launched himself through the air at me.

"Hey, Mom!"

I caught him and cradled him against me as gently as if he was made of spun glass. I looked at Jane, who was all smiles, leaning against the door frame, arms crossed, as if she had no cause to leap across the porch at any second to stop me from biting Danny.

I buried my face in Danny's hair and discovered that my darling boy did not smell as beautiful as he looked. *Phew.* Sweat, sunscreen, citronella, smoke, fried fish, singed sugar, and an undercurrent of exhaust. Danny stank to high heaven, something I wouldn't have noticed before. Human mothers had to overlook a lot of interesting odors. It was going to take time to adjust to my vampire nose.

"Hi, baby," I said, putting all the strength I had into not recoiling.

Danny shivered. "Your cheek is cold, Mom."

"Sorry," I said, leaning back and looking at him, taking in every detail all over again. "It's the air-conditioning. You're a big, tough outdoorsman now. You're not used to modern conveniences."

"You're so weird," Danny huffed, though he was grinning broadly. I laughed and pressed my forehead to his as the last sliver of fear evaporated from my chest. I made Danny smile. He called me weird. This was a very normal interaction for us. We were going to be OK.

"Danny, get down!" Marge yelped as she climbed out of the truck. "You know your mama's not strong enough to hold you like that."

Oh, right, because I was supposed to be seriously ill. I made a big show of struggling under Danny's weight, letting my knees buckle as I wobbled and set his feet gently on the ground.

"Did you have fun with Papa and Mamaw?" I asked, grinning at him.

"Yeah, we went fishing and made s'mores and went riding on Papa's four-wheeler."

Well, that explained the smell of exhaust.

I gave Les Stratton the extreme side-eye. My father-in-law was still a strapping man at sixty, with a thick head of salt-and-pepper hair and Rob's brown eyes. If I ever wondered what my husband might have looked like if he'd survived to old age, all I had to do was look at Les.

That was a rather gross thought.

"Les, I've asked you not to put him on an ATV. He's small for his age. It's not safe," I told him.

Les dismissed my concerns like he always did. "Ah, Robbie and I used to do it all the time at his age. It's fine. Trust me. When you've been at parenting as long as I have, you'll be able to tell the difference between real danger and worrywartin'. Besides, I have to teach the boy how to be a man."

It struck me that Rob had learned much of how to be a husband from Les. Dismissal. Condescension. And when that failed, falling back to the old "I'm a man and therefore know better than you, silly woman" stance. There were times I really wanted to punch my father-in-law in the kidneys.

Of course, if I did that now, I would probably kill him. Still, something to consider.

At the moment, I simply wanted them away from the house before they figured out that there was some-thing different about me. So I was willing to let his mansplaining go . . . for now.

"What do you say to Mamaw and Papa for taking you camping?" I prompted Danny.

"Thank you!" Danny picked up his backpack and ran into the house, going past Jane without a second look. He'd gotten used to all sorts of people coming into the house to help care for me. We were going to have to do something about his stranger awareness.

Marge patted my cheek, and I was overwhelmed by the scent of White Shoulders. White Shoulders and blood—warm, delicious, sweet blood that would taste like the cinnamon Marge always sprinkled on top of her coffee. I could sense it, pulsing through her veins, throbbing at the juncture of her neck and shoulder. My mouth watered at the thought of sinking my fangs into her neck and drinking deep. I could almost feel the warm tide of it slipping past my lips.

"Libby," Jane said in a warning tone. It seemed that Jane did not appreciate the violent slide show going on in my head.

My fangs dropped. My mouth clamped shut, and I took a tiny step back. An expression of hurt crossed Marge's features. I concentrated on unappetizing thoughts and willed my fangs to go away. Roadkill. The smell of Danny's sandals at the end of the summer. James Franco's paintings.

"You must have gotten your rest while we were gone," Marge said. "You're looking much better. Still a bit peaky, mind, but better. Your skin doesn't look so dull. And did you do something new to your hair?"

"I had it done," I said, nodding, letting the buttery waves bounce around my face. I couldn't help it. Marge had been after me to "spruce myself up" for months. Because "you're looking a little frumpy" is just what someone with a terminal disease wants to hear. "Do you like it?"

"Was it Tammy, over at the Beauty Mark?" Marge

asked, peering closer at my face, as if she was trying to figure out what sort of moisturizer I was using to give my skin that flawless undead porcelain glow. If I said yes, that my new look was the result of Tammy's work, Marge would be in her chair the next day, grilling my poor hairdresser.

"You using a new makeup, too?"

"Uh . . ."

But I was saved by the nosy father-in-law. Les gave a sort of chin nod at Jane, who was hovering by the front door. "Who's this?"

It made sense that Les was giving Jane the "I think I recognize you from church, but I'm not quite sure" look most Hollow residents did when we ran into someone new. Heck, I barely recognized Jane when I crawled out of my grave. She was a few years ahead of Rob and me in school. And Jane's appearance had changed quite a bit since she'd dropped out of the Hollow's "daytime" social circles.

"Oh, this is Jane, from the PTA. We've got the Pumpkin Patch Party coming up, lots to plan," I explained airily. It seemed that once you had no pulse or blood pressure, lying came a lot easier. Yay for me and my already slippery morality.

"School hasn't even started yet," Les noted. "And you haven't been able to help at the school in months."

"PTA business never stops," Jane supplied helpfully. "And Libby has been feeling better lately. I'll bet in the next few weeks, you'll see a real turnaround. Right, Libby?"

I stared at Jane, who was smiling as if butter

wouldn't melt in her mouth—which, given her lower body temperature, was plausible. She seemed to be enjoying this just a little too much.

"It's not fair to give her false hope," Marge admonished Jane.

"I *am* feeling better," I told Marge, and before she could object, I called after Danny. "Honey, come tell Mamaw and Papa good-bye, and then it's time for bed!"

"I can stay, give him a bath and help put my baby down to sleep," Marge offered, still eyeing Jane.

"I'll be fine," I assured her. "I need to get used to doing things on my own again."

My mother-in-law edged toward the truck, wearing her suspicious face, but for once in our relationship, she chose discretion over interrogation. Vampirism might have some benefits I hadn't even considered yet.

"You know, it's at times like these that I'm grateful my in-laws died a century before I met their son," Jane said, waving cheerfully as the truck backed out of my driveway. "Next time, marry an orphan, sweetie."

"No one likes a gloater, Jane."

Vampirism adds an additional layer of challenge to parenting, an already challenging prospect. As your child develops from a baby to a toddler to the child who makes you cringe when he gets near a microphone in public places, so you must develop, too.

—*My Mommy Has Fangs: A Guide to Post-Vampiric Parenting*

It's going to sound super-creepy, but I spent my first night with Danny watching him curled up on his bed in his Spider-Man pajamas. I sat on the floor with my hand on his chest, watching it rise and fall. It was as if I'd never seen my son before, and I couldn't stop looking at him.

Jane was just down the hall, going over some inventory reports for her shop, keeping one ear open for any suspicious "bite-y" sounds. But really, sitting there in the dark, quiet home, listening to my son breathe, it felt like any night before I died. It felt strange to me that my life had changed in such a major way, but Danny hadn't noticed a difference. I wondered if it was the blessing of being so young or if I had managed to cling to the most stubborn parts of my humanity. I hoped that was it.

What if no one else saw the change in me, either? Part of me wanted that, like somehow I could pretend nothing had happened and keep people from finding out that I was a vampire now. That was reasonable, right?

OK, no, no, it wasn't. I knew that I was going to have to tell them eventually. But I wanted to get Danny settled into our new routine, get him in school, and demonstrate that I could take care of him even with my new "condition." So when my maternal fitness inevitably came into question, I would have some parental street cred built up. My son was never going to have a normal life. First he was poor Danny whose father had died. And now he was poor Danny whose mother was a monster. I contemplated starting a savings account for his therapy as soon as there was some extra money in the budget.

Besides, I knew how Half-Moon Hollow residents talked about their neighbors who'd been turned. Like it was something the new vampires brought on themselves. Like it was something that could never happen to *them*. Frankly, it was the same way my classmates whispered about girls who got pregnant in high school. I didn't want the whispers to affect Danny. I didn't want people to stop talking when I walked into the same Walmart aisle.

I supposed there was some advantage to gaining a reputation as a creature of the night. There wasn't much about my appearance that was intimidating to vampires or humans. My wardrobe consisted mostly of jeans, weather-appropriate cardigans, and Keds. Would it damage my position if the other vampires saw me dressing that way? Would they not take me seriously? I mean, Jane wore pretty dresses, but she was still somehow quite intimidating. And Dick dressed in jeans and smartass T-shirts, but there was still this edge of menace, as if no matter the time of night, he would know exactly how and where to hide your body.

Should I go out and buy leather pants and boots? I didn't want to be picked off because other vampires perceived me as weak.

No. Moms should not wear leather pants, even when they had a good reason.

I watched my son's chest rise and fall. Our usual babysitter, Kaylee Dickson, would come over early in the morning as planned to keep Danny all day. I'd left her a note stating that I'd had a particularly bad reaction to a treatment and would probably sleep most of the day. That was the story I planned to stick with for most of the first week. There was no reason to freak her out.

Kaylee was a sweet girl, sixteen and possessed of all the scatterbrained, optimistic charm that involved her not asking a lot of detailed questions about why I only needed her during the day. But she was also fiercely protective of Danny, was an excellent storyteller, and had gone on a vegan health-food kick after reading *The Jungle* for her advanced English class, so Danny couldn't con so much as a Fruit Roll-Up out of her. He'd survived the whole summer on Tofurky and carob cookies.

I'd timed my turning carefully, just as summer was ending but before Danny started school, so I would have some time to adjust before his classes began. Kaylee was already coming over in the mornings to help him with breakfast and getting dressed. She'd agreed to keep doing that after school started and then drive Danny to the elementary school.

Wait.

I pulled my cell phone from my pocket, ignoring the multitude of missed calls and e-mails that had come in while I was underground, and checked the calendar. I opened my Internet browser and pulled up the school's Web site.

I had to register Danny for first grade in two nights. It was inevitable, I supposed, that when you made a change like this, something would slip through the cracks, but I couldn't believe I'd forgotten about school registration—the annual refiling of paperwork that I'd already filled out the previous year, just so the school district had updated parent signatures. It was my belief that this practice was a conspiracy by notary publics to keep their industry afloat.

School registration—a big, crowded school building full of people and their smells and their noise and their tempting blood. And kids running around. And people who would try to recruit me into volunteering for stuff. This did not bode well, in terms of what sort of vampire parent I was going to be.

I rubbed Danny's back and gave myself a cross between a pep talk and a "come to Jesus" scolding. I knew this sort of thing was coming. It was all part of raising a child. Dang it.

Danny ran ahead of me in the hallway, his lime-green T-shirt disappearing into the crowd of people milling around in the school's maze of classrooms. The school staff had gone all out with the decorations this year, festooning the hallway in blue, gold, and white streamers, balloons, and tissue puffs. A huge mural of Happy the Half-Moon Howler Pup had been added to the entrance over the summer, his blue sweater stretching over a chest puffed up with Howler pride. Beyond that, not much about the building had changed since I was a student here.

I could only be grateful that my illness had gotten me off of the PTA's social committee the previous spring, so I wasn't obligated to organize this insanity. I'd tried to come up with several different scenarios in which I could register Danny for school without leaving the house before sunset—calling the school and claiming I was too sick to come in and asking the administrators to just fax all of the permission slips and registration documents over for a signature, or asking Les and Marge to take him and sign the documents for me. But those didn't paint me as a very good parent, and I didn't want Les and Marge to gain any foothold as potential legal guardians. Frankly, I was surprised they hadn't shown up for registration just to make sure they made contact with Danny's new teacher . . . who wasn't in the classroom or anywhere that I could see.

So far, I'd managed to duck my in-laws' calls for two days. I texted to assure them that I was fine. Danny was fine. We were both resting up for the beginning of the school year.

Danny, a social bumblebee by nature (he refused to be called a butterfly, too girlie), was in heaven, darting back and forth between his kindergarten classrooms to talk to his former teachers. Every former classmate he saw was treated to a big hug and an interrogation about his or her summer. I hung back, pleased to watch him play tiny politician while I wrestled with my senses. This was a considerable development from the skirt-hugging kid who had only started morning preschool a few months before Rob died.

I was not in top shape for this little outing. For days, I'd been having recurring dreams about my blurry-faced sire. At first, it was just a repeat of my turning, the same sweet nothings he'd whispered to me while I was dying. And then it progressed to new, more intimate scenarios. Sitting on my kitchen counter while he stood between my thighs. Cuddled up on the swing on my front porch. Sprawled across a large, unfamiliar bed while he traced every vertebra of my spine with his fingertips and spoke soft nonsense to me. But I never saw his face. It was like I was compelled not to look him in the eye. Even while he held me, he kept his face tucked into the crook of my neck or buried in my hair. It was warm and lovely and made me so happy, knowing that there was someone who cherished me this much. And naked. We were usually naked.

It was confusing, feeling that much for someone who was a virtual stranger. I knew that it wasn't real. I didn't know this man. He didn't know me, much less love me. But to be yanked out of that sweet illusion every sunset into a world where I was unsteady and uncertain was disorienting. At least, that was the rationalization I used for being so damned late for Danny's school registration.

We were coming in late, driving in Jane's sunproof vampire-mobile she called "Big Bertha, Jr.," during the final (increasingly sunless) minutes of the registration window. At this point, most of the parents had finished their paperwork and were standing around socializing while their kids ran around like feral cats. As usual, the sight of all those complete family units, mothers and fathers herding their kids around in tandem, made my chest a little tight for Danny's sake. Danny had never seen his dad put up a tent in the backyard for a campout. He would never know what it was like to have his dad coach his Little League team. He would never be a big brother. While I'd survived being a fatherless only child, I'd hoped for something better for my son. Now I simply hoped that having one parent who whole-assed it was better than one absent parent and another who less-than-half-assed it.

Considering that this was my first crowd situation since I'd been turned, I thought I was doing pretty well. While the combination of sights, smells, and sounds was overwhelming, I distracted myself by cataloguing all of the odors in my head. Paste and new crayons and floor wax and kid sweat. I'd glutted myself on bottled blood as soon as I rose for the night. I even swigged a sample of HemoBoost on the drive over. (Definitely not a repeat purchase. It tasted like a combination of old dirty pennies and that stuff you find dried on the corners of your mouth in the morning.) Thanks to that vurpy experience, I was more nauseated than hungry. My fellow parents were safe.

Jane was trailing behind me at a casual pace. And when people questioned the presence of a childless vampire at a school event, she simply responded that the Council was looking into opportunities to partner with the county's schools and provide support. It seemed plausible enough, and Jane was generally known as a reasonable, non-murdery citizen, so they accepted the explanation.

Miss Steele hadn't put a lot of effort into decorating like the other teachers had, but the room was clean and organized and chock-full of informational posters about addition, subtraction, nouns, and verbs. Miss Steele herself was nowhere to be found, but that wasn't unusual. There were so many different parents with so many different needs, and teachers spent a good deal of registration night running around the building, chasing down paperwork.

Dorothy Steele had been a first-grade teacher when I attended Half-Moon Hollow Elementary School. Approaching ancient even then, she hadn't been a cuddly nap-time and handprint-turkey sort of teacher. She'd been stern, no-nonsense. But I left her class with impeccable penmanship and a thorough knowledge of my times tables, material far above my grade level. Without her, I might never have achieved the math proficiency I needed for accounting. But telling her so probably would have irritated her. Miss Steele had never been one for emotional displays.

I settled into the tiny child-sized chair in front of the desk marked "Danny" on a cheerful fire-engine-shaped name tag and marveled at the sheer number of labeled folders waiting for me. Basic information forms asking for address, phone number, e-mail, Social Security number, Twitter handle, and shampoo preference. Forms to authorize Danny's lunchtime food choices and put money in his account. Forms to approve his use of the school's Internet. Forms to enroll him on the bus route. Forms that promised that I would not hold the school responsible if one of his classmates pushed him off the top of the monkey bars and broke his collarbone. (It was a pretty specific form, in terms of liability.)

I spent thirty minutes filling out the papers, signing my name over and over again as Danny's sole legal guardian. Instead of putting Marge's and Les's names down as Danny's emergency contacts, I wrote down the name of the local Council office daytime liaison. It felt wrong, but considering my uncertainty about my in-laws, I couldn't risk them being able to come retrieve Danny from school while I was out for the day.

This had been so much easier last year, when all I had to worry about was keeping Danny occupied while I tried to fill out his mountain of kindergarten paperwork. I still hadn't explained to Danny that I'd been turned. I just couldn't seem to gather my nerve. There was no good time to work that into a conversation. *Hey, sweetie, could you turn off* Ninja Turtles *long*

*enough for Mommy to tell you that she's one of the un-
dead and your life has changed forever?*

For right now, I was in a holding pattern, adjusting
to my new life, and it was working for me. I felt like I
was balancing a house of cards on my palm and any
movement would bring it down.

"Mom, look what we got!"

I turned to find a blue-frosted "HMHES" cupcake
being shoved into my face. Now, under normal preturning circumstances, my main concern would be getting blue frosting out of my sweater. But since human
food smells absolutely repellent to vampires, I was far
more focused on the fact that Danny was waving what
smelled like a freshly deposited cow pie directly in
front of my face. I gasped, whipping my head back
away from the treat. The overreaction merited a few
curious looks from other parents, so I worked to main-
tain control over my gag reflex.

"Mom, what's wrong?" Danny asked. "Don't you
want a bite?"

I would rather watch one of those "eyebrow waxing
gone wrong" videos on YouTube than take a bite of
that thing. I wheezed, "It's all yours, sweetie."

"You're not on a diet, are you?" Danny said, shaking
his head. "Katie Hannan's mom is always on a diet, and
Katie says she never smiles anymore."

"Maybe you shouldn't repeat the things your friends
say about their families," I told him.

Breathing through my mouth, I finally noticed the
little boy in a camo hoodie and scuffed sneakers standing behind Danny.

"Who's this?"

"This is my new best friend, Charlie," Danny said, slinging his arm around the boy's shoulder. Charlie kept his cupcake-free hand tucked into his pocket but seemed pleased by Danny's show of bro-fection. Charlie had wide, mischievous brown eyes and sharp features, the sort of impish face that would get him labeled the class troublemaker for years to come. He had an admirable blue frosting mustache on his upper lip.

"It's nice to meet you, hon. Are you new here?"

Charlie shook his head. "No, ma'am. We moved here after my birthday. My birthday's in February. Dad says I can have a party at the Knight's Castle this year."

Well, that explained why I'd never met Charlie. I hadn't been able to volunteer at the school since the early spring semester. It also revealed that Charlie's father was a very brave man. The Knight's Castle was a medieval-themed indoor play complex with inflatable bouncy houses, video games, a snack bar, and, for that extra level of noise and stink, pony rides.

I pulled a wet wipe from my purse and dabbed at his frosting facial hair. I'd expected him to object, or at least wriggle a little, but again, he seemed pleased by the attention, tilting his face from side to side to make sure I'd cleaned away everything.

Danny was bouncing on his toes, though I couldn't tell whether it was from excitement or in an attempt to hide the fact that Charlie towered a full head over him. "Charlie says I'm invited to his party this year, Mom. Can I go?"

"You're handing out invitations already?" I asked Charlie, who shrugged and dug his toe into the floor.

"Danny already invited me to his party," Charlie said.

"Of course he did." Danny issued invitations to his next birthday party all year round. He planned his cake, theme, and color scheme at least nine months in advance. "And I hope you can come."

"Mom, Miss Lisa is doing story time in the library. Can I go?"

God bless Lisa Stewart, the school librarian. With her endless patience and carefully organized arsenal of distracting stories, she'd taken pity on us all. She was the one who'd recognized Danny's above-average reading level and encouraged him to find authors like Aaron Reynolds and Chris Gall to appeal to his sense of humor. Those books had helped Danny stay entertained during the worst nights of my treatment. I would be forever grateful.

"Can I go, Mom?"

"Sure, baby." He scampered off with Charlie, and I was reminded, once again, that no matter how messed-up the consequences, I'd made the right choice being turned. I could be gone right now instead of watching my son making a new friend. I organized the paperwork carefully and retrieved the *three-page* list of school supplies he would need for the year.

I took a deep, unnecessary breath before walking out into the hall, fortifying myself for the onslaught of human noise and smells. Several of the parents called out to me, waving, smiling, telling me how glad they were to see me up and around. Mark Walsh, the school principal, who had been instrumental in keeping me in touch and informed about Danny's academic and emotional status even when I was too fatigued to make a damn phone call, stopped me to remind me that the staff was there to help us with anything we needed in the new school year.

Jane was leaning against the wall, texting, waiting for me by the nurse's office. She was frowning as she peered down at the screen.

"Council business," she told me, shoving the phone into her pocket. "Are you done?"

"No, now I have to go to the cafeteria and find all of the right people to give the right pages to and then commando-roll out of the fire exit before I get recruited for the homework helper program. I love helping kids understand math, but I'm not willing to let the sun evaporate me in order to do it," I said quietly.

"That seems reasonable," Jane said. "Maybe we can find some online tutoring program for you to help with if you find you miss it a lot." She shuddered as a rowdy group of kids stampeded by, waving blue "Go, Howlers, Go!" foam fingers. "You know, there are times when I'm really glad the childe I got had already graduated by the time I turned him. I'm not sure I would have survived all this. You're well suited to it, though. You haven't flinched once."

I grinned. "Thanks, Jane."

"Libby!"

Casey Sparks, a petite brunette with a sassy pixie cut, was bustling down the hall toward me.

"Friend or foe?" Jane whispered.

"Friend," I whispered back, adding, "Ish."

Of all the parents I knew through school, I was probably closest to Casey. We'd worked together on the raffle committee for the Pumpkin Patch Party, the school's annual fall festival and biggest fund-raiser of the year for the PTA. Working that thing was like serving in the armed forces together. It changed a woman.

Casey and I occasionally met for coffee, and when I got sick, she'd brought some casseroles over to the house. With my symptoms and her four kids, that was about as much as either of us had time for. And honestly, I didn't know how to offer more.

Casey threw an arm around my shoulder and squeezed me tight. I hugged her back with a fraction of my strength for fear of hurting her. Leaning away from the potential temptation of her pulsing throat, I ran through the list of things I was supposed to be doing—breathing, blinking, smiling—and tried to do them at a regular, human pace.

"They must have the air-conditioning cranked up pretty high—your hands are freezing!" she exclaimed.

My smile stretched tight. Actually, the air-conditioning was struggling under the body heat of so many people walking through the building while the doors were standing open. Everybody else's forehead had a fine sheen of sweat. I supposed Casey was trying to be polite about my less-than-stellar immune-system-slash-everything-else. "Well, the system must be catching up from being off over the summer."

"Wow, you're looking really good," Casey said, holding my hands and stepping back so she could survey me. "That new treatment seems to be a little easier on you. Have you been taking supplements or something?"

Remembering the horse-pill iron supplements I'd choked down that morning, I said, "Yep, vitamins and supplements. Health shakes. That sort of thing."

Synthetic blood was a sort of smoothie, right? A meaty, metallic smoothie.

"Well, you look great. So did Danny get Mrs. Roberts this year?" she asked. The highly coveted first-grade teacher was a miracle worker with behavioral problems. Her class reading-comprehension test scores were through the roof. And she'd managed to make the first grade's Earth Day play interesting three years in a row. All the parents wanted their kids to be in Mrs. Roberts's class, so much so that the school stopped taking assignment requests as a matter of policy.

"No, he got Miss Steele," I said quietly, nodding toward the empty classroom. "I'm sure he'll be fine. I was when I was in her class. How about Peyton? How is she liking her last year of Sunnyside?"

Peyton was Casey's youngest, a pink-obsessed princess obsessed with the Little Mermaid. She had cried, cajoled, and attempted bribery to get her mother to let her skip a year at Sunnyside preschool, Danny's "alma mater," so she could join her oldest siblings at big-kid school. Casey was a stronger woman than I, because I don't know if I would have been able to say no to that level of cuteness. Or whining.

"Mrs. Bloom," Casey said, her pink-glossed lips bending into a frown.

I winced. Danny and Mrs. Bloom had not gotten along well when she'd been his teacher. Mrs. Bloom seemed to be of the opinion that four-year-olds should be seen and not heard, which was an odd stance for someone who spent all day talking to four-year-olds. "Well, I'm sure it will be fine."

"When Danny had Mrs. Bloom, you told me I should pray for her retirement or a falling cartoon safe before Peyton got to the four-year-old class."

"I think I said cartoon piano, but OK. And maybe she was just having an off year when Danny had her."

"I don't think you're allowed to have an off *year*," Casey said. "A week, sure. Maybe a month. But not a year."

"It will be fine," I said. "Just ask Peyton a lot of questions when she gets home so you're prepared for the phone calls."

It felt wrong to be gossiping about teachers in what amounted to "faculty housing." But I also knew that this happened in every hallway in every school in America. For every wonderful, talented, dedicated teacher out there, there was the one who triggered the fight-or-flight response during parent-teacher conferences.

"If you're feeling up to it, let's meet up for coffee once the kids are in school," Casey said.

"Sure."

As she walked away, I bit my lip. I hoped she liked drinking decaf at night. I relaxed a little, now that I didn't have to play human quite so convincingly. I was suddenly so tired. Tired and kind of depressed that no one here knew me well enough to see how much I'd changed. The last time I was here, I looked like the walking dead, dang it, and now I was practically a mom supermodel, and people seemed to think it was because of some magic herbal pill. I just needed a few minutes. A few minutes of peace and quiet and fewer smells.

"You're looking pretty tired, hon. Why don't you take a little break?" Jane suggested, nodding toward the closet near the music room marked "Janitorial Supplies."

"Thanks. I'll be right back," I said.

I ducked into the closet, using just a teensy bit of my vampire strength to wrench the doorknob's fifty-year-old lock off of its pins. Promising myself that I would send the school a check to replace it, I leaned my forehead against the cool wood door and tried some of the relaxation techniques the nurses had suggested at the chemo center. I pictured warm, yellow sunlight filtering through the ceiling and relaxing my frazzled nerves. I pictured a warm beach, sand shifting underneath my back as my toes curled and uncurled under the grainy surface. I imagined the scents of coconut suntan lotion and ocean salt wafting toward my nose. I felt a pretend breeze against my skin. And I heard a voice, low and loving, calling my name. I'd heard the voice before, whispering in my ear while I was unable to breathe. He told me that everything was going to be all right, that this was part of it, and when I woke up—

Suddenly, the door popped open and smacked me in the forehead, knocking me back on my heels.

"Oof!" I cried, clutching my face. Thank goodness I had rapid healing powers, because I was pretty sure I'd just sustained a concussion.

"Are you OK?" a gruff voice demanded.

"What the hell— Who are you?" I demanded.

"I'm the guy with the keys to this closet. Who are *you*?"

My eyes went wide. *This* was the school janitor? What happened to Ernie Houser? When I attended Half-Moon Hollow Elementary, the janitor had been a sweet old man who had a fluffy white walrus mustache and whistled "My Old Kentucky Home" through the gap in his front teeth.

The contemporary school janitor was made from a slightly different mold. Tall, lean, almost wiry, with respectable cords of muscles rippling over arms covered in a swirling cloud of colorful tattoos. His face was long and lean, with sharp features only softened by a scruff of white-blond beard and longish darker blond hair that brushed against the collar of his T-shirt. His eyes were a defiant blue. If Thor had a pissed-off, tattooed younger brother, he would be the guy blocking my exit from the supply closet. And yeah, he might have fit the bill for some of my more tawdry biker fantasies, but given the way he was glaring at me, I got the distinct impression that he didn't want me touching him or his . . . hog.

"I came in here for a fresh shirt," he said, nodding toward the flannel shirts hanging neatly from hooks on the closet wall. "The air conditioner was on the fritz . . ." He stared down at the ruined doorknob. "What the hell did you do to the door?"

"Nothing!" I exclaimed, but I hid my hands behind my back as if it would keep me from being caught red-handed.

"What are you even doing in here?" he demanded. "You don't have any good reason to be in here, damaging school property. What the hell is wrong with you parents? Ya know, just 'cause you pay taxes doesn't mean you *own* the school!"

My mouth was hanging open in response to his rudeness. I was sure my vampire impression of Munch's *The Scream* was super-attractive. "I got turned around."

"Well, turn back around and get out." He jerked his thumb toward the open door behind him as he shrugged out of his sweat-stained gray Half-Moon Hollow Howlers T-shirt and into a blue cotton uniform workshirt with "Wade" stitched on the breast pocket.

My jaw dropped. Who the hell was this guy, and who did he think he was, bossing me around? Nobody had talked to me like this in . . . well, I couldn't remember the last time someone talked to me with such an irritated tone, certainly not since I became a tragic terminally ill widow. I'd been treated with kid gloves lined with cotton balls for the past two years.

And holy Hades, he had even more tattoos underneath the shirt. Even with my super-vision, I couldn't take in the details in the brief glimpse I got. Still, I got a good look at the big picture, and the picture was pretty damn nice. Long, sinewy arms, a broad chest, and a flat stomach tapering to hip bones that jutted out just a few inches above the waistline of his worn jeans.

How perverse was it that between the pretty face, the tattoos, and the surliness, I was actually beginning to feel the faint stirrings of attraction? Fine, they weren't so much faint stirrings as a deep, reverberating echo between my thighs, like a super-dirty version of those Tibetan meditation bells. It was certainly stronger than anything I'd felt in years. For a while, I hadn't been certain that all of my parts were still in working condition. Was this a side effect of vampirism? Unprecedented skankiness in response to hostility?

And I had been staring at him this whole time, which was starting to become awkward.

"Are you always this grouchy?" I asked.

"Only when nosy soccer moms invade my damn space! Now, get out!"

"Just as an FYI, in case the policy manual is outside your reading-comprehension level, most school employees don't strip in front of parents."

As soon as the words left my mouth, I regretted them. Why had I said that? That was mean. But my insult hadn't even fazed "Wade," who was waving me toward the door. "Keep walking, Bree."

"My name isn't Bree."

He scoffed. "Your names are always 'Bree' or 'Krissy' or 'Elizabeth.' And then you slap it on everythin' you own, including those stupid little stick figures you stick on the backs of your minivans."

"It's Libby," I shot back.

"Which is short for Elizabeth. Thanks for proving my point."

Actually, it was short for Liberty, because I was born on the Fourth of July and the pain meds made my mom all weepy and patriotic. But Sassy Janitor didn't need to know about that.

"Do us all a favor and try to develop a nicer attitude before the kids come back to school."

"I don't need to. The kids know better than to go where they're not wanted!" he shot back as I walked out to find a bemused Jane standing outside the closet.

I would not walk down the hall of an elementary school flipping double birds at a school employee, even if that hallway was empty. That was not something classy mothers did, living or undead.

"You couldn't have stopped him from going into the closet?" I asked drily.

"I was distracted by text messages," she said, sounding not at all apologetic. "You have a thing for tattoos, huh?"

"Don't read my mind without my permission!" I hissed quietly. "That's just rude!"

"Hey, I only got half of the picture before you managed to shut me out. How did you do that, by the way? Meditation exercises?"

"Do what?"

"Shut me out of your head," she said. "The only other person who can do it is Nola, and she has an unfair magical advantage."

"I'm not sure what you're talking about," I said. "Let's just get out of here before I make a bigger scene."

"Eh, there's so much background noise no one really noticed the muffled voices coming from the closet."

I stopped in my tracks, turning on my heel and shouting toward the now closed closet door, "And my face is *fine*, by the way! Thanks for asking, jerk."

Danny was still happily rolling about on the magic story-time carpet in the library when I found him, completely engrossed in Miss Lisa's narration of *Pete the Cat: Rockin' in My School Shoes*. Jane took a deep breath as we entered the library, as if she missed the smell. Afterward, I tried to give her some space as we walked to the car. She looked a little weepy. Danny filled up the silence with chatter about his new friend Charlie, Pete the Cat, Charlie, the cafeteria, Charlie, the music room, and Charlie. Charlie was apparently the source of all things cool. He had a dog named Ratchet and a collection of snakeskins and arrowheads.

"So I take it you're excited about this year, buddy?" I asked him as I buckled his seatbelt.

"Yup. Charlie and I are going to be in the same class. We're going to play pirates at recess. But close the door, Mom. I don't want anybody seeing that I still use a Bubble Guppies booster seat."

I nodded and saluted as I closed the door. The poor kid had always been a little sensitive about being smaller than the rest of the kids in his class. He considered his continued use of a preschool-brand booster to be on par with thumb sucking or needing a sippy cup. But he hadn't outgrown it yet, and booster seats weren't cheap.

"I'm proud of you," Jane told me. "That was a lot of sensory input, and you handled it beautifully. And you didn't even show any signs that you'd been turned. Do you know how hard that is? I barely got through a first visit with my mama, and she kept trying to force-feed me pot pie!"

"Thank you, vampire Yoda," I said. "Do I get my 'first outing' merit badge?"

"No, but I'm going to ignore the fact that you're sassing your mentor. You should consider that a gift."

"I do," I told her solemnly.

"Drive safe," she called as she walked toward her tank of a car, an SUV she called Big Bertha, Jr. "I need to swing by my place, and then I'll see you at the house."

"I always drive safe. It's a minivan." Just as I turned toward the car, which had been moved to the school while I slept by a helpful human Council employee, I tracked a flash of hot pink in my peripheral vision. My head whipped toward the movement, a predatory instinct that made me more than a little uncomfortable. About twenty feet away, Ashlynne Carson, the little sister of one of Danny's classmates, was chasing her wayward "Welcome Back to School" balloon as it floated toward the parking lot. Ashlynne's mother, Candace, was busy talking to Mr. Walsh and didn't see her daughter in danger. And Nina Paltree was backing her huge Yukon out of its space and had no clue that Ashlynne was behind her. In fact, it seemed like no one was watching Ashlynne at the moment.

Without thinking, I sprinted the short distance at top speed. I caught Ashlynne under her arms and scooped her up, springing to the side, out of the path of the car. It would have been a graceful rescue had my foot not caught on the curb and sent me sprawling across the sidewalk. I wrapped my arms around Ashlynne's squirming body, rolling across the pavement and taking the brunt of the impact on my back.

"Ow," I grunted as Ashlynne and I rolled to a stop.

"My balloon!" the little girl wailed. "You made me miss my balloon! I want my balloon!"

"Everybody's a critic," I mumbled.

It seemed that while no one had seen me barrel across the parking lot at superhuman speeds, everybody had seen me take a dive on the pavement. Typical. Candace scrambled across the sidewalk and pulled Ashlynne from my arms. I could barely make out her "thank you"s through her alternate sobbing and fussing at her daughter. Nina drove the Yukon away, unaware of the drama left unfolding behind her.

A few other parents huddled around Ashlynne and her mother, while Principal Walsh and Casey ran to help me.

"Libby! Are you OK?" Mr. Walsh helped me to my feet. With every movement, I discovered new bits of gravel buried in my knees and palms.

"I'm fine," I assured him, even as I hissed in pain. Once again, vampirism did not stop the pain response. If anything, I think my sensitive nerves felt it more acutely.

"I'll go get Nurse Anne," he called over his shoulder, jogging into the school building.

"Oh, careful, hon," Casey said, turning my hands over. "You've got some pretty good scrapes on your hands. Let's get you to the nurse's office, and she can clean those . . ." We watched as the wounds on my palms closed on their own. The bits of gravel skittered across the pavement as the healing flesh pushed the rocks out of my skin. "Up." I watched the color drain from my friend's face as she backed away from me.

"Casey . . ." I began.

"Don't." Casey held up her cross necklace as if that would ward me off. (It wouldn't.) "I *knew* you seemed too healthy. You moved too fast. You were too pret— I knew something was wrong."

"There's nothing wrong," I told her.

"Oh, sure, nothing's wrong," she scoffed. Her head snapped toward Mr. Walsh, who was following Ashlynne and Candace into the school.

"Casey," I said, with a little more warning in my tone than was probably wise.

"I don't know anyone who is a vampire," she said. "And I don't want to know you."

And with that, I watched as the closest thing I had to a friend climbed into her car and drove away.

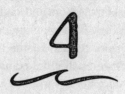

4

Your relationships with other members of your family will change, just as the rest of your life has changed. And if you thought those relatives questioned your parenting decisions before, just wait until they find out you're a vampire.

—*My Mommy Has Fangs: A Guide to Post-Vampiric Parenting*

I knew it was only a matter of time before Les or Marge showed up at my door. Casey was a serious gossip.

I'd expected to have more than forty minutes, though.

When Mr. Walsh emerged from the building with Nurse Anne, enormous first-aid kit in hand, I'd had to explain that the emergency medical care wasn't necessary as I'd done my healing all by myself. There was no time like the present, I supposed, to update them on my new condition. Mr. Walsh spent a grand total of two seconds looking vaguely uncomfortable with the idea of a vampire parent before clearing his throat and handling the situation with his usual aplomb. He assured me that this wouldn't change my son's educational experience at the school and said to come to him if I had any problems. He'd even understood when I'd requested that he not release Danny to his grandparents. He'd dealt with much more complicated custody situations than mine, though in most of his cases, the parties involved had pulses. And while Nurse Anne remained silent, as I was leaving, she slipped a card into my hand detailing the meeting schedule for the Newly Emerged Vampires Support Group.

Still, I'd barely had time to get Danny showered and in bed before I heard a truck screeching through the cornfield and onto my driveway. I sighed, plucking Danny's dirty clothes from the floor and switching on his Captain America night-light before I closed his bedroom door. I walked down the hallway, listening to the slap of Marge's house shoes against the concrete walkway. For a short woman, she was moving at a pretty good clip.

Dear Lord, I prayed, *please grant me the grace to explain this situation to my mother-in-law without permanently damaging our relationship. And if that's not possible, please keep me from ripping her throat out, because that's the sort of thing that will go on my undead permanent record.*

Before Marge could pound on my door and wake my son, I pulled it open, startling her out of her furious posture for a second and making her step back. Marge was wearing one of her old cotton summer nightgowns. Her carefully dyed dark brown hair was up in pink sponge curlers, a nighttime ritual she still kept up, even with the invention of much more convenient hairstyling tools. I doubted she could get to sleep without the tight sensation against her scalp.

Les was standing near the truck, practically vibrating with rage. But he was silent, unable to do anything but stand there, glowering at me.

I opened the door just enough to stretch my arm across it, barring Marge from barging in. "Hi, Marge. I wasn't expecting you. Everything OK?"

There was always the off chance that my in-laws were mad at me for non-vampire-related reasons.

"What have you done?" Marge shrieked, a pink roller dangling near her ear.

OK, maybe not. I sighed. "I got better."

"Don't you play flippant with me, Libby Stratton! You got yourself tangled up with some vampire, and he gave you his *disease*."

And while she was sort of right on some counts, I couldn't help but be a little hurt that she was implying that I'd picked up an STD from an ill-advised hookup. Honestly, where was my vampire Yoda when I needed her? What would Jane do?

"How could you do that?" Marge continued without waiting for an answer. "Was it an accident? Were you attacked?"

"I didn't go looking for a good time, Marge," I said as calmly as I could. "And I wasn't attacked. I made this choice so I could see Danny grow up. I knew you would try to talk me out of it, so I didn't say anything to you."

"You're damn right I would have tried to talk you

out of it!" she yelled. My eyes went wide. In the eight years I'd known my mother-in-law, she'd never cussed once. "I cannot believe you could do something so stupid and selfish. There's no going back from this, do you understand? You can't take it back. How are you going to take care of him? How are you going to be a mother when you can't even wake up during the day? What if he gets hurt and starts bleeding? Will you be able to control yourself?"

It hurt to hear my mother-in-law voice all the fears I'd had tumbling in my own head since I rose. I couldn't blame her for feeling this way. If I were in the same position, I might react the same way. And if I'd felt any sort of hungry twinge for Danny's blood, I would have packed his bags and sent him on to her house. But I hadn't. Danny was safe with me. And her fears were something she was going to have to work through if she wanted to spend time with her grandson. I wasn't going anywhere.

Just then, Jane rolled up the driveway in her SUV and screeched to a halt next to Les's truck. I saw Les's hand start toward his cab, but as Jane hopped out, she warned him, "Whatever you're thinking about grabbing, don't."

In a flash, Jane was at my side, blocking the door. "Mr. and Mrs. Stratton, I'm Jane Jameson-Nightengale with the local Council office. I understand that you're upset right now," she said in a tone so smooth and even her little spiel had to have been thoroughly rehearsed. "Finding out that your loved one has made the transition to vampire can be a very confusing and upsetting time, but the important thing to remember is that Libby is still the same person you've always known. She just has a few new interesting skills. We have several chapters of the FFOTU meeting locally that could help you cope with the changes within your family. I have a brochure here that lists all of the meeting dates and locations." Jane whipped out a slick brochure featuring the triangular logo of the Friends and Family of the Undead.

Marge stepped back as if Jane had offered her a dead rodent. "I have no interest in spending more time with *your kind*. I know what happens at those meetings. A bunch of people sitting around lying to themselves about not being upset at what their family has turned into." She snorted. "And as for her being the same person? The girl who married my son wouldn't have done this to herself. She's obviously lost her mind."

"Well, I can see that the gentle, political approach isn't going to work," Jane muttered. "OK, look, I understand that you're worried about your grandson, but I've stayed with Libby for the last few days, and she hasn't made one move toward Danny with blood on her mind. The thought of hurting him makes her physically ill. You will not find a more devoted parent than your daughter-in-law. Look at what she went through to stay with her son."

"Well, you'll pardon me if I don't take your word for it that Danny's safe. I'm not going to leave my grandchild alone with someone who drinks blood for *food*. We tried to be patient with you while you were sick, Libby, but all you've done is prove that you're not a good influence on our grandson. He's going to go home where he's safe. I simply can't trust you with him."

I chose not to address the fact that she called her house Danny's "home," because there simply weren't enough hours in the evening to unravel that particular rat's nest of dysfunction. So I kept it simple. "You will not take my son from me," I told her. "Cancer didn't take him from me. I sure as hell won't let *you* do it."

"Well, if you think we're going to stand for this, you're even crazier than you let on!'" Marge barked, starting toward the door as if she could push past both of us. Jane very gently caught her arm and pushed her back. Marge's dangling curler bounced loose and skittered across the porch into my azaleas.

"You don't have a choice. I'm his mother. *I* have custody," I told her. "I'm more than willing to let you visit Danny anytime you want. I don't want him to lose his relationship with you. But if you try to take him from me, all bets are off."

"I'm not going to let you *decide* when I see my own grandson," Marge spat. "We're taking you to court. We're going to sue you for full custody."

"And she will have the full backing of the Council's legal department," Jane said, sighing. "You should know that unless you can prove that Libby represents a danger to Danny, you will have difficulty taking custody from her."

"Do you honestly think that a judge in Half-Moon Hollow will give Danny to her instead of us?" Marge demanded. "You must not be from around here, young lady."

"Yes. In fact, there have been several cases in this district of responsible undead biological parents retaining custody over living relatives who filed without reasons beyond 'I don't want my kinfolk living with vampires.'" Jane drawled that last bit in an accent so insulting it couldn't possibly be seen as an endorsement of Marge's position. "And for the record, I grew up in this town. I'm Sherry Jameson's daughter." She turned to me. "How is it possible that your in-laws are the only people in town who *don't* know me?"

I shrugged.

"Well, then, shame on you for helping her get involved in this mess!" Marge shouted.

"Calm down," I whispered fiercely. "You're going to wake up Danny!"

Les moved toward his wife before I could, speaking for the first time since they'd arrived. His voice was so tense and quiet I was afraid his vocal cords would snap. He tugged her arm gently, pulling her toward the truck. "Come on, Marge."

"This isn't over!" Marge cried as Les loaded her into the passenger seat.

Les didn't even look at me as he climbed behind the steering wheel and spun out of the driveway.

"Well." Jane sighed, watching their taillights disappearing into the distance. "It looks like you're going to need that rental a little sooner than you thought."

I nodded, wondering how Danny was going to handle the separation from his grandparents and moving right before the beginning of the school year. His first day of school was Tuesday. (Starting midweek was a lovely quirk of the Kentucky school system.) It seemed very unfair of me to be forcing so many changes on him in such a short period of time. I hoped all those comforting platitudes I'd heard about the resiliency of children were true.

"Lucky for you, the Council happens to know of a recently vacated unit that already has all of the required vampire conveniences. It's located closer to Danny's school and has a registered nurse living in the unit next door, should Danny have any medical emergencies."

"That . . . sounds pretty perfect," I said, lifting a brow. "What's the catch?"

"You will be under close Council surveillance . . . and Dick will be your landlord. But on the upside, moving is much easier when you have superstrength."

"I can live with that," I told her. "And I've been packing for weeks."

I was nearly moved into the Victorian-turned-duplex five days later when my in-laws served me with a very official-looking eviction notice. Kaylee was wringing her hands at the stove when I rose for the night. The white envelope lay on the table with a red "OFFICIAL NOTICE" stamp blaring under the kitchen lights.

It was funny that my brain didn't immediately hop onto "past due bill" when I saw the red stamp. My second night as a vampire, I'd opened my online banking profile and found that it showed a significantly higher balance than I'd expected before I went underground (so to speak). I'd set up all my bills to pay automatically out of the account while I was "out." And while my utilities were all paid up, the considerable insurance money I'd promised my sire in exchange for turning me was still there. The check I'd written for "cash" had not been cashed.

What the hell did that mean? Who turns someone just for fun?

In other developments, the move was coming together more quickly than we'd expected. The new apartment needed very few repairs after the departure of the last tenant, a conscientious vampire who'd given up his lease to move closer to his girlfriend's college campus.

This was the first home I'd have that was my own. *I* paid the rent. *I* controlled the décor. Unless Dick suddenly decided to turn the place into a bed-and-breakfast, we weren't going to be kicked out. There was a tremendous freedom in that.

So much more about my life had changed, beyond my pulse and my diet. I had friends. I had people I could trust with my feelings. I didn't have to put on a brave front or pretend not to be hurt or upset when the occasion called for it.

Danny was upstairs, sorting his toys into "keep," "store," and "donate" boxes. I was fortunate that he seemed to view the move as an adventure, particularly when I described the old restored house with its turret bedrooms and time-worn wooden stairs. He'd always wanted a house where he could slide down the stairs on his butt. It was a dream come true for him.

Beyond the fact that it was necessary, I hoped the

move would be good for my son. Sure, he would start school the day after we moved into the new place, but living in the more rural "farming district" of the Hollow, Danny didn't have any nearby friends his age. Living closer to the school, he had a better chance of developing playmates. He'd asked several questions about his grandparents and how they felt about the move, but I'd been able to distract him with promises of painting his room whatever color he wanted and spending time with "Mr. Dick."

The good news was that the move and keeping up with my contracted bookkeeping work kept me distracted from any weird bloodthirst issues I might be having. Being a vampire mom wasn't that different from being a human mom—it was all about multi-tasking.

But as I made my way into the kitchen for my evening cup of blood, it seemed that Kaylee didn't share my semioptimistic view on life. She was slumped over my stove, stirring a pot of spaghetti and wheatballs while she gnawed on her bottom lip. With Kaylee, I knew that this news could be anything from the death of a grandparent to the cancellation of her favorite teen demon-hunter show. I hoped she was just worried about getting into trouble for accepting the eviction notice.

I opened the official envelope and scanned its contents. It was nothing unexpected. I was being notified of my "breach" as a tenant. Since Rob and I had never actually signed a lease or paid rent, I could only assume that my "breach" involved my not breathing anymore.

I had thirty days to contest or vacate the premises, something I wasn't all that concerned about since I would be ready to move within the next twenty-four hours. I supposed this was the first volley in Les and Marge's suit for custody: prove that I couldn't provide a stable home for Danny on my own. I couldn't help but be somehow proud that I'd anticipated this.

"It's OK, Kaylee, really." I sighed, downing my breakfast. "I was expecting this."

"You were expecting my mama to say I can't babysit for you anymore, Miss Libby?"

"No," I said, pursing my lips. "I was referring to the eviction notice."

"That's what that is?" she cried. "Well, that's not right. I told my mama, I don't care if you're a vampire, you're a good person. Personally, I think it's kind of cool. You look better. You feel better. And you've never hurt me. I don't figure you're going to start now. But Miss Marge's been calling around, telling people that you've gone crazy and started biting people. I tried to tell my mama that just wasn't true, but she said she didn't feel safe with me taking care of Danny anymore. I'm really sorry. I talked her into one more night, but I told her it was because you had to go out and buy Danny's school supplies. She wants me home by nine."

I tamped down the panic welling in my chest. The next day was Danny's last official day of summer vacation, and he was going to wake up without supervision, in a house where I was technically dead down the hall. There was no way that could go wrong.

Danny ran into the kitchen and threw himself at

my side. Because my feet were planted, he bounced off my hip like a rubber ball. I shot my hands out at vampire speed and caught him by the elbows before his head could smack against the corner of the countertop. His eyes went wide with shock as I lowered him gently into a kitchen chair.

"You OK, sweetie?"

"Wow, Mom, you moved quick," he whispered.

I gave an uncomfortable, clipped laugh. "Yeah, well . . . Mom's been taking her vitamins every morning."

"Like the orange ones that get stuck in my teeth?" he asked with a grimace.

"Yep, and if you want to be super-fast, you better take them, too."

Danny had on his skeptical face, which made it a perfect time to change the subject from my unprecedented catlike reflexes.

"So why did you come barreling into the kitchen like a cannonball whose mother never taught him good manners or common sense?" I asked.

He had the good grace to look sheepish for a grand total of three seconds. "OK, so, when you buy my new backpack, make sure it's not a baby backpack. No puppies or construction trucks or anything like that. Transformers or Avengers, and if they don't have those, maybe *The LEGO Movie*. But that's it." Danny tugged on my T-shirt until I dropped to his eye level. "That's *it*, Mom."

"OK," I said. "Any other instructions?"

"No lunch boxes. Nobody brings lunch, Mom. Everybody eats the cafeteria food, even though it can be gross sometimes. And I know you like to get me those little erasers shaped like pizza slices, but Carson ate them last year and started to cry 'cause he thought he was poisoned, so that's not a good idea," he said.

"Got it."

"And no fat crayons. Everybody knows those are little-kid crayons. I need the skinny crayons."

"OK, Danny."

"And no—"

"Danny!"

Having finally made me bark at him, which was his goal all along, he burst out laughing and scampered off to his room.

I shook my head and asked Kaylee, "Are you sure you want to give all this up?"

Kaylee promptly burst into tears.

I blew out an unnecessary breath. "Oh, boy."

While I drove into town, I mulled over the Danny situation and the fact that I would have no help in less than eight hours when he woke up. My first thought was to call his grandparents. It was an instinct born of years when calling anyone else to watch Danny— because I felt guilty asking for babysitting help every time we talked—caused disagreements with Rob and his parents, because they didn't like the idea of anyone else watching Danny. Kaylee was only trusted because her mother went to Les and Marge's church.

Again, it occurred to me how small my friend circle was now that I didn't have other moms I could call for help. I doubted very much that Casey would be willing to watch Danny, since she seemed to be running some sort of gossip campaign about me.

Relinquishing the problem to my hindbrain for a thorough mulling, I pulled into the Walmart parking lot and brought the three-page school-supplies list out of my enormous mom purse. While I was walking to the entrance, I added several things we would need for the duplex: ice trays, a rug for Danny's new bathroom, a countertop blood warmer, plus cracker packs Danny could put in his backpack for snack time. It was a far more interesting array of items than any of my preturning shopping lists.

It was nice to know that despite everything that had changed in my life, Walmart remained the same. I turned toward the special-dietary-needs aisle, the "vampire supplies" area where the undead could shop for fang floss, synthetic blood, and specialized sunscreen. I'll admit I got a little overexcited at the number of new products now available to me. I dropped a tube of White Fang dental whitening gel into the cart, next to Hershey's Special Blood Additive Chocolate Syrup and ReNu Skin revitalizing crème, because you never knew when you would suffer accidental sun exposure and need to regrow your epidermis. I might have overshopped a little, especially when one considered the metric ton of school supplies I was about to purchase, but so far, Casey's and Marge's calls hadn't affected my bookkeeping business. I was going to consider that a good sign . . . or a sign that my clients were afraid to snatch business out from under a new vampire.

I turned toward the school-supplies section, praying that there was a Transformers or Avengers backpack left on the rack. While I dropped boxes of tissue, hand sanitizer, plastic bags, and paper towels into the cart, I tried to remember when exactly this stuff had become a parent expense. I turned the cart around the corner and *crash*—I ran right into another cart.

"Oh, I'm so—you!" I growled, my eyes narrowing at the tattooed arm in front of me. Grumpy Janitor was no less attractive in Walmart's harsh fluorescent lighting. He smelled of iron and citrus, the earthy scents of the garage clinging to his clothes. Those two things should *not* have smelled good together, but God help me, they did. His dark gold hair was slicked back, revealing those devastating blue eyes. The less shaggy appearance made his face open up . . . and his face was openly hostile.

He was wearing worn jeans and black work boots with a T-shirt that read "HMH Custom Cycle Parts." And a sneer. "*You.*"

And, of course, he appeared to be holding the last Avengers backpack in the store.

"So, what, now you're runnin' people down in the grocery store?" he demanded, throwing the backpack into his cart. "Seems like you're always standin' in my way somehow. What's your problem?"

"*My* problem?" I exclaimed. "You ran into *me*. Just like you ran into me at school the other night. Do you have any manners at all?"

"I've got plenty of manners for people that deserve 'em. What the hell are you even doin' here?" he demanded. "Who waits till two days before school starts to buy their kid's school supplies? I thought your type updated your school-supplies shoppin' list progress on Pinterest and shit."

"*You're* shopping for school supplies two days before school starts!" I cried, looking pointedly at his ill-gotten backpack. His cheeks flushed pink, and I tried really hard not to find that adorable. I had to actively command my nerve endings in naughty places *not* to tingle. Also, why didn't I know what to do with my hands?

And he wasn't even my type. While Rob hadn't been all that considerate, he'd at least put on a show of politeness every once in a while. He didn't actively disdain people to their faces.

"Also, I deleted my Pinterest account months ago."

"And I'm here because I bought the wrong backpack. I guess it's against some sort of kid law to carry a Minion backpack after kindergarten," he grumbled, pointing to a bright yellow backpack featuring one of the small yellow underlings from *Despicable Me*. I grimaced. Danny had been rabid about Gru and the Minions when he was in kindergarten but declared the cartoon was for "babies" just after his fifth birthday. There was no greater insult. But I would not commiserate with the Hot Cranky Janitor, no matter how acutely I felt his pain.

I wondered how old his kids were and how old they would be when they got their first tattoos. Also, I wondered how his rough hands would feel against my skin. And where was the kids' mom that he ended up shopping for a replacement backpack at nine o'clock on a Tuesday? Was he a single parent like me?

I glanced down at his hands. He wore silver rings on several fingers. One depicting a motorcycle running along the band, another showing an elaborately carved sugar skull, another made to look like heavy chain link. But none of the pieces screamed, *My baby's mama put a ring on it*.

While I was staring at his manual accessories, his eyes flicked down to my cart and suddenly went wide. I followed his line of sight to the fang-whitening kits.

He smirked at me. "Ohhh, so you're *that* mom."

"*That* mom?" I asked, cocking my fist on my hip.

"The woman who went nuts and got herself turned into a vampire because she was tryin' to avoid gray hair and crow's-feet," he said, smirking. "Just so ya know, hair dye is cheaper."

My jaw dropped. *That's* what the other moms at school were saying about me? Had they not seen me struggle through the last year with their own eyes? And they thought it was OK to tell one another that my reasons for being turned were cosmetic? I suddenly felt no guilt at all for skipping the room-mom meeting the night before. Let some living mom without a reputation for insane vanity take care of the class parties this year.

And this guy—it wasn't that I didn't appreciate his lack of preconceived notions.

The Hollow's gossip circuits ran in concentric socioeconomic circles that never touched. The beauty-parlor circuit ran on a totally different level from the trailer-park-kitchen circuit and even further from the country-club circuit. (Yes, Half-Moon Hollow had a country club. It doubled as a catfish farm, but we had a country club.) Without a sensationalist story in the local paper about a murder trial or some county commissioner getting caught with his pants down, the stories rarely reached all levels. It was sort of refreshing meeting someone who didn't feel sorry for me. He wasn't afraid of me. He was annoyed with me based on personal experience alone. And I had to respect that. But still, screw him and his comments about crow's-feet.

"No, n— What? That's just freaking rude. I'm not going to take that from someone who has the name of his favorite motorcycle on his arm," I shot back.

He frowned in confusion and glanced down at his forearm, where he had "Harley" tattooed in flowing, elaborately shaded script. His arms were a mishmash of styles. Golden Japanese koi swam in and out of the crease near his elbow. A bit of cursive peeked out from under his sleeve, but I couldn't make out what it said. A vintage pinup mermaid curled up on his other forearm. I couldn't help but wonder where else he had ink and felt sort of sad that I would never find out.

"That's not my— That's my son's name!" he exclaimed.

"You named your son Harley? Please, *please* tell me his middle name isn't Davidson."

"It's Wade," he deadpanned. And suddenly, I remembered seeing the name "Wade" stitched on the front of his shirt at school.

"After you, *of course*. And do you also have a daughter named Chlamydia because it sounded pretty?"

Anger flashed across Wade's handsome features, but instead of lashing out, he just shook his head. "Were you always this bitter? Or did ya get that installed with your new plastic-surgery fangs?"

"Look, jackass, you don't even know me. And every time you talk to me, you just spout more hostile bullshit. Why don't you just stay on this side of the school-supplies aisle, and I'll stay over there, and we can avoid each other. I don't know how much more of your *charm* I can take."

He grinned, showing surprisingly bright and even teeth. I wasn't sure if I wanted to smack that beautiful smile off his face or yank him close so I could kiss it away. These were not normal thoughts. He was not my type. And I was already conflicted enough with all the naked sire dreams. I did not need this.

"Oh, it's not charm. I just don't like ya much," he drawled.

"Trust me, I've deciphered your subtle social cues," I shot back, pushing my cart toward the notebooks and folders. I turned on the heel of my sensible Keds and called, "By the way, you do realize that I could literally reach down your throat and hand you your own spleen, right?"

A horrified expression dawned on his face, as if he had not, in fact, considered that.

"Just making sure," I said, smiling just enough to let my dropped fangs show. "You know, so your mouth doesn't write a check your ass can't cash."

"Lunatic," he muttered under his breath.

"I heard that!" I called as he stalked off.

I managed to recover most of my dignity as I checked off the rest of Danny's lengthy school-supplies list. I was still trying to figure out what it was about Wade the Angry Janitorial Engineer that set my fangs on edge so easily. Was it because he reminded me so much of my childhood? Because he was the first person to express real and honest reactions to me in years? Or because he was the first person who seemed to be able to take it when I snapped at him?

I didn't think any of those reasons painted me in a particularly positive light.

I checked out and walked out of the store a ridiculous amount poorer. But the good news was that I was no longer afraid to walk across a dark parking lot by myself. There was an extraordinary amount of freedom in that. I was practically skipping to my van, even with the enormous number of shopping bags I was carrying. Despite its being a relatively nondescript gray, I was able to find the van easily, thanks to the decal on the back that read "I like big books and I cannot lie." It helped separate my car from all of the other mom-vans with stick-figure families on the back. I had briefly thought about getting a zombie stick family, but considering the whole dead-husband-slash-vampire-mom thing, that was probably unseemly.

And while I found the van easily enough, I also found that there was a motorcycle parked incredibly close to my driver's-side door. As in, I couldn't open the damn door. It was a beautiful bike, a sleek black classic Harley-Davidson with a swirling silver pinstripe along the gas tank. But while I could appreciate the aesthetics, I also wanted to drive my car home as opposed to jogging. I loaded the grocery bags into the back hatch and considered using my vampire strength to pick up the Harley and move it. But I'd read somewhere that touching a man's bike was a big no-no in the motorcycle world, and the last thing I needed to do was piss off a random Hells Angel in a Walmart parking lot.

I would not crawl to the driver's seat from the back gate of my van. I wasn't sure my skinny jeans would hold up to the strain. I could crawl in from the passenger's seat, but I wasn't actually sure that I could back out of the space without hitting the bike. And while I wasn't so worried about being beaten up by a biker, I probably couldn't afford to replace a vintage Harley.

Wait. Harley. Oh, crap.

"Whatever crazy-ass evil thing you're planning to do to my bike, just back away and do somethin' else. Crack my kneecap or do the spleen-rippin' thing, but just leave my bike alone."

"I wasn't going to hurt your precious bike," I shot back as Wade dropped the backpack into a saddlebag slung over his bike's seat.

"You were thinkin' about it," he said, pointing his finger at me.

"I—I was not," I insisted. "I couldn't afford to replace it, so I was fighting down the urge."

He quirked an eyebrow and actually smiled at me. A real, sincere, mockery-free smile that actually made me want to smile back. I bit back the urge, but it was there. "So why are you standin' here, eyein' my bike in a suspicious fashion?"

"Because you parked it so freaking close to my van that I couldn't even get into it."

"Well, I only parked so close because I got distracted by the 'big books' sticker!" he exclaimed.

"What?" I cried.

"It was funny!"

I laughed, pinching the bridge of my nose and trying really hard not to like the cranky redneck. When I looked up, he was still grinning at me. I let loose a shocked gasp. "You're enjoying this, aren't you?" I accused. "You *enjoy* winding me up, like some sort of backward, backwoods form of flirting. You've got one of those weird fetishes where you can only get turned on by the sound of a woman yelling at you while pelting you with balloons filled with banana pudding."

Wade went pale, and his full mouth fell open. "I'm tryin' to come up with a smartass comeback, but my brain seems to have gone 'TILT.'"

I snickered. "That's not the first time I've had that effect on a man."

"I don't doubt it," he drawled.

A smoother, more cultured voice sounded behind me. "Is this man bothering you, miss?"

I turned to find a tall, dark-haired man standing behind us, giving Wade a strong case of side-eye. He was certainly the kind of guy you'd want coming to your rescue—handsome and well dressed in dark jeans and a navy dress shirt rolled at the elbows. His eyes were dark, and his features were even and sort of dignified in that old-fashioned matinee-idol way. Given that I was pretty sure he was a vampire, it was entirely possible he *was* an old-fashioned matinee idol. He looked vaguely familiar, but I couldn't quite place him.

He looked vaguely familiar and yet so out of place in the Hollow. But somehow I was glad that he'd stopped to check on me. It gave me hope for the male gender. How wrong would it be for me to play injured party so this gentlemanly vampire would slap Wade around a little bit?

Pretty wrong.

Wade's face, roguishly handsome though it might have been, could not stand up to a vampire whooping. So instead, I asked, "Do I know you?"

Wade had stepped between me and the newcomer and interjected, "Hell, no, I'm not botherin' her."

Mr. Gentleman gave Wade a withering stare. "I think I'll let the lady answer that."

"It's fine," I assured him. "Just a minor parking disagreement between fellow PTA members."

Wade's brows rose, as did the vampire's. "Really?"

"Look, buddy, we're not lookin' for an audience, so keep walking," Wade told him, making a shooing motion with his arm.

I ignored Wade's rudeness, saying with saccharine sweetness, "My friend here was just asking me if I thought that his huge motorcycle could be considered a sign that he might be overcompensating for something. And I told him, 'Don't be silly, everybody knows that Corvettes are the classic compensation vehicles.

Motorcycles are more of a midlife-crisis sort of purchase.'"

Wade cleared his throat. "And I told her that she was right, it was way more interestin' to ride around town in a van that could carry a freakin' basketball team. I mean, you have *one kid*, but really, drivin' a barge is the smart thing to do."

"Don't pick on my van," I retorted.

"Don't call my bike an overcompensation. I don't need to compensate for anything."

"You sound a little defensive there."

"I swear, woman, you are the most frustratin' person I have ever met."

"Are you sure you're all right?" the vampire asked.

"We're fine," Wade and I chorused, glaring at each other. And it seemed that we were back to square one in terms of hostilities. It was nice to know we could agree on something, even if it was how much we irritated each other. The vampire stared for a few more beats and then walked away, frowning.

"Just let me back out, and you can climb into your mom-mobile," Wade sniped, slinging his leg over his bike. I sincerely wished that wasn't as sexy as it was. Maybe he would have one of those dorky full-face shield helmets that made him look like Darth Vader. Nope, no such luck. The half-helmet, black with a flaming motorcycle wheel painted down the side, just made him look hotter.

"It's always a pleasure to see you," I told him, my voice dripping with sarcasm. "Remember, red lights are for quitters."

Wade backed out of the space with the Fred Flintstone shuffle, then started his bike. Under the roar of his engine, he was muttering some rude words he thought I couldn't hear. I smiled, waving as I opened my door.

I sighed, starting my own engine. I wasn't entirely sure what had just happened, but it made me smile. I *never* talked to people like that, much less attractive men. I was not a firecracker. One of the things my late husband had liked most about me was what he called my "sweet nature," which boiled down to me not complaining about his shenanigans and letting him do whatever he wanted. I did not simultaneously flirt with and insult attractive men on motorcycles. It was Wade's fault, I told myself. Becoming a vampire couldn't have changed my nature this much. There was something "special" about his personality that activated the rude, reckless bits of my DNA.

Maybe I should have let that chivalrous vampire slap him around after all.

5

You will have to find a way to make compromises with your child's living relatives. It's a difficult process, but remember, one day those difficult relatives will be dead, and you will not.

—*My Mommy Has Fangs: A Guide to Post-Vampiric Parenting*

I was probably the first vampire ever to say this, but God bless the World Council for the Equal Treatment of the Undead. By the time I arrived home, Jane had already heard about Kaylee's defection through the Hollow gossip mill and had sent a trusted Council-approved sitter to my house to wait for Danny to wake up. Petite, with chicory-colored skin, wide brown eyes, and a cloud of dark, perfectly spiraled curls framing her face, Kerrianne Union was the divorced mom of a fifth-grader at Danny's school. Her mother, Diana, lived with her, so she was free in the mornings to come over and help Danny get ready for school, then carpool both kids.

I'd met Kerrianne in passing at a few school events, but I'd always been in such a rush that I hadn't made time to get to know her. But now, sitting at my kitchen table with a cup of coffee clutched between her hands like a predawn lifeline, Kerrianne was brusque and no-nonsense, like Mary Poppins in a "Purple Rain" T-shirt.

"I won't be starting this early every day," she told me. "But I figured you'd feel better goin' to bed knowin' who's taking care of your baby."

"You're not wrong," I told her while I packed up. "I really do appreciate your coming over at the last minute."

"Well, a job is a job, and the Council is a good employer to have," she said, stirring her coffee even as I leaned away from the brew. I was sure it smelled heavenly to her human nose, but to me it smelled like Danny's socks marinated in raw sewage. "They don't trust anybody, so once you pass their crazy stringent background checks, you're golden. They pay a fair wage, and they pay on time. I earn enough from part-time work that I can take care of my daughter."

"And you don't mind working for vampires?"

"Aw, hell." Kerrianne snorted. "They're not any more evil or violent than the average human. At least they're up front about what they want. And did I mention they pay on time? That's a big priority for me."

"You mentioned," I said, laughing softly as I taped up a box of kitchen stuff.

"I don't mind working for you. I figured you seemed pretty nice at those PTA meetings, and you'd probably carry that through to your unlife. From what I've seen, people who were assholes when they were alive stay assholes when they're vampires. Besides, we're on the prize solicitation committee for the Pumpkin Patch this year, so we might as well get to know each other."

"Argh." I groaned. The prize committee was in charge of calling area businesses and asking for special lots for the festival's raffle and silent auction—gift certificates, free services, and, occasionally, special perks like sports tickets. I'd served on the committee last year. It was like being a telemarketer, only a telemarketer who was asking for really annoying loans. People started ducking me at the grocery store. I took a bottle of Faux Type O out of the fridge and glugged it down without warming it. "That is the *worst*."

"I know." She sighed. "And personally, I'm a little uncomfortable with the word 'solicitation.'"

"I can still say no," I insisted. "I can use my scary vampire powers and tell them I'm unavailable this year."

"Your scary vampire power is getting out of volunteer 'opportunities'? I'm not sure if that's lame or awesome."

I giggled, spitting a dribble of blood over my chin.

"Whoops, party foul. Don't waste good blood, hon," Kerrianne said, shaking her head. "Don't be that girl."

"I think we're going to get along fine," I said, holding my bottle up.

Smiling, she clinked her mug against my bottle. "Just fine."

Danny adjusted to the move, Kerrianne's presence, and his first day of school like he did all things: quickly and with enthusiasm. He loved his new room in the

Victorian's "tower," his new big-boy planet-themed sheets, and sliding down the stairs on his butt. He also insisted that it was the *perfect* place for us to live because a Bigfoot lived in the backyard.

"I've been watching it for the last couple of nights through my bedroom window," he told me solemnly. "I could see him, clear as anything. Last night, he waved at me!"

This claim might have seemed like cause for some concern for the average mom, but this was not the first time my Bigfoot-obsessed son had sworn he'd seen a hominid creature from a distance. His insistence that he'd seen a Sasquatch while camping with his grandpa the previous summer led to Les insisting that "the boy needs less reading and more man's work." My response was to buy Danny a children's book on cryptids and a "Caution: Bigfoot Crossing" sign for his bedroom door.

But there were other adjustments that weren't so easy. Danny didn't understand why I couldn't spend more time with him now that I was "feeling better." As much as he liked Kerrianne and her daughter, Braylen, he didn't understand why they drove him to school in the mornings instead of me. He missed baking with me, a B.C. activity we'd both enjoyed thoroughly, but I was too afraid of how the food smells might affect me to give it a try. And I was even more afraid of explaining it all to him for fear of scaring him.

Danny was a sunny kid, so it was difficult to suss out when something was bothering him. But it didn't shock me to find him on the porch a few nights later, staring at fireflies dancing in our new front yard one evening, instead of sitting at the kitchen table with Braylen, practicing his math flash cards like usual. Kerrianne was at the stove, her dark hair wound into a high, loose bun as she stirred something that involved neither wheatballs nor tofu. This alone would make her Danny's favorite sitter ever.

I shuffled into the kitchen with the Knight's Castle monthly financials under my arm, desperately seeking a caffeinated blood blend called Plasmaspresso. It was the only thing that brought me up to Danny's level first thing in the evening.

"He's out on the front porch, Miss Libby," Braylen told me, her big brown doe eyes solemn. Braylen was a sweet girl, tall for her age, with a cute overbite that she would eventually grow into. "He did not have a good day at school. You should ask him about lunch."

"He was on a four today," Kerrianne added. I drew my lips back in a wince. The kids' daily behavior was rated on a scale of one to five, pushing up their rating with the severity of their disruption. One meant no problems. Five meant a call home from the principal's office. Danny had never been past a two.

"Wow," I marveled. "What did he do?"

Braylen pinched her lips together, as if she couldn't bear to tattle.

"Honey, I need to know what I'm walking into here," I told her, my tone gentle.

"He *may* have thrown a cup of applesauce at Mrs. McGee when the class was getting ready for snack time."

"That is . . . What?" I stormed out to the porch. "Daniel Robert Stratton, what on earth?"

But I stopped in my tracks when I saw the tears streaking down his cheeks. My son did not cry unless something was bothering him deeply. Though my crazed, angry "Hulk Mom" instincts demanded that I track down the source of those tears and *SMASHSMASHSMASH* it out of existence, I dialed down my righteous (irrational) mom anger and plopped down on the step next to him.

"Danny, what happened at school today?"

Danny tucked his face against his knees and shook his head.

"Danny, why did you throw applesauce at Mrs. McGee?" I asked gently.

Mrs. McGee was a grandparent volunteer who had been lurking around the building since *I* was in elementary school. She wasn't exactly a cuddly, cheerful soul. And she didn't seem to like children all that much. Her own grandkids had graduated from high school years before. I wasn't sure why she even bothered volunteering, other than to fill her empty hours. Frankly, I wouldn't have minded tossing an applesauce at her myself a time or two, but I was sure that wasn't the most responsible thing to tell one's delinquent son.

"Danny, talk to me." I rubbed a hand down his arm. Slowly, he lifted his head and pierced me with his big blue-green eyes.

"Mom, Mrs. McGee said you were a monster. What did she mean?"

I was going to *drown* Mrs. McGee in applesauce. "What did Mrs. McGee say, honey?"

"We were making family trees in class on big pieces of construction paper," he said. "Everybody was so busy that Mrs. McGee came in to help us, 'specially with writing the names."

I nodded. I'd known about this assignment. Miss Steele had asked the parents to send in a list of relatives and their correct name spellings to help the kids construct their trees.

"I spent a lot of time drawing my trunk, so I was one of the last ones to get done. Everybody else was getting ready for snack time. Mrs. McGee was writing the names on my tree, and she kept talking about how one side of my tree was almost empty. And how it was a 'shame' that you didn't have more names for me, because you didn't even know who your daddy is. And she said it would have been better if you just left your side blank and gave me to Mamaw and Papa. She said that you went looking for, uh, 'ankneesyfix,' instead of what God wanted you to do. You should have just died, but you'd gone and turned yourself into a monster. And that's when I threw my applesauce at her."

"Danny."

"Well, Charlie left it out on my desk for me! It was right there! And she was asking for it, Mom. She was being mean."

"I'm not disagreeing with you, hon. But why didn't you just go to Miss Steele if Mrs. McGee was hurting your feelings?"

"Miss Steele was busy helping Anna with her tree. And I was so mad I just didn't think to get up and tell her."

"Hmm." I buried my nose in Danny's hair, praying for the strength and patience to deal with this situation correctly.

"What did Mrs. McGee mean, Mom? What's a 'an-kneesyfix?'"

I took a deep breath, even as my fangs ached to stretch from my jaw, to tear and bite into the evil old biddy. I couldn't help but feel this was my fault on several levels, not just because of my undead altered state but because of my inability to fill out my half of Danny's family tree. I barely had information on the parent I did know. And I could only imagine how it felt for Danny to put question marks in place of his grandfather's name. I allowed myself to feel just a momentary flash of guilt and hurt. Guilt because I couldn't give Danny a second set of grandparents to love and spoil him, hurt over one more reminder that my father had run off, leaving me with those blank spaces.

But Danny didn't care about me or my abandonment issues. He needed answers now.

"I think she means that Mom's different now. And she doesn't know how to deal with it."

"Why not?"

"You know how Mom got real sick a while ago?"

Danny nodded, wiping at his cheeks. "Yeah, when you went to the hospital and you were so tired all the time?"

"Well, I was *very* sick, and I wasn't getting well. And I found some people who could help me feel all better. But to do that, I had to change."

"Change, like, how?" he asked, leaning into me while I stroked his back.

I took a deep, unnecessary breath and braced myself. "Honey, I'm a vampire."

I waited for him to wrench away from me, to cry or yell or laugh. But all he did was snuggle against my arm and grumble, "Yeah, duh."

Well, that was anticlimactic.

"Do you know what that means?" I asked.

Danny stayed silent, and when I poked his arm, he said, "You've told me it's rude to say 'duh' more than once, Mom."

"It's rude to say it once, Danny."

"Oh, sorry. But yeah, I know what it means."

"So you figured that out already, huh?"

"Well, yeah, you were only coming out at night, and you haven't eaten anything in a week. We talked about vampires during Undead American Appreciation Week at school last year. I'm a kid, Mom, I'm not stupid."

"Fair point," I said. "Remind me to start spelling things around you again."

"I'm learning to read."

"Well, there goes my whole parenting strategy." I sighed dramatically, making him roll his eyes.

He picked at the cuff on my blue thermal shirt. "Is it fun, being a vampire?"

"Sure. I feel so much better than I did before, which

was the whole point. I can take care of you much better now. The only problem is, like you said, I can't go out during the day, but that's a small price to pay if it means I get to stay with you. It's going to be different for a while, but we'll work it out."

Danny stared at me, speculative. "Do you have fangs?"

"Yep."

"Can I see?"

This was the part I was dreading, Danny seeing me as something different, changed from the woman who baked him cookies and made his Halloween costumes. I was terrified that he would reject me, even if it was something as simple as being afraid of my fangs. But he had a right to ask questions and see the big picture. Biting my lip, I nodded and let them drop gradually, so it would feel less like I was springing something at him. Plus, in the corner of my brain, I still worried a little that moving my fangs too quickly would trigger some sort of instinctual feeding frenzy. But even when Danny reached up and touched his fingertip to the sharp point, I didn't feel any temptation. I did worry about whether he'd washed his hands since he'd left school.

"Are you going to try to bite me?" he asked, lifting my lip so he could get a better look at my canines.

"No," I said, pulling his hands away from my mouth. "Never."

"Can you still make me pancakes for dinner?"

"I will try my hardest."

"What does blood taste like?"

"Like meaty Diet Coke," I responded, laughing when he made a face of absolute disgust. "I'm sticking to bottled fake blood for right now. It's OK, but I definitely don't want you trying it."

Danny shrugged. "OK, then. Can I have SpongeBob macaroni for dinner?"

I stared at him. "That's it?"

He shrugged. "Yep. You're not going away. You're not sick anymore. And you're not going to bite me. That makes me happy. I mean, I don't like that I can't see you during the day. But vampires can do cool tricks, right? Like turn into bats and stuff?"

"No," I told him. "That's just in cartoons."

Danny crossed his arms over his chest and stuck out his bottom lip. The pouting force was very strong with this one. "Well, that stinks."

"But I'm super-fast and super-strong. When I get hurt, it heals right back up."

"Like Superman?"

"Yeah, sort of," I said. "Watch."

I stepped off the porch and took off at top speed, running a lap around the house and skidding to a stop in front of him.

He launched to his feet and cheered. "Cool! Can you fly?"

"No, but watch this." I bent at the knees and sprang up as fast and as far as I could, clearing the roof of the house and landing on the lowest sturdy branch of the oak tree by Danny's bedroom window. Danny cheered and whooped, while I did a backward flip off the branch and landed gracefully on the ground.

"I wish I could take you in for show-and-tell," he said.

"Well, it would be really entertaining until the sunlight made your mom burst into flames and traumatized the whole class."

"Probably," he admitted, standing up and brushing the dust from his butt.

"So we're OK?" I asked, tugging at his hand until he fell into my lap. He squirmed, too old in his mind now for cuddles.

"Yeah."

"And no more throwing applesauce at school personnel, OK? If you're upset with an adult, you go to Mr. Walsh, or you come home and tell me and I'll take care of it."

"Are you going to take care of Mrs. McGee?"

"Well, not in the way that you seem to be implying. I'm not a hit man."

Danny's eyes went wide and innocent. "I don't know what you mean."

"I think you do."

"Fine." He sighed. At the front door, he paused. "Vampires don't eat, right?"

"Not solid human food, no."

"So you won't be able to eat my Halloween candy?"

"No."

"Or my Christmas-stocking candy?"

I sighed, pursing my lips. "No."

"Or the ears off my chocolate Easter bunny?"

"Daniel Robert."

"I'm just checking!" he exclaimed.

"Sweetheart, I cannot eat your candy anymore," I told him. He gave me a Cheshire cat grin. "Stop smiling so much."

"But I'm happy."

"Go get your dinner."

I clicked my tongue as he announced to Kerrianne that I'd approved of pasta shaped like a talking sea sponge. "I'm raising a future supervillain."

I pulled my cell phone from my pocket to call the principal. He'd given me his personal cell-phone number to call in case of issues like the one with Mrs. McGee.

Scrolling through my phone, I found several voice-mail messages from the Council office daytime liaison. She was calling to set up a meeting time with my in-laws, who had contacted Jane's office to try to arrange mediation for the custody of one Daniel Robert Stratton.

I was so glad that Danny was inside, because the string of curse words that came streaming out of my mouth would surely be repeated at school, resulting in my son progressing beyond behavior level four to at least a seven.

When I called Jane in a panic, she assured me that the notice was a good thing, that it was less likely to end in a courtroom or in bloodshed if they were willing to mediate. Of course, I was the first custody case she'd ever handled, so I wasn't really sure on what she was basing this comparison. But it made me a feel a little better.

I was a bit disappointed in the plain gray conference room of the Council offices. I expected something a bit more *American Horror Story* meets *Mad Men*, particularly after Jane described the insane number of Hello Kitty office accessories she'd had to toss out of her predecessor's office. But maybe the vampire officials were trying to put visiting humans at ease by lulling them into a boredom coma. Nondescript gray carpet, gray laminate table, gray chairs, but no windows. The rest of the Council complex was decorated in a similar fashion. I wondered if the lack of windows and other indicators of time of day were as much an effort to trick employees into higher productivity as to avoid unpleasant sunlight exposure. Like Vegas, with duller furnishings.

The main advantage of the setting was Les and Marge's abject discomfort. Marge clutched her purse in her lap as if some vampire had been waiting for centuries to snag her Vera Bradley bag and its bottomless supply of coupons. Les just sat across the table, arms crisscrossed over his chest, glaring at me. Because I'd become a vampire specifically to annoy him.

I'd dressed carefully in my most respectable "mom clothes," or what had passed for my respectable mom clothes before I was sick. My teal sweater set and khakis were baggy from the weight I'd lost, but they were pressed, clean, and appropriate.

I hoped that this meeting would end more amicably than current attitudes around the table would indicate. I didn't want to deny my in-laws visitation or access to Danny, but I refused to let them take over parenting him. He was *my* son. But for now, I was wary about weekend visits or even ice-cream trips. On some level, I just didn't trust them to bring him back to me.

"Our mediator, Miss Dwyer, will be here shortly," Jane's very human receptionist, Margaret, assured us. Margaret was a graying, humorless woman with all the personality of dishwater, but she was kind and almost deferential to me, offering a variety of soothing herbal blood blends while we waited.

"If she's not here in ten minutes, we're out of here." Les grunted. "We don't spend time in buildings run by vampires after dark."

"We'll try to get you home as soon as possible," I told him.

"Oh, because you're running the meeting, are you?" Les said, his mouth twisting into a sour line.

I sighed. "I didn't say that, Les, really. I'm just trying to—"

"Oh, we know what you're 'just trying' to do," Les interjected. "We know all about how you're ruining our grandson. Weird hours at home, no proper meals, outbursts at school."

I lifted a brow. How did my father-in-law know about my outburst in the custodian's closet?

Wait, no, he probably meant Danny and Mrs. McGee. Mr. Walsh and I had a phone conference about the Applesauce Incident and agreed that while Danny's reaction had been inappropriate, Mrs. McGee would not be allowed to continue to volunteer at the school if she couldn't keep her opinions about vampires to herself. Mr. Walsh was willing to let her go over the incident—in his opinion, this was no different from a volunteer spouting slurs about other ethnic or religious groups. But honestly, Mrs. McGee was an institution at that school. Politically, I didn't think I could afford to be the parent who insisted on her removal. So she had one more chance. After that, Mr. Walsh could toss her out on her ancient butt.

"That was one incident of misbehavior at school, not even worth a visit to the principal's office. And Danny is supervised in the afternoons by a Council-approved, CPR-certified child-care provider who prepares healthy, balanced meals," I told them.

At the mention of this, Marge sort of quavered, as if the idea of someone else cooking for her grandson was somehow the cruelest cut of all. I added, "You should know that if you're going to call my parenting into question, you're going to have to find something a little more serious than a classroom tantrum."

Les sneered. "And you should know that we're not screwing around with visitation. We don't want a judge to think we're happy with that. Our lawyer told us to hold out. It's going to make it easier for us to go for full custody of Danny. Our boy deserves to be raised in a normal, human home with normal, human parents."

"But you aren't his parents. What sort of insane lawyer gave you that advice?" I demanded.

"None of your business," Les said, smiling nastily.

I stared at my father-in-law, wondering how he'd managed to keep this level of petulant rudeness under wraps for so many years. Sure, he'd been a condescending mansplainer, but he'd generally been the "nice to your face, but ask other people to 'redirect' you when you weren't around" type since Rob and I started dating. Marge cleared her throat, her dark, almost starched curls bouncing as she leaned across the table.

"Look, I don't see any reason why we can't all be reasonable here," she said, her tone wheedling. "We all want the same things. We all want Danny to have a happy, normal childhood."

"Everybody needs to stop emphasizing the word 'normal,'" I told them. "There is no normal anymore; there hasn't been since vampires became our neighbors instead of myth. This is the new normal. And y'all need to deal with it."

I cleared my throat. I was losing myself, reverting back to my old accent as I grew more upset. I needed to calm down. If I lost control in this session, it would be one more justification for Danny to be removed from his home.

"We just need to work together to find a compromise," Marge continued, as if I hadn't spoken. "Libby doesn't want to disappoint us, I'm sure. You want us to have a cordial relationship, don't you?"

How did Marge manage that sweet tone, considering her nightgowned hissy fit outside my home just days before? Were we pretending that had never happened? Because I didn't know if I could do that. And I certainly noticed her not-terribly-subtle implication that we could only have a cordial relationship if I was willing to bend to their wishes.

"We just have to work out a schedule. You'll get

Halloween with Danny. I'm sure your people love Halloween. And we'll take Thanksgiving and Christmas. You can just sleep in those nights."

I frowned. "Why wouldn't I want Danny to spend Thanksgiving and Christmas with me?"

Marge tittered nervously, looking to Les for validation, but all he did was roll his eyes and stare at the ceiling. "Well, you wouldn't want Danny to miss out on spending the holidays with his relatives on my side. Besides, it would be an awfully small celebration if it was just you and Danny. Family has never been as important to *you* as it is to most people," Marge said. "And besides, it's not like you're going to eat anyway."

Ouch. I mean, she wasn't wrong about the eating thing, but ouch.

It wasn't unusual for my in-laws to cite my limited genealogical tree. I'd never been allowed to forget that I'd married into an expansive, storied McClure County family. But they normally did it in a far more passive-aggressive, less "steal your child like something out of a Grimm tale" manner.

The aforementioned very late Miss Dwyer finally arrived and did her best, going around and around with us on suggesting pickup schedules and potential weekends. But Les and Marge—or at least Les—wouldn't have it. He insisted that there would be no visitation schedule. They wanted total custody or nothing.

After Les refused yet another carefully constructed suggestion from Miss Dwyer, I will admit that I lost my temper a little. If "a little" meant snapping a fancy fountain pen in half with my thumb and splattering black ink all over the carpet. I took a deep breath and resisted the urge to wipe my smudged hands against my khakis.

"Les and Marge, you need to understand that if and when you see Danny, it will be on my terms. If we can't come to some sort of resolution, you may not be able to see him at all." I knew I was using my "explaining to Danny why playing with matches is wrong" voice, but I didn't care. They'd lured me to mediation under false pretenses. They had it coming.

While Marge was downright unsettled by this statement, Les didn't even twitch. "We're not worried about that," he said, his gray mustache bristling as he smirked.

I hid my stained hand under the table and very carefully asked through my clenched fangs, "If you didn't plan on cooperating, why did you bother coming to mediation at all? You were the ones to call the Council office and request this meeting in the first place."

Les shrugged. "Our lawyer said that this was the best way to show that we were trying to be reasonable."

If and when I found out who was representing my in-laws in this farce, that attorney might just be my first human chew toy.

Be very careful approaching children's social events. They will be fraught with dangers, including birthday candles, unsecured silverware, and clowns.

—*My Mommy Has Fangs: A Guide to Post-Vampiric Parenting*

I dumped yet another bag of gummy feet into a camouflage paper bowl and wondered how I'd gotten myself into throwing a Bigfoot-themed sleepover for a cabal of first-graders.

Danny was officially turning six, and it was his dearest wish to have a big-boy sleepover. We'd spent months discussing the best snacks to serve and the best games to play. He and Kerrianne spent most of the week creating an elaborate pillow fort in his new bedroom to house this sugar-fueled spectacular. He'd been pushing for it since he was four, but overnighting with a group of grumpy toddlers was a bit beyond even my mothering skill level, so I'd been able to put him off. But this was the year. We'd agreed that when he hit first grade, when it was almost guaranteed that his friends were potty-trained and could feed themselves, I would be willing to host them. Danny resented the "almost" guaranteed, but we shook on it and everything.

At least I was a nocturnal creature now and had a ninety percent chance of outlasting them, sleep-wise. But I'd woken up with a weird heavy feeling in my stomach that evening, a feeling of impending dread that had nothing to do with not picking up the cookie cake on time or the fact that I could only find one age-appropriate Sasquatch-related movie for the kids to watch. It turned out there were a lot of super-creepy, violent movies made about Sasquatch. *Harry and the Hendersons* was the least emotionally scarring option.

I couldn't put my finger on why I was so unsettled. I tried to invite Les and Marge for cake and ice cream, at least, hoping to bridge the gap a bit with a magnanimous, slightly underhanded gesture. But they hadn't returned my numerous calls. My conscience was clear, at least.

I may have overprepared a little bit, abusing my renewed Pinterest account to find Bigfoot-themed printables and games. I'd arranged for a moonlit Sasquatch hunt in the backyard, leading to a big footprint near the tree line that the boys were going to fill with plaster. I'd thought about ending it with a Bigfoot-shaped piñata, but I wasn't comfortable with the idea that if you loved something you should hunt it down and beat it with a stick until delicious surprises fall out.

We'd followed the school's unwritten party policy of inviting every boy in Danny's class. The administration would not tolerate a child doling out party invites like a tiny Perez Hilton. The problem was that I didn't

know how many kids to expect. None of the mothers
had RSVP'd. This was not unusual. In the Hollow, an
RSVP phone contact was just the number a mother
called to inform the hostess how many of the guest's
uninvited siblings would also be attending.

So why did I have this weird "Carrie before the
prom" feeling pressing on my chest?

An hour after the party was expected to start, I got
my answer. Not one single kid had arrived. Not one.

Danny was collapsed on the couch, his jeans and
flannel shirt rumpled from his rolling around on the
cushions, waiting for his friends to arrive. His little
Outback hat had been thrown to the ground, forgotten. He'd started out so excited, bouncing on the balls
of his feet while he waited at the front door for cars to
roll down the driveway, and then slowly wilting into
the pile of disappointment lolling on the couch.

It took iron control over every single muscle fiber in
my face to keep a calm, cheerful expression for Danny's sake. I couldn't believe this was a coincidence.
In all of the birthday parties Danny had attended, I'd
never seen this happen. At least two or three kids
showed up for every party, even in the homes where
it was rumored that a meth lab was operating. I could
not believe that this was not somehow connected to
the fact that I was a vampire now. Danny was being
shunned because of me.

"You put directions to your new address in the envelope, didn't you?" Kerrianne whispered, refreshing
the ice in the cooler full of sodas. "Maybe they don't
realize you moved."

"I printed the directions in red, in all caps," I whispered. "I can't believe this! I can't *believe* the other parents would pull this. I've seen their kids through accelerated reader testing and field trips to the freaking petting zoo and the Christmas programs—oh, my God, how many times can I loan out my dead husband's bathrobe as a shepherd's costume—but now, I'm trying to throw my son a freaking birthday party and they can't be bothered to show up?"

Behind me, I heard a quick intake of breath and realized I wasn't being nearly as quiet as I thought I was. Sure, the gasp I heard, but I didn't pick up on his little feet shuffling across the carpet? Stupid inconsistent vampire senses.

"What do you mean, Mom? Do you mean no one is coming?" Danny asked, his lips trembling.

"No, not at all, sweetheart. I'm sure people are coming. They're just running late," I assured him, trying to keep the anxious note out of my voice.

"You're sure?" Danny sniffed.

"Absolutely. There will be people here before you know it, lots of them."

"OK." He sighed. "Can I have a cookie while I'm waiting?"

I tried to weigh the pressures of proper parental nutrition standards versus keeping my son calm on what would no doubt be one of those traumatic birthday incidents he'd discuss in therapy ten years in the future.

"Half a cookie," I told him.

"I'll take it," he said, nodding sharply and marching into the kitchen.

"Hey, does celebrating this birthday mean that you're going to stop introducing yourself as being 'five and five-sixths'?" I yelled after him.

"Mah-ommm."

"I see we've reached the stage where I embarrass you just by having the power of speech. I have leveled up in motherhood!" I raised my hands in a semitriumphant pose until he was completely out of earshot. I dropped my arms.

Right, I would make this happen.

I turned to Kerrianne. "I need bodies. And I don't mean in the creepy vampire way."

Kerrianne gave me a crisp salute, and we both pulled out our cell phones and started dialing.

Once again, my friendly local Council representative came through. Jane activated some sort of vampire phone tree, and within fifteen minutes, I had guests pouring through the front door. Kerrianne called her mother, who dropped Braylen off with the makings for s'mores and *Finding Bigfoot* on DVD. Jane and her tall, dark, and ridiculously handsome husband, Gabriel, arrived first, and Gabriel distracted Danny by asking endless Bigfoot-related questions. (Gabriel's secret vampire power was clearly picking up on party themes.) Jane fixed me a *large* double-vodka Especially Bloody Mary, for which I would be forever grateful. I didn't even know you could mix liquor and blood together, but you could, and it was freaking transcendent.

Jane's human childhood friend, Zeb Lavelle, arrived with his wife, Jolene, and their twins, Janelyn and Joe.

A vampire named Sam Clemson and his girlfriend, Tess, arrived with several warmers full of dessert blood from Tess's restaurant, Southern Comforts. Iris Scanlon and her husband, Cal, brought a four-foot-tall stuffed Bigfoot with a big blue bow tied around his neck. I didn't even know where one would find a stuffed Bigfoot, much less on last-minute notice, but Iris ran one of the most successful vampire concierge services in the Southeast, so it stood to reason she knew people who could procure weird items on the fly. I would remember that for Danny's next birthday. Who knew what the theme would be by the time he was seven?

I hoped Danny didn't notice that said guests were strangers and several hundred years outside the expected age range. In my desperation for guests, I'd even called Les and Marge *again*, but they didn't pick up either of their phones. *Again*. It would be the first birthday with their grandson they'd ever missed. I would take time to feel like a horrible person when I wasn't in such a social panic.

As much as I fretted over the birthday boy's mood, once "Mr. Dick" arrived, Danny was so excited to be showing off his stuffed Sasquatch he couldn't care less who else was there. The vampires stood around my parlor, talking and laughing, filling my home with joyous noise while they sipped their blood. They'd all gamely donned their "Sasquatch-hunt" outback-style bush hats and pretended to nibble at their cookies, because Danny didn't quite grasp the whole "vampires can't eat solids" concept.

"I hope Danny doesn't overwhelm him," I told

Dick's vampire wife, Andrea, as Danny used his favorite vampire as a not-quite-living jungle gym.

"He loves it," Andrea assured me. "He missed out on his own son's childhood years, so spending time with kids now is a sort of privilege for him. He can't get enough time with Jolene's twins."

Dick Cheney had a kid. Holy hell. I would file that under questions I would ask Jane when I wasn't surrounded by birthday-party chaos.

"When are we going to start the Sasquatch hunt, Mom?" Danny called from the couch, where he and Dick were going over the *Young People's Guide to Cryptozoological Wonders*, a softcover volume Jane had found in her shop.

"What's a Sasquatch hunt?" Gabriel asked out of the corner of his mouth. "And will it hurt? Because if it hurts, I say we put Dick in charge."

I grinned at Jane's husband and wondered what karmic debt had been owed to Jane that she'd found a partner in life who fit her personality so well. The doorbell rang, distracting me. I opened the door to find a woman in peach nurse scrubs with unruly dark hair standing in my doorway. A tall man with sandy hair and a crooked smile was standing behind her, holding a bright blue gift bag.

"Sweetheart!" Dick crowed, hitching Danny on his hip and dashing across the room so fast even my vision couldn't track him. He handed a squealing Danny off to me while he threw his arms around the brunette, lifting her off her feet with the force of his hug. "Oh, I have missed you so much, Nola. I think you've grown!

Are these summer visits to Ireland really necessary? Can't ya just tell the whole McGavock clan just to move their asses to Kentucky?"

"Yes, Pops, I'll tell my Irish family to abandon their ancestral lands and move to the land of the Yanks because you have separation anxiety," she said, her odd lilting accent muffled by her burying her face into his shoulder.

The sandy-haired man snorted at her comment and shook Dick's free hand. "And you saw us a week ago when we got off the plane. And three days ago. And yesterday."

"I know, Jed, I'm making up for lost hugs," Dick said, not relaxing his grip.

"Is that your girlfriend, Mr. Cheney?" Danny demanded, his blue eyes narrowing suspiciously at Nola. "Because I thought you were married to Miss Andrea. I like Miss Andrea. She looks like a Disney princess."

I had mentioned my son's ability to pick up on potentially awkward social situations and zero in on them like a hawk, yes?

For a second, Dick looked completely horrified. Nola's head popped up from Dick's shoulder, and she let loose a great, braying laugh. Andrea took pity on both of them and said, "Danny, honey, this is Nola. She's Mr. Cheney's granddaughter. Several times great-granddaughter, but we shorten it for convenience's sake."

Danny's eyes tracked between Dick, who was in his mid- to late thirties, and Nola, who was *maybe* pushing the bottom of that range. "I don't think that's possible."

"It is, trust me," Dick assured him. "And I haven't seen my lovely granddaughter for *two months* because she just *had* to go visit her family in Ireland."

"Let it go, Pops."

"There are some really nice rentals right here in the Hollow. They could relocate. You could get them a group rate," he noted.

Nola's voice was flat as she said, "Grandpa Richard."

Dick winced and took Danny by the hand. He told him, "When she uses my proper name, that means I'm in trouble. Let's go get you another cookie, huh, bud?"

"There are cookies?" Jed asked brightly, following them to the snack table. "Do I get a cool hat, too?"

"You brought me a present, so yes!" Danny crowed.

Nola closed her eyes and shook her head. "Give me strength."

"The infamous Nola," I said, stretching out my hand to shake hers. "Nice to meet you!"

Nola grinned broadly, snapping out of her prayers. "Sorry, we should have stopped in days ago, but I've been settling back into my work schedule at the clinic, which is always difficult after getting back to the States."

"I'm glad to meet you. Jane said you were a nurse, but she didn't mention the connection to Dick. I'm sure we'll be taking advantage of proximity the next time Danny wakes up in the middle of the night throwing up."

"Does that happen often?" she asked.

"One time, I did it off of Seth Perkins's top bunk," Danny boasted, running across the room and climbing up my leg. "It was *amazing*."

"Not for the kid on the bottom bunk," I told him, hoisting him onto my hip.

"Well, Danny, distance vomiting notwithstanding, happy birthday to you," Nola said, extending her hand for a shake. "Thank you for inviting us. I've never been to a Bigfoot birthday party before,"

Danny shook her hand firmly and whispered, "It's the perfect spot for one, and do you know why?"

"Tell me," Nola said, grinning.

"Because there's a Bigfoot living in the backyard."

Nola's dark brow winged up. "Really?"

Danny nodded. "Uh-huh, I've seen him out my window."

Nola glanced up at her boyfriend and gave a sort of exasperated roll of her eyes. "You don't say."

"Yep. And we're going to catch him tonight," Danny declared. "Mom got all of the equipment."

Nola grinned suddenly. "I'd say you have a better-than-average chance. Now, I didn't have time to go shopping for a present, but I'd like to give you this." She pulled a Mason jar from the blue gift bag with a flourish. An empty Mason jar.

Danny, who had been schooled thoroughly on the proper response to presents—*any* present—glanced up at me and smiled very sweetly before responding, "Thank you very much, Miss Nola. I can use it to catch lightning bugs."

Nola offered him an approving pat on the head. "Well, what lovely manners you have, birthday boy. And it's funny that you mention lightning bugs, because this jar contains a night-light."

Nola put her hands over the jar and closed her eyes. She seemed to be muttering something under her breath, but even my keen vampire ears couldn't make sense of the words. A warm, golden-green glow fluttered to life inside the jar, reflecting brightly in the blue depths of Danny's eyes.

"Whoa," he whispered. "What is that?"

"A *very special* night-light," Nola told him solemnly. "Whenever you are in your room and trying to fall asleep, it will glow until you drift off. But be very careful with it. If you break the jar, it won't work anymore."

"How did you do that?" he asked.

"An old family trick," she said. "Take good care of it, OK?"

He nodded, carefully cradling the jar to his chest and running up the stairs toward his room. "Yes, ma'am. Thank you!"

"How did you do that?" I asked her.

"Old family trick," Nola repeated with a shrug. "Will you excuse me? I need to go talk to my wayward boyfriend for a moment."

"Sure." I watched her walk away and wondered what exactly she meant by "old family trick." Was she a witch? A fairy? Were there other supernatural creatures out there besides vampires? It stood to reason that if we were real, there were other beasties out there, lurking in the dark. Maybe Danny's claims to have seen Bigfoot weren't so impossible after all.

I shuddered as the doorbell rang, and I opened it, expecting more undead revelers. Imagine my surprise to find Wade the Cranky Janitor standing at my door, cheerfully wrapped present in hand, standing behind the little boy my son had dragged around like a rag doll on school registration night.

What the hell?

My jaw dropped, and fortunately, I was left unable to say anything to hurt the little boy's feelings. Wade's eyes narrowed before he smirked at me. "Crazy closet lady."

"Of course." I saluted him. "Cranky maintenance man."

"Charlie!" Danny cried, running across the living room and throwing his arms around his friend. "You came!"

The little boy grinned and hugged Danny. "Yeah! I'm excited! I've never been to a sleepover party before."

"I'm real sorry we're late," Wade said. "Harley was having a problem with his inhaler, and we had to make a last-minute visit to his doctor. I didn't want to take any chances before a sleepover. I've got his sleepin' bag and stuff in the truck. I thought I'd keep 'em there for a while. Give him a chance to bow out graceful-like if he changes his mind about sleepin' over. This is new territory for him."

I eyed Wade carefully. What did he mean by that? Was he really concerned about his son's big-boy face? Or did he not want his son sleeping at my house because he didn't want to leave him in my care? He had to have known whose house he was coming to when he saw the invitation. Oddly enough, I didn't remember filling out an invitation for a "Harley."

"Danny, I thought you said your friend's name was Charlie."

"I thought it was, too," Danny said as he helped Harley shove a straw into a chilled Capri Sun. "By the time I figured out I was wrong, I was used to calling him Charlie, so I stuck with that."

I turned to Harley, smoothing the strawlike blond cowlick from the back of his head. "Why didn't you correct him, hon?"

Harley shrugged and sipped his juice. "I didn't wanna hurt his feelings."

"You don't have to let someone call you the wrong name to be polite, Harley."

"Oh, OK," Harley said, nodding his head as if this was a big revelation.

"And Danny, make an effort to call him by the correct name. How would you feel if someone called you Fanny every day?"

Danny's face twisted in disgust. "Ew, no."

Harley snickered. "Fanny."

Danny pointed a finger at Harley's face. "Don't even think about it."

Harley pinched his lips together, but his little shoulders shook with repressed laughter.

"Harley, why don't you and Danny go get some food? There's plenty of hot dogs over there. Kerrianne will help you with your plates."

"There are more adults at this party than I expected," Wade observed.

"Not all of the kids came," I said. "In fact, Harley is the only kid who came, so my friends are here to even out the room a little bit. You should know that most of the people here are vampires. So if that bothers you, you should find a way to make your excuses without hurting Danny's feelings."

Wade scoffed. "Hell, no, it doesn't bother me. I know Jed from the gym. We went to Nola's clinic once when Harley had an asthma attack. I've done some special modifications for Dick at my shop, which I'm not supposed to talk about 'cause of some paperwork I signed. They're all nice enough."

Nola's hunky boyfriend walked over and handed Wade a beer. "Hey, man, come on in."

"I thought you worked at the school. How do you find the time to work in a garage?" I asked.

Wade frowned at me. "I don't work at the school. I'm a volunteer."

"You clean the school for free?"

"I don't actually clean the school," he said. "I own my own shop, so I make my own hours. I'm at the school almost every day, mostly in the mornings. I help the kids take their reading-comprehension tests in the library. I try and fail to control the chaos in the cafeteria at lunchtime. And yeah, when the occasion calls for it, I help out with maintenance."

"So why are you so territorial about the supply closet?"

"That's where I keep my stuff," he said. "You get thrown up on enough times, you learn to store extra clothes in a handy spot."

"Yikes."

He pursed his lips, making the golden-blond beard

undulate over his cheeks. He nodded toward his son. "You'd think after nursin' that one through every one of his stomach flus, I'da learned the signs of Vesuvius about to blow."

I laughed, watching Danny drop an Outback hat onto Harley's head while Harley scarfed down a hot dog. "It seems that our sons are inseparable."

"It does."

"So we might as well try to get along."

"I s'pose."

"Do you ever give answers with more than two words?" I asked. "I mean, I've heard you string together more words, but that was when you were yelling at me, so I figured that might be special circumstances."

He smirked. "Sometimes."

"Well, that's still one word. But I'll take it. Libby Stratton," I said, offering him my hand.

"Wade Tucker." He shook my hand, and I yowled in pain as my skin came into contact with something that burned and itched and stung all at the same time. Fangs sprung, I yanked my hand out of his grasp and stared at the dirty gray streaks across my fingers. I looked down at Wade's hand and saw that he was wearing several silver rings.

"Huh," Wade said, pursing his lips as I worked to get my fangs back into my mouth.

"It's a problem," I admitted, shaking my injured fingers. "OK, so you want to stay for a while and help us plow through an insane amount of beef jerky and foot-shaped cookie cake? Almost eighty percent of the guests cannot eat solids, so you'd be doing me a big favor."

"I don't think I can pass up an offer like that," he said, shrugging.

I grinned and turned to the kids. "OK, boys, are you ready for your 'Sasquatch hunt'?" I asked, using that hypercheerful voice only mothers who'd suffered through birthdays could fully understand. The boys abandoned their plates and bellowed a mighty hunters' roar, dragging Dick and Braylen and Sam and Gabriel out to the backyard. The rest of us followed this brave battalion of cryptozoologists. I handed each boy his own binoculars with green Saran wrap over the lenses to make them look like night-scope goggles. They also got a flashlight and a butterfly net and beef jerky to sustain them on their perilous backwoods safari. Danny had his little camouflage digital camera strapped around his wrist, just in case he needed photographic evidence.

I wished I could accurately describe the heart-melting adorableness of fully grown, supposedly vicious vampires holding hands with little boys as they were dragged through the bluegrass, hunched over and searching for Sasquatch sign by moonlight. Wade and I followed at a casual pace. We exchanged grins every time the boys crowed over the clues. They loved the jerky wrapper I'd left by the rain spout, the faux fur I'd tangled around the rosebushes, the Swiss Rolls I'd dropped as Sasquatch scat. (Don't judge me.) I tried to guide the boys toward the huge footprint I'd made in the softened earth just beyond the border of the yard, but my hints weren't quite blatant enough. Before I could drop a more anvil-sized verbal clue, Danny yelled, "What's that?"

In the distance, I could make out a tall, furry shape near the tree line, at least eight feet tall, with long, apelike arms covered in reddish-brown fur. Danny gasped, and the shape's head whipped toward us. Its yellow-gold eyes flashed in the moonlight, and I sprinted across the grass to plant myself in front of the boys.

I clamped my hand over my son's mouth and glanced around, wondering why the other vampires didn't seem all that alarmed by the appearance of a Bigfoot in my backyard. Dick was freaking smirking at me. You didn't smirk in front of Bigfoot. It was just asking for trouble.

I didn't smell anything. It seemed completely wrong that this hulking, fur-covered creature was standing upwind of us and the only scent I could detect was a touch of sweat and Polo cologne. I stepped toward it, a growl forming on my lips, and Nola put her hand on my arm, smiling gently and shaking her head. "It's OK," she whispered. "Really."

What in the flaming hell was going on here? Was this some sort of weird initiation into the vampire world? Social acceptance through cryptid pranks? Reluctantly, I loosened my grip on Danny and let him wander closer to the mystery guest.

"Look at him, Mom," he whispered reverently. "He's real."

"Take a picture," Harley hissed through the hand

clamped over his mouth. I noticed that he'd hung back, clutching at my shirttail and watching the proceedings from around my hip.

"Oh." Danny fumbled with the camera, but before he could raise it and hit the right buttons, the creature let out a low sound, a cross between a *moo* and a *bark*. He—I was assuming it was a he—made a strange hand-jerk gesture toward Danny and then lumbered into the woods.

It wouldn't do, I suppose, for Bigfoot to pose for a selfie with the birthday boy.

"Let's go after him!" Danny said, still trying to aim his camera at the retreating Sasquatch.

"Er." I struggled to find the right explanation that wouldn't scare Danny but would drive home the "don't go running off into the woods alone in the dark" lesson.

"I don't think that's a good idea," Harley supplied. "It looked like he's just eaten and taken a crap. He's probably off to bed. You don't want to interrupt a Bigfoot's bedtime, Danny. It's dangerous."

"Solid logic," I told Harley.

"Harley, we've talked about usin' the word 'crap' like that," Wade said pointedly.

"Sorry, he'd just taken a dump," Harley amended.

I snickered but managed to hide it with a cough. I knew how much it annoyed me when other parents found Danny's particular brand of "forthright humor" charming.

"Aw, man!" Danny cried, snapping a photo of our now empty backyard. "I could have had photographic evidence. But Mom, he *waved* at me. Did you see? He *waved*."

"Bigfeet love birthday parties," I told him. "They love cookie cake. It's a scientific fact. And you know what? It's almost time for cookie cake and presents. How about you and Harley go inside and wash your hands?"

"OK!" Danny dragged Harley back into the house. Wade's poor son was going to have NBA-length arms come morning.

"That was awesome," Jane told me. "You're totally planning Jamie's next birthday."

"Darling, Jamie is almost twenty-one years old," Gabriel said as he followed her through the back door. "He's a little mature for streamers and goodie bags."

"But I missed so many of his birthdays!" Jane protested.

Without a word, Wade wandered toward the tree line, as if he was considering following the creature into the woods. I might have worried, but Wade struck me as a particularly capable guy, as in, when the zombie apocalypse finally happened, I expected to see him rolling through town in a tow-truck-turned-tank, picking off zombies with a potato gun modified to launch grenades. And he would probably look crazy hot while doing it. Stupid effective cheekbones.

While I contemplated this disturbing postapocalyptic image, Jed jogged around the corner of the house toward my side of the yard, shrugging back into his shirt. When he realized I was watching him, he stopped in his tracks.

"I have so *many* questions," I said, shaking my head.

"So, yeah." Jed grimaced as he finished buttoning his shirt. "I'm a shapeshifter."

"That's a thing?" I exclaimed.

"'Fraid so," Jed said. "I have this little genetic quirk that lets me take on the appearance of just about any livin' thing, real or fictional. It's like being a werewolf but having more options. For the longest time, my family thought we were cursed, but it turns out we just happen to have a couple of extra genes thrown in. Jane and Nola thought Danny would get a kick out of it. I'm sorry for not checkin' it out with you before. I didn't mean to make ya uncomfortable."

"So . . . when Danny thought he saw Bigfoot out of his window the other night . . ."

He grimaced. "That was me. But to be fair, I wasn't in Bigfoot form. I've been playing around with an ape-werewolf hybrid creature. You know, trying to keep things interesting. Nola's helped me figure out that I'm more in control of my shifts when I'm not bored."

"Could you maybe not do that where Danny can see you?" I suggested. "Or if you do, pick a non-scary, non-emotionally-traumatizing form? Like a giant bunny or something?" I asked.

"You don't think he would find an unnaturally large bunny lurking outside of his house to be traumatizin'?" he asked, and when I gave him my mom look, he added, "I'm just sayin'!"

"I'm sending him to your front door when he has nightmares," I told Jed.

Jed pursed his lips and nodded. "Fair enough. I'm gonna go get a beer. Shiftin' takes it out of me."

"Wait, Jed, what did you mean by werewolves?" I called after him. "Are werewolves a thing, too?"

He just smiled his adorable redneck smile and ducked inside the house.

"Jed?" I yelled. "That's not an answer!"

"Man, when you throw a party, you throw a party," Wade said, carrying a beer across the lawn. "Where do you even find a Sasquatch impersonator? And what kind of person makes a livin' pretending to be a Bigfoot? That musta been an interestin' Craigslist ad."

"You'd be surprised what you can find online." I chuckled awkwardly. "Look, I really appreciate you being so open-minded, bringing Harley here in the first place and then sticking around when you realized most of the guest list was, uh, pulse-challenged."

"Hell, I told ya, I don't care about that," he scoffed. "You're clearly crazy about your kid, and your friends seem nice enough. My family are all humans, and they can be a bunch of assholes."

"I'm just glad you added more words after you said 'crazy.'"

"We did kind of get off on the wrong foot, huh?" Wade blushed—honest to God, blushed—and even in the silver light of the moon, I could see the rich pink hue spread across his cheeks. The spread of blood through his tiny capillaries did strange things to me. I wanted to follow that blush's path across his cheekbones with my tongue. I wanted to see how far it spread. Did he blush all the way down?

And he was still talking while I was ogling his circulatory system. I decided to tune in before I embarrassed myself.

"I'm sorry I was such a jackass when we met. School registration is always sort of hard for me. It's like a punch in the face, seeing all those big, happy families. Signing all that stuff as Harley's only parent-slash-guardian, it was like being reminded over and over that I'm doing this all alone. I got pissed off, and I took it out on you, and that's not fair."

"I can understand that," I told him. "And that night at Walmart?"

"Well, you did compare my son's name to chlamydia," he noted.

"Touché."

"It would be better, I think, if the two of us could find a way to get along, for the boys' sake," he said. "If nothin' else, we could stop cussing at each other every time we make eye contact."

"I would like that." I stuck my hand out to shake. "Truce?"

"Truce," he said, extending his hand with the rings. Then, remembering the silver issue, he switched and offered me the safer hand. His closed his fingers around mine and pumped my hand gently. His callused, warm skin felt heavenly against my own, like sliding into a bath with just enough heat to sting a little. He didn't seem to mind how cool my skin was, turning my hand over in his.

"Huh," he said, studying our joined hands.

I withdrew my hand from his, rubbing it against

my denim-covered leg. "So do you have family around here?"

He cleared his throat. "Yeah, but I try to steer clear of them. My family are a bunch of screw-ups. Mostly on my mom's side. My dad was a pretty great guy. He's the one who was into motorcycles, showed me everything he knew in the garage. But he died when I was eight, and Mom ended up moving to Garden Vista. She brought home a bunch of 'uncles' who got more and more messed-up with every year. I got a couple of half brothers and sisters running around the Hollow. I try to keep them away from Harley, so they don't try to borrow money off him. Hell, if they thought he had a twenty in his piggy bank, they'd take a hammer to it. And then call him a 'selfish little jerk' if he got upset over it.

"Growing up the way I did, I didn't want Harley seeing that shit. I wanted him to have somethin' normal and soft. I wanted him to know that when he came home from school, I would be there. I would be sober. And he wouldn't have to be afraid when I walked through the door."

I stared at him. If only he knew exactly how much I identified with that statement. When I was pregnant, I told myself it would be different from how I'd grown up. My baby would know how much I loved him. He'd have homemade birthday cakes and Christmas stockings that weren't a knotted-up grocery bag. I would read him bedtime stories and take care of him when he was sick.

It wasn't that my mom hadn't cared. She'd worked

night shifts at the Twelfth Street Launderette to pay for our lavish accommodations in the Garden Vista trailer park. I couldn't say there was much animosity between us. We just weren't particularly close. I knew she liked to paint. I knew her favorite color was purple. I knew she liked to listen to Stevie Nicks on the rare occasion that she cooked. But there were no long talks or maternal advice. The mothering gene was just missing in her, I guessed.

Mom seemed to be resigned to me, like some part of life that she had to accept—aching feet or the late-stage breast cancer she was diagnosed with at age thirty-seven. And even then, her dying process was very matter-of-fact. She just told me that her life insurance wouldn't amount to much and not to let a preacher speak over her at any sort of funeral. After a couple of door-to-door evangelists had informed her that she and her bastard baby were headed for hell unless she joined their church that very Sunday, she'd never had much use for organized religion. And that was it. She might as well have been breaking a lease.

I had a much closer bond with kindly old Mrs. Patterson, who babysat me from the time Mom went back to work after her three unpaid weeks of maternity leave. Mrs. Patterson taught me to read by age four. She taught me how to make basic meals without the stove after Mom decided she couldn't afford having Mrs. Patterson watch me every night and ten was old enough to take care of myself. She was the one who had to explain the birds and the bees to me when I started my period and ran to her trailer crying. Her trailer, which was apparently right down the row from Wade's. And I'd never even met him.

"I grew up in Garden Vista," I told him.

Wade burst out laughing. "Bullshit."

I raised my right hand in a swearing gesture. "I *did*. We lived in the little blue-and-rust number at the end of the sixth row."

Wade snickered. "I haven't seen you at any of the alumni dinners."

"Well, I took myself off the newsletter list. I married a nice boy, cleaned up the accent a little. I worked hard in community college and bought myself a word-of-the-day calendar to help beef up my vocabulary. My mother-in-law says you can hardly tell I grew up in a trailer now, which she *thinks* is a compliment. She doesn't really mean anything by it, but she doesn't have a real strong filter when it comes to condescension."

He laughed. He was standing so close I could feel every warm breath whispering along my skin. I could make out every hair on his head, the golden sheen taking on a blue cast in the moonlight. The most insane urge took hold of my hand, to reach out, stroke my fingertips along his face, run my thumb along his full bottom lip. I wanted to kiss him, to bury my face in his iron-and-citrus-scented hair. I wanted to feel those rough hands stroking down my back. I wanted to trace the path of his jugular with my tongue, feel the warm spill of his blood into my mou—

Uh-oh.

I could feel my fangs lengthening in response to my

sexy, bloody thoughts. My fangs were out. And I was alone, with a human, whose child was playing inside my house because I'd promised his father that they were safe with me and my vampire friends. Damn it. *Damn* it. I pressed my lips together, as if that could hide my unfortunate dental boner, and tried to think of something unappetizing. Something that would kill my libido.

The night before my wedding, Marge visited my apartment, gave me a pink lace nightie that looked just like the one she'd worn on her wedding night to Les, and tried to give me the "wifely duty" talk.

Aaaaaand away went the fangs.

Now that any trace of desire for anything had been thoroughly murdered, I was able to take a step back from Wade. I held my breath to keep that delicious scent of man and blood and leather from invading my senses again.

"I can't believe I don't remember you," he said.

"I pretty much kept to myself when I was a kid," I said. "It's sort of a pattern with me."

Wade glanced back at the crowded, noisy house. Just inside the window, I could see the vampires watching Danny and Harley play. "Until now."

Just then, Jane stuck her head out of the back door and called, "Hey, Libby!"

When she saw the two of us standing so close, she did a quick double take and stepped back into the kitchen. "Sorry."

"It's OK, Jane. What's going on?"

"Well, the boys are threatening some sort of cookie

coup if you don't get in here. Gabriel wants to try to negotiate, but I think Dick is secretly slipping them contraband candy to support their cause." Jane ducked out of sight, calling, "Their blood sugar levels have given them the strength of ten men."

"We'd better get in there," I murmured. "I know they're nice kids, but they can't be trusted to make rational decisions right now."

Wade nodded, stepping back. "Yeah, we're not allowed back at Chuck E. Cheese after the cotton-candy incident at Emma Perry's birthday party."

"*Harley* is the kid who took out Chuck E.?" I gasped.

"Kids will do regrettable things for tokens." He sighed, shaking his head. "I tried to turn it into an object lesson about violence and greed. But I just ended up bannin' him from playin' any of those *Grand Theft Auto* games, ever."

"Seems reasonable."

As a living parent, you may feel pressure to make sure your child "measures up" in terms of intelligence, athleticism, or popularity. As a vampire parent—let's just say that it's not appropriate for children to compete in terms of vampire virtues.

—*My Mommy Has Fangs: A Guide to Post-Vampiric Parenting*

Why had I said yes?

I'd told myself that I didn't have time to volunteer for the PTA this year, that I needed to focus on my complicated home life and adjusting to my liquids-only diet. I could have declined when Chelsea Harbaker, PTA president and all-around terrifying personality, called to confirm my nomination to serve on the Pumpkin Patch Party's prize committee. But for some reason, I'd said yes. Some perverse urge had me agreeing so I could prove to these snotty wenches that I was still the same committed, involved parent I was before, that being a vampire didn't make me less of a mother. Also, I thought it wouldn't hurt for people to see me working diligently on school projects while my in-laws tried to convince the community that I was a dangerous slacker mom.

So now I was sitting in the cafeteria of the elementary school, with a little paper placard in front of my seat that read "Libby Sutton—Prize Committee." That's right. They spelled my name wrong. And I was without Kerrianne to amuse me with smartass asides, because *she* had an excuse not to come to the meeting. She had to work. Of course, she had to work for *me* so she could keep my child as I attended this meeting. It was a "damned if you do, relieved because you get out of attending a boring meeting if you don't" situation.

I was barely listening to Chelsea drone on about the importance of the Pumpkin Patch Party to the community, the long-standing tradition and the fund-raising capacity for the PTA. I couldn't focus on the lists of tasks to be done when I felt like a weird little rock in a stream, with conversation flowing around me and people passing me by. But I didn't feel quite so alone as I had when I was human.

The wonderful thing about Jane's friends was that when they said "Call me," they meant it. And if you didn't call them, they called you. I had a coffee date scheduled with Andrea that week. Nola had offered to take Danny to Children's Day at the local Civil War history museum the coming weekend. Gabriel asked me to come by the Nightengale house for dinner, ostensibly so I could look over the payroll for a string of frozen-yogurt shops he owned and determine whether one of the regional managers was being dishonest with reported overtime. But I think he and Jane just wanted to see me without the Council mantle on her shoulders.

The Half-Moon Hollow vampires friended me on Facebook. They added me to their group texts. I got the impression that I had somehow been marked as part of their pack.

It was a little overwhelming, having this many people reaching out to me when I was so used to a small social circle. But they didn't breach my boundaries. They listened when I said no.

Which was more than I could say for Chelsea Harbaker.

While Chelsea was preaching, I took my little paper placard and slashed through "Sutton" in bright, blood-red Sharpie. Under my corrected last name, I drew a little smiley face . . . and then little red triangles under the smiley's mouth. And a little drop of blood.

"Libby?"

Oh, hell.

I looked up and found Chelsea looming over me. Her blond hair was artfully sculpted around a round face with Kewpie-doll lips and big baby-doll blue eyes. When she spoke, you could practically hear cartoon chipmunks and birds scampering away in terror. It was like Snow White and Satan had an evil, chirpy blond baby.

Believe it or not, I'd been comforted by my interactions with Chelsea, because, so far, she'd treated me with just as much condescension as she had before I was turned. She was consistent, and for that, I was grateful.

"Do you have the list of local businesses you need to solicit for raffle prizes and donations?"

I wished she would stop using the word "solicit." It was unseemly.

I cleared my throat, shuffling through the papers in front of me. "Yes. I have the list. And the sublists. And the list of sublists."

"Are you and Caroline—"

"Kerrianne," I supplied.

She sniffed. "Yes, Kerrianne. Are you two able to handle it, or do I need to assign a few more people to your committee?"

Behind her, I saw several eyes go wide and my fellow parents shaking their heads. I schooled my lips from the smirk that wanted to form. "No, thanks. We'll do just fine."

"I expect a report from the committee at next week's meeting," she singsonged.

Next week? I would have to do this again next week?

I sighed, glancing around the room again, as if Wade had somehow materialized in the last five minutes. I hadn't realized how much I'd hoped he would attend this meeting until I saw that he wasn't there. We'd actually managed to build a shaky rapport after the birthday party. It would have been nice to see a friendly face, but it would appear that even he had his limits in terms of parental volunteering. I did, too, but was forced to ignore them for the sake of pending litigation. That was something reasonable parents did, right?

Chelsea eventually ran out of things to drill the various committee heads about, and we were dismissed. Some people shot out of their seats and ran for the door. Others milled around in the room to chat. I tried to hold on to a bit of my dignity and split the difference.

A few of the moms were friendly. Jenny Marcum and her cousin, Penny Bidcombe, stopped me to ask how Danny was faring after the incident with Mrs. McGee. In my now weekly calls to the school, I'd found out that Mrs. McGee hadn't gone near Danny since Mr. Walsh informed her that I was aware of her opinion and "displeased" that Danny had overheard her. So I couldn't report much beyond "I indirectly threatened a septuagenarian." But it was nice that they'd asked. Penny and Jenny, whose mothers were sisters with an odd sense of humor, had daughters in Danny's grade. I'd have liked to think they would have allowed the girls to attend a birthday party at my house, but because of Danny's girl-cootie-phobia, I supposed we wouldn't know for a while.

"Soooo, Libby, how are you?" I turned to find Marnie Whitehead standing behind me, smirking. Marnie's son, Brian, had been on the invite list for Danny's party. I desperately wanted to ask where the hell she and her son were on Friday night, considering that my son had continued to sit next to "Buggy Brian" at lunch even after his well-known and unfortunate head-lice outbreak the year before. But I bit my tongue.

Also, as an aside, I was really tired of people asking how I was, with their heads tilted to the side. It was becoming annoying.

"Just fine," I said, with my sweetest smile.

"Really? Because I've heard Les and Marge are planning to sue you for custody of Danny," Marnie said. "I just can't imagine how I would feel if someone tried to take Brian from me. I would be so stressed out if I were you."

"Well, it's a good thing that you're not me. But really," I said, all easy smiles and wide eyes, "everything's just fine with Les and Marge."

Just at that moment, because the conversational gods hated me, a man in a plaid shirt and jeans tapped me on the shoulder. It was unusual to see dads at this sort of thing, which was part of the reason I'd assumed that Wade was a school employee. I gave him that same easy, empty grin. "Hi, can I help you?"

"Liberty Stratton?"

"Most people call me Lib—" My sentence was cut off as the man in plaid slapped an envelope into my hand.

"You've been served."

My mouth hung open as the man strode away as if the hounds of hell were on his heels.

If vampires were capable of blushing, my face would be on fire at that moment. I unsealed the envelope and scanned the contents. Les and Marge had used a lot of scary legal terms to file for full custody of Danny.

I folded the papers back into the envelope and stuffed them into my back pocket, all the while schooling every muscle in my face into a relaxed, untroubled expression. I would not let these people see me worried or upset. I would not be fodder for the gossip mill—well, any more than I already was. I would walk out of here with my head held high and have a snotty, gross, undead breakdown in my van like a grown-ass woman.

"So I guess things with Les and Marge aren't as OK as you think they are," Marnie said, clucking her tongue.

"I don't know what you're talking about, Marnie," I said, all sweetness drained from my voice. "That was just a little warning from the Council. They get really cranky when I bite random civilians without provocation. Of course, if I *had* provocation, they'd probably let me slide."

I swept the tip of my tongue over my elongating canines and gave a very pointed look toward Marnie's jugular. She went bone-white and took a step back. Behind me, I swore I heard Penny snicker, but she covered it with a cough.

"Good night, y'all," I said, patting Jenny's arm. I glanced at Marnie's neck again, making her retreat even farther.

I walked out into the parking lot, teeth grinding as I searched through my enormous mom bag for my keys. I shouldn't have been surprised. I knew my in-laws were going to file suit. It was the next step in the natural progression of this sort of legal situation. I just didn't expect them to serve me at a freaking PTA meeting. Had they done it because they wanted to make sure there were witnesses or because they wanted to make sure I was embarrassed in front of the other parents? It wasn't as if my evening schedule was unpredictable.

I could feel the fear and anxiety dragging me under the oily surface of paralysis. My hands were so cold and numb I could barely keep my grip on my purse. How was I going to fight them? How was I going to keep my son with me? Hell, how was I going to drive home?

So distracted was I that I didn't even notice the footsteps falling behind me for several moments. When I did, I stopped, listening to make sure I wasn't just hearing some other parent hightailing it out of the meeting. I turned and scanned the parking lot. A dark, exceptionally tall shape stood waiting at the end of the row, watching me.

"Jed, if this is another Bigfoot sighting, they're getting kind of old," I called. "You could at least shift to something interesting, like a land squid or a *chupacabra*."

The shape didn't move. It was hard for even my vampire eyes to make out details because he was dressed in relentless black from head to toe. He was even wearing a ski mask with strange meshlike coverings over the eyes.

We didn't get a lot of ninjas in Half-Moon Hollow. And I'm pretty sure Jed would have responded. So I wasn't quite sure how to react here. Was this some sort of test from Jane to determine whether I would survive a parking-lot attack? Couldn't I just roll around in a gym with a practice dummy or something?

The figure cocked his head to the side, staring at me like some predatory creature considering his best approach. I dropped my bag and kicked out of my sandals.

I could do this. Sure, I had no fighting experience, but I had superstrength and speed on my side. Then again maybe this guy did, too. He could be a ninja *chupacabra* for all I knew. But I could survive this. I'd gotten through a trailer-park childhood, cancer, and ostracism from soccer moms.

I flicked my fingers at Mr. Chupacabra in the international gesture for "bring it."

I could make out the shape's long legs gathering for a leap, as if he was going to throw himself all the way across the parking lot in one jump. But across the pavement, someone blasted a horn and yelled, "Come on! I've got to get home before *Scandal*!"

More parents were filtering out of the school entrance. Brake lights flickered red across the darkness. I whipped my head back toward the dark figure . . . who was no longer standing at the end of the row. I scanned the parking lot, but there were no wayward ninja creatures lurking about.

I whipped my head around, searching for signs of El Chupacabra. But all I could see were my fellow parents and a sea of SUVs and minivans.

Great. Now I was having delusions.

Scooping my bag from the ground, I climbed into my van and slammed the door, locking it tight. And thanks to every woman-in-peril movie I'd ever seen, I knelt backward in my seat to check the back of the van to make sure no one was lurking there.

Jane had made it very clear that if I was confronted by any assailants, masked or otherwise, I was to come to her immediately and tell her every detail. After texting Kerrianne to tell her I would be a little late, I put my van in gear and pulled out of the parking lot, heading downtown.

Jane's shop, Specialty Books, had started a sort of revolution on Paxton Avenue. She'd taken the original occult bookshop space and expanded into the former adult-video store next door to create a thriving store for readers living and undead. The next thing we knew, a children's consignment shop had opened down the street, and a specialty embroidery business, then a gourmet cheese and wine shop and an artisanal candle store. The neighborhood that had once been an embarrassment to Hollow residents was on the verge of being a bit hipster. I wasn't even nervous about parking my van outside of Specialty Books, but it took a long time for me to work up the courage to walk inside. I sat in my van, watching people walk in through the front door.

There were a lot of people gathered there. I could barely make out the well-stocked maple shelves through the elaborately lettered window. Opening the door, I was greeted by a mishmash of voices and smells. The shop managed to be quirky and cozy at the same time, with its tranquil purple-blue walls and the twinkling star-shaped light fixtures dangling from the ceiling. While it was modern and clean, the candles, the ceremonial items, and the antique maple-and-glass sideboard that served as a checkout stand kept it earthy.

Jane was pushing the comfy purple chairs into a semicircle just beyond the shiny coffee counter, where Andrea reigned supreme. She refused to let Jane near the large, rather intimidating copper cappuccino machine ever since some sort of incident involving a steamed-milk explosion. One man with broad shoulders and a prominent sloping forehead stood at the bar, glugging down some espresso-blood concoction that left a faint red ring around his thin upper lip. When I passed by, his watery blue eyes followed me, sending a shiver up my spine.

"What are you doing here?" Jane asked, grinning. "I've been trying to get you to come to one of these meetings for weeks!"

"Meeting?"

"The Newly Emerged Vampires Support Group," she said, waving her hand at the people milling about the shop. "We started it up as a sort of spin-off program of the FFOTU. And since people were used to meeting here already, we found room in the shop's schedule."

"This is a support group?" I asked, frowning as I watched the vampires chatting, laughing, sipping their bloodychinos. I'd attended a few support-group meetings at my treatment center. They'd been considerably less cozy. "It looks like a book club."

"We try to keep it loose and comfortable," she said. "And since you clearly didn't come here for the meeting, what's going on? Is Danny OK?"

"He's fine," I assured her. "But you told me to tell you if anything strange ever happened, and I am here to file a report in an official capacity. Very official."

Jane's posture straightened, and her face went grim. "Come with me," she said. "Andrea, could you get things started?"

With a nod to Andrea, Jane escorted me to an office at the back of the shop, small and snug, with a dark wood desk that occupied most of the space. A shelf behind the desk was littered with framed photos of Gabriel and Jane, Jane's childe Jamie, Dick and Andrea, and the rest of Jane's friends.

In a very businesslike manner, Jane and I sat down, and she questioned me. It was a very gentle interrogation but an interrogation all the same. She left no detail unexamined, down to the possible brand of the ninja's ski mask.

"You did the right thing, coming to me immediately," Jane said. "It means you are smarter than ninety percent of the vampires in the Hollow. Sidebar, please tell Gigi Scanlon I told you that, and make sure I am there when you do it, so I can see the expression on her face. I can't guarantee that we'll be able to find this guy, but at least we'll have a paper trail."

"Very comforting," I told her drily as she led me out of the office, arm around my shoulders. "Oh, by the way, my in-laws have filed suit against me for custody of Danny. And I am filled with bone-quaking terror."

"Actually, I have good news on that front," Jane said. "Your in-laws' petition has been directed to Judge Holyfield in the local family court. Judge Holyfield has written several legal-journal articles on the rights of undead parents and the importance of keeping family units together as long as the parents, living or undead, are responsible and fit. So you have better than a fighting chance in this. I don't want you to worry. We might be able to nip this thing in its early stages."

I nodded. It was fortunate indeed that the Council was paying for my defense in the custody case, because the legal fees would have drained the comfortable but not exactly fluffy cushion that stood between us and homelessness. It was also fortunate that I wasn't the state's, much less the Hollow's, first case of a grandparent trying to claim custody of a grandchild from a vampire parent. I did not want to live through this case on the front page of the *Half-Moon Hollow Herald*.

"I'm a mother. Worrying is basically how I pray," I told her. "Wait, when you say the case was 'directed' to Judge Holyfield . . ."

"Sweetie, you don't want to know," Jane told me. "Let's just say that as a local Council representative and the wielder of all of its questionable resources, I'm glad to finally wield for the sake of good."

"Thanks, Jane."

The storefront had gone very quiet as the tall man from before, the bloodspresso chugger, stood with his back to us, espresso cup in one hand, while he weepily explained how he couldn't find friends in the undead community.

"It's just so lonely," he whispered, shoulders heaving. "I don't understand why I can't find friends among other vampires. I'm a nice guy once you get to know me."

The reek of desperation could have something to do

with it. Men who have to point out that they're nice guys are very rarely actual nice guys, I thought, rather loudly, so Jane could hear me. But she didn't respond. Weird.

"Who is that?" I whispered.

"That is Crybaby Bob," she said. "Crybaby Bob is one of our newest members and a little nervous about finding a support system nearby. And by 'nervous,' I mean a person-shaped sieve constantly leaking tears. Hence the accurate but somewhat mean nickname."

"You're not going to try to set me up with Bob, are you? Because I'm not ready for undead playdates."

Jane shook her head and whispered, "Bob is needy as hell and working my last nerve. He's been a vampire for three years. You'd think that would be time enough to take the training wheels off of his fangs."

"I just need someone who understands me!" Bob sobbed.

Jane cringed, and I mouthed, *Wow*.

I drove home, sipping on a blood-coffee-chocolate concoction Andrea told me was a guaranteed "better mood in a bottle." I knew better than to ask questions, so I simply listened to Norah Jones and sipped my vampire Prozac while I slowly, calmly guided my van home. Because getting pulled over for speeding while drinking from an open blood container would not help my chances of keeping Danny at home.

From the highway, I could see an unfamiliar shape on my front porch. Kerrianne hadn't texted to warn me of visitors, and Jed wouldn't have let someone loiter on our shared porch. Frowning, I threw my van into park and jumped out, running toward the house with more speed than I could safely put on my engine.

I skidded to a stop in the gravel drive, crouching slightly.

Sitting on my front porch, cool and crisp as you please, was a man in a light blue dress shirt, sleeves rolled at the elbows. The even matinee-idol features were now brightened by a warm smile that crinkled the corners of his dark goatee. It was Mr. Gentleman, the vampire who had intervened in my conversation with Wade in the Walmart parking lot. And as the wind changed directions, the scent of sandalwood drifted toward my sensitive nose.

There was something familiar about him, and not just from that one incident in the parking lot. I knew him somehow. His smile filled me with what I could only describe as a warm, giddy sort of peace.

Attempting to keep some semblance of cool, I cleared my throat. "So did you just walk around, sitting on all of the front porches in town until you found mine?"

He snorted, and the warm, flirtatious smile bloomed into something more like delight. "Oh, I have my ways. Your babysitter made it very clear that I wasn't welcome in the house. And if she hears one distressed sound out of you while we are talking, she's going to, and I quote, 'pepper my ass with salt and silver buckshot.'"

I looked over at my front window, where Kerrianne waved . . . what looked to be a shotgun. Where did she get a shotgun? Did Jed loan it to her? Then again, this was Kentucky. A better question would be where *couldn't* Kerrianne get a shotgun.

For the record, answers to that question would not include the local bait shop, the church rummage sale, or the quilters' guild luncheon. We would have to have a long talk about my concerns about gun safety and proximity to Danny some other time.

"She's a smart lady, my babysitter."

"Are you all right?" he asked. "That had to be frightening for you earlier, seeing that weird guy in the parking lot with the ski mask."

"How did you know about that?"

"It's a long story."

"Well, I would love to stand out here with you and try to figure out your cryptic quips, but I have other things to do. Enjoy your night." I took the steps, light on my feet, but he caught my hand as I passed.

"So do you remember me?"

He stood, close enough for me to appreciate the warm amber notes of the cologne he wore. I pulled back, but he used the instability of my momentum to pull me near. His lips were so close to my temple I could almost feel the soft brush of his beard against my skin. "Please, remember me."

A rush of images flooded my brain. Hands sliding up my throat to cradle my head. Cheap, thin motel sheets stained with tiny specks of blood. Lips at my ear, whispering that it was all right to be afraid. That this part was always difficult, but when I woke up, I would be like him, strong and beautiful.

Cool, strong hands curled around my elbows, catching me before my knees buckled under me. I surfaced from the strange memory fog and found Mr. Gentleman staring down at me, his lips quirked into an amused smirk.

Holy hell. No wonder he seemed so familiar. This guy was my sire.

Be careful of the connections and friendships you form in the world of the undead. Just as when you were living, you want to be careful of the influences you allow around your children.

—*My Mommy Has Fangs: A Guide to Post-Vampiric Parenting*

He was real. The man from my dreams, the matinee idol with the warm eyes and the naughty smile. He was standing right in front of me. He was real.

I remembered more and more, even as a thrill fluttered through my belly, hot and fast. I remembered his long, muscled arms winding around me, cradling me gently against his chest. I remembered him distracting me with stories—stories of his near-idyllic childhood in Cleveland in the 1950s and the *Ocean's Eleven*–style heist gone awry that led to his being turned, along with his best friend, Max. It had taken the pair almost thirty years and several schemes before they paid off the debt to their vampire "creditor." Someday, he promised, he would introduce me to Max, who he was sure would love me before he even met me.

My sire was every bit as physically imposing and, well, devilishly sexy as my dying brain had imagined. But he'd also been oddly considerate, comforting almost, in a way I hadn't expected. He'd honestly tried to make my transition as painless as possible. It wasn't his fault there was no such thing as a painless vampire birth.

My sire clasped my hands before sliding his own up both my arms.

"Well, you turned out just as I'd hoped," he purred. "A simply divine creature.

"I'm sorry I missed your transition. Mrs. Nightengale made it very clear what would happen to me if I came anywhere near you. But I think I've given her warnings a respectable amount of consideration and am now going to ignore them."

"Well . . . I have questions."

He grinned, even as I pulled my arms out of his grasp and stepped back. "I knew you would."

I began counting the queries on my fingertips. "One, what the hell do you think you're doing here? Two, who the hell are you? Three, how did you find my house? Four, are you aware that the Council told me never, ever to talk to you? And five, just to reiterate, who the hell are you?"

"Do you want my name or some deep philosophical explanation of who we really are on the inside?" he asked, his breath feathering across my neck as he circled me. It took all of my strength not to shudder under that whisper of sensation over my skin. "We're so much more than our names, aren't we?"

Even though I was ninety percent sure he'd stolen that line from a postmodern *Dracula* remake, I couldn't help but duck my head as he rounded me like a predator. And when he smirked, I wanted to lick that little divot over his lips.

Seriously, I was going to have to have sex soon, or I would be making some very unfortunate decisions.

"You, sir, are the devil in a Sunday suit," I told him.

He spluttered. "What?"

"The very picture of charm, drawing me in, lulling all those natural alarms that go off when a woman hears a line of bull."

"I don't think I should be flattered, and yet, somehow, I am." He stared at me for a long time, and the tension seemed to ease from his frame.

"So what can I do for you . . . ?" I asked. "There was a pause there, which was a chance for you to tell me your name."

"Finn Palmeroy," he said, reaching out to shake my hand. Given the whole wanna-lick-the-upper-lip-divot reaction, I didn't trust myself to touch him. So I gave him a nod—a friendly nod but a nod. He handled this miniature snub with grace. Hell, he looked pleased.

"I guess you already know my name, given that you tracked me down like a deer."

"Yes, Libby, I know a little about you but not much. I checked your driver's license before I buried you at the park."

That was right. I'd asked him to bury my purse with me. Because I didn't want to have to go back to the motel for it. The absolute absurdity of our situation hit me with full force, and I burst out laughing. I giggled until tears ran down my cheeks, and I had to brace my hands against my knees to keep from collapsing to the gravel. He watched me, his head cocked to the side as if he'd never seen someone laugh before.

"That is *such* a weird sentence to leave someone's lips." I sighed, plunking my butt down on the steps. He slid down next to me with much more grace. I put an appropriate amount of distance between us as I wiped at my eyes.

"Our relationship did have a strange beginning, didn't it?"

"We don't have a relationship," I told him.

"I'm your sire."

"In the eyes of the Council, Jane Jameson-Nightengale is my sire. You're like a biological parent without any rights. You're a vampire deadbeat dad." That particular phrase, I noticed, made him cringe. "Now, what are you doing here?"

"I just want to see how you are. I've never made another vampire before. I didn't expect such a feeling of obligation about your well-being. Not knowing how you're doing left me feeling unsettled."

"Well, I'm doing just fine. My bloodthirst is well under control. I haven't had one violent outburst. I'm keeping my at-home business running, and I've only lost a client or two. I'm practically a functional member of undead society."

"I knew you would turn out well."

"Because you learned so much about me in the time between meeting me in a cheap motel and biting me?"

He shook his head. "Your ad, the one you put on the

Internet. I could tell, just from the way it was written, that you were a decent person. Desperate but decent. Decent people generally turn into decent vampires."

"I've heard that from Jane."

"Decent vampires have to be careful, however. You could be seen as weak by other vampires."

"Jane mentioned that, too," I told him. "So who are you, Finn Palmeroy? Jane has made a few unflattering comments, but I think I should consider the source a bit biased."

"Thank you for that." He cleared his throat. "What do you want to know?"

"Why did you respond to my ad? How did you even find it? Do you plan on invoking some sort of weird sire privilege that involves me killing someone or not spending time with people you don't like?"

"That's a really broad scope of sire privileges," he noted.

"I like to cover my bases."

"I don't know if I should tell you all that. A guy likes to have a bit of mystery about him."

"Trust me, you've got mystery by the pant-load," I muttered, making him snicker.

"OK, I can tell you that, like Dick, I'm an entrepreneur. I use my connections to help people find what they need, no matter how obscure. This was my line of work before I was turned, and let's just say that my being turned stemmed from a miscommunication with a client. The market was a bit more diverse before we came out of the coffin, but I have a few special skills that help me along."

"We'll just ignore the fact that the word 'miscommunication' was in invisible air-quote marks, and I'll ask, skills like what? Is it your vampire power? What is it? Is it weird, like being able to guess what's in a sealed envelope or talk to squirrels?"

He waggled his eyebrows. "That would be telling you."

"It's not the ability to guess underwear colors, is it? Because that eyebrow waggle is making me wonder."

"Air of mystery," he whispered.

"And why did you answer my ad?"

"Because I don't have the chance to do the right thing very often," he said. "And that's all I'd like to say for now."

"Will you expand on that in the future?"

"When the time is right." He nodded and twined my fingers together with his. "So I have a question for you. Are you ready?"

I shifted in my seat and nodded. "Shoot."

"What was your last meal?"

"What?" I cackled. "That's the big personal question you want to ask me? Of everything you could ask, *that's* what you want to know?"

"Come on." He chuckled. "Your last meal. You knew death was coming. You planned it out. I mean, everybody asks themselves, if they were on death row, what would they choose as their last meal? It's like a personality test."

"What was yours?"

"You tell me first," he countered.

"You show me yours, I'll show you mine."

"I was hoping for something a little more revealing when you used that phrase for the first time," he said. When I lifted an eyebrow, he took a small leather notebook out of his pocket and handed me a piece of paper. "OK, we'll write them down. And then we'll exchange them."

"OK." I dug a few things from my giant mom bag at my feet—toy trucks, lip balm, an extra phone charger, old contact solution—to find a pen.

"Is that purse like the TARDIS, bigger on the inside?" he asked as I dropped the kid debris onto the porch floor.

"Oh, if I was a bigger nerd, that would be so sexy," I told him, making him do the eyebrow thing again.

"That is a *Star Wars* LEGO man," he said, nodding toward the action figure I'd unearthed from my purse.

"Nice try." I scribbled my Last Supper menu on the scrap of paper. It took me twice as long as his, which I made a grab for. He snatched the paper out of reach and shook his head.

"Same time," he reminded me, and we slowly exchanged papers. His eyes bugged out as he read down the list. "Roast turkey, dressing, hash brown casserole, green beans amandine, honey-glazed ham, potatoes au gratin, deviled eggs, pot roast, buttered carrots, marshmallow Peeps (purple), pumpkin pie, red velvet cake, an entire sixteen-piece box of Vosges Wink of the Rabbit truffles, and half a bottle of Chardonnay. Good grief, woman!"

"I went off several of my medications just so I would have the appetite to eat all of that," I said proudly.

"It's just so much food," he said.

"I knew I was going to be missing holiday meals for the rest of my life, so I was trying to eat them all at once. I had to special-order the Peeps from a seasonal candy site on the Internet."

Finn was still staring at me. I shrugged and read from his paper. "A porterhouse steak, mashed potatoes, and a slice of chocolate cake? That's kind of boring."

"I'm a man of simple tastes. I'm still trying to imagine you eating all that," he said. "You're so tiny."

I laughed, a genuine, tinkling amused note that made him join in. I let that hang in the air between us, because I was about to say something he would not enjoy as much. "Look, I don't need you to guide me or mentor me or anything like that. I have a support system and, if I want, a support group, Lord help me. I'm doing just fine. Besides, I'm pretty sure the Council told you to stay away. Dick and Jane both have some . . . not nice things to say about you. They probably wouldn't be very happy with me for talking to you."

"Do you always do what you're told?" he asked.

"When it involves being told what to do by scary older vampires, yes."

"Oh, we're going to have some fun, you and I," he told me. He leaned close, and—thinking he was going to kiss me on the mouth—I ducked my head. Unfortunately, he had leaned at the last minute to kiss my cheek, and my feint had put my mouth on a direct path with his. It was just a peck, really, a friendly, soft press of his lips against mine.

Holy hell.

Even though it only lasted the length of the heart-beat I no longer had, I felt it all the way down to my toes. He tasted smooth, like old wine, and seeped slowly into my senses. It was sliding slowly under cool, crisp sheets, soothing every single cell of my body. Just as the spicy flavor of his kiss had settled into my mouth, I pulled away. I pressed my fingers to my lips and fought the urge to giggle hysterically.

"Right," I said, clearing my throat while I wobbled to my feet. "Not impressive at all."

But instead of being insulted by my critique, he simply grinned wickedly as I backed toward my door.

"Some fun," he said again.

It was at times like these—counting out individual adhesive glitter letters in front of a giant display at Copy Shack—that I wondered whether it was a positive thing that I could run errands at any time of the night. The Copy Shack was the only office store in town now, since the Council office stopped masquerading as a Kinko's and actually put the agency's real logo on the door. And because of the laws of elementary-school project timing, I was there at ten P.M. considering just how much glitter was too much glitter for a first-grader's homework.

I'd woken up that evening to my son beating on my cubby door, asking where I'd put his poster board for his special assignment. A special assignment that was, of course, due the next day. He had all of his photos of him fishing and playing with LEGOs, and he'd printed out his three-sentence "essays." But he needed a poster-board canvas on which to paste his master-piece. I normally kept a supply of poster board on hand for just such occasions, but lately I'd had other things on my mind.

Danny needed poster materials for the "superstar project" for Ms. Jenkins's art class. The students had to make a poster featuring art and mini-essays about things at which they excelled, what made them "super-stars." It was a project focused on color scheme and self-esteem bolstering, so it landed in Ms. Jenkins's ed-ucational sweet spot. Danny swore he'd told me about it. And while I was sure I'd never heard him mention any such thing, I went on the glitter run, because that's what moms did.

Fortunately, the Copy Shack had a large selection of poster board and adhesive letters for parents who needed to help produce grade-saving projects at the very last minute. I double-checked the list to make sure I got all of Danny's must-have materials and heard the now-familiar squeak of work boots behind me, accom-panied by the smell of iron and citrus. I smiled, turning to find my favorite smartass mechanic standing behind me, hands stuffed in his pockets, giving me a smirk that drew a little dimple on the left side of his mouth.

It was normal to be overwhelmed with the urge to lick someone's cheek dimple, right?

"Do you only run your errands at night?" Wade asked.

"I *can* only run my errands at night. What's your excuse?"

"Superstar project?" we chorused, and then burst out laughing.

"Danny swears he told me." I sighed. "But I honestly don't remember him asking me for neon green poster board and glitter stickers. He doesn't ask for glitter stickers very often, so I think I would remember."

Wade snorted. "At least Harley admitted that he forgot."

"Well, apparently, there was a note in their backpacks, so neither one of us is off the hook."

Wade grimaced. "Damn it."

I helped Wade pick appropriate supplies for Harley's project, and we checked out and lugged our purchases to the parking lot. Despite the fact that I had superstrength, Wade insisted on carrying my bags for me. There was an old-fashioned sweetness to that, which, while not exactly progressive, touched the wearier parts of my heart. I was so accustomed to doing things on my own that a little gesture like that had a lot more impact than I expected.

I was actually sorry that we reached my van. I so rarely got to see Wade when it didn't involve the kids. It was nice to be able to talk to him without being interrupted with requests for juice boxes.

We stood near my van, plastic shopping bags twisting in Wade's hands, neither of us willing to drive away. A strange feeling of anticipation seemed to seep up from my belly to my chest, this desperate, longing ache that made me feel like I was coming out of my skin. I didn't know whether that ache would be eased by getting closer to Wade or farther away, I just knew I needed something to happen. Quickly.

Was this how teenagers felt when they were falling

in like with someone? No wonder they acted so insane all the time.

Maybe it was because he sensed my mind wandering, but suddenly, Wade abandoned his story about a frustrating customer, who didn't seem to understand that you had to put oil in a motorcycle to keep it running, to say, "So I'm gonna ask you out. Probably not dinner, since you don't eat. But I was thinking a movie. The old drive-in at Possum Point is showing a bunch of John Candy movies next weekend. And who doesn't like John Candy?"

I stared at him for a long time, blinking, and a smile slid across my face. "Crazy people."

"Exactly. I thought maybe bein' outside might keep you from gettin' sick at the smell of popcorn. And besides, you probably feel cooped up, havin' to stay inside all day. So we'll take my bike, spread out a blanket, and watch John Candy shoot a grizzly in the ass with a shotgun lamp."

It sounded like the best date I could imagine. Hell, he'd actually put some thought into what I would enjoy, which was more than I could say for the handful of men I'd previously dated. But there was Finn to consider. He hadn't exactly asked me to go steady, but it seemed sort of rude to go out with someone who wasn't my sire . . . without my sire's approval. That seemed backward.

Right, respond to social situations like a normal person. I could do this.

"And just to clarify, this does not involve the boys?"

"No. This is one-on-one, grown-up time," he swore,

holding up his fingers in a mock Boy Scout salute. "Noncrazy John Candy fans would call it a date."

I laughed. "Wade, I haven't been on a date since . . ."

"Since you were turned?"

"Since my husband died," I admitted.

He took a step closer to me. "Are you saying no because you don't want to spend more time with me?"

"No."

"Is it because you don't want me?" he asked, stepping forward again, head cocked to the side, studying my reaction as he closed the distance between us. And my reaction was to take a step back until I bumped into my van.

I shook my head. "Definitely not."

He nodded, keeping his eyes locked on mine, which seemed inadvisable, considering the whole apex-predator thing. He leaned toward me, wrapping his big, warm hand around my left hip and pulling me a bit closer. "I'm gonna kiss you now."

"Thank you for the heads-up." I murmured as my tongue darted out to moisten my lips. Thanks to my heightened senses, I could hear the increase in his heartbeat, scent that edge of excitement spreading through his system in the form of pheromones. I was more than flattered by his response.

I looked forward to kissing him like kids look forward to Christmas. What the hell was wrong with me? I was a grown woman with a child. I should not be all giddy and giggly. In that moment, I wanted nothing more than to kiss him. I wanted to know what it was like to kiss Wade Tucker. But he seemed content to hover just outside of my reach, rubbing the tip of his nose along my cheek, letting the bristles of his beard tease my skin.

I moaned softly as his hands slid down the small of my back and braced around my hips. I threaded my fingers through his hair, pushing it back from his face as I stared into his eyes. Hesitant, I pressed forward, letting my lips slide along his in a sort of glancing blow, just a taste. Where Finn's kiss was cool and sly, a tease with a promise of more, Wade laid out everything he had to offer, consuming my mouth with his warm, sweet force.

I withdrew, and he followed, growling softly and crossing his arms behind me to draw me closer. He pulled my bottom lip between his teeth, nibbling gently before nudging my lips apart and deepening my tentative kiss.

I twisted my hands in his hair, sliding up the hood of my van as he leaned in. His palm skimmed down my thigh, wrapping it around his waist. I gasped into his mouth, and he took the opportunity to skate his tongue against my growing fangs. He pulled back, and I panicked a bit, clapping my hand over my mouth. But he was giving me the filthiest grin, rubbing the reddened tip of his tongue over swollen lips.

I swear, my panties spontaneously combusted right there.

"Excuse me!" someone shouted. "This is a public place! There are *children* present!"

The spell was broken.

My eyes went saucer-sized, and Wade reluctantly let

go of my leg. We turned to see an incensed man loading his towheaded children into a blue pickup truck. He looked vaguely familiar, in that "I think we've met before, but I can't guarantee we liked each other" kind of way. I couldn't put a name with the face, but given the way he was glaring at me, he seemed to know me. Great. My already tarnished reputation needed an addition like "parking-lot hussy."

"Seems to me the problem is you've got your kids out past ten on a school night, Roy!" Wade shouted back, stepping between me and the angry dad.

Roy. I sighed, thunking my head between Wade's shoulder blades. Roy Pannabaker. He was a high school classmate of Rob's, come to think of it. And he had come to the funeral, overflowing with condolences and within five minutes asking what I was planning to do with Rob's fishing tackle and tools.

"Go home, Wade!" Roy shouted.

"You get your kids home, Roy!" Wade hollered. "And you can forget about me fixing your carburetor at cost next time!"

Roy muttered something under his breath that super-sensitive ears only picked up as "mash-hole" and squealed out of the parking lot. Both of my hands were on my face now, and I was giggling, actually giggling. When I thought about it, that made sense, because I had just made out in a parking lot like some high school hussy. Wade seemed to find it pretty damned funny, too, because he was leaning his forehead against my neck, shoulders shaking with laughter.

"I can't believe I just did that," I said, gasping.

"Well, ya didn't do it *alone.*"

If Rob had been confronted with such a public scene, especially in front of someone he knew, it would have been recriminations and griping all the way home. But Wade just shrugged it off.

I so wanted to date Wade Tucker.

"Now." Wade reached to my driver's-side door and opened it for me. "Next weekend?"

"Yes," I told him, letting him hand me into the van like something out of a Regency novel. He shut the door as I started the engine. "I would love to . . . And next time, remove Roy's carburetor altogether."

It wasn't until I got home that night (and had helped Danny complete a spectacular poster, if I did say so myself) that I had a sort of hormonal epiphany. I'd kissed two men in the course of two days. I'd never kissed two men in the course of *two years*. I hadn't even dated since Rob died, much less kissed anybody. And now I was stringing along two perfectly nice men—OK, at least one perfectly nice man, because I wasn't sure about Finn. At the very least, I was engaged in a more than platonic relationship with both of them, which was way more than I was used to.

I had no clue how to feel about this, so I took what I was sure was an emotionally healthy route: I didn't think about it at all. I had other things to worry about, including maintaining the appearance of a responsible, engaged parent and trying to be an actual responsible, engaged parent. I just pushed it to the back of my mind. That would work, surely. Because Finn was supposed to keep his distance, and if he kept his distance, I could ignore the whole thing.

When I was human, I processed my stress through baking. It came in handy whenever the school had a fund-raiser. And with running my home business, raising an active child with last-minute art projects, managing my bloodlust, and meeting with the Council's (cordial but still scary) appointed custody lawyers, I had plenty of stress to work through. I woke up just before sunset, equivalent to a predawn wake-up call, to whip up a special batch of my famous triple chocolate chip from-scratch cookies, which had been *the* biggest seller at the Back-to-School Night bake sale the year before. I could blame those cookies for my sudden "indispensability" when the PTA needed someone to run the cakewalk at the Christmas Carnival.

Back-to-School Night was held about halfway through the first quarter of the school year, which gave the teachers a chance to get to know the kids enough to determine whether they were in for a year of "Your child is a joy to have in class, *but* . . ." notes home. It was also the setting for the PTA's first volley in the yearlong attempt to raise enough funds to provide all of the little things the school needed but couldn't fund through the district's provided budget—field trips, playground equipment, matching T-shirts for the robotics team, that sort of thing.

So there I stood, cooking for the first time in our duplex's kitchen, trying to prove my worth to people who didn't really like me all that much. And it didn't feel right to make Kerrianne do my penance just because she happened to be human, especially since Kerrianne's mother was keeping the kids so we could both meet with our kids' teachers. Frankly, she was doing me a favor, because if Danny were present during baking, he would be sneaking raw dough from the bowl when my back was turned. We did not have the time to visit the ER for his inevitable salmonella.

Yawning as twilight seeped into my kitchen, I dropped softened butter into my KitchenAid, watching as the paddle beat it together with the sugar until it was a fluffy yellow dream. Just watching it go round and round in the bowl made my mouth water. Damn, I missed cookies. And cake. And doughnuts. Basically, all of the baked things.

Hmm, maybe it was better that I was turned. Even if I hadn't gotten sick, my terrible sweet tooth would surely have led to health complications later in life. I sniffed at the mixture. It didn't smell quite right—rancid, maybe? I checked the date on the butter carton. I still had weeks before the expiration date. Maybe my vampire senses were a little oversensitive?

Cracking the shells with one deft hand, I dropped eggs, one at a time, into the creamed butter and sugar, and each one was like a stink bomb exploding in the mixing bowl.

"Augh!" I could taste the awfulness in my mouth, like I'd inhaled garbage. "Oh, my God, no!"

Vanilla. The sweet scent of vanilla would make this better. I opened the bottle and poured it into the batter without even measuring. It turned the bowl into a dark brown, mushy mess, spinning at top speed into baking oblivion.

"Worse, this is worse." I wheezed, shaking my head as I dumped the over-vanilla'd cookie vomit into the sink and turned on the garbage disposal. And that's when I realized I didn't have a garbage disposal.

I slid along the cabinet until I collapsed to the floor and promptly burst into tears. That's how Jane found me. She came into the kitchen and saw me weeping and wiping at my bloodied cheeks with a dishtowel. She slid down next to me on the floor, handing me a paper towel to mop up my tears. "Whatcha doin'?"

"I can't bake!" I whimpered.

"Well, you know most vampire powers are more, you know, 'super' in nature. You're not going to suddenly be able to bake just because you're undead."

"I could bake before!" I exclaimed.

"Oh," Jane said, frowning. "Well, then, this situation is officially beyond my frame of reference . . . Is it OK to ask why you're so upset over not being able to bake?"

"Because this is the most basic thing a mother can do for her son, and suddenly I can't do it anymore!"

"First of all, baking is *not* simple. I've watched Tess do it, and it's complex and terrifying. Second, you do a lot of things for your son. Birthday parties, volunteering for his school, and I don't know, changing your entire physical form so you can raise him. If you go to the grocery store and buy a couple dozen cookies, I don't think he'll notice."

"I can't take store-bought cookies to the bake sale.

I'll be even more of a pariah among the other mothers than I already am!"

"Am I going to have to get out the spray bottle?"

"No!" I told her.

"I never get to have any fun," she muttered. "Fine, you're going to wash your face, because there's bloody tears running down your cheeks, and that's super-disturbing. And then we're going to get Dick to bring by some of those gas masks they use on *Breaking Bad*, because I'm sure he has them, and we're going to make some fricking cookies. We're going to make so many cookies that those PTA wenches can't refuse them without looking like jerks."

"Thanks, Jane." I sighed. "Did you have this many meltdowns when you were a new vampire?"

"More," she told me. "Of course, someone was generally trying to kill me at the time, but I'd say your legal battle with your in-laws is comparable."

"Thanks. My baking angst almost let me forget about my legal battle."

"Well, I might have good news on that front."

She handed me a legal-sized envelope marked with the seal of Marcus K. Holyfield of the local family court system. I ripped open the envelope, skimming the very official-looking letter at vampire speed. Judge Holyfield was issuing an order stating that there was to be no interference with my custody of Danny while it was under review, since I'd always shown myself to be a responsible parent. That meant that unless I'd given them written permission—which clearly I had not—Les and Marge were not to contact Danny's school or doctor, and they were not to demand visitation or show up at the house uninvited, or there would be unspecified, but potentially scary, consequences.

"How?" I asked Jane, eyes wide. "How is this happening so quickly . . . and in my favor?"

Jane pursed her lips. "Apparently, Judge Holyfield was not impressed with some of the statements Les made about your 'wanton and unholy state' in his petition. I believe they got their notice two days ago. It took a while for your letter to wind its way through the Council office mail maze. Other than that, you probably don't need to know which strings are being pulled and how. I'm just happy to be using those strings for good instead of the Council's usual death, mayhem, and general evil tomfoolery. Now, feel better?"

"Much," I said. Before I rose to wash my face at the sink, I sniffed and confessed. "I have something to tell you. My sire, Finn Palmeroy, was here the other night when I came home."

"I know, but I appreciate your telling me," Jane said. "He came by the shop to inform me that he'd made contact, despite my orders that he stay away. And I asked him *again* to keep his distance because of the custody case. Trust me when I say that if Les and Marge find out you've been spending time with Finn, it will not do you any favors."

"Why do you hate my sire so much?"

"I don't hate him. I just don't trust him. I don't trust anyone who will turn somebody for money. Frankly, he reminds me a little of Dick, back when I first met him, without Dick's personal integrity. And you need to understand that I am trying really, really hard not to make Finn *more* attractive by forbidding you to see him and giving him the Romeo factor. So I'm trusting your judgment to stay away from him."

"But you did forbid me to see him," I pointed out, resisting the urge to tell her that Finn had not, after all, taken the money from my account in exchange for turning me.

"No, I forbade him to see *you*. I'm asking you nicely to take my advice into account. Totally different."

"Fine, but I don't see how you could make Finn *more* attractive," I murmured.

"What was that?"

"Nothing."

Jane and I obtained the gas masks from Dick's questionable contacts and made several batches of brookies, a recipe Jane found on the Internet labeled "moron-proof." It basically involved spooning brownie batter (from a mix) into a cupcake pan and dropping bits of premade cookie dough into the batter. The dough sank into the batter while it baked, and when it was done, you had perfect golden-brown bits of cookie baked into brownie cups. While they looked beautiful, the scent made my vampire senses revolt. We bagged the cooled brookies into packages of three and packed six dozen of them into my car just in time for me to skid into the school parking lot by eight.

I hauled the bags of baked goods through the front entrance of the school, past Happy the Howler Pup, and deposited them on the elaborately decorated bake-sale table. Blue and white and black streamers were twisted into bunting against a bright blue plastic tablecloth, bracketing a sign that read "SUPPORT THE HMHES PTA!" The table was chock-full of Bundt cakes and bags of brownies and cookies. A few mothers had been brave enough to try decorated cupcakes with spiky frosting creatures that could be either Howlers or . . . Scottie dogs?

Casey Sparks and Chelsea Harbaker were manning the table, wearing their bright blue "HMH Howler Mom" T-shirts and matching hair bows. They were all bright smiles and welcoming faces until they turned around and saw me standing there.

"Oh, Libby, hiiiiii," Casey drawled, barely able to refrain from flinching. She looked to Chelsea, who had a better poker face.

"Hi. I brought some brookies for the sale, bagged and priced," I said, putting my bags on the table. "I've got to duck into Miss Steele's class for my conference."

Casey shook her head, biting her lip. She glanced around, though I wasn't sure whether it was to look for moral support from the other mothers or some handy pair of decorative pinking shears she could improvise into a weapon. "Well, I—"

"I'm sure they'll be just fine," Chelsea said, taking the bagged brookies and moving them to the worktable behind her. "Thanks, Libby."

"Anything to help the kids," I said, smiling sweetly. It wasn't my fault that my fangs slipped out just the tiniest bit when I did it.

OK, maybe it was. But Casey's skittishness was pissing me off.

Miss Steele was waiting for me in her classroom, of course. And she checked her watch as I walked in, even though I was *precisely* on time for our 6:55 appointment. That was Miss Steele's way. She wanted to make sure you knew you were being monitored and measured, so you worked your butt off to avoid a failing grade. She was one of the few teachers who attended every monthly PTA meeting and special session, as if she didn't trust us to behave properly during the meetings and get the necessary tasks accomplished without supervision. If Chelsea Harbaker had strayed from the agenda the least little bit, I had no doubt that Miss Steele would have whacked her on the knuckles with a ruler. (Kentucky's laws against corporal punishment didn't hold much sway with Miss Steele.)

"Mrs. Stratton." She sniffed. "It's good to see you up and about. I've never believed in long-term convalescing. Too much lying about leaves the body weak and soft."

"I will try to remember that the next time I'm diagnosed with a terminal illness," I told her.

She didn't bother with even a courtesy smile, gesturing to the child-sized chair in front of her little grading table, because sitting in that wouldn't be humiliating at all. She'd used the same antique sewing desk as a grading table since I was a kid. It had ornate wrought-iron legs with flourishes of shells and feathers. It had surface area for only so many stacks of paper, so Miss Steele graded tests quickly to make room. There was no hope for a delay in grading if you thought you'd done poorly.

"Thank you for seeing me, Miss Steele. How is Danny doing?"

"As well as one could expect, in this world of video games and tablets and instant gratification. His reading and math skills are above-average, though every child is considered above-average these days. If you stopped to consider the math involved there, you would scream."

It was more difficult than I expected to keep a straight face in light of this little diatribe. This was a far cry from the Back-to-School Night of the previous year. Danny's teacher, Mrs. Dodge, had practically given a PowerPoint presentation overflowing with praise about Danny's progress over the past month, including penmanship, coloring accuracy, and number of days without a bathroom accident.

"I'm sure he told you that he and his friend, young Mr. Tucker, had to be separated."

I pinched my lips together. "No, he did not."

"Well, their frequent chats in class proved to be a distraction, for the two of them and their classmates. Mr. Tucker now sits in the front row nearest the door. Your son sits farthest from the door."

I cleared my throat, hoping that I was not, in fact, smiling in response to this news. I didn't think Miss Steele would appreciate that. "I'll talk to him about it."

Miss Steele waved a dismissive hand. "To be frank, I'm more concerned about a conversation he had with young Mr. Ramos last week. Mr. Ramos told Danny that his dad could beat up Danny's dad if Danny's dad wasn't already dead. Before I could point out the inappropriateness of such a statement, Danny responded that you could sneak into Mr. Ramos's house while they were sleeping and bite his whole family."

My mouth dropped open. *Oh, Danny.*

"I never—I don't even know where he got such an idea," I spluttered. "Why didn't you call me? Or at least send a note home? I think a death threat to another kid's family merits a *note*."

"Well, considering the 'dead dad' remark, I do think Mr. Ramos got as good as he gave. And he hasn't made any bullying statements to his classmates since, so I think we should sit back and see how it plays out. Being so small for his age, I believe Danny needs to learn how to handle these situations on his own."

"You will call me if *he* bites someone, though, right?"

"I don't think it will go that far. Besides, I believe I can channel his energy into more creative pursuits. As you can see, your son is very fond of drawing. "

She slid a large piece of paper across the desk. A crude crayon sketch showed me and Danny standing in front of our new house, with a large brown apelike figure looming in the background. And instead of a big yellow sun in the corner of his drawing, Danny had drawn a white moon, surrounded by black. He'd drawn his family at night. With Bigfoot.

Of course.

"If he does his work quietly and correctly, I allow him to draw when the rest of the class are practicing their recorders. His talents do not, unfortunately, extend to music."

"He really hates the recorder," I said, my tone apologetic.

"The recorder hates him back," she retorted. "That is the sum total of my report. Well done so far this year, to you both. I do, however, feel that I should inform you that Mr. and Mrs. Les Stratton have contacted me, both at my school phone number and on my personal landline, requesting updates on Danny's progress. Because they are not listed as Danny's legal guardians, I refused to release that information. I don't care that my mother was a friend of Marge's mother or that Les's fishing buddy serves on the school board. I will not be bullied into violating school policy or my personal ethics."

I kept my face still and calm, even when the gears in my head started to turn. "Would you mind if I ask when they contacted you?"

"Yesterday morning," Miss Steele told me.

Yesterday morning, after they'd received the notice from the judge informing Marge and Les that they were not supposed to contact the school, much less demand copies of Danny's academic records. Surely their lawyers had told them that. Had they not understood, or did they just not care?

Frankly, I would almost welcome the intrusion if their crap decisions kept them from taking Danny away from me.

"And if they proceed with their threat to subpoena school records as part of their custody case, I would like you to know that the only review the court will see from me is my usual report of sufficient classroom performance and adequate behavior. Nothing more. Nothing less."

"Thank you, Miss Steele."

I rose, and she shook my hand, with more strength than you would expect from a woman approaching her eighties. "I never did like Les Stratton," Miss Steele muttered as I walked out of her class. "He's managed to be a pompous ass since birth."

Of all the places I'd expected support, Miss Steele was startling, to say the least. Snickering, I caught up to Kerrianne in the hallway. She looked tired but bemused as she linked her arm through mine.

"How's Danny doing?"

"Talkative, occasionally threatening to his classmates, but intellectually salvageable. How was your conference?" I asked.

Kerrianne smirked. "Oh, the usual. Braylen's a joy to have in class, *but* could I please do something about her reading those Percy Jackson books tucked inside her grammar textbook while the rest of the class is diagramming sentences?"

"You would think the teacher would be happy that Braylen is reading, instead of, say, diagramming obscene sentences on her desk with a scented marker."

Kerrianne snorted. "Well, the other students can see Braylen doing it, which is openly challenging Mrs. Morgan's authority. Also, it's disrespectful, even if Braylen is doing well in the class. So we're going to have to talk about it."

We paused as another woman shouted, "He drew *what* on another boy's face in Sharpie?" from a nearby classroom.

"It could be worse," Kerrianne conceded.

Nodding, I agreed. "It could be worse."

As we approached the bake-sale table, I couldn't help but notice that my brookies were still piled up on the worktable, not set out for sale. In fact, they were piled up next to the crumpled masking tape and table decorations, as if Chelsea and Casey were about to toss my contribution out with the trash.

Really?

I'd spent—hell, Jane had spent—the better part of two hours baking those damn brookies, and they couldn't be bothered to set them out? When the rest of the table was damn near empty? I'd known some of these vipers for years. *Years*. And now they wouldn't take my damn bake-sale contributions? Because I was a vampire? Were they afraid I'd slipped something into the brownie batter? Or was it just my general condition that "contaminated" the food?

"Hold my purse," I told Kerrianne, striding toward the table.

"Nothing good ever followed that statement," Kerrianne whispered harshly.

"Chelsea, Casey, is there a reason my brookies are on the back table, instead of being set out for sale?" I asked sweetly. "It seems like you've sold just about everything else."

Chelsea was about to speak, but Casey interjected, "I guess no one's in the mood for brownies tonight."

A few heads turned our way. Parents gathered in the entryway, who had been muttering to themselves about their kids' progress reports, were now staring at the spectacle of Libby Stratton getting her brookies thrown back in her face. I was grateful, for once, that I was incapable of blushing, because my face would be on fire.

I glanced down at the platter to the left labeled "Brownies," which was practically decimated. "Mmm-hmm."

"We can bag them up so you can take them home," Casey offered.

Now, under normal circumstances, in a normal town, that comment probably wouldn't have stung. But here in the Hollow, bake sales were a big fund-raising business. Why? Because no treat was left behind. If a male Hollow resident saw that his wife's or girlfriend's cupcakes were about to be left on the bake-sale table, he would step in and buy leftover treats. It was a little bit like that scene in *Oklahoma!* where the cowboys bid for their sweethearts' picnic baskets to publicly declare themselves a couple. It secured extra cash for the charity raising money, helped the lady in question save face, and gave the men a chance to beat their chests a little bit. In previous years, it hadn't been an issue, because my triple chocolate chip cookies always got snatched up. But now . . .

I smiled sweetly, fangs fully extended, making Casey recoil. "You know what? Why don't you take those bags of baked treats, wrap them up in craft paper, tie them with a pretty raffia bow, bend over, and shove them up your—"

A rough hand wrapped around my bicep, squeezing gently. "Actually, I was just thinkin' a brownie would hit the spot."

I looked up to see Wade giving Chelsea and Casey

his best "aw, shucks, ma'am" grin. While Casey had drawn back, patting the worktable behind her to check for her purse, Chelsea's smile ratcheted up several degrees, and she stepped closer to the bake-sale table, leaning over ever so slightly to give him a better view of her V-necked cleavage.

"Oh, well, then you'll have to try my brownies, Wade, double fudge," Chelsea practically purred. I arched an eyebrow. Chelsea was married to the main morning DJ for the local Christian-music station. Despite her husband's cheerful on-air persona, I sincerely doubted that "Brother Happy" would be at all happy with the way Chelsea was staring at Wade's tattooed arms. Frankly, *I* didn't like the way she was staring at Wade's tattooed arms.

"Actually, I got a hankerin' for cookies and brownies all wrapped into one, so why don't ya just give me those brookies back there?" Wade drawled.

"That's fine." Chelsea, a bit deflated, asked, "How many?"

Wade pulled his wallet from his back pocket, letting the chain that kept it in place slap against his thigh. "All of 'em."

Chelsea's baby-blue eyes bugged out. And I'm sure mine were twice as big.

"All of them?" I whispered as Wade dug cash out of his wallet. "Wade, that's fifty dollars' worth of brookies."

Wade dropped the bills into Chelsea's hand. "And?"

"I'm not going to let you spend fifty dollars on my cooking," I hissed. "That's throwing good money after bad."

"I'm sure they're gonna be delicious," Wade said, just a little too loudly. The few parents who *weren't* side-eyeing the proceedings had turned around to watch Wade's transaction. I watched helplessly and accepted my less-than-stellar offering in return.

Wade stretched his hand out to me. "You ready to go, darlin'?"

The angry vise grip I had on my jaw was the only thing that kept it from dropping open. And Chelsea looked like she was about to fall over from shock. For all intents and purposes, according to Hollow tradition, Wade Tucker had just openly declared that I was his girl.

Stunned silent, I cleared my throat and slipped my hand into Wade's warm human hand. He took the brookies in his free hand and led me past Kerrianne, whose equally shell-shocked expression was giving way to a sinister grin.

"See you later," she whispered sotto voce. "And you're gonna give me details, woman."

"Mmm-hmm," I murmured. As soon as I figured out what the hell had just happened.

Once we cleared the front door, my shoulders sagged from the tension of my ramrod posture. I sighed, rubbing my free hand over my face. Wade's hand slipped around my waist, and he guided me toward my minivan.

"I can't believe I keep letting them get to me, when I've got so many other things to worry about. I can't believe I baked those damn brookies. Do you have any idea how bad brownies smell to a vampire's nose?

I feel like I've been rolling around in toxic sludge for the past couple of hours."

"Ah, screw 'em," Wade told me, nudging me against the hood of my van and dropping the brookies gently to the ground. "I'll eat every one of those damn brownie-cookie things."

He was standing so close, bracketing my legs with his thighs and pinning me to the van. I laughed when he took my hands in his, lacing our fingers together as his hair fell forward over his forehead. "So I guess I'll be picking you up from the hospital when you get sick from cocoa overload."

"It'd be worth it if it took that miserable look off your face." I could feel his breath against my mouth, like I could swallow his words, breathe him in.

"You know what buying all those brookies means in the Hollow, Wade. You know what people are going to think, especially after Roy seeing us in the parking lot the other night—which, by the way, seems to be a bit of a pattern with us. And I don't want things to become . . . difficult for you and Harley because you're getting lumped together with me."

"Darlin', I don't know if you've noticed, but I ain't exactly the Hollow's idea of a model citizen. If you think people give you the cold shoulder around here, you should see how quick they clam up when the tattooed guy comes strolling into the Quik Mart. Besides, ya don't have a husband to step in and defend your bakin' honor. I thought you'd appreciate the help."

"I do, I just . . . It's been a while since anyone . . . I do appreciate it."

"You never really talk about him. Your husband."

"And you don't talk about Harley's mom," I countered.

"Should we?"

No. Absolutely not. I did not want to hear about the beautiful woman who had given birth to Harley and walked away, breaking Wade's heart. Because then I might have to track her down and break her face. "I don't know. Isn't it sort of early to share our tales of woe?"

"We've survived a Bigfoot birthday party and made out against your minivan at a shoppin' center. I'd say we're due some backstory. Did ya love him?"

"I thought I loved him, in the beginning. I was young, and I was stupid, and I thought that being loved by someone meant that they stuck around, that you didn't fight with them all of the time. I didn't exactly have a great role model on which to base a comparison. I married him because I thought that was what I was supposed to do. We dated for more than a year. He proposed to me at one of his family's famous Fourth of July barbecues. Just knelt down in front of me and sixty or so of his nearest and dearest and shoved a ring at me. And then compounded the pressure by saying the ring was my birthday present. How was I supposed to say no?"

"Ya say, 'No, thank you, I don't wanna marry you because I don't think I love you,'" he said, doing a very poor job of impersonating me.

"Well, when you are a woman in her twenties living in a small town and you have been dating a man for a year, if he proposes to you in front of his family, you have to have a pretty good reason for saying no. Like 'he's a compulsive-gambling hoarder who parades around in my underwear when I'm at church.' Something like that. I knew we didn't have a lot of passion between us, but I thought we had a firm foundation, one of those slow and steady couples who make it for the long haul. You know? But the longer we were married, the more he became like his father, and the more he expected me to be like his mother . . . and I knew I'd made a mistake. But we had Danny, and I . . . just made the best of it. And then he passed away, and I'm still not sure how to feel about it."

Wade was still giving me side-eye.

"OK, Mr. Judgy, how did you end up president of the Cranky Single Parent Club?" Apparently, my need to protect myself from information was outweighed by my need to redirect his focus.

"Well, I wish I could say it was some great tragic romance like yours." He smirked at me. I scratched my nose with my middle finger, which he seemed to find hilarious, given the way he cackled. "But ta be honest, Lisa Ann was just some girl I dated for a couple of months. Nothing serious, just 'Hey, you're here, I'm here, and our parts match up.'"

"Ew."

"You asked."

"I should have clarified which details I was asking for," I mumbled.

"Sooner or later, we just lost interest," he said. "I stopped callin', and she moved on. But a couple weeks later, she shows up with a pink plus sign on a stick. She didn't believe in 'options,' said she was keepin' it. I had my doubts, I'm not going to lie. But when a Tucker screws up, he pays the price. So I gave her money for the doctor's appointments, baby things, vitamins. Hell, I even asked her to marry me. She said no, thank God. And she got real quiet at the end, just when I was really starting to think of that bump under her tank top as a real little person. She just shut herself off. Wouldn't tour the hospital. Wouldn't take those breathin' classes. Wouldn't talk about what was gonna happen after he got here.

"That baby was born, and he was a Tucker, all right. There was no denying him. Not that I would have anyway. I took one look, and that was it. I was in love with my boy, and it was deeper than anything I'd ever felt in my life."

I smiled with the silly sort of kinship only another parent would understand. "And Lisa Ann?"

"Checked out of the hospital the minute she was allowed, signed the papers sayin' she didn't want him. She told the nurses that I could give him up for adoption if I wanted to, but she was done."

"And you never saw her again?"

"Naw. She moved to Nashville, last I heard, waitin' tables in some karaoke bar. We don't need her. A mama who's going to ditch and run when things get tough? That's worse than no mama at all. Besides, we do just fine on our own. Can't say it doesn't pay off. 'Cause in return, I get this." He pulled a drawing from his back pocket. It showed a little boy and a bigger man, both with bright yellow hair, sitting on a motor-cycle, big smiles on their faces.

"Aw, that's beautiful. I got this." I pulled out Danny's drawing.

"Is that Bigfoot?"

I nodded. "Yes, it is."

He guffawed. "That's awesome."

"But it never gets any easier, does it?" I sighed, look-ing at Danny's "nighttime family."

"Do ya ever get mad, that ya had to go through all this to keep your son?"

"I'm not one for 'why me's,'" I told him. "I mean, why *not* me? When people hear that someone they know is sick, they want to hear something that person did to bring it on themselves. Something they did to de-serve it, you know? Like 'She was a two-pack-a-day smoker' or 'He worked with radioactive waste' or 'He's the Nielsen family that kept *According to Jim* on for so long.' They're looking for something that will separate them from whoever's suffering, because they need to tell themselves that it's not going to happen to them. But honestly, I was a nonsmoker who stayed away from the sun and processed foods and hair dye. My only crime was faulty genes. There are times when I wonder if I've done the right thing. I mean, there were times when I was human that I was absolutely sure I was the worst mother in the world, but at least then, I didn't pose a direct threat to my son. I question myself constantly."

"That's the job, the doubtin'," Wade said with a shrug. "When Harley was a baby, 'bout two months old, I got him to sleep almost through the night through a combination of a warm bath, a big bottle, and a whole album's worth of Kenny Rogers songs. I felt like the smartest man alive. And the very next day, he started hollering like he was about to explode. Nothing would soothe him. Late-onset colic, the doctor called it."

"It happens sometimes," I said.

"Well, it was friggin' awful. The next six months were like one of those psychological experiments you see in horror movies, the ones with the sleep deprivation and the hallucinations? One morning, I stumbled into the pediatrician's office—in my sweatpants and my huntin' boots—after being up all night with Harley screamin' his head off, convinced that my baby had one of those exotic diseases people catch in the rainforest. The doctor actually sent me down to the radiology department for a full workup—X-rays, scans, the whole bit. And while we were waiting for the results, I changed Harley's diaper. I pulled his foot out of his onesie, and the doctor noticed that his big toe was just about purple. He had a 'hair tourniquet' wrapped around his big toe. It happens sometimes when hair gets trapped inside the baby's pajamas in the dryer. The doctor cut the hair loose, and Harley stopped cryin' all at once. I felt like the biggest idiot on the face of the planet. All that fuss over a damn hairball. And then I thought about all those hospital bills I was about to get, over some stupid hair. I will admit, I started cryin', big boo-hoo sobbin' right there in the middle of the exam room. It was not my manliest moment by a long shot. But the doctor patted my shoulder through the whole thing and gave me a piece of advice."

"And what was that?"

"Bein' a parent is a constant cycle of gettin' yer ass handed to ya. Anytime you think you're ahead of the game, that you got it all figured out, that's when reality pops up and bites ya."

"A man with a medical degree said that to you?"

"I'm paraphrasin'," he said, shifting his shoulders.

I laughed. I couldn't remember the last time someone—besides Jane—let me babble on like that. Wade actually listened to me, and he didn't try to "fix" me. And while he did make the occasional grand gesture, like mass brookie consumerism, he recognized my need to handle things on my own. He didn't try to tell me what I could be doing better or step in to take care of a problem for me. I could handle a little more of that in my life.

"Well, stop it. You being helpful is downright disorienting. And while we're at it, stop calling me darlin'. It does funny things to my brain." I smacked at his arm, making him laugh again.

He pressed a kiss to the side of my head, still snickering. "And that's why I do it."

Just because you have joined a new community, that doesn't mean that everyone you meet in that community is going to get along. Try not to interfere with established feuds between vampires. Those situations have a tendency to take out bystanders.

—*My Mommy Has Fangs: A Guide to Post-Vampiric Parenting*

Chelsea Harbaker had her revenge, upping the deadline for my donation collection for the Pumpkin Patch Party by two weeks. It was a maneuver that was both elegant in its effective simplicity and super-bitchy.

So I was spending the evening at Specialty Books with my two favorite vampire ladies. Jane and I were going over a list of businesses in the chamber of commerce listing. We were dividing the list into two sub-lists, one of businesses most likely to donate raffle tickets and auction lots for the Pumpkin Patch Party and the other of businesses that would be good targets for me to approach for my bookkeeping operation.

Les and Marge were not pleased with me for reporting their breach of Judge Holyfield's freshly released order. I could feel their displeasure as more of my clients—most of whom knew Les and Marge—had been dropping off my roster with excuses like "I'd be more comfortable with someone I can contact during the day" or "I've been friends with Les for twenty years, so . . ." Meaning I'd lost about ten percent of my client base in the last week.

According to Kerrianne, Les had been grousing to his cronies at the Coffee Spot that Judge Holyfield was obviously a shameless liberal, biased toward the undead. In a town as small as the Hollow, that was bound to get back to the judge eventually. I decided to take the opposite tack, so I would be able to meet the judge's eye when we finally saw him. To show that my little family was being influenced by the most stable vampires in the region, Danny was sitting at the coffee bar, enjoying a large hot chocolate and telling Mr. Dick and Mr. Gabriel all about his latest schoolyard adventures with Harley. I noted that he did not mention his three-day TV ban as a result of his emotionally scarring threats to Chase Ramos.

Danny loved Miss Jane's "magic shop," with its mysterious candles and ritual items and the strange herbal smells. And if I wasn't careful, he was going to talk Dick out of a third chocolate chip cookie.

Andrea slid into the seat next to me and shook her head over my two-page list of neatly handwritten business names.

"Never accept the prize committee position," Andrea told me in a sage tone. "That way lies madness."

Jane shrugged. "I tried to tell her."

"Not helpful," I told them both, sipping a particularly nice bottle of Plasmatein, a blend of synthetic blood and proteins that was supposed to stave off bloodthirst for longer periods of time.

"I don't get it," Jane huffed. "I mean, I was turned years ago, and I'm not facing the sort of prejudice you are. Sure, my former boss was a bit of a jerk about filling out my undead benefits paperwork, but all I had to do was make a few veiled threats, and she fell right in line."

Dick protested, "Yeah, but you basically stuck to the nocturnal community. You got a job in a bookstore in a seedy part of town. You made friends in the vampire community. It's easy to ignore someone who's sticking to their own kind. Buttercup here is going to PTA meetings and cooking for the school bake sale. She's rubbing her fangs right in their faces."

"You do realize that I'm standing right here, yes?" I said, waving my hand, making Dick and Gabriel laugh. "And I am not rubbing anything in anybody's face. And at least I'm not engaging in front-seat make-out sessions with my sire at a Cracker Barrel, Jane."

"That happened *one time*," Jane said, holding up her index finger.

"Besides, I don't think Finn's ever been to a Cracker Barrel," Dick added.

"Finn?" Gabriel's eyes went wide. "*Finn Palmeroy* is your sire?"

"Why does everybody say it like that?" I exclaimed.

Andrea cleared her throat. "Finn has a bit of a reputation among vampires. Also, Jane, Dick, why didn't you tell us Finn was Libby's sire?"

"We took a vow of confidentiality," Jane said.

Dick shrugged. "Also, it sort of slipped my mind."

"What kind of reputation?" I asked.

"What's a nice word for 'shady as hell'?" Andrea asked.

"Dick Cheney," Jane said just as Gabriel asked, "*Is* there a nice word for 'shady as hell'?"

I might have laughed if they weren't talking about the guy who'd turned me while I was unconscious. I hoped there weren't questionable pictures out there on the Internet.

"I think I find that offensive!" Dick exclaimed. "No, seriously, I do find that offensive, Jane. You know how hard I've worked to turn over a new leaf. I haven't sold a counterfeit UK promotional product in months!"

"Dick!" Jane exclaimed. "You know I'm kidding!"

"No, I don't know that, Jane. Just like you don't know whether I'm 'kidding' when I throw out every coffee drink you make at the shop to protect our customers from food poisoning!"

Dick flounced off into the back room. He honest-to-God flounced. I'd never seen a vampire flounce before. It was considerably less intimidating than everything else I'd seen vampires do. Jane stared after him and turned to her husband, who shrugged and then gestured toward Dick's back.

"That wasn't more insulting than what I usually say to him," Jane protested.

"You make me apologize to Jamie when I say the wrong thing," Gabriel noted.

"That's because you say the wrong thing so frequently. I only say the wrong thing every once in a while."

Gabriel said nothing, merely lifted an eyebrow and stared at his wife.

She added, "When it comes to *Dick*, I only say the wrong thing every once in a while."

Gabriel's eyebrow did not change position.

"Miss Jane, when you hurt someone's feelings, you should say you're sorry," Danny informed her solemnly. "Miss Steele says that not saying you're sorry 'only compounds the rudeness.' I'm not sure what that means, because when we asked, she told us to look it up on Google when we got home. And I forgot."

"You're setting an example for Danny," Gabriel told her, smirking to beat the band.

Jane groaned. "Fine."

With all of the enthusiasm of a petulant teenager, Jane flung herself from the chair and followed Dick into the stockroom. "Dick! Danny says I have to say I'm sorry!"

"They've been like this ever since they started working together at the Council," Gabriel said with a sigh.

"As much as I sympathize with the Council's internal squabbles, can we get back to the fact that my sire has a Keyser Soze reputation?" I asked.

"He's not violent," Gabriel said, quickly putting his hands over Danny's ears. "Well, he's not always violent.

He considers it the last resort, a sort of rudeness he doesn't want to stoop to."

"So more Hannibal Lecter than Keyser Soze. That's much better."

Gabriel didn't disagree with me, which I didn't find comforting. "Finn has made a lot of money over the years for himself and his backers using a systematic sort of ruthlessness that makes even the Council hierarchy balk. He is unsentimental and efficient and has no qualms."

"Has no qualms about what?" I asked.

"Anything." Gabriel's expression was neutral despite his conflicted tone. "I didn't say he was unlikable. He can be quite charming, actually. I just wouldn't trust anything that comes out of his mouth, unless he's telling you how his actions will directly benefit him."

"So why would he turn me?" I asked. "If he's this cold, ruthless businessman, why in the world would he respond to an online ad and turn me?"

Gabriel shrugged. "Your guess is as good as mine."

"Should you go back there and try to smooth things over with Dick and Jane?"

Gabriel shook his head emphatically, finally unclamping his hands from Danny's ears. "No, I should not."

"You're much better at earmuffs than my papaw," Danny informed Gabriel. "I could hardly hear anything."

Gabriel gave Danny a regal little nod.

"So on to less awkward subjects. How's Wade?" Andrea asked in a tone too casual to be authentic.

"He's fine," I said lightly.

Andrea sighed. "Yes, he is."

Jane poked her head out of the stockroom doorway, having apparently heard this comment over the commotion of Dick's hissy fit. She and I both stared at Andrea for a long moment.

Andrea shrugged. "I have a soft spot for sketchy characters with hearts of gold. And you two were just so adorable at Danny's birthday party. It's hard to believe he's the same guy you were screaming at in a janitor's closet."

"I wasn't screaming. I was projecting my voice. Loudly. And Wade isn't sketchy," I insisted quietly, checking to make sure Danny wasn't listening. "He's just not what I'm used to."

I expected some commentary from Jane, but she was staring at the door, with a "kill it with fire" expression on her face. I followed her line of sight to the door and saw my sire strolling into Specialty Books like he didn't have a care in the world. He'd dressed up for the occasion of startling the hell out of me, wearing a dark blue suit and a crisp white shirt. And his short dark hair seemed especially slicked back. And I was smiling at him, in front of my mentor, who likened him to poison ivy.

Oh . . . shitballs.

"Hey, man," Dick said, emerging from the stockroom to shake Finn's hand.

"Dick!" Jane barked.

"What?" Dick sighed. "I don't get to spend time with a lot of former colleagues."

Jane gave Dick an even more pointed look. Dick's heaving sigh was downright petulant, giving Danny a run for his money. At last, she relented. "Fiiine. But this is not helping your whole 'I have changed' shtick."

Finn gave Dick's shoulder a manly pat and sauntered over to the table, standing behind me. He put his hands on my shoulders and seemed to relax, as if he was relieved to be near me again. It was sort of flattering but, at the same time, off-putting, considering Jane's opinion of him.

"Mrs. Nightengale, you're the one who summoned me here. Surely you're not surprised to see me."

Jane's whole character seemed to change in one roll of her shoulders. She went from the quirky, funny lady who let my son scramble all over her like a beanbag chair to a strange queenly creature, glaring across the table at Finn like he'd sunk her armada without even offering a half-assed apology. Her posture was ramrod straight. Her mouth was grim. And her voice was frosty. "I am surprised to see you, considering that I asked to see you *tomorrow night*. When Libby isn't here. I think you two have already spent enough time together."

"Really?" Finn gave me a cheeky wink. "I don't think so."

Oh, Oprah, I prayed, *just let me sink through the floor so I don't have to be present for this awkward conversation.*

"So uncomfortable," Andrea whispered. I bit my lip and nodded.

"Did you just not *hear* me when I forbade you to see your childe, or do you suffer from some sort of auditory-processing disorder?" Jane asked.

"Actually, I appealed your decision to the North American Council offices in Cleveland," he said, handing Jane an official-looking envelope. "I offered several character references and a considerable donation. They've granted me conditional visitation rights."

Suddenly, I understood how Danny felt, with the "adults" in the room talking over my head. I was pretty sure Jane and Finn were going to start spelling the big words soon. Also, why did I not know that the North American Council offices were in Cleveland?

And because he could sense conversational tension like a shark scents a distressed seal, Danny slid off his bar stool and climbed into my lap. "Who's this?"

My son studied Finn for a long moment, then leaned close and whispered, "I don't trust him, Mom. He's got a bad-guy beard. He's probably from an evil dimension."

My first-grader knew about the *Star Trek* Evil Beard Dark Parallel Universe. Lord, save me from my sci-fi precocious son.

"Mr. Wade has a beard, too," I reminded him.

"Not the same thing," Danny insisted. "Mr. Wade's beard goes all the way up his cheeks."

Andrea bit her lip so hard I was afraid she would draw blood. I glanced at Jane, who threw her hands up in the international gesture of *I tried to warn you*.

"What is this?" Finn asked, his eyebrows arched.

"This is Danny. My son," I said, staring at him, challenging.

Finn shook his head and in an amused tone told me, "I know he's your son, Libby. And I know he's the reason you wanted to be turned. I meant, what is this about a bad-guy beard?"

"All the bad guys on my cartoons have beards like that," Danny informed him, pointing to the neatly trimmed goatee on Finn's chin.

"Danny," I warned quietly, pulling my son's hands out of biting range. But to my surprise, rather than looking annoyed, Finn snorted and knelt down to Danny's eye level.

"No, no, it's true, cartoon villains are partial to facial hair. It's a scientific fact," Finn agreed. He extended his hand to Danny. "But you'll find that in real life, the villains are a little harder to spot. Nice to meet you, Danny. I'm Finn."

Danny gave Finn's hand a manly shake. "I'll be watching you."

That delighted grin broke across Finn's face again. "I wouldn't expect anything less."

"Why don't you go start on the downtown section?" I asked Danny, scooting him toward Dick as I stood.

"Nice to meet you, Mr. Finn," Danny said, running toward his favorite vampire.

"What if I shave it off?" Finn called after Danny.

"I'll still know it's there!" Danny yelled back, making Finn snicker again.

"Sorry about that," I said, my lips twitching.

"I can respect a healthy reluctance to trust a strange man with designs on his mom," Finn said with a shrug. Jane made a disdainful grunting noise, which Finn ignored. "What's the downtown section?"

"My son is recreating Gotham City. Out of biscotti."

"No one eats the biscotti," Andrea muttered.

"Because they're like cookies, only drier and harder to eat," I told her.

"Well, this complicates things." Finn sighed.

I pursed my lips. I had been expecting this. Dating when you had a child was complicated. I hadn't actually done it yet, what with the deadly disease and all, but even when I had been well and felt strong enough to take off my wedding ring, the moment I mentioned my son to a man who seemed interested in me, I could see the shutters behind his eyes close. I was disappointed that I saw the same from Finn. I'd expected more, somehow, as if he should have better perspective because of his immortality.

"Because after seeing you with your son, now I have to like you as a person, too," Finn said, as if this was a great burden. "And here I was hoping for a relationship built on chemistry and dimples."

"Aw." Andrea sighed. When Jane glared at her, she cleared her throat and said, "Right, back to the coffee bar where it's safe. Come on, Jane."

Andrea caught Jane through the crook of her elbow and tried to lift her from her seat. When Jane resisted, Andrea picked up the envelope and waved it in her face. Jane screwed up her face with disgust but allowed Andrea to haul her away.

"What are you doing here?" I whispered, which was pointless, because all of the vampires in the shop were going to hear me regardless of what I did.

"I wanted to see you, and I wanted to make clear to Jane that her embargo wasn't going to stand. As long as you don't have a problem with me visiting you, the Council shouldn't be able to stop that." At that, the tiny demitasse cup Jane was holding shattered in her hands. We turned to look at her, and she smiled blithely, shuffling the shards of porcelain from her fingers. Finn rolled his eyes and cupped my chin in his hand. "Do you . . . want me to visit you?"

"I don't know," I told him.

"Hey, this is an important part of a relationship, right? Awkwardly introducing each other to the lesser-known areas of our lives? How else would I know about your son's passion for cookie architecture or that your first name is Liberty?" When I groaned, he added, "I saw it on Jane's paperwork."

"Is that what this is, a relationship?" I asked.

"I'd like it to be the beginnings of one."

"Then I think you should know that I'm seeing someone else."

Finn scoffed. "Yes, your motorcycle enthusiast. I have heard tales. I like my chances on this one."

I snorted. Of course Finn would see himself as the natural choice over Wade. He wasn't being snobby or rude. That was just who he was, confident and secure in himself to the end. Part of what made him so charming was what made me want to smack him.

"So, Danny's father?" Finn asked. When I raised my brows, he added, "I didn't get a *thorough* look at your file."

"Passed a few years ago."

"It's not going to be easy on you, you know, taking care of a child on your own," he said.

"It's never been easy."

"But growing up without a father, you know how hard that's going to be on Danny as well."

"Are you trying to make a point, Finn?" I asked, my voice going several degrees colder.

"I'm just wondering, do you ever regret not knowing your father?"

"I regret not applying myself more in geometry. And most of my fashion choices during my adolescence. But it's hard to regret something you've never had."

"I was just curious," he said.

"Well, be curious about something else," I snapped. I regretted my waspish tone, but I didn't like being asked these questions by someone I barely knew. And I was getting tired of explaining myself—to the Council, to the courts, to the PTA.

But Finn seemed unaffected. He grinned cheekily. "OK, I'm curious about what you will be doing next weekend, as I would like to take you out to an interesting little spot that serves specialty blood. Perfectly legal specialty donor blood."

"Next weekend, I have plans," I told him, thinking of my date with Wade.

"And the weekend after that?"

"I may have other plans," I said.

"You're not going to make this easy for me, are you?" he asked, dark eyes twinkling.

"You don't want me to make it easy for you. That wouldn't be fun for you."

He moved in fast, giving me an unexpected peck

on the lips, which made me take two steps back. He grinned, despite my sudden movement. "See, you already know me so well!"

Several nights later, I stood at the kitchen window, watching the moonlight filter through the tree limbs, painting the elaborate landscaping in the backyard in a silvery wash. I would miss the flowers, come spring. It was a small sacrifice, but I would definitely miss the bright colors of the day. I thought about a poem we'd read in high school about Persephone's garden and the elaborate, but false, flowers she'd constructed out of gems and precious metals the god of the Underworld gave his lonely, depressed bride to try to keep her happy. I wondered if this was some ancient Greek fable to explain seasonal affective disorder.

Jane had insisted that I attend another Newly Emerged Vampires meeting the night before and she made me sit next to Crybaby Bob, with his decidedly unposh London accent, who ended up crying every time he was asked for an update on the strained relationships with his family.

"I just miss them all so much," Bob blubbered, slugging down what had to be his fifth bloodyccino since we'd started the meeting. "It's not fair that they've cut me off from the whole family. I'm not allowed to go to Christmas this year, can you believe that?"

Frankly, I was surprised Bob's family hadn't set him on fire just to prevent his whining.

Despite Jane's best efforts, membership in the NEV group was a mixed bag. I was starting to make some friends, but the meetings weren't a lot of fun. I still didn't know what my vampire power was, but Jane insisted that was normal. I was, however, learning lots of new tips and tricks for ignoring human food smells, so I could feel like I was more a part of Danny's dinnertimes. Andrea even gave me a polished egg-sized pink quartz crystal to keep in my palm, so I could picture all of my discomfort and negative energy being absorbed into its milky surface.

And as an added bonus to NEV membership, there were several vampire-owned businesses in town that not only wanted to use my bookkeeping service but were also happy to donate items to the Pumpkin Patch raffle. This was increasingly important, as the deadline was looming and businesses that had supported the event for years had suddenly instituted "budget cuts" when I called.

Somehow I'd cobbled together a network of supportive people—Kerrianne, Jane, Andrea, Miss Steele, Mr. Walsh, Wade. In fact, when Kerrianne wasn't available, Wade and I had come to depend on each other for babysitting help.

For instance, tonight I was home, watching the kids. Wade was working on a special project at his shop, some custom part for a special-order bike that he wanted to finish in time for the weekend so we could keep our drive-in plans. So I was keeping Harley for dinner and homework time. Wade had promised to take the boys to see some very loud, obnoxious cartoon the next week to even things out.

I was composing a list of excuses for why I couldn't

go to the next NEV meeting—new-fang cramps, Danny had homework, emergency meeting of the Pumpkin Patch committee, *Dancing with the Stars* marathon—when a large figure emerged from the trees in my backyard. I suppressed a grin, wondering what exotic shape Jed had selected for this evening. Fins? Fur? Fangs?

I stared at the shape lumbering about in the backyard. It would seem that he'd gone with none of the above. In fact, he looked downright human, which was sort of boring. He was a tall human, with a broader build, but still human. I lifted my hand to wave. After a long moment, he waved back.

"This form needs some work," I muttered.

"Mom, I don't think Harley feels too good."

I turned to see Harley and Danny standing behind me. Harley's cheeks were flushed, and his blue eyes were glassy as marbles, a quick descent from the condition I had found him in when I rose for the evening. Kerrianne had mentioned that Harley had been a little "draggy" when she'd picked the kids up from school. I should have known that was a child-health red flag for impending immune-system meltdown.

Harley sneezed loudly and looked utterly miserable.

"Your shoes are tight," Danny told him, patting Harley's matted blond hair.

"I don't think tight shoes makes you sneeze," Harley said, sneezing louder, even as I wiped at his dripping nose with a tissue.

"Your shoes are tight again" was Danny's reply.

"*Gesundheit*, honey," I reminded him, laughing. "It's

Gesundheit. It means 'bless you' in German. Why don't you get Harley a juice box from the fridge?"

"That makes more sense," Danny reasoned, fetching the juice and poking a straw into the box. Harley let loose one final ear-splitting sneeze. I grabbed the digital ear thermometer from the medicine cabinet.

"Bless you in German," Danny told him.

"No, that's not—" I shook my head. "Never mind."

"My head hurts," Harley said, crossing to the sink and leaning his face against my arm. His forehead was burning up. I didn't need a thermometer or vampire senses to know that he had a fever.

"Harley, honey, I think we need to get you into a cool bath. Danny, grab my phone off the charger. We need to call Mr. Wade, OK?"

I carried Harley upstairs to the guest bath, running a tub as cool as I thought Harley could tolerate. According to the ear thermometer, his temperature was 102.3, not dangerous but definitely not a symptom to ignore, particularly with his asthma.

I let Harley put a pair of Danny's swim trunks on, for both our sakes, before he climbed into the tub. His poor little lips were quivering, and his teeth chattered, even though the bathwater was lukewarm. As I dialed Wade's number, I called to Danny to knock on Miss Nola's door and explain the situation.

"Hey, baby doll, everythin' OK?" Wade yelled over the whine of machinery in the background. I set the phone to speaker.

"No. I'm sorry to bother you, but Harley's not feeling well. He's got a fever and a runny nose."

"You put him in a bath yet?"

"I'm in here now, Daddy, and it's cold!" Harley shouted irritably.

"That usually works, but he'll fight you like a pissed-off cat," Wade said.

"Really? He didn't give me any trouble, other than some pitiful looks."

Wade harrumphed. "Clearly, he likes you better than me."

"Clearly."

Nola, bless her, was there in a flash, medical bag in hand, and took the phone from me so she could ask Wade some questions about Harley's asthma medication. I kept myself busy mopping Harley's head with Danny's Ninja Turtles loofah.

Once Harley's tooth chattering was reduced to a less castanet-like state, we let him out of the tub and dried him off. Danny had already fetched his favorite Ninja Turtles pajamas, which were about a size and a half too small for Harley, but the poor baby didn't complain.

"You, sir, have a nice, solid upper-respiratory infection going," Nola informed him after examining him. "It's nothing too serious, but it's probably a good thing we caught it before it got worse."

"Am I going to have to take medicine?"

"I'll call Dr. Hackett and ask him to call something in to the pharmacy," Nola told me. Harley groaned, and Nola brushed his damp hair back from his forehead. "I'll make sure they add the bubble-gum flavoring, OK, darlin'? Can Wade pick it up?"

I nodded, and Danny suddenly sneezed, spraying the side of my face with spit and who knew what else. Nola handed me a wet wipe and then curved her hands under Danny's jaw, feeling his lymph nodes.

"If I didn't know I was immune to whatever bio-hazards are on my face right now, I would be really upset," I told her, wiping at my cheeks. "Nope, I am upset either way."

"Danny, do you and Harley share everything?" Nola asked, carefully cupping her hands under Danny's jaw to feel for swelling. "Like your pencils, your hats, maybe your water bottles?"

Danny nodded. "Harley finished his drink before I did at lunch today. It's nice to share."

I groaned, dropping my head. "Of course."

"Well, he should fall victim within a day or so. Lots of fluids for both of them," Nola told me. "Rest, cartoons, bland soft food. And I will bring by some coloring books tomorrow describing how not to share germs."

"Too late," Danny grumbled.

By the time Wade arrived, I could tell that he was already sliding toward infection himself. His symptoms mirrored his son's to an eerie degree, down to the glassy blue eyes and flushed cheeks. He was congested, and I could feel the slight difference in his body temperature without even touching him. And he looked like he was about to fall over from exhaustion.

Harley and Danny were conked out together in Danny's room. They'd spent most of the evening on the foldout couch in the living room, dosed up on Tylenol and ginger ale and enough *Dexter's Laboratory* to drive me slightly insane. I impressed even myself by hauling both of them upstairs under my arms without breaking a sweat. All mothers should have vampire upper-body strength.

"You don't look so good," I told Wade, handing him a can of ginger ale from the fridge.

"I don't get sick," he protested, shrugging out of his denim work jacket. "I've got the Tucker constitution."

"Well, I don't know if you should take Harley home. He's sick. Danny's halfway to sick. You're getting sick. And I can't get sick. So if you stay here, when you inevitably fall under the germ spell, you're not left without support."

"I'm telling you, I don't get sick," Wade growled, sprawling back on the foldout couch.

"I'll remind you of those words in twelve hours when you're sniffling and whining for juice." I propped his foot against my thigh and wiggled his work boot loose. His leg dropped like dead weight to the floor as I repeated the process with his other foot.

"I never whine. I'm a Tucker," he muttered.

I was smiling, even as I rolled my eyes and pulled the sheets up to his chin. "Yep." I kissed his warm forehead. "You're a regular badass."

It didn't take twelve hours for Wade to sniffle. It took three. But to his credit, he didn't whine for juice. He politely requested a Budweiser.

"I don't think beer is the answer," I told him, dropping two Tylenols into his palm for his five A.M. dose.

"It's the answer if the question is 'What's cold and delicious and makes ya forget that ya feel like your head's about to explode?'"

"Well, it is hard to argue with that logic."

"I really don't feel good," he mumbled, pulling me down to sit so he could drape his arms around my waist and bury his face against my thighs.

I giggled, cupping my hand around his bare neck. "I know."

"I don't want you to have to take care of me."

"I know. And I appreciate that."

"You're a really sweet girl, and your hand feels nice on my neck."

"Thanks. You're a nice guy."

He rolled onto his back and sort of sleepily leered up at me, through the dark gold hair that was tossed over his eyes. "And you're so good to Harley. You treat him just like you treat Danny."

I pushed the hair back from his face. "He's easy to love. He's a good boy. He's a good friend to Danny."

"And you're funny and you're smart and you call me on my bullshit." Wade grinned loopily. "And ya have a pretty fantastic rack."

"There it is," I scoffed. "How much of that Coldaid stuff did you take?"

He held up two fingers to measure a little bit and then slowly expanded his fingers until they measured a shit ton. He pursed his lips. "You're right. That's not a very nice thing to say, is it?"

"Probably not."

"OK, ya have the greatest rack in the history of racks."

"Is that much better?"

"Is it the word 'rack' that bothers ya?" he asked, squinting at me.

I shook my head, still petting his hair like I was stroking a feverish cat. "I'm not sure."

"Will ya ignore the 'rack' comment and lie down here with me?" he asked, lifting up the blanket. I looked down at his flushed, feverish face. I couldn't catch his cold. There was no reason *not* to slide under those blankets. Shaking my head, I crawled onto the couch next to him. He rolled over, slinging a leg over mine and snuggling his face against my chest. "Oh, you feel nice and cool." He sighed, combing his fingers through my hair. "And ya smell nice. You always smell nice, like those white flowers. The ones that only come out at night?"

"Jasmine?"

"Yeah, jasmine. It's pretty, and you're pretty."

"Thanks." I chuckled, patting his sweaty head. "I try."

"And I really like you," he mumbled into my side. "Like more than a friend or one of them 'friends with benefits' things. I like you a lot more than I've liked anybody in a long time."

"That's really nice to hear, Wade. Because I like you, too."

"Gonna ask ya to be my girl."

My eyebrows shot up. "What does that mean, exactly?" I asked.

No response from Wade.

I craned my neck to peer down at him. Wade's eyes were closed, and his mouth was open in a light snore. "Of course."

• • •

The boys ended up waking for their own doses of Tylenol just before dawn. They crawled onto a pallet I made up on the floor near the foldout couch and went back to sleep. I stayed with them, watching them doze, until the sunlight crept over the horizon. I had to get down to my little basement hidey-hole. I knew I had to go. But I made up reasons to stick around, leaving bottles of water and juice boxes for everyone by the sofa and leaving little Post-it explanations about how to use our remotes.

I watched as Wade rolled over to the far side of the mattress, fumbling around blindly until he found Harley with his hand. He rubbed the space between Harley's shoulder blades, in a gesture that seemed to comfort him as much as it did his son. And then, absently, he reached over and patted the top of Danny's head.

I heard the jangle of keys at the front door and jumped up to let Kerrianne into the house. I pressed my fingers to my lips. She nodded and followed me into the living room.

"Welcome to the plague house," I whispered. "Danny will not be going to school today. Also, you have a few new inmates."

Wade's head rose from the pillow, hair all askew and still squinting. "Hi, Kerrianne."

"Wow. I knew one day I would stumble into your house and find Wade all stupid and disoriented, but I thought it would be under dirtier circumstances."

"Easy," I warned her.

"Don't worry. I'll take care of them," Kerrianne told me. "I've got the day shift."

"Are you sure?" I asked, yawning. "You're no use to your family if you're sick, too. This could be the beginning of one of those horrible outbreak movies that ends in a zombie apocalypse."

Kerrianne scoffed. "Oh, I'm fine. Unlike Cliché McTough Guy here, I'm smart enough to use hand sanitizer and megadoses of vitamin C. I don't rely on the Tucker constitution to defend me from germs."

"Does everybody but me know about the Tucker constitution? Is it on the Internet or something?" I asked.

"Wade may have referred to it a few times. He's a legend in his own mind."

Wade shook his head. "That's not very nice, Kerrianne."

"Yeah, well, I can't ogle you if you're all snotty and gross. You need to think of my needs before you do something dumb like this," she shot back.

"Oh, come on, you can still ogle him from the neck down," I chimed in helpfully.

"I'm lyin' right here, ya know," Wade grumped.

"I'm sorry, sweetie." I crouched close to him, sitting on the chair near the couch and running my fingers along his cheek. He leaned into the caress like a cat and made a rumbling noise low in his throat. Kerrianne's eyebrows rose at the sight, but she said nothing.

"Better. Not awesome. But better," he said. "And I don't remember a good portion of last night, so I'm hopin' you'll have the decency not to post any incriminatin' videos on YouTube."

"Just for my private collection, then. Got it."

"Very funny," he said, weakly batting at me with his hands. "How are the boys?"

"They've been napping for a while," I said, nodding toward their motionless forms. "You should probably get them up for some juice and meds in an hour or so. But for now, just enjoy the peace and quiet. Danny's a bit of a whiner when he doesn't feel well."

"Yeah, pretty soon Harley is going to want his own pajamas, his own toys, that sort of thing," Wade said, patting his son's head.

It struck me that Harley and Wade would be going home soon, maybe even tonight. And that made me sad. I liked having them here in the house. It felt more like a home when Danny had other humans around, other people who needed to eat and could go out during the day. I felt more secure with Wade there, and . . . it just felt *better*. I'd looked forward to rising for the evening, knowing that he and the boys would be waiting upstairs. And the fact that I was desperately attracted to Wade, well, that didn't hurt.

"I'll get some breakfast started," Kerrianne said.

"My colds are cured by bacon!" Wade told her. "And more bacon!"

Kerrianne replied, "Oatmeal for everyone!"

"Bacon-flavored oatmeal?" Wade asked, his tone hopeful. He looked up at me, his eyes all pitiful. "She's just making regular oatmeal."

"I know, the very nerve," I said, rubbing my hand on his back. "I miss bacon."

"Maybe they could make bacon-flavored blood

someday. I'm sorry you have to see me like this," he said, waving his hand at his blotchy face.

"It's not so bad," I told him. "It's actually kind of nice, you letting me see you all vulnerable and pathetic. Rob always went to his mom's when he was sick and stayed for days at a time. Said her chicken soup was magic or something."

"Rob was a dumbass. And was the 'pathetic' really necessary?"

"You're begging for bacon-flavored oatmeal, so yes, it was."

The boys stirred, almost simultaneously. Danny sat up, blinking blearily. Harley buried his face in his dad's ribs and pulled the covers over his head. Seeing this, Danny rolled off the pallet and ambled around to my chair. He climbed into my lap and tucked his face into my neck.

"I hate everything," Danny grumbled against my skin.

I laughed, hugging him tight. I could feel the weight of the sunrise, a wave of fatigue dragging me under. But I wanted to stay. I wanted more time with everybody. It seemed unfair, that I had to give up the daytime, that I missed out on so much of their lives. But I guessed this was the sacrifice I'd made for more time. A girl couldn't ask for everything.

"Thanks for taking care of us all night, Miss Libby," Harley said.

"There had to be some advantage to this vampire thing, like being able to stay up all night with you," I said. "Well, that and the whole immunity to your gross germs."

"The gloatin' was definitely *not* necessary," Wade warned.

"What are you going to do, sneeze on me?"

Wade made a face that was downright diabolical. "Might." ·

"I already tried it," Danny told him. "Didn't work."

"Dang it. New plan, boys. We lick random objects in the room and don't tell her which ones are contaminated." At this, the boys cheered. Well, they cheered as much as two sick boys could muster.

"And with that, I bid you good day," I told them. "I'm going to bed."

"Aw, come on, Mom!" Danny whined.

"I said good day!" I exclaimed, streaking toward the basement door. I took one last look at the boys, Danny hanging off the back of the chair while Wade and Harley sprawled on the couch. Sleep-rumpled and slightly snotty, they waved at me. I blew them a kiss and closed the door.

"I'm going to lick the remote!" I heard Danny exclaim.

I poked my head out of the basement doorway. "Don't lick the remote!"

Boys were so weird.

10

Though you will go through an instinctual withdrawal from people you don't completely trust, remember that your child needs contact and support from the living world, just as you need support from the vampire world. Also, there are only so many homes that can support a panic room.

—*My Mommy Has Fangs: A Guide to Post-Vampiric Parenting*

Someone was knocking on my basement door.

Why was someone knocking on my basement door?

I sat up slowly from the single bed I'd set up in my little underground sleeping compartment, slapping my hand around my nightstand, searching for my cell phone. It was 5:56 P.M. The sun was barely down. Why the hell was someone trying to wake me up?

Danny?

Was Danny feeling worse? His fever had broken the night before, just after Harley's, but it could have spiked again. I sprang up from bed, stumbling as the sheets tangled around my ankles. I didn't need a light to maneuver toward the stairs. I'd kept the basement as simple as possible, just a bed and a nightstand and a framed photo of me and Danny, convincing myself that it wasn't really my bedroom, just a place where I slept while the rest of the household lived aboveground in the potentially fatal sunlight. All of my clothes and shoes and toiletries were upstairs in the master bedroom. Unfortunately, that included my hairbrush, and my hair was falling over my face like something out of *The Ring*.

I yanked the door open to find Kerrianne gnawing on her bottom lip. "What's going on?"

"Your mother-in-law."

"She's here?" I exclaimed. "Has she tried to take Danny? Is he talking to her now?"

Kerrianne shushed me. "Yes, she's here, but she's out on the front porch. I didn't want to let her in without talking to you first."

"Close all the blinds," I said. "I'll be out in a second."

"OK. Also, you might want to think about taking care of this area," she said, waving at her head.

"That's my whole face," I told her.

She nodded. "Yes, it is."

Several minutes later, I had thrown on jeans and a cardigan and was trying to look respectable as I sprinted to my front door. I was maybe eighty-two percent awake, but that was as good as it was going to get. Kerrianne passed me a freshly warmed bottle of synthetic blood as I whipped through the kitchen.

She was a wonder, that Kerrianne.

"Hi, Mom!" Danny cried as I passed the foldout couch. I paused to kiss the top of his head and gauge his temperature. I guessed it was slightly less than one hundred degrees. Wade and Harley, it seemed, had recovered enough to drive home.

Marge, as promised, was waiting outside my front door, holding an enormous CorningWare container of something that smelled like old socks—to me, at least. She was wearing her "Number 1 Grandma" sweatshirt and a tremulous smile.

I stepped out onto my porch, crossing my arms over my chest and shivering slightly. The air was finally starting to turn crisp after the remaining heat and humidity of September had ebbed away. Fall would be blowing us over before we knew it. Danny was still debating his costume choices for Halloween but felt pressure to narrow it down since most kids wore their costumes to the Pumpkin Patch Party. He and Harley were trying to coordinate, of course, and while Danny was lobbying for characters like Ninja Turtles or Avengers, Harley was pushing for something clever, like Danny dressing as toast covered in peanut butter and Harley dressing as toast with jelly. Danny was trying to undermine the idea by claiming it was rude to the kids who were allergic to peanuts.

They'd spent hours debating this matter from their sickbeds, to the point where I started coming up with fake "bookkeeping emergencies" so I could hide in my room with my laptop . . . until Kerrianne figured out what I was doing and gave me some super-judgmental looks.

"I heard that Danny is sick," Marge said.

"You're not supposed to be here, Marge. Not until

we get everything settled with the courts," I said. "I can't believe I have to put it this way, but I don't feel comfortable talking to you without a lawyer present."

"I know, I know, but I couldn't bear to think of Danny being sick without anyone to take care of him."

"Danny has people to take care of him. The fact that you think I would leave him without someone to care for him while he's sick, that's probably why we have to have lawyers involved when we speak," I told her, my voice ice-cold.

"You know that's not what I meant."

I gritted my teeth. When Rob was alive, I let Marge get away with a lot of comments and criticisms under the guise of "not what I meant" because it was too hard to convince her that regardless of her intention, insults still hurt. Rob always told me to just let it go because "that's just how she is." Well, I was done letting it go. I was done playing nice. I was held accountable for every damn word I said. Marge deserved equal treatment.

"No, I don't. Your court summons made it clear what you think of my parenting skills."

"I didn't come here to start any ugliness, Libby. I just wanted to bring Danny some of my chicken soup. It always made Rob feel better when he was sick."

"Danny is not Rob. He's a different little person entirely."

Marge stared at me with a bewildered expression on her face and then suddenly turned chalk-white. She dropped her CorningWare as she sank heavily onto our front-porch swing. I caught the container before it hit the floor and handed it off to Kerrianne, who was waiting just inside the door. She made a wincing face as she whisked the soup away but did not offer an escape from this horribly awkward conversation.

"Do I need to call someone for you?" I asked.

"Is that—is that why you got yourself turned into a vampire?" Marge wheezed, fanning her clammy face with her hand.

"Please stop referring to it as getting myself turned," I told her. "You make it sound like I contracted a social disease."

"Is that why you wanted to be turned? Is that why you're fighting us so hard on the custody case?" Marge amended. "Because you didn't want us raising Danny? Because you think we're trying to replace Rob with our grandson?"

She sounded more hurt than angry. And to be honest, the idea of hurting her seemed so much more painful than her being angry with me. But she needed to hear this, and I needed to say it.

"I didn't trust you," I told her. "Well, not so much you but definitely Les. You take him fishing, you talk about how much *Rob* enjoyed a certain spot or how *Rob* always liked using a cane pole. You watch Rob's favorite childhood movies with him and eat Rob's favorite foods. You don't bother learning Danny's favorite childhood movies or Danny's favorite foods. That's not fair to him, and it's really unfair to you, because you are missing out on the opportunity to get to know who he really is. Because who he is, is really freaking amazing."

"I can't believe—I can't believe that after all these years, this is what you think of me. As a mother, I would think you would understand what it would be like to lose your son. I would think you would understand how hard that loss would be."

"I did think about it," I told her. "I thought about it every day. I still think about it. So you should understand how desperate I was to make the decision I did. And you should think about how desperate I am, now that you and Les are trying to take Danny from me."

Marge's dark eyes narrowed. "Are you threatening us?"

"Not at all," I told her. "I just think you need to consider this from my point of view. Consider how different this situation could be. If you two would just compromise, figure out a way for us all to be in Danny's life instead of trying to make it an all-or-nothing situation, we might be able to get through this without destroying the relationship we have. Because as it stands, you two are doing a pretty good job of convincing the courts that Danny would be better off with me."

Marge shook her head, biting her lip. "Les would never allow it. He's convinced he's doing the right thing, bringing Danny to stay with us. He's going crazy, ignoring the court orders, saying he has every right to check up on his grandson and no judge is going to stop him. And it just keeps getting worse every time the judge sends one of those letters. He would be furious knowing I'm here talking to you. Getting Danny home with us has become his whole reason for living. I've tried getting him to talk to somebody, but he says he knows he's doing the right thing."

I sagged against the porch railing. This wasn't new or unexpected information, but it was still distressing to find out that your worst suspicions were true. "I'm really sorry to hear that."

"I'm sorry it's come to this," she said. "In a million years, I never would have guessed our lives would turn out so . . ." My mother-in-law was polite enough not to finish that particular thought, which I appreciated.

"What, vampire daughter-in-law wasn't on your list of potential outcomes when you watched me toddle down the aisle?"

Marge made an undignified noise that sounded suspiciously like a laugh. And against my better judgment, I said, "If I let you in to see Danny, could you talk to him without upsetting him or pumping him for information? Without reporting back to Les or the judge? Just a regular visit with Mamaw?"

Marge's eyes brimmed with tears, and she nodded frantically. "Yes, I could do that."

"Could you do it without telling Les about it? Or anyone else?"

Marge's head stopped mid-nod. After a long silent moment, she said, "Yes, I could do that."

I was trapped in the vampire version of *Adventures in Babysitting*. I remembered watching that movie when I was a kid and thinking, *Wow, Elisabeth Shue's night could not possibly get worse*, and then being proven wrong over and over again. Nostalgic déjà vu was a bitch.

It started off easily enough. I had to drive to Murphy

to pick up a packet of gift cards for gas at a service station owned by a student's grandfather. Considering it was more than five hundred dollars in gas cards that would be raffled off, I didn't think it was asking too much for me to drive an hour to pick them up. Wade had to work late on a special order, so Harley was keeping Danny company with Kerrianne and Braylen.

I hoped I'd made the right decision, letting Marge visit with Danny. They'd both enjoyed it enough to warm even the cockles of my still heart. They fell right back into their dynamic, without a mention of their separation. Danny simply kissed her cheeks, told her about his new friend Harley and their "sick-person campout." He showed her his new room and his new Ninja Turtle and asked for a bowl of her soup. It was as if he'd seen her just a few days before.

For purely selfish reasons, I hoped that renewing Marge's visits with Danny would somehow result in Les going the opposite of crazy and dropping his suit. But I also hoped it would give Danny a greater sense of security, one more thing in his life that hadn't changed. Because with the direction things seemed to be going with Wade, I couldn't help but think that something in our lives was about to change all over again.

Just as I reached the far east side of town, my van's dashboard lit up in an explosion of color, beeping and flashing like one of the video games I refused to let Danny play. I couldn't tell *which* of my warnings was going off; I just knew that my engine was very angry with me and I should probably do something about it soon.

I glanced around, trying to determine my exact location. I was just inside the town limits, on Cary Street. Because the street was lined with storage facilities and used-car lots, there was no traffic at this time of night. In fact, the only motion I could make out nearby was a lone pedestrian walking down the middle of the street toward me, which didn't make me feel entirely safe. I mean, as a vampire, I had a higher-than-average chance of surviving a mugging, but that didn't mean I wanted to test the theory.

I could park my van here, lights and alarms flashing, and call Jane or Dick or Wade—wait, Wade's shop was on this side of town. I pulled my phone from my purse and Googled the address of HMH Custom Cycle Parts. I was only two miles away. Maybe I could make it without my van catching fire?

I gently guided my poor vehicle around the corner, while the dashboard continued to bleat and flash. By the time I pulled into the shop's parking lot, the van's alarm system was going off for reasons I couldn't quite figure out. I was surprised to find that instead of a mechanic's shop, it looked more like an engineering firm. A clean, quiet blue building with an unassuming, unlandscaped entrance. The exterior didn't even have a garage door, more of a freight entrance.

Wade came out the front door, a scowl on his face. When he saw me climbing out of the van and frantically clicking the keyless remote, his expression switched to one of concern. He rushed over and yelled over the noise, "Hey, what's going on?"

"I don't know!" I shouted as he ducked into my car

and popped the hood. He started yanking and pushing, all the while looking very competent. "I was just driving along, and everything was loud and bright and—"

Suddenly, the blaring horn died. Wade straightened, looking triumphant.

"Oh." I sighed. "That's better."

"That's gotta suck when you've got superhearing, huh?"

"You have no idea," I told him.

"What are you doing out on this side of town? I thought the boys were with you tonight."

"Well, Kerrianne decided to show the boys how to make homemade pizza, which made the house smell to high heaven. I made my escape to drive over to Murphy to pick up some stuff for the Pumpkin Patch. And then my car had some sort of tantrum."

Wade commenced poking things in the engine. "Yeah, I think the motherboard for your computer system has short-circuited. And your brake line looks a little worn. But I'm not sure. I can have my guys take a look at it. Terry loves that kind of thing."

"Oh, no, I couldn't. You said you had a special project to work on tonight."

"Eh, we've reached a stopping point. And frankly, the guys could use a change of pace. They're starting to get a little punchy, which is never good. I'll give you a ride over to Murphy while they take a look at it. We've probably got the parts you need right here."

"What is it exactly that you do here?"

He grinned at me but didn't answer. "Just hold on a second."

He jogged back into the building, and a few minutes later, the freight door opened. Two men came walking out—a tall man of solid build and a much shorter man with a rounded belly that hung over his belt. They were both young, the taller one much younger than me, with faint acne scars still spotting his cheeks. But they were moving swiftly toward me, as if eager to meet me. In fact, the shorter of the two had his arm outstretched before he was anywhere close.

"Hi!" he exclaimed. "I'm Terry. Are you Wade's lady friend?"

"I am his friend," I agreed, adding awkwardly, "who is a lady."

"He said you're having some trouble with your motherboard?" the taller man asked. Standing two heads taller than me, he was practically a giant, with high cheekbones and a prominent forehead. He looked like he should be swinging a broadsword somewhere instead of handling the comparatively tiny mechanisms of my engine.

"That's Junior," Terry supplied cheerfully. "He doesn't stand much on introductions."

"It's no problem, really," I said. "Now that it's turned off, I can just have it towed to the dealership. I'm sure it's just a problem with a spark plug or something. I don't want to bother you when you're working on something else."

"A spark plug? You have no idea what you're lookin' at, do ya?" Junior asked me, his expression not quite friendly.

"It's . . . an engine," I said.

"I thought you were a vampire," Terry exclaimed. I couldn't help but notice Junior's face going from irritated to downright livid at the word "vampire."

"That doesn't mean I know how to fix cars. It's not like they download information into our brains like in *The Matrix*."

"Well, I, for one, am glad I finally found something you're not good at . . . besides socializin' with the normals," Wade teased as he approached with two motorcycle helmets in hand.

"Oh, hush," I told him, making Terry raise his eyebrows. "I'll show you my accounting software sometime and let you try to make heads or tails of it."

Wade scoffed. "The difference is, I know my limits. And that limit is long division."

"Hardly," I muttered.

"Y'all see what you can do to fix up the mommobile. I gotta get this little lady to Murphy."

"But your project—" I said, grimacing guiltily when I saw the irritated expression on Junior's face.

"It'll keep," Wade told me. "The boys get their overtime, one way or the other. And Terry's savin' up for an engagement ring for his gal, aren't ya, Terry?"

Terry ducked his head, and his rounded cheeks flushed pink.

"Well, OK, I need a ride, but that doesn't mean I'm going to ride on that thing!" I exclaimed. "I'll probably go flying off the back when you hit a bump or something."

"You're a vampire," he said, strapping on his own

brain bucket. "You're invincible. If anything happens, you'll just heal up anyway."

"That won't save my pride," I told him, watching Junior carefully as he eyed my van. Well, great, now I had to worry even more about my brake lines.

I threw my leg over the motorcycle, thankful that I'd worn jeans and a thick canvas jacket, and slipped my arms around Wade's waist.

"Hold on tight," he told me, squeezing my hands.

"Oh, don't worry," I told him.

It was curiously pleasant to ride along on the motorcycle, the vibrations sending little thrills up and down my spine. I propped my chin against Wade's shoulder and for a few precious moments let myself forget my legal troubles, Danny's needs, the Pumpkin Patch, the million little tasks I had to accomplish to keep our lives running. I wrapped myself around Wade's back, enjoying the warmth seeping through his clothes to my chest. I closed my eyes and took in his metallic, citrus scent. And I just enjoyed the experience of flying down the highway.

It took a few minutes for me to feel the first drops of rain against my skin.

It appeared that Wade and I were about to be caught in one of the Bluegrass State's sudden "change of season" thunderstorms.

Within minutes, we were being battered by sheets of rain, which quickly soaked through my clothes. Tree limbs whipped over our heads like hysterical mothers throwing their arms up in the air over ungrateful children. The wind changed directions, throwing leaves and debris into the mix, so now we were battered *and* blind.

"I've got to pull over!" Wade yelled over his shoulder. Even my ears could barely pick up his voice over the roar of the storm. But we were on a deserted highway in the middle of nowhere. There was no convenient Starbucks where we could take shelter. In the distance, against the backdrop of lightning, I saw the outline of some sort of structure.

"There!" I yelled, pointing over Wade's shoulder. He nodded and sped toward what looked like an old tobacco barn, leaning under the weight of disuse. Before Wade could stop, I leaped off the back of the bike, skidding in the mud and yanking the old barn door open. Wade slowed, his brake lights casting an eerie red glow around the empty barn.

Tobacco farmers used to use outbuildings like these to smoke the leaves after they were harvested, great billowing piles of burley painting the interior walls with the tar grime and a rich scent that still hung in the air years after western Kentucky's farmers all but abandoned the state's traditional cash crop. The barns were usually located on the far outreaches of the farms, to keep the smell and fire risk far from the farmers' homes. Now this barn was being used to store old tractors and what looked to be an inordinate number of old rusty scythes spread out on antique tables, which was . . . concerning.

"This is why people drive cars, with roofs and windows and stuff!" I exclaimed as Wade shut off the engine.

"Well, if I knew I was going to be carrying a passenger through a storm, I woulda taken my truck to work tonight."

"Don't make your meteorological miscalculations my fault," I teased. "How far did we get?"

"About halfway," he said. "No sense in callin' anyone. We'll just wait it out."

"Or be sacrificed by the scary tobacco cult that clearly holds its meetings here." I put my cell phone on flashlight mode and held it up so Wade could see the tables full of scythes.

He recoiled. "Yep. We live in a strange town."

I nodded. "So just you and me. In a tobacco-torture-cult barn."

"Can't say I don't know how to show a girl a good time."

"If you try to tell me that we should 'get out of these wet clothes,' I will smack you. A lot."

Wade laughed and jostled me with his shoulder. "Smartass."

"My appeal is ninety-two percent sass-based."

"I wouldn't say that." Wade shook the water out of his hair. "It's more a sixty-forty split."

"Oh, really? And does the other forty percent depend on my 'greatest rack in the history of racks'?"

Wade's blue eyes bugged out of his head. "That wasn't a dream?"

"Oh, no, it was very real." I laughed as he dropped his head to his shoulder and groaned. I giggled, giving his shoulder a comforting "sorry you made an ass out of yourself" pat.

"Thank you for not killin' me in my sleep," he muttered against my damp skin.

"Eh, you're cute, and you smell nice, so I think I'll keep you."

"That's all of my good qualities?" he muttered. "Thanks a lot."

I laughed, tilting his chin up so he had to meet my gaze. "OK, you are a good man and an excellent father. You are funny and smart and kind, and you listen to me. No one has ever really *listened* to me before. And you remind me that these insane things I'm doing, I'm doing them for the right reasons. And you just drive me crazy sometimes with how pretty you are, which I don't think should be overlooked, in terms of a virtue—"

Wade closed his mouth over mine, effectively shutting me up. His hands, warm and alive, slid under my wet jacket and pulled me closer, so I could feel the beat of his heart against my own silent chest. I threaded my fingers through his damp hair, rubbing my thumb over his pulse point. It jumped with every stroke.

He broke away, chuckling softly as he backed me toward one of the tables. I could feel my nipples drawing tight and hard against the wet fabric of our shirts. I felt desire flicker between my thighs, and for the first time in years, I knew that desire was about to be fulfilled. Waves of an entirely different sort of hunger rolled through me, and I could feel my fangs stir, aching to break through and strike at Wade's neck. The very idea of his sweet, warm blood flooding my mouth, into my throat, made me moan, even as the more human, rational parts of my brain rebelled.

I turned my head, capturing his lips to distract myself from the temptation of his jugular. I growled in appreciation at the taste of his mouth, cinnamon gum and the hint of smoke. He took advantage of this, sliding his tongue across my lips to dance with my own. He spread his hands over my ass and lifted me, wrapping my thighs around his waist. He hitched me up, raking my aching center over the growing bulge behind his zipper.

"We need to get you out of those wet clothes," he rumbled against my lips as he carried me across the room to a table only half full of deadly farm implements. Laughing, I smacked at his arms, even as he spread me out over an empty spot on the table. He pushed at my wet jacket, protecting me from the rough wooden boards with its damp, heavy material. He rubbed his thumb across my bottom lip, raising his eyebrows, as if to ask permission.

I nodded and kissed him, hoping I was giving him some idea of how much I wanted him, how much I wanted to touch and be touched, how glad I was that it was Wade here with me. He propped my ass on the edge of the table and pushed his wet jacket back, letting it drop to the ground. His fingers splayed across my collarbone, tracing its curve down to the swell of my breasts. He kneaded them, teasing the nipples through the wet cotton of my shirt. I moaned, arching into his hands, bucking my hips. My ankles locked at the small of his back, trapping him against me. He tried not to let the wince show, but it was clear I was hurting him. I relaxed my legs from their vise-like grip, and he fell against me, face tucked into the valley of my cleavage.

I retreated, embarrassed by my lack of control, pulling my hands back and uncrossing my ankles. But Wade caught my thighs in his hands and wrapped them back around his hips, thrusting ever so slightly against me, showing me that his want for me hadn't waned one bit. He reached for the button of my jeans, popped it loose, and dragged the stubborn denim down my hips. I was grateful that I'd worn one of the nicer pairs of panties I owned, cornflower-blue sateen with strategic lace panels. The warmth of his palm spanned between my hips, over my mound, and I sighed in contentment.

Grinning, I reached for his shirt, pulling it gently over his head. No matter how many times I saw his sculpted, inked upper body, I would never stop admiring the curves of his toned torso, the way his tattoos accentuated the length of his arms. I traced them with my fingertips, the flashing golden flames of the phoenix curling over his shoulder, the curve of antlers from the deer skull on his forearm, the graceful dance of lettering on his ribs.

He caught my wrist, urging my hand down his belly to his zipper, and I made quick work of it. My panting joined his as I slid my cool fingers under the elastic of his underwear and wrapped them around the hot length of him. Groaning, he bucked forward, and his hands abandoned my breasts, landing hard beside my shoulders to brace himself.

The noises he made were fan-freaking-tastic. I

could hear them, even over the howling of the wind and thunder outside.

He was kissing me again, making me forget my nerves, teasing my opening with warm, rough fingers, working me into a state of shameless, shaky need. I guided him toward me, sure that if he wasn't inside me soon, I would die all over again. Growling softly, he slid home. I sobbed, throwing my head back and whacking it against the table as I rolled my hips, desperately trying to bring him closer.

He cradled my crown in one hand while he secured my ass on the table with the other. I clung to his shoulders, undulating against him. The more I moved, the tighter that delicious tension coiled inside of me. I could feel the coil of excitement gathering, building to something I couldn't quite name but desperately needed. And in focusing on that feeling, I let my control slip.

Being so close to Wade, surrounded by his lovely human smell, the sound of his pounding pulse, it made my mouth water all over again. I could sense his blood flowing through his veins, under all that golden skin, mere inches from my lips. I could practically taste the tangy, warm throb of it over my lips. My fangs extended, stretching farther than I'd ever felt them go.

Just a little nip, a cold, hissing voice seemed to whisper in my head. *He'll hardly miss it. And it will be soooo good.*

I licked my lips, tracing the line of Wade's jugular with my eyes to find just the right spot to sink my teeth— Then I froze suddenly, sitting up and clamping my hand over my mouth. My throat was positively *burning* with thirst, and in my rush to get out the door earlier, I'd barely had breakfast. The synthetic blood I'd planned to drink during the evening I had left in my van. I didn't want to feed from him. I'd managed to keep to my strict "vampire vegan" policy so far . . . and damn, he smelled like everything that was good and delicious in the world.

I would drain him dry.

I panicked, scrambling away from Wade, nearly uncoupling us. He frowned, holding on to me. When he saw me clutching my hand over my fangs, his golden brows rose, and he slowly peeled my hand away from my face. He kissed me, deliberately pressing his lips against each of my canines. He edged his mouth along my jaw, nipping and biting until he reached my throat. This left his neck exposed and vulnerable to my mouth.

"I don't want to hurt you," I whispered.

Wade shrugged, moving his hips and nudging against an absolutely wonderful spot inside me that even I didn't know existed. "So don't."

I keened, digging my fingernails into the table. Panting, I licked my lips and tentatively scraped my fangs against his skin. Wade clutched me to his chest, preparing for the pain. I could feel the table buckling under my fingers as I concentrated on being gentle. My teeth sank into his vein, and warm, fragrant blood burst into my mouth.

I had missed out on a *lot*. Real, warm human blood straight from the source was better than any food, drink, or drug ever devised by man. I was drinking stars. His life was flowing into my mouth, satiating every taste bud, wetting my parched throat. And he never missed a stroke, moving over me as I drank from him. I could feel every cell in my body, his body. I could feel everything. I could feel *more*.

Grunting, Wade picked up the pace, slamming his hips into mine. I curled around him, drinking deep. I had to stop. I didn't want to hurt him. I didn't want to take too much. I didn't— Wade reached between us, arm bent at an awkward angle as he circled his fingers just above our joined bodies. I wrenched my face away from his neck as that coil inside me snapped and my whole body seemed to seize. I threw my head back, howling, as a racking climax burst through me. I felt the table crumble in my hands as I rode out the waves of pleasure.

Wade followed me over the edge, hips bucking, face buried against my collarbone. I collapsed back against the table. I stroked my hands down his back while his breathing settled.

Despite the cold and the wet and the adjacent serial-killer training ground, I could stay sprawled across that table forever. His weight on top of me only added to my contentment as I came down from my high. Maybe this was some sort of side effect of drinking real blood? Was this why "live-feeding" vampires seemed to be less angsty?

"Did I take too much?" I asked. "Do you feel OK?"

"I can't feel my face, but I don't think that has to do with the blood drinkin'," he muttered against my cleavage. He slowly withdrew from me but kept me propped against the table, comfortably bearing my weight.

I lifted his head so I could inspect his wound. I was rather proud that I had only made two small punctures over his vein, leaving barely a swipe of blood on his skin.

"I feel fine," he assured me. "Better than fine."

"Are you sure?"

He nodded. "Barely felt it. Are you sure you got enough?"

"Yeah, I didn't have to drink as much as I normally do."

"That's what you get when you go organic," Wade said.

I snickered, batting weakly at his back. "That's so wrong. And unless you're a vegan who uses one of those salt-rock things as deodorant, I don't think you count as organic."

"So was that your first time?" he asked.

"Having sex in a death barn? Yes."

"Drinkin' blood from a human," he said.

"Yes, you took my fang-ginity," I told him. "Sorry about that. I didn't feed properly before I left the house."

"You've gotta take better care of yourself, Libby," he said. "You run around takin' care of everybody else but you. I know you're immortal and all, but I think that only counts if you're a fully functionin' vampire."

"I know, I know." I sighed, tracing the path of the koi that swam along his arm.

"You can ask," he said.

"Didn't this hurt? I mean, clearly, you kept going back, so it couldn't have been that bad, but . . ."

"Oh, no, it hurt like a bitch," he said. "But it was a good hurt. And I love all of 'em. I'm assuming you don't have any."

"No. Rob didn't like them, thought they looked trashy. And I don't think I could get one now, since I basically heal up within seconds of getting a wound."

"That's a shame," he said. "Because I think you would look insanely hot with ink."

"I'm insanely hot without ink," I countered.

"Of course you are," he said. Leering a little, Wade bent, rummaging through his pants pocket, and pulled out a black Sharpie. He balanced my ass on the edge of the table as he methodically wrote something along the curve of my rib cage.

"If you're writing 'Property of Wade,' I will punch you in the throat," I told him, craning my neck as I tried to make out what he was writing.

"Nope." He bit the tip of his tongue while he finished his work with a flourish.

He hitched up his pants, crossed back to the bike, and grabbed my purse. "Use your mirror thingy to look."

"Thank you for not going through my purse," I told him, plucking my compact from a side pocket. "Also, thank you for knowing that I have a reflection."

"I may be a redneck, but I ain't fool enough to go through a woman's purse uninvited. And everybody knows that vampires have reflections."

It took me a second to figure out how to read Wade's neat handwriting backward, but I eventually read, "I had sex in a death barn, and all I got was this temporary tattoo."

"Wow," I said, shaking my head.

"Hey, a girl's first tattoo, that's a milestone. That, your fang-ginity, and your first barn sex all in one night. I'm just glad I was here for it."

"Well, it's been so long since I've had sex, you might get credit for taking my actual virginity," I muttered into his neck.

"How long?" Wade asked, smirking down at me.

"About two years . . . two and a half . . . three. It's been three years since I've had sex," I told him. "Oh, my God, this is pathetic."

"Nah, it's not pathetic—three *years*?" he marveled. "How is that possible? Your husband's only been dead for *two* years."

"Well, the last year with Rob was . . . distant."

"Were y'all living in the same state?"

"My marriage was far from perfect!"

"You know, every time I think I like ya just enough, you go and say something like that, and I like ya even more."

"There is something very wrong with you," I told him as he helped me right my clothes.

"And you love it," he said, kissing me.

"Yeah, I kind of do. Which means there's something wrong with me, too."

I was proud of myself, knowing that I'd said I loved *it* and not him. I hadn't melted into a postorgasmic puddle of overenthusiastic-to-the-point-of-being-sad confessions of affection. I'd come out of my first sexual experience (involving another person) in three years with about seventy percent of my dignity intact. Even if I had, technically, had sex with him before our first actual date.

I liked my relationship with Wade. It was comfortable and fun and seemed to meet both of our needs for now. Would I like to see it grow into more? Absolutely. But with things being so unsettled with my custody case and my attachment to Finn, I didn't know if I could handle "more" right now. Barn sex and sassy banter were my current limit.

Wade smirked, offering me his hand as if he were a knight aiding a lady stepping down from a carriage and not the girl he had just ridden hard and put up damp. He helped me slide into my jacket and carefully folded the collar under my chin. "I think the rain's let up a little bit. Do you want to make a break for Murphy?"

I grinned at him, toying with the buttons of his own jacket. "Would it be weird if I said no?"

"Well, as much as I am sure I would enjoy round two, I'm gonna have to get some juice and a cookie in me, or my whole standin'-upright situation is gonna get ugly."

"Yeah, I should probably start carrying an emergency blood-donor pack in my purse for next time," I said.

"You sure you don't already have one in that giant-ass bag?" he asked wryly. "And it's kind of nervy of you to assume there'll be a next time."

I gasped. "First of all, that's a fair statement about

my bag. But who said that the donor packet would be for *you*?"

"Oh, so you're going to just bite me and drop me?"

"Well, if you didn't like it, I'm sure I could find someone who—"

Wade caught my wrist and yanked me close for a hot, demanding kiss. "I liked it," he told me, his voice stern. "Trust me, I liked it."

"Good. Let's go get you that cookie."

I had officially taken the evening off. Between work, Les and Marge, the Pumpkin Patch madness, and whatever I was doing with Wade, I felt like I'd been missing too much time with Danny. So I'd sent Kerrianne home at sundown, made Danny's favorite chicken nuggets with a bandanna tied around my nose, and spent the evening watching him run around our front yard, searching for Bigfoot tracks. Eventually, he got tired of chasing his own tail like a Jack Russell terrier and joined me on the front-porch swing, where we read *Pete the Cat and His Magic Sunglasses* (six or seven times).

I was proud of my progress—having Danny sit on my lap, letting my chin rest on his sandy hair without a twinge of worry about whether I would be tempted by his blood. Now that I'd experienced live feeding and connected it to sexy Wade-based feelings, there was no way I could consider it in any way related to Danny. Ever.

"Mom, who would win in a fight, a werewolf or a vampire?" Danny asked, flipping through his copy of *Bigfoot Cinderrrrrrella*.

"Well, sweetheart, there are a lot of Web sites devoted to this debate, but I'm not really sure."

"But werewolves have fangs and claws, and they're super-fast," Danny reasoned.

"And vampires have fangs, and they're super-fast. And they're super-strong," Finn noted, stepping onto our porch.

My sire had just walked onto my front porch mid-conversation, as if it were totally normal for him to drop by in the middle of the night. I smiled, because I couldn't think of any other expression that wouldn't convey, *Oops, I slept with some other guy since the last time I saw you.*

While I was the master of multitasking, I was not good at this semi-sort-of-juggling-two-men thing. Surely this was going to come back and bite me in the ass. I knew that on the scale of potential evil I could do as a vampire, it was pretty minor. Still, I knew I was going to have to make it clear to one of them at some point that he was relegated to the friend zone.

I just had to figure out which one it would be.

Finn returned my smile, looking at me like I was something precious, which was not helping me in terms of friend-zone designation. It was the sort of expression you'd hope to see on the face of a husband and father returning home at the end of the day to find his wife and child waiting for him—except that he wasn't Danny's dad . . . or my husband . . . or even my significant other . . . and he was a dead guy.

"Yeah, but vampires can't go out during the day. All a werewolf would have to do is rip the lid off your coffin, and you'd be dead," Danny scoffed, but there was mischief in his eyes. He was teasing Finn, testing how far he could push the big bad vampire and not get busted for being rude to a guest.

And Finn was playing along, blithely ignoring my son's sass. He sat next to us on the porch swing, careful to put a respectable distance between himself and Danny. "You make a valid point."

"Does that mean I win?" Danny asked me.

"I think it means you and Mr. Finn are at a tie," I told him.

"Miss Steele says there's no such thing as a tie, that's something new-age parents made up to keep from hurting their kids' feelings when they lose."

I snorted. "That sounds like something Miss Steele would say."

"But that's OK," Danny said. "Because I don't want Mr. Finn's feelings to be hurt because he lost."

"I'm not sure that's the case," Finn said.

"So Mr. Finn, do you drink blood from people or bottles?"

"A bit of both."

"How old are you?"

"Most vampires don't like to answer that question."

Danny nodded. "Neither does my mom."

"Easy," I warned him.

Finn chuckled. "You ask a lot of questions, don't you, Danny?"

"Mom says that's my job. How am I supposed to learn anything about the world if I don't ask questions?"

"I seem to recall mentioning something about being polite when learning about the world," I muttered.

"I could be worse," Danny noted. "Hayden McTieg shoves people off their chairs when he says hello."

"That's true. I should lower my standards to McTieg levels." I snorted. "Danny, how about you go brush your teeth and get ready for bed?"

"Actually, before you go up, Danny, I have something for you," Finn said, digging a small blue-wrapped package out of his jacket pocket. "I noticed that you really like LEGOs."

Without hesitation, Danny popped the small blue box open and gasped. "Mom! Clutch Powers!"

Danny showed me the dark-haired mini-figure inside the box, dressed in painted-on blue jeans and a leather jacket. Clutch Powers was the main character in a LEGO adventure movie that Danny watched over and over until we could both quote the DVD from memory. But despite his numerous notes to Santa and birthday requests, I had never been able to track down a mini-figure Clutch, not even on eBay.

"This is the best present ever!" Danny exclaimed. He threw his arms around Finn's waist. "Thank you, Mr. Finn!"

And so Danny explained to Finn why this was such an awesome present and why Clutch Powers was the greatest character created since the invention of literature. And they debated the merits of LEGOs versus the Lincoln Logs that Finn had played with when he was growing up. Finn was a little stiff at first, but he managed to approach Danny from the level my son appreciated most. He didn't want to be talked down to or patronized or treated like an adorable brainless moppet. He just wanted you to talk and listen.

"All right, sir, it is bedtime for you," I interrupted at last.

Danny huffed in protest. "But I wanna talk to Mr. Finn some more!"

"You'll see him some other time."

"OK." He sighed. "Good night, Mr. Finn. Thank you for my present." He held up his hand for Finn to give him a high five.

The corner of Finn's mouth lifted as he slapped it. "Good night, Danny."

Danny scrambled off the couch and up the stairs like a monkey.

"He likes me!" Finn exclaimed, sounding downright giddy.

"You brought him a rare LEGO. You could burn down our house, and he would still look at you all googly-eyed."

"Don't ruin this moment for me," he said, shushing me.

"Just wait until you step on one of them with bare feet," I muttered. "I don't do that very often, by the way. Let him talk to men that I'm . . . I don't even know what to call what we're doing. I don't know you. I don't know what your intentions are. Just don't—don't hurt him. Don't be nice to him because you're trying to show me what a good guy you are. For that matter, don't hurt me. Because if you do, I'll have to—"

He kissed my cheek, running his hands along my

hair. His nose twitched, and for a second, I worried that he smelled Wade on me. But his tone remained smooth and even as he purred, "I would expect nothing less than the no doubt very creative and terrifying threat that is about to fall from those lovely lips of yours, but it's not necessary. I don't want to hurt either of you. That's the last thing on my mind. And as far as using him? I like Danny. I mean, I don't have a lot of experience with kids, but he's not an unpleasant little person. I can adjust. And he's part of you, an important part of your life. How could I not want to get to know him better?"

"Let's just . . . we need to take things slow in the 'getting to know you' area, OK?"

His lips quirked. "Does that cover occasional kissing?"

"It might," I said. "But not in front of Danny, because he's six, and kissing in all forms grosses him out."

Finn nodded. "Cootie-phobia."

"Exactly." I giggled as he leaned in, brushing his mouth against mine. That same feeling from my dreams, the emotions I'd experienced when I was turned—acceptance, excitement, a thrill of fear—all came rushing back to me. It was a shockingly gentle kiss, questing, searching for some bit of softness in a world that had been just a bit too hard on him. I worried that he might be able to smell Wade on my skin, taste him in my kiss. But Finn simply pulled me into his lap, nibbling on my bottom lip as his hands traced the lines of my back. And then I recalled the feeling of Wade's lips against mine, and I clutched at Finn's shirt, prepared to shove him back.

But he retreated on his own, sliding his hand along my arm as he settled back in the seat. "So how's my favorite vampire accountant?"

"I am doing well," I said.

"Still have plans for the weekend?"

"Yes," I told him. My date with Wade was cemented, with babysitters and everything. If nothing else, I really wanted a romantic outing with him that didn't involve a death barn. "I'm assuming this is an unsanctioned visit?" I asked.

"I left Jane a voice mail," Finn promised. "Which she will not get, because according to Dick, she doesn't understand how to use her voice mail."

I sighed, letting my head drop to his shoulder. "Why do you risk pissing her off just to see me? Why do *I* risk pissing her off just to see you? Is it just that you're my sire? Is this why I feel drawn to you?"

"No," he said, stroking his thumb along my cheek. "At first, there is an instinctual bond between the sire and the childe, to help the new vampire trust their mentor enough to get them through the transition. But it fades once the new vampire feels more settled in their new life. Most of the sire's privileges after that? Rules designed by the Council to keep older vampires in power and younger vampires in line. Look it up in any of the guidebooks."

"Oh, trust me, I will," I told him. "Maybe your influence over me got extended because we didn't get that time together at first? Maybe that explains the warm fuzzy feelings and the dreams."

"Dreams? There were dreams?" Finn's smile widened.

"I will never recap them."

"Mom!" Danny yelled from upstairs. "I can't find my ninja pajamas!"

At the sound of my son's voice, I slid out of Finn's lap. "Well, of course you can't, they're ninja pajamas! No one sees ninja pajamas."

I got silence from upstairs. Finn stared at me.

"I thought it was funny," I told him before calling to Danny. "I put them in your top drawer."

"I'm still a little stung by the refusal to recap. I'm really not so bad as all that, am I?"

"Yes!" I exclaimed, laughing. "You are completely untrustworthy. You haven't told me why you answered my ad. You haven't even told me why you've stuck around and continued to see me, despite Jane threatening you with some very creative retribution."

"I told you, your ad made you sound like a good person. I wanted to help you."

I stared at him, silent and stone-faced.

Finn cleared his throat. "You're not going to let this go, are you?"

"No."

He sighed. "OK, cards on the table. I turned you because of your talent."

"You needed a discreet bookkeeper?"

He chuckled and cupped my cheek in his palm, settling a very serious gaze on my face. "Your vampiric gift."

"I don't have a vampiric gift," I told him. "Jane said it would probably manifest itself within a few months of my changing. But nothing so far, and for some reason, she can't get a read off me. "

"That's because you're a stabilizer."

"What?"

"When you're around, you suppress the gifts of the vampires around you. Jane can't always read your mind. I'd bet she couldn't read the mind of any human or vampire within twenty yards when you're around. She's just so focused on trying to read you that she hasn't noticed."

"Well, that's a crappy power!" I exclaimed, unable to contain the disappointment of being told I was the psychic equivalent of a candle snuffer. "I was hoping for something cool, like telepathy. I would have settled for the squirrel thing!"

"No," he said, holding my hands between his. "It's an incredible gift, especially to someone like me."

"Why?"

"My special ability involves a sort of mental possession. I can travel into other people's heads, read their thoughts, see what they've done, what they plan to do. Occasionally, if the person I'm occupying is highly suggestible, I can move them around, physically, a little bit like a puppet."

"Have you ever done that to me?" I demanded.

"I try not to invade my hosts' privacy."

"That's not really an answer."

Still not responding, he said, "My ability has become more unpredictable lately. I'm not sure why. It's becoming . . . more. The door is swinging both ways. For months, when I've gone into other people's heads, some of them have made their way back into mine. I'm losing consciousness in the middle of conversations while my mind goes on walkabout and I drag people in. I am walking around my apartment during the day, copying the morning routines of my neighbors. The day before I turned you, I woke up in my hallway, inches away from walking into a beam of sunlight."

"How is that possible?" I asked.

"Our talents change over time. They grow and mutate. Your friend Jane couldn't read the minds of vampires when she first rose, but now she's able to read our thoughts easily, unless there's some complication like your gift. My talent is just changing faster than I can control it."

"And how does my gift work? How am I helping you?"

"Because you are suppressing my power. You're stabilizing me."

"How?"

"Without even trying, which is the best sort of gift," he said. "Think about it. You're one of the most stable people I've ever met. You're nurturing and solid. It only makes sense that you would provide an anchor for the people around you."

"But how did you even know that this would be my completely passive and useless-to-me gift? How did you know to turn me?"

"I was in the Hollow, months ago. You were sitting at a coffee shop at the hospital. I was visiting a human acquaintance who had gotten into a, let's say, *disagreement* with a business associate."

"So many of your stories involve violent disagreements."

He poked my side, continuing as if I hadn't said anything. "I passed by the coffee shop, and I saw you there. And you looked so very miserable. I don't think I'd ever seen a human look so hopeless in all my life. I felt something for you. And I hadn't felt anything for anyone, besides myself, in a long, long time. I couldn't help but slip into your head, to see what was making you so unhappy."

"So you *have* been in my head."

Still no acknowledgment that I'd spoken. "I could sense it, that latent power, bubbling under the surface of your blood, the ability to suppress the abilities of the vampires around you," he said. "You were my salvation, my solution, and you didn't even know it. I settled into your memories, learning more about you. I saw you fighting with your husband, just before he died. I saw you sitting in the doctor's office, receiving news about your test results. I saw your little boy sleeping and your terror at never being able to see him grow up. And before it even fully formed, I could see the birth of the inspiration for your plan to become a vampire. I knew you were going to follow through with it. And if you weren't careful, you would either find some brutish vampire who would take advantage of you—or, worse, a human who would take advantage of you. So I stayed close to you. I dipped into your mind a few more times and made sure I was the first to answer your ad."

"So you've been in my head *multiple* times?"

"And . . . I may have hired someone to hack the Web site to disable your ad so you wouldn't get any other answers," he admitted.

"That is the least disturbing thing you've told me so far," I groused, rubbing my hands over my face. "So you only turned me to save your own ass?"

"It's not that different from you seeking someone to turn you so you would have more time with your son."

Damned if he didn't have a point there. I couldn't help but feel deceived, though. I'd thought that he'd done something for me for the sake of doing something good, but he'd done it because it benefited him. It felt like that episode in high school when Hal Morrow asked me to Homecoming only to ask me to do his math homework the next day. He'd made me feel special only to yank it out from under me. Finn was an enigma wrapped in a riddle coated in misdirection. He was a burrito of dishonesty.

Wait.

"I *did* have cancer, didn't I?" I demanded, sliding out of Finn's lap. "You didn't find some way to fake my medical test results so you could manipulate me with this insane vampirism idea?"

"No. I'm devious, but I'm not evil."

"That remains to be seen," I muttered. "So you've been hanging around because being in my presence is sort of like a booster shot for controlling your power?"

"Well, yes, but that's not why I want to spend time with you!"

"You know, you could have just told me this at the beginning. You could have just said, 'I need a supernatural supplement from your aura.' And I wouldn't have minded. You didn't have to put on this charming act, the whole 'seduce the schoolmarm' thing. You didn't have to—"

"This isn't an act!" he swore. "I do want more time with you. I didn't want to tell you because I didn't want you to think that was the only reason I turned you. But I also didn't want you to hear this from Jane before you heard it from me. Frankly, I'm surprised she hasn't told you already."

I stood up, putting space between myself and my sire. For the first time since meeting him, I wanted Finn out of my presence. Stat. I wanted to throw Wade up in his face. I wanted him to know that I didn't need him in order to feel special. I didn't need him in order to feel loved or appreciated.

"I need some time to think about this," I said. "I appreciate your honesty, half-assed and delayed as it may be, but at the same time, I don't. If you need a booster, I'll meet you at the bookshop, and you can soak up my rays or whatever for a few minutes."

"You're upset."

"I'm glad you're picking up on that."

"I didn't tell you this to hurt you," he said, rising. He moved toward me but seemed to think better of it. "I'll see you soon."

As Finn disappeared into the woods near my house, I flopped back onto my swing, whacking my head against the backing. Ouch.

I didn't have the time or the emotional resources for a pity party. I was a grown-ass woman. I was a mother. Mothers didn't pout. At least, the good ones didn't.

"I thought you liked Mr. Finn, Mom." Danny poked

his head out around the screen door. He was carrying a freshly popped bag of extra-butter microwave popcorn, his favorite snack since I'd taught him how to use the microwave. It smelled like sour milk and oven cleaner to me, but Danny was chowing down like I would never allow him to have hydrogenated yellow food dye again.

I closed my eyes and inhaled deeply, despite the disgusting popcorn smell. This was what I'd dreaded, the idea of men drifting in and out of Danny's life. Danny deserved stability. "I do like Finn, hon. But sometimes even grown-ups fuss at each other."

"Does that mean that he's not going to bring me any more LEGOs?"

"If anything, he might bring you *more* LEGOs."

"That would be OK," Danny conceded, climbing up onto the swing and settling against my side. The smell of his snack was making me gag, even if I craned my neck so far away that I felt a vertebra pop. "So Finn's the guy who made you into a vampire, huh?"

"How do you know that?"

"You used the word 'sire' the other day when you were talking about him with Miss Kerrianne," he said. "I hear Miss Jane say it when she's talking about Jamie. So he's like your vampire daddy?"

"I don't really know how to answer that."

"It's weird."

"Yes, it is," I admitted. "But no matter who comes into our lives or goes out of our lives, it's never going to change the way I feel about you. I might make new friends, I might start dating someone, but you will always be first for me, got it?"

"You mean you're going to start dating Harley's dad?"

"Wha—how—why do you say that?"

"Because when you look at each other, your eyes get all googly, like Madison's stupid cartoon kitty-cat folder."

I snorted. "Sometimes I wish you weren't so smart."

"And Madison says that means you like someone as more than a friend," Danny told me, tilting the popcorn toward me. I shook my head and turned it so the popcorn was facing downwind.

"Is Madison pretty smart about this sort of thing?"

Danny nodded, his face solemn. "She knew that Mr. Brinker and Miss Hershell were going steady before any of the grown-ups figured it out."

"Well, it doesn't matter if Mr. Wade and I start dating; it will not affect whether you and Harley can play together. And it won't affect whether Mr. Wade likes you. You're a great kid, and everybody loves you."

"Except for Madison," he said. "She says boys smell."

"Except for Madison," I amended as Danny offered me his popcorn again.

"I can't eat popcorn anymore, baby. I can't eat any food."

"Oh, OK," he said, with a glimmer of mischief in his eyes as he moved the popcorn closer to my face.

"Are you taunting me with popcorn right now?"

"What does 'taunt' mean?"

"Waving the popcorn in front of my face because you know I can't have it."

"Then, yes, I am taunting you."

11

It's important to take time for yourself, develop your own interests as hobbies. One day, your child will grow up, and vampires with empty-nest syndrome tend to be destructive.

—*My Mommy Has Fangs: A Guide to Post-Vampiric Parenting*

Being taunted with popcorn was not easier when the smell came drifting from dozens of cars. However, I had a very thoughtful escort.

For our drive-in date, Wade had packed blankets for us to set up in the back of his truck, plus a cooler full of drinks, including a wide range of bottled blood. The Possum Point Drive-In had a very liberal policy regarding outside food, because there was no on-site concession stand. The owners had tried to establish a hamburger stand early on. But the facilities were overwhelmed by the local population of possums, which broke into the concession every night and destroyed everything in search of food. After several failed extermination attempts, the owners brought in Popcorn Pete, a retired ice-cream-truck driver who converted a hot dog cart to sell popcorn. Possums were less likely to hit a moving target. And the critters were a little afraid of Popcorn Pete, who was surprisingly mean for someone who chose to make his living selling treats to children.

"You know I only drink one or two bottles a night, right?" I asked, marveling at the number of brands resting on "my side" of the ice chest. Wade was busy plugging in a baby-bottle warmer he'd rewired for his car-charger port. All around us, families and couples were spreading blankets in the backs of truck beds and settling in for an evening of old-school fun. The last orange-pink streaks of the sun had disappeared over the horizon as we were leaving my house, meaning the movie would start in just a few minutes.

"I know you're not going to drink all of that, but I didn't know what you'd like," Wade said.

"That's adorable," I told him as I climbed into the truck bed. I was in a buoyant, giddy mood. I'd woken up to a day's mail that included a very official-looking letter from the local family court. Danny was to meet with Judge Holyfield under the supervision of a state-appointed chaperone in two weeks. The letter, which was addressed to my in-laws and to me, included some very strong language about appropriate adult behavior and following the court's instructions. Specifically, Judge Holyfield wrote that he "didn't appreciate certain parties ignoring previous instructions and certainly didn't appreciate accusations of bias toward either party." He made it clear that we would discuss that behavior when we next met and that any dramatic shenanigans would not be tolerated in his presence.

While I wasn't exactly thrilled by the idea of having to take Danny to court, it certainly sounded like the judge was unhappy with Les. And I figured it was unlikely that a judge would assign custody of a child to someone who couldn't be trusted to behave himself. And even if Les and Marge ended up with scheduled visitation, I would find a way to live with it. I was hopeful. Still somewhat romantically confused but hopeful.

"I'm not adorable," Wade protested. "I am manly and grizzled and have no emotions. None."

I rolled my eyes, lifted a bottle of Faux Type O, a sort of "Classic Coke" version of synthetic blood, and handed it to him. He dropped it into the bottle warmer and grabbed a Ziploc bag from his glove compartment. Inside was a bright red bandanna.

"Are you planning to chloroform me? Because this sort of ruins the surprise."

"Just wear it around your neck, smartass," he said, tying the bandanna under my chin.

"Again, I appreciate your going outside of the box in terms of first-date gifts, but why?"

Wade nodded at Popcorn Pete, who was rattling his cart along the row of cars, yelling, "Popcorn! Buy it or don't, I don't give a damn."

I watched in horror as dozens of customers lined up, buying their little red-and-white-striped bags of popcorn and spreading through the lot like the spores of a particularly stinky dandelion. That synthetic sour-milk smell seemed to be coming at me from all sides.

"Here." Wade gently pulled the handkerchief over my nose, and the nauseating popcorn miasma was smothered by the spicy, warm scent of . . . Wade.

My mouth went from wincing to watering in seconds. It was like being wrapped in a bubble of Wade's delicious scent. I was instantly calmed and comforted and crazy aroused all at the same time. I knocked the blanket out of his hands and hauled him into the truck bed with me. I rolled on top of him, straddling his hips as I lowered my face to his. And realized that my bandanna was still in the way. Wade laughed, pulling the red material back down under my chin so he could plant a hot, sweet kiss on me.

"Better?" he asked.

"You sealed it in the bag so it would smell like you," I said, giving him an "aw" face.

He shrugged. "You seem to like the way I smell."

"I love the way you smell, which on any other date would seem like an off-putting thing to say."

"Being thrown around like a rag doll by my gal is extremely hot but pretty damn emasculatin'," he muttered against the soft skin of my jaw.

"Well, get used to it," I told him, turning his head so I could nibble at his lower lip. He groaned and rolled his hips under me.

"Is that your vampire talent?" he asked. "Slappin' guys around but lookin' so cute while you're doing it that they don't mind?"

I laughed and, realizing that we were still very much in view of people in neighboring cars, sat up, straightened our clothes, and scooted against the back of Wade's cab so we could watch as the titles to *The Great Outdoors* began playing. "No, my vampire talent is very boring. I'm a stabilizer."

"What's that?"

"I suppress the talents of other vampires near me," I told him as he wrapped his arm around me, settling my head against his chest. I tucked my hair under his chin, burying my nose in his shirt.

"Well, that's not . . . OK, yeah, that's pretty boring. But how do you even know that you're doing it? It could just be a fluke."

"My, uh, my sire told me all about it. He was the first one to figure it out, because I was suppressing his talent."

"How did he manage to figure it out when Jane couldn't?" Wade asked, winding my gold hair around his fingers and watching it uncurl when he released it. I opened my mouth to tell him the story about Finn seeing me at the hospital coffee shop. But then Chet Ripley pulled his family car in front of the Loon's Nest, and it seemed rude to keep talking. And even though I was watching one of my favorite childhood movies, I couldn't help but wonder, how *did* Finn figure out that I was a vampire damper? I had never heard of a vampire's talent being "latent" when he or she was still human. In all the reading Jane had forced me to do, the books stated that vampire powers manifested *after* the newly turned vampire changed. It seemed impossible, even with Finn's special head-hopping power, for him to sense what I could do.

Why hadn't I questioned it? Why had I simply believed what he said, even when I'd learned so much to the contrary? Why did I want to believe the best of someone who hadn't done anything to deserve my trust?

Finn had lied. Or at the very least, he had stretched the truth to the breaking point. Again. I was getting really sick of Finn treating conversations like a taffy pull. I was sick of half-truths and shadows and meeting on his terms.

And here I was, spending my date with Wade thinking about Finn.

I was going to have a conversation with Finn Palmeroy. But first, I was going to watch John Candy shoot a bear in the butt with a shotgun lamp.

I stomped through the lobby of the Holiday Inn and bypassed the elevator in order to scale the stairs and work off some anger. I'd barely been able to concentrate on what was a perfectly lovely first date with a desirable, extremely fang-worthy man because I'd been too busy turning over all of the possibilities in my head. I'd come up with a dozen plausible explanations that didn't involve Finn lying to me, but somehow they just didn't seem as believable, as likely, as that he was manipulating me. Finn was too charming, too smooth. Hadn't I learned by now not to trust the easy path? Why hadn't I seen this coming? Why hadn't I listened to those warning bells?

And because I wanted to catch my sire off-guard for once, I kicked in his hotel-room door and walked in without an invitation. Finn looked deliciously casual, stretched across the bed, going over some paperwork. He didn't even seem that startled to see me busting into his hotel room like the cops. He just grinned brightly and hopped to his feet.

"Libby!" he exclaimed. "This is a pleasant surprise."

"Don't start," I growled, shoving a hand against his chest as he moved closer. "How did you know what my vampire talent would be?"

Finn frowned, but I could see a flicker of dread in his eyes. "I told you, I saw you at the—"

"No, don't feed me your bullshit story about seeing the fragile cancer patient at the hospital and feeling moved to help her. Vampire powers don't manifest in humans, no matter how powerful. Everything I've read says so. Now, how did you know I would be able to suppress your wonky brain-walking?"

Finn took a deep breath and started again. "I saw you—"

"Nope!" I shouted at him.

"I knew you—"

I shook my head. "Nuh-uh."

"I read your ad—"

"Try again."

"What do you want me to tell you?" he demanded.

"I want you to stop lying to me!"

"Fine! Fine, you want to know why I turned you? I turned you as a favor to your father!" Finn shouted.

The world seemed to tilt on its axis. I felt a strange, tight pressure at my chest and sank into the desk chair, my hands cold and numb. My fangs slid out so quickly it hurt. "I'm sorry, what?"

"Libby, let me explain, please."

Finn took a step closer, and I shot him a vicious look. "Don't you come any closer to me." He froze in his tracks, hands raised. "Now, talk."

"I'm a friend of your father's."

I couldn't even begin to give voice to all of the questions bouncing around my brain. How did he know my father? How did my father know about me? Why had he never come forward to meet me? Why had he sent Finn to spy on me? Why was Finn telling me this now? What did this mean?

"If you're making this up, Finn, so help me, I will find a way—"

"I know. I don't have to be a psychic to see how violent your reaction would be. I'm a friend of your father's," Finn said.

"And his name is . . ."

A frisson of doubt slid over his features.

I bared my fangs at him and growled.

"Max!" he exclaimed. "His name is Max Kitteridge, and for right now, that's all I should tell you."

Somewhere, in a less angry, frantic corner of my brain, I remembered Finn telling me stories to comfort me while I was being turned—stories about his buddy, Max, and the trouble they used to get into. He was telling me stories about my *father*, and I hadn't even realized. Betrayal, hot and acidic, burned through my chest.

"And you didn't think this was something you should tell me? You didn't think I should— I've never even *met* my father. I don't know what he looks like.

I know nothing about him. And you knew this whole time? How am I supposed to feel about that?"

"I know, it was wrong. I tried to find a way to tell you, but there's no easy way to fit 'By the way, I'm your long-lost father's best friend since we were both human' into the conversation. I barely got the chance to get to know you myself, so how was I supposed to tell you that? Libby, from the moment I saw you, I wanted to know you. And that had nothing to do with your father or you being sick or your talent—"

"What do you mean, 'since we were both human'?" I interrupted him in a tone that made Finn wince. "Are you telling me that my father is a vampire, too?"

He cleared his throat and took a cautious step closer. "Yes."

"And the whole thing about my talent being able to suppress yours? Was that a lie, too?"

Finn ran his fingertips along my arms, and I jerked them out of his grasp. He cleared his throat again. "Oh, no, that's true. Just being near you has given me a whole new grasp on my control. But I didn't realize that was what was happening until after you were turned. Your father sent me to town to check on you. And I did see you at that coffee shop, and I did see inside your head and see how desperate and sick you were. I went to your father, told him what you were thinking of doing, and he sent me to intervene. He wanted to turn you himself, but he thought you might find that confusing, meeting him and going through all the changes at once. He wanted to make sure you were safe, not left with some creep you met over the Internet."

"Yes, it would have been tragic being saddled with someone I couldn't trust as a sire," I deadpanned.

Finn cleared his throat. "I was supposed to leave you alone after I turned you. But I couldn't."

"Right, because I was a solution to your problem."

"But that's not why I couldn't leave you. I want you, Libby. I want to spend time with you and be part of your life. I know you're upset with me now, but if anything, this is something to celebrate. Your father, Max, he wants to be part of your life so much, but he wanted to give you time. You can have more people in your life who understand you, who love you. How is this bad news?"

"And I'm sure you told him to stay put, give me more time, while you figured out how to best take advantage of my talent."

"No, you don't understand," he protested.

"Oh, no, I think I've got a pretty good grasp of the situation," I growled at him, getting up and yanking the battered hotel-room door open. "You stay away from me. And you tell my father . . ."

The unfamiliar word seemed to choke me, solidifying in my throat like a stone.

"What do you want me to tell him?" Finn asked, his voice so soft and gentle it broke my heart. "I'll do anything you ask of me, Libby, just please, listen to me."

"Tell my father he's about thirty years too late."

12

It's important to carve out time in your schedule to volunteer at your child's school and extracurricular activities whenever possible, if for no other reason than to remind the other children that your child's parent can definitely beat up their parent.

—*My Mommy Has Fangs: A Guide to Post-Vampiric Parenting*

There was a very short pirate standing in my living room. He was wearing a black tricorn hat, a puffy white shirt, and a little vest with skulls on the lapels, but no pants. He adjusted his eye patch over his left eye, which was difficult, considering that he was holding his plastic sword.

"I'm ready for the Pumpkin Patch Party, Mom," Danny announced while I was packing the last of the party supplies into my shoulder bag, including two extra bottles of HemoBoost. I would not suffer another emergency feeding situation in front of the PTA.

"You look great, Captain Danny," I said, giving a jaunty little salute.

"Thank you."

"Could I persuade you to put on pants?" I asked, waving in the general direction of his Underoos.

Danny pulled an indifferent face. "I don't know if I feel like it."

"It's an important part of the costume. And what is with your sudden aversion to pants? This is the third night in a row we've had this conversation."

"Did pirates wear pants?" he asked, climbing onto the couch.

"Pretty much full-time."

"OK." He sighed, sounding very put-upon as he padded up the stairs in his little pirate boots. "Is Mamaw going to be there tonight?"

"I'm pretty sure she will be. And Harley, too. And I am one hundred percent sure he will be wearing pants. You guys will be hanging out with Braylen and Kerrianne while Mom and Mr. Wade run the games. And then we're coming back here for *The Great Pumpkin* and hot cocoa."

"Sounds good!" he called. After a few minutes, he yelled, "Hey, Mom, did pirates wear sweatpants?"

"I can't help but think this conversation is going to be the highlight of my evening," I grumbled to myself as I carted the bag of party stuff out to the van. "Also, I don't know if I should let my child spend so much time with Dick Cheney."

Like the biblical plagues of old, the Pumpkin Patch Party was finally upon us. I guessed I should be grateful that because of bursting-into-flames issues, I didn't have to help with setup. By the time I arrived, the games were set up, the popcorn was popped, and the inflatables were . . . inflated. Chelsea Harbaker and the other moms had done a remarkable job strategically placing hay bales and pumpkins so the front of the school actually looked like a place people would come to sort out their fall harvests. The actual pumpkin patch, run by Marnie Whitehead and provided by McDonough's Tree Farm, was spread out over the front lawn. At the end of the night, each participating kid could buy a pumpkin for a dollar, a ridiculously low price for their future jack-o'-lanterns, but McDonough's was happy to get rid of some of its "irregular" specimens.

Wade had been busy helping some of the other dads put together the dunking booth and the ring toss and other carnival games that were actually designed to allow the children to win. As for me, I'd been wrapping up all of the raffle issues, including redesigning the tickets at the last minute because it turned out the state had some scary, heretofore unknown laws about charity-related gambling and what was supposed to be printed on the tickets. I was not going to jail for the Pumpkin Patch Party.

Danny ran ahead of me, eager to find Harley among the kids whose parents had arrived early to volunteer. The air smelled, frankly, repugnant, between the popcorn and the caramel apples and the mulled cider. I was sure it smelled heavenly to the humans, but it was like walking through a Wicks & Things where all of the candles were garbage-scented.

It was nice, but somehow a little disturbing, that this Pumpkin Patch Party looked almost exactly like the Pumpkin Patch Parties I'd attended as an HMHES student. The same booth banners, the same games, the same families milling around, seeking good old-fashioned entertainment.

If I returned years from now with Danny's children, would anything have changed? Would Chelsea, who seemed to be having some sort of nervous breakdown by the snow-cone machine, still be there, trying to organize everybody into oblivion?

And suddenly, I was struck with an image of myself, the exact same age but wearing Marge's "Number 1 Grandma" sweatshirt. And it made me shudder.

"Miss Libby!" I turned to see Harley running at me full-tilt, dressed as a ninja. His straw-blond hair stuck out at all angles, mussed from the ninja hood draped around his neck. As I caught him, I noted with some discomfort that the costume included ninja throwing stars.

"I'm a ninja, Miss Libby!" Harley cried. "Where's Danny? I want him to see my costume."

"You bought that costume purely for the throwing stars, didn't you?" I asked Wade as he approached, even as a pleasant warm sensation spread through my chest at Harley's easy affection. This was a far cry from the shy child who'd refused to correct Danny's butchering of his name for the sake of politeness.

"It's nice that you know me so well," Wade said.

"I was talking to *him*," I informed him. "Or so I thought."

"Dad made me leave the nunchuks at home," Harley informed me. "I gave myself a bloody lip."

"It was for the greater good," I told Harley.

"That's what Dad said!" Harley exclaimed.

"Your dad's a pretty smart guy," I said. "Kerrianne and Danny are over by the bouncy castle if you want to find them."

Harley wriggled loose from my grip and ran toward the bouncy castle. "Thanks, Miss Libby!"

Wade's eyes followed Harley until he reached the "safety" of the inflatables and Kerrianne's company. Wade leaned close, nuzzling his cheek against mine before planting an open kiss against my mouth. "Hi."

I was smiling when he pulled away from me. "Hey."

"I missed you while you were serving your tour with the pumpkin brigade," he said, sliding his hand around my waist and settling it just above my ass. I snuggled against him, not even minding the public ass pat. As much as I lusted after Wade, I'd come to appreciate his more internal qualities even more since Finn's coerced confession. Wade was honest and considerate and trustworthy. And had I mentioned honest? I'd come to understand that I needed a bit less drama and a bit more Wade in my life.

"You, too. It's sort of insane how much I'm looking forward to watching a Charlie Brown special with you and the boys later," I told him, pecking him on the lips.

A few of the parents, including Chelsea and Casey, had stopped in their tracks to stare at the spectacle of the vampire mom and the biker dad making out near the dunk tank. "Move along, people. Nothin' to see here," Wade barked at them, prompting an instant return to whatever task they'd dropped in order to gawk at us.

"That's going to take some getting used to," I muttered.

"I wouldn't worry about it," Wade said. "Now, did you have a healthy 'breakfast' when you rose for the night?"

"Yes, definitely," I promised. "And I brought some snack bottles, just in case."

"Well, that's a shame. I was thinkin', maybe later, after *The Great Pumpkin* when the boys have gone to sleep, you might have another 'emergency.' I've been eatin' a lot of cookies and drinkin' a lot of juice in preparation."

"Don't use me as your excuse to eat cookies," I chided. "Don't endanger your abs in my name."

Wade hooted. "I see how it is. You only want me for my body!"

"Oh, yes, I thought I made that clear with my seductive opening comments in the janitor's closet," I purred.

"You know, we can always visit that closet later, after everybody's gone home," he said, hooking his fingers through the loops on my jeans.

"Why would I be here after everybody else is gone?"

"I sort of volunteered you for the cleanup committee."

My jaw dropped as I stammered, "Wh-why? Why would you do that?"

"Because we haven't been able to spend a lot of time together lately. And you weren't able to help set up, what with the whole sunlight thing. The other moms were more than willin' to throw you under the bus, by the way."

"Bitches." I tried not to pout, really, I did.

"It will give us some time alone together and let the boys work off their sugar high while they're on Kerrianne's watch."

I glanced over to the caramel-apple stand, where Danny and Harley seemed to be wrapping their caramel-coated fruit in cotton candy. "Good call," I conceded, sticking my finger in his face. "But for the record, this is not a date. You do not get credit for planning this."

Wade snapped his teeth, barely clamping down on the tip of my finger. I yelped, laughing and yanking my hand away. He laughed and kissed my cheek. "You just wait, I'ma date the hell out of you."

"That's not a declaration or an answer of any sort."

"Crazy girl," he scoffed. "I gotta get goin'. I'm needed over at the cakewalk."

"Better you than me."

"Maybe later, I'll win you one of those big stuffed elephants at the ring toss," he said. "Come on, boys! Let's go cheat some ladies out of some cakes."

I laughed as Wade led our sons to diabetic crisis, but the happy expression on my face died quickly as Chelsea and Casey minced their way across the "fairway" toward me with matching "approaching an uncomfortable conversation" expressions on their faces.

What had I done now? PDA with Wade within view of their impressionable children? Or just walking while undead?

"Libby, hiiiiiii," Casey intoned.

"You really need to learn to use fewer 'i's when you're feeling awkward," I told her.

Casey's eyes went wide. "I'm sure I don't know what you're talking about."

"Mmm-hmm."

Chelsea cleared her throat and tossed her golden hair over her shoulder. "Libby, we're just a little surprised to see you here, that's all."

"Why?" I asked. "I organized the raffle and the auction, and apparently, I'm the cleanup crew."

Casey managed to look guilty for a second, or possibly scared. In truth, all of her expressions just read "vaguely gassy."

"It's just that your presence is making some of the other parents uncomfortable," Chelsea whispered. "Safety concerns, you know."

Casey added, "They're afraid you'll attract the wrong element."

I glanced around at the other parents, who didn't seem to be noticing me now that I wasn't making out with Wade in front of their kids.

"Is it them I'm making uncomfortable or you?" I asked Chelsea. "Because it seems to me that you were plenty comfortable with me doing all your crap work, driving all over creation to pick up gift cards and gift baskets and two hundred pumpkins. Do you have any idea how long it takes to load two hundred pumpkins into a minivan?"

Chelsea stammered an answer, but I cut her off.

"Save it. It occurs to me that the best thing for me to do would be to just walk away from the PTA, to save us all this tension and discomfort. You don't want me here. And honestly, this experience hasn't been as rewarding as I'd hoped."

Casey's face brightened considerably. "Really? Oh, that's a shame."

"But screw that noise. If I want the PTA to change and be more friendly for parents with supernatural needs, I'm going to have to be that change. I'm going to have to run for PTA president."

Chelsea's cherubic cheeks went bone-white, and she made a noise that sounded like a choking giraffe.

"And given the number of people you've railroaded over the past few weeks for the sake of the Pumpkin Patch Party, I think I can get the votes."

I turned on my heel, smirking to beat the band, and as I ducked behind the dunking booth, I ran right into my father-in-law, who looked downright smug himself.

"Libby."

I hadn't seen him face-to-face in months, on advice of the Council. The difference in his appearance was startling. He'd lost weight, especially in his face, where his cheekbones seemed more prominent, and his eyes were underscored by dark circles. He was grinning at me, but the smile didn't reach his brown eyes. They were as flat and glassy as a shark's. Frankly, the effect was creepy, and I took a step back from him. Predatory pride be damned.

"I was hoping to see you tonight," he said.

"Really?" I asked. "Why would that be, Les? According to my lawyers, you've been pretty reluctant to talk with me in any rational, civil way."

"Well, I just didn't know how to communicate with you before," Les said. "I think I've figured it out now."

"Again, I say, really?"

"Sure. I'd like to meet with you and your Council rep on Monday to work out the details, but I think we can come to an agreement."

I stared at him, long and hard. Was my father-in-law completely high? We'd spent the better part of two months going round and round over the very basics of a simple visitation schedule, and suddenly he had some sort of epiphany to go forth and be a proverbial thorn in my side no longer? Why hadn't Marge mentioned this on one of her handful of secret visits to our house? Had one of Jane's vampire friends fiddled with Les's brain? Was that a secret vampire power, emotionally manipulating controlling old men? It was still cooler than my vampire power.

"So what time is Danny heading home?" Les asked casually.

"In a bit. I don't want him staying up too late."

"But you've probably got cleanup duty after everything shuts down, right? Most of the parents do," Les said, his tone too casual to be genuine. "I'm assuming that the sitter the Council hired will be with him tonight. You're not just going to leave him alone in the house, right?"

"Why do you ask?"

Les shrugged, sliding his arm around Marge's shoulders as she sidled up next to him. She creased her brow, looking between Les's contrived relaxed posture and my face-full-o'-tension. "Just want to make sure our grandson is taken care of."

"I've always taken care of Danny," I told him. "No matter what. He's a happy, healthy little boy. And if you're interested in spending time with *him*, instead of trying to reshape him into the boy you think he should be, I think we'll be able to iron out an arrangement. But you are his grandparents. That's your role. I'll respect your role, if you respect mine."

For a second, Les's easy demeanor dropped, and I saw the rage simmering underneath the surface. His dark eyes focused on me with a sharp hatred I could feel like heat on my skin. His lip drew back in a snarl. I was afraid he was going to take a swing at me, not because I was worried about him hurting me but because beating an old man into the ground, particularly an old man who was suing me for custody of my son, was not going to help me in court. But as soon as the rage had appeared, it ebbed. Les's face relaxed, and his hand was hanging loose at his side. "Well, you never know what could happen," he told me, walking away without a word to his wife.

"What was that about?" I asked Marge.

"I don't know." She sighed. "He's been behaving so strangely for the past few weeks. I'm starting to worry about him."

"He mentioned that you two have come to a settlement agreement?"

Marge frowned and shook her head. "Not that he's told me. In fact, he's stopped returning our lawyer's calls."

"I'm worried, Marge."

"I'll keep an eye on him. I'll see you in a few days?" she asked quietly. I nodded. "Thanks, honey. You take care of yourself."

My first instinct was to find Danny, to make sure that Les hadn't decided to snatch him from the Pumpkin Patch Party and spirit him away to Grandpa Brainwashing Land. Zipping around the fairway at vampire speeds, it only took me a few minutes to find my son, bouncing his heart (and most likely his dinner) out in the inflatable castle with Harley. Part of me cringed, seeing my slightly undersized son bouncing around the vinyl with boys twice his height, pinging between them like a grinning ping-pong ball. But I knew he needed to be bounced around a bit. I needed to let him fall and get hurt and fail, because otherwise, he would never learn how to get back up.

That didn't stop me from cringing when a collision with Harley sent him sprawling against the mesh walls, under the feet of two third-graders. Kerrianne called for Danny to get up before he got turned into "people jelly," and he gamely obeyed, waving and hooting all the time.

"Hey, hon. How is your voluntary servitude?" Kerrianne asked me.

"Could you take Danny to your house tonight?" I asked. "Les was being, well, weird as hell earlier, and it made me nervous."

My lack of greeting or response to her "servitude" jibe brought Kerrianne to attention immediately. "Of course. I'll tell Wade we're switching locations."

"Thanks. I feel better knowing you'll be somewhere unfamiliar to Les."

"Hey, did I hear that you were planning to run for PTA president next year? Are you really planning to run?"

"Oh, hell, no. I wouldn't touch that job with a ten-foot pole. But Chelsea doesn't need to know that. I want her to spend the next year thinking I'm going to wrestle her power away in some bloody vampire coup."

"Well, it's working. Chelsea is having kittens over by the cotton candy."

"Excellent," I drawled, steepling my fingers together like a *Simpsons* villain.

"Hey, is Finn planning on showing up?" she asked.

"Decidedly *not*," I said. "I've asked Finn for some space."

"Because you and Wade finally did the deed?"

"No, and how did you—"

"Oh, please, you came back from that thunderstorm with obvious deed signals all over your face. Not to mention the dirt on the back of your jacket and the smudges on his jeans. Frankly, I'm a little hurt that you didn't immediately dish with me over it. You know how I feel about Wade's ass. I need some vicarious information. Come on, it was bone-shaking, wasn't it? It had to be."

"That recap is not going to happen at a children's carnival," I told her.

"I knew it!" Kerrianne crowed as I shushed her. "He couldn't have a mouth like that and not know what to do with it."

"You are not an emotionally well woman."

"Fine," she groaned. "At least, tell me why you're not speaking to Finn at the moment."

"He told me some things about why he turned me,

and it was . . . upsetting," I said carefully. "I don't want to like him. But he has just enough charm to make him dangerous. I get all confused, and I forget who I'm dealing with."

"You are the master of vague. Tomorrow evening, after we have washed the caramel from our kids' hair, you and I are going to sit down with a bottle of that vampire wine, and you're going to spill your guts."

I gave her a dutiful curtsy. "Yes, ma'am."

"For right now, I have to keep my daughter from conspiring with your boys to cheat at ring toss."

"How do you cheat at ring toss?" I asked.

Kerrianne shrugged. "They have a system."

When the last wad of cotton candy had melted into sugar goo on the last child's cheeks and the last raffle prize had been given away, the parents of Half-Moon Hollow could not have disappeared faster if they were paid magicians. A few intrepid fathers stuck around long enough to pack up the booths and shut down the PA system, but other than that, the random debris, the game pieces and leftover prizes, and the litter were my problem—well, mine and Wade's.

"I'll take the huge-ass mess on the left, you take the huge-ass mess on the right," he told me.

"You volunteered us for this, you lunatic!"

"I assumed it would be more packin' up teddy bears and cleanin' up smashed pumpkins. Givin' us enough time to roll around on those hay bales back there."

"Well, that's what happens when you assume." I laughed, giving him a smacking kiss. He caught me around the waist and held me there, sliding his hands up my back until they were cupping my jaw. As usual, I felt *everything* in Wade's kiss. There was no artifice or holding back, just playful warmth and affection and this thing he did with his tongue that made my toes curl. Wade was laying it all on the line for me . . . and I was giving him a big whopping lie by omission.

Reluctantly, I pulled away from him, swiping my tongue over my lip. "There's something I need to tell you."

Wade kissed the curve of my chin, the bristles of his whiskers tickling my sensitive skin. "What's that?"

"I've been seeing my sire." I closed my eyes, wincing, as if he were going to detonate at the news. When he said nothing, I opened one eye and checked to make sure he was still there.

"OK," he said, nodding.

"I mean, I was *seeing* him, as in more than a mentoring relationship, though thanks to some pretty disturbing revelations on his part, that's pretty much over, because I think I would want to hit him in the face with a folding chair if I saw him again. I haven't slept with him, though there have been some very intense dreams—never mind. The important thing is that I need to be honest with you about it."

"OK."

"Please stop saying OK!"

"Well, what am I supposed to say?" he asked, laughing.

"Tell me I'm a cheater who cheats! A woman of loose character! A betrayer of trust!" I cried.

"Libby, honey, have I asked you for a commitment?" he asked. "Have I given you my fraternity pin and asked you to go steady?"

"If you have a fraternity pin, I will never trust my judgment of people again," I told him. When he gave me a pointed look, I sighed. "You said you were going to ask me to be your girl, but no."

"OK, then, so we're not exactly committed yet. You haven't broken any sort of promise to me. Of course, once we are, I'd expect you to be faithful, just like I will be to you. But I know how important sires are to vampires. Hell, Jane married hers. I'd rather you figure out now whether you want to be with him than a couple of years from now. And once you figure out how you feel about those upsetting revelations and the fact that he'll never be as good in bed as I am, you and I will ride off into the sunset."

I snorted. I needed him to make a joke like that at this very moment. I needed to laugh, because otherwise, I was going to cry. "So you're going to see other people?"

"Well, I'll put it this way. I haven't dated more than once or twice since Harley was born. I doubt that's going to change now."

"Thanks, Wade." I sighed.

"You're still gonna be my girl," he said, kissing my forehead.

"There are no other men like you in the world," I told him.

He scoffed. "'Course not. When he made me, God bronzed the mold and retired it." He kissed the tip of my nose and, closing his mouth over mine, laid a kiss on me that stole the unneeded breath from my lungs. He pulled me against him, hands roaming to my denim-covered butt and giving it a none-too-gentle squeeze.

"What are you doing?" I asked, grinning up at him.

"Just givin' that other guy somethin' to live up to."

"Nice," I said, shaking my head.

He shrugged. "Gives me time to plan my next move."

"OK, master manipulator, you go get your truck to haul away the prizes and stuff, and I'll run litter patrol."

"That's going to take you a while," he said.

"I've got it," I told him, snagging a rake from a decorative display. (Yes, really.) As Wade disappeared into the darkness, I bolted across the schoolyard at top speed, dragging the rake behind me. I darted back and forth over the grass in tight rows, picking up the litter as I went. Eventually, I had a huge pile of it in the middle of the grass, waiting to be bagged.

"Vampire speed finally pays off!" I exclaimed. "Wade, I beat you! I'm already done! I invite you to marvel at my efficiency." I did a little victory dance, complete with rake spins.

Unfortunately, these rake spins were witnessed by a man lurking at the edge of the schoolyard—a tall man in dark pants and sweater and a black ski mask, with a squarish head. Someone didn't get the memo about Pumpkin Patch costumes being a kid thing. Or this was the same *chupacabra* creep who'd lurked all over me after the PTA meeting weeks before, which was more likely.

El Chupacabra sauntered over to me, and I put my rake on my shoulder like a baseball bat, crouched in a ready stance. Even through the mask, I could tell that he wasn't breathing. He didn't have a heartbeat. Which meant he was a vampire, too. There went any advantage I might have had. I had literally never been in a fight before, not even a catfight at the Laundromat, which, I will admit, was unusual given my upbringing.

I worried about Wade. Was he OK? Had El Chupacabra hurt Wade so he could corner me? The man stopped just outside of rake range, waving his hands over my face. I lifted an eyebrow. "Can I help you?"

The man tilted his head, staring at me through the ski mask with baleful black eyes. An odd, acrid smell, like old burnt coffee, hit my nostrils, and I reeled back. He held his hand closer to my face, apparently expecting some reaction, but got nothing. He even shook his hand, all jazzy and fluttery, before trying it again. But I felt nothing. Maybe this was part of my stabilizing gift? He had a power he was trying to use to subdue me but couldn't because I was shutting him down?

Maybe my power didn't suck so much after all.

Then it seemed that he had decided to handle things the old-fashioned way, because he produced a stake from behind his back and lunged at me.

I ducked (thank you, vampire reflexes) and yelled, "Who the hell are you, jackass?"

Danny believed I was a superhero. I could do this. I could survive a fistfight . . . in which one of the parties had a stake. Right. Mustering all the upper-body strength I had, I shoved his hands aside and whipped my head forward, smashing my forehead into his.

Ow.

Effective. But ow.

He stumbled back, but I still had to sidestep the stake and, using the rake, shoved the man aside while he was off-balance. A bit more dazed than I would expect, he side-swung again, and I blocked with the rake handle. I swung back, using the rake fan like a giant palm, slapping him back and forth across the face.

He grabbed the fan and shoved it toward me, the rounded end of the handle catching me right in the sternum. I panicked, looking down and expecting to see the handle sticking out of my heart and my body disintegrating to dust. But I was just bruised . . . in a really embarrassing location. Stumbling away and rubbing at my battered chest, I still had the presence of mind to hang on to the rake handle.

Yay for me.

My opponent, who was still a little addled from his rake-slapping, struggled to his feet and limped toward me. When he got within range, I swung the rake over my head and whacked him over the face with the handle. He grunted, swinging his leg forward and planting his foot on my chest, knocking me to the ground. I gasped, rolling out of the way as he lunged, stake down, and got his wooden weapon stuck in the dirt. I scrambled to my feet and kicked the man in the ribs, sending him sprawling across the grass.

Dropping the stake, he ran at me, hands outstretched and curled, as if he was going to strangle me. I took a few steps forward and tripped him with the rake. He'd built up so much momentum that he actually dug a furrow into the lawn, only stopping when he hit the fence near the playground.

If I survived this, I was going to hold on to this rake. It was clearly a lucky rake.

My opponent did not appreciate being splattered all over the grass via lawn tools. He bounced up onto his feet and yelled, "Crazy bitch!"

When I took exception to this, swinging the rake over my shoulder like a bat again and marching across the grass toward him, he leaped to his feet and ran off into the night.

"Rude," I muttered.

Wade's voice sounded behind me. "I leave you alone for five minutes, and you dig a trench in the school's front yard?"

I turned to face him, and he shrank back at the sight of my bruised face and torn clothes.

"Honey, did ya trip over the rake?"

13

You should be just as respectful to authority figures and public servants, even if you can now drain them dry. Because your kids are watching you. Also, because it's still illegal to drain authority figures and public servants dry.

—*My Mommy Has Fangs: A Guide to Post-Vampiric Parenting*

I woke up the next evening feeling oddly vulnerable. The bruises left behind by El Chupacabra were long healed, but the sensation of having a rake handle jammed into my cleavage remained.

Just after my assailant had flounced off into the woods, Wade had come rolling up in his pickup truck. Seeing me bent over at the waist and bleeding from my mouth (I wasn't sure how *that* happened), Wade had hopped out of the truck and run to me. Even though I was already healing, he was furious that I'd been hurt while he was driving around gathering game booths.

He'd driven me home immediately, Pumpkin Patch equipment be damned, and helped me clean up before Kerrianne brought Danny and Harley home. As promised, we watched *It's the Great Pumpkin, Charlie Brown* and drank hot cocoa. Well, I had blood mixed with a very strong dose of whiskey, but it made me feel nice and toasty. The kids fell asleep with their swords and throwing stars clutched against their chests. (Harley thought the Great Pumpkin was pretty sketchy and wanted a defense system.)

I should have called Jane. I should have driven directly to the shop and reported the incident. But I just wanted to get home, to see my son and try to feel normal. After I'd put Danny down for the night, Wade insisted that I send her a text, which I did after he watched me bolt every window and door in the duplex. Long, long after he watched me bolt the doors and windows . . . as in, right before I went to bed for the day. But knowing that she would come running, risking sun exposure, if I gave her too many details, I'd kept my text vague. *"Incident" after the Pumpkin Patch Party. Need to discuss tomorrow night and fill out report.*

I was not proud of myself, but I just couldn't face questions and paperwork at that moment.

The next night, I ran my fingertips over my forehead, checking for a head-butt dent, as I shuffled toward the basement stairs. On the bottom step, I heard the sound of a strange male voice coming from my living room. I didn't think my feet touched the wood on my ascent back to the basement door. I shoved the door open and skidded across the linoleum on my socked feet. At the sound of Kerrianne's calm, measured voice, I paused to take stock of the situation.

I poked my head around the corner and peered into the living room. Kerrianne was sitting on the couch while Danny talked to a lanky man with graying blond hair in a Half-Moon Hollow Police Department uniform. I recognized Sergeant Russell Lane from two years earlier, when I'd waited outside the emergency room for news after Rob's accident. Lane had all sorts of questions about whether Rob had a drinking problem (no), if he had problems sleeping (no), whether he texted while he drove (yes, even when Danny and I were in the car with him and I begged him not to do it). He was not particularly helpful in terms of a public servant. Any comfort he offered me was in the vein of "I'm sure this wasn't your fault, ma'am, just because he was driving home late from work and probably very tired from working overtime. I'm sure supporting his family didn't lead to his untimely death." (He was actually coming home from practicing with his employer's softball team, but thanks for trying.) So really, I wasn't very happy about the idea of him talking to my son without me.

I crept to the door, listening carefully from a position where Sergeant Lane couldn't see me. Kerrianne noticed the movement in the hallway and opened her mouth to speak, but I pressed a finger to my mouth and shook my head. She nodded and focused on Sergeant Lane.

Danny was fascinated by all of the big-boy toys on Sergeant Lane's police belt, poking at his Taser. "Can I play with that?"

"No," the policeman told him. "Not until you're at least ten."

"OK." Danny sighed, and then Sergeant Lane handed him his flashlight, flicking it on. "Cool."

"Danny, how do your mom and your grandpa get along?" the policeman asked. "Are they always nice to each other, or do they fight sometimes?"

I raised my eyebrows. Had Les called the cops on me? I'd barely spoken to him the night before, and if anything, he was the one behaving in a creepy, vaguely threatening manner. Did this have something to do with the custody case? Maybe he was all smug and weird because he'd called child protective services to review my fitness as a parent. What the hell was this?

"They used to fight sometimes," Danny said. "Papa said that I should be living with him and Mamaw, but Mom said no. That made Papa mad. And he said mean things sometimes, which made Mom mad."

"How mad?" Sergeant Lane prodded.

Oh, Lord. This was not the time for Danny's unique interpretation of conversations. Using my vampire speed, I ran into the living room and stood behind Danny. My son was used to this by now and didn't so much as flinch. Sergeant Lane, on the other hand, stood up so fast he nearly knocked over the rocker he was sitting in, and his fingers were already flipping the safety catch from his gun holster. I closed my hand around his wrist to stop him. "That won't be necessary, Sergeant Lane."

"Hi, Mom," Danny said as the officer's blue eyes narrowed at me. "This is Russ. He's a policeman. But he won't let you touch his gun. I already asked."

"Trust me, baby, *I* would know better than to touch a gun in a room with a six-year-old in it," I told him, releasing Sergeant Lane's arm as he tugged away from me. "Danny, honey, why don't you run upstairs and watch some *SpongeBob* before dinner? I need to talk to Sergeant Lane."

"Really?" Danny asked. "You never let me watch cartoons before dinner."

"So it's a treat," I said.

Danny went tromping upstairs before I could change my mind.

"I'll just go into the kitchen and warm up Danny's dinner," Kerrianne said, practically sprinting into the kitchen.

I crossed my arms and dropped my fangs. I wished I could say that it was some attempt to be badass, but honestly, I was just pissed off, and I hadn't eaten yet. Sergeant Lane winced at the sight of my dental aggression, making me smile.

"Have you been questioning my son without me being present or giving permission?" I asked him. "I'm not an attorney, but I've watched enough *Law and Order* to know that's not OK."

"I was just making conversation until you woke up," he said, clearing his throat.

"So I'm assuming this has something to do with my in-laws?" I asked.

Sergeant Lane smirked at me. "You could say that. Is there anything you'd like to tell me about your in-laws?"

There were a lot of things I'd like to say about my

in-laws, but this was starting to feel like a trap. "Is there something *you'd* like to tell me about my in-laws?"

He sighed. "Mrs. Stratton, it is my duty to inform you that your father-in-law, Les Stratton, was found dead this morning."

For just a second, I was sure I'd heard him wrong. I damn near fainted as all of the bones in my body seemed to go liquid. "What?"

"Les Stratton was found outside the Cellar, that vampire bar on the other side of town, his blood drained, with severe wounds to his throat. The coroner estimates his time of death around two A.M. Can you tell me where you were at two A.M.?"

Ignoring his question, because I wasn't about to tell him that I was recovering from a schoolyard *chupacabra* ass-kicking, I sat heavily on my sofa. My brain felt like it was moving too quickly from this current crisis to what it meant for my custody case with Danny to how to handle telling my son. It was like my brain refused to focus on one thought for too long, because the overwhelming emotion I felt at the moment was gratitude. I felt bad for Marge. And I felt terrible for Danny, who had adored his papa. But overall, I just felt relieved that I wouldn't have to spend every minute of every day worrying about Les trying to take my son from me.

What was wrong with me that I felt such ambivalence every time a Stratton man died?

And suddenly, a thought occurred to me.

"Did you just question my son about his dead grandfather without Danny even knowing Les has passed?"

"'Passed' isn't exactly the term I would use," Lane told me. "It's too peaceful. Your father-in-law was savagely attacked. He was barely recognizable."

"Keep your voice down," I hissed. "I don't want this to be the way Danny finds out that his grandpa is gone."

"Again, that's a very peaceful word for it. 'Gone.' It's odd, isn't it, that you become a vampire and suddenly the man who was trying to take custody of your son is exsanguinated?"

"Yes, it does seem odd to me, since I can't imagine doing harm to Les. And it makes even less sense to me that you seem to think that I, a recently turned vampire, would kill someone in a distinctly vampiristic fashion and leave him out in the open where anyone could find him. That wouldn't exactly throw the suspicion off of me, now, would it?"

Sergeant Lane's face went slack for a second, as if the blatant oversight of motive had just occurred to him. Sherlock Holmes he was not.

"And where were you last night around two?" he asked again.

"I believe that I'm going to refrain from answering questions until I've contacted my local Council representative, which is a right guaranteed under the Undead Civil Rights Act," I responded.

An expression of extreme irritation flashed across Sergeant Lane's features. I smiled sweetly, my lower lip dragging on my fangs.

"I've already called them and explained. They're on their way," Kerrianne yelled from the kitchen. I turned my head toward my babysitter, who beckoned me from the hall where Sergeant Lane couldn't see. I nodded.

"If you'll excuse me for a second."

I crept down the hall to the kitchen, where Kerrianne was standing, wringing her hands.

"Kerrianne, what the hell?" I hissed.

"I didn't know what to do, other than call the Council, but none of the reps was awake yet," Kerrianne said.

"Sorry, I'm just being asked to absorb a lot of messed-up information at once. I'm sorry."

"It's all right. Badges just make me nervous," Kerrianne groused. "Wade's been calling me all day, asking me to check on you, even though I reminded him several times that you were kind of literally dead to the world. He also said to tell you that he went back this morning and put everything away so those PTA witches wouldn't fuss at you. Only he didn't say witches. I'm assuming you know what he's talking about."

I nodded. Wade had taken the time to put away the stupid Pumpkin Patch games in the midst of all the chaos I'd dragged him into. I was going to have to be careful, or I was going to fall head over fangs for that man.

I paced around the kitchen, watching Kerrianne cook and listening to Danny's cartoons while Sergeant Lane cooled his heels in the living room. After what he'd done, I wasn't about to make him any more comfortable in my home. How could this be happening? Les was dead, and I seemed to be suspect number one. What if I went through all of this only to lose my son when I went to jail for a murder I didn't commit? Should I just run with Danny? Take him away from everything he knew so we could escape the scrutiny?

Maybe it would be better for Wade and Harley—and Finn, for that matter—if we did leave town. Maybe they would be better off if we just ran far away so my crazy didn't contaminate their lives like some horrible movie virus.

I was considering escape routes to Mexico when I heard footsteps beating a staccato rhythm across my porch. Jane and Dick didn't even bother knocking on the door. They just walked right in. They looked wind-blown, as if they'd run all the way across town to get to me because driving would have meant breaking several traffic laws. Aw. That made me feel loved, as did the heretofore unseen murderous expression on Dick's face when he looked at Sergeant Lane.

I would not want to be Lane at this moment.

"Sergeant Lane," Jane said, her tone supremely frosty. "How have you not been fired by now?"

The lanky officer looked less than thrilled to see my local Council rep. And that made me sort of happy. He bristled, drawing himself up to his full height, which was still about an inch shorter than Jane. "I don't think—"

"That's the problem, Sergeant Lane, you don't think. From what I hear, you've been questioning one of my constituents without a Council rep present. And you compounded that dumbassery by questioning that vampire's child without his parent's consent."

"You're just peeing all over the Constitution from

both sides of the Undead Civil Rights Act, aren't you?" Dick growled.

"I'm going to need you to come downtown with me to answer some questions," Sergeant Lane said, attempting to grab my arm. I sidestepped him, sliding between Dick and Jane.

"You do realize that our police station isn't actually downtown, right?" I asked him.

"Just tell me where you were last night," Lane spat.

"I was here, at home, with my son."

"And I'm assuming that there's no one who would be able to corroborate this?" He sneered. "That seems convenient."

"I don't know if it's occurred to you, officer, but innocent people don't need alibis. However, Wade Tucker and his son were here until about midnight, if that helps."

Jane smirked and waggled her brows at Dick. He scowled and handed her a twenty-dollar bill.

"That still leaves you two hours to drive to the Cellar, kill your father-in-law, and get back to your house before the sun came up," Lane insisted.

"Assuming, of course, that I would leave my son alone in the house, which I would not do. Ask Kerrianne. Ask anyone at Danny's school. I don't put my son's safety at risk."

"Oh, trust me, I've already talked to people at Danny's school. And they had some very interesting things to say about your change in attitude since you were turned. You're more aggressive, less patient, mean-spirited."

"I see you've been talking to Chelsea Harbaker," I muttered.

"No, a Mrs. McGee."

"Figures," I huffed.

"Do you have any evidence that Libby had anything to do with Les Stratton's death, other than 'I can't think of anyone else'?"

"Not at the moment, but I'm sure we'll find something," Lane said.

"Well, until you do, you will leave Mrs. Stratton alone. You will not contact her or question her without myself or Mr. Cheney present. And you will not approach Danny Stratton, ever. If I find out that you have been harassing either of the Strattons, I will be on your supervisor's front step faster than you can say 'mall security.'"

"Fine," Sergeant Lane said, shutting his little notebook with a snap. "Don't leave town, Mrs. Stratton. I will be coming to see you soon."

"Good evening, Sergeant Lane."

As the patrol car pulled out of my driveway, all of my bravado melted, and I practically sagged against the front door. My hands were shaking, and I thought I was going to throw up what little I had in my stomach. I felt Jane's hand on my back and heard some distant murmuring in the kitchen.

Dick was holding a mug full of synthetic blood in front of my face. I let him put it to my lips and drained the entire thing in one gulp. How was I going to explain this? How was I going to prove my innocence to the people who could keep me out of jail? Sure, Dick and Jane were supporting me in the face of law enforcement now, but what if there was some circumstantial piece of evidence that linked me to Les's death? What would happen when supporting me was no longer in the best interest of the vampire community?

"Jane," I said, wheezing, "I know this is going to sound cliché, but I didn't do it."

"I believe you," Jane said, nodding.

I straightened, my shoulders slowly relaxing. "Really?"

"I've been accused of murder . . . how many times now?" Jane asked.

"Two or three times," Dick estimated, flopping down on the couch.

"Right. And every time, I didn't do it."

"There was that one time," Dick said.

"That was in self-defense, and technically, all I did was Taser her."

Dick snorted. "While she was soaked in lamp oil."

"My point is that it would be stupid of you to spend all of this time in mediation, battling your father-in-law, only to murder him. It would bring the police right to you. And you are not a stupid person. You would not risk your custody of Danny. So now you have to lie low and say nothing. We have to do some damage control and try to find out who, besides you, wanted to see your father-in-law dead."

I shrugged. "Me, most of the U of L fans in town, the people who had heard his 'caught a ten-pound bass on a kid's Snoopy reel' story more than once . . ."

"That's a long list," Jane said.

"Well, we'll look into it. You just sit tight, and don't do anything else to draw attention to yourself. No arrests for public intoxication. No shoplifting undies from Walmart," Dick told me. "No swimmin' naked with Wade in the memorial fountain."

"Have *you* been talking to Mrs. McGee?"

"Now, before we start our *Scooby-Doo* routine, is there anything we should know about?" Jane asked. "For instance, why did you send me a maddeningly vague text right before bedtime about an 'incident' at the Pumpkin Patch Party and the paperwork it would require?"

"Oh." I sighed, burying my face in my hands. "I forgot all about that. I was sort of attacked by a masked figure while I was cleaning up the Pumpkin Patch debris last night. I'm pretty sure it was the same guy lurking in the school parking lot a few weeks back. He tried to stake me, but I fought him off. With a rake. He ran away into the woods."

Jane's lips disappeared as she pinched her mouth shut and exhaled loudly from her nose. She nodded, jaw clenching and unclenching. "And you didn't think that *maybe* you should have reported this right away instead of sending me a cowardly text right before sunrise?"

I winced and offered, "I was traumatized?"

"Dick," Jane said wearily, "get my spray bottle."

"Jane, no!"

Hours later, I sat outside Les and Marge's house in my minivan with Kerrianne's funeral potato casserole riding shotgun. While I'd loved the carb-based grief fuel when I was human, tonight I had to ride with the windows down just so I could tolerate the smell. This was what Southern people did in the face of death, no matter what their social class. They heard about someone passing. They threw together a casserole to sustain the mourners during their time of need, and they called on them to deliver the covered dish and their well wishes. And if they happened to pick up a tidbit of gossip about the bereaved or the strange circumstances of the death, all the better.

Just because I was a vampire now, that didn't mean I was going to give up on tradition.

I hadn't told Danny about his papa yet. I didn't know how. He was so young, and he'd lost so much already. It seemed cruel to take something else from him. In addition to that stress, I wasn't sure I was doing the right thing contacting Marge. But I wanted to continue the tentative relationship I'd rebuilt with her. I didn't want Les's death or my being a suspect in that death to derail the progress we'd made.

My life was complicated.

I leaned forward and tapped my forehead against the steering wheel. "Please, Lord, please don't let this be one of those decisions I end up regretting a lot."

Balancing the warm Pyrex in one hand, I knocked on the front door, a formality I'd insisted on even when Rob was alive. I didn't want Les and Marge to feel comfortable just walking into my home unannounced, or vice versa. Of course, they did it anyway, but I tried to communicate how I felt about the issue with this little quirk.

An older woman, a friend of Marge's I vaguely recognized from my in-laws' annual holiday party, opened the door. Her blandly pleasant smile evaporated as she realized who was on the front stoop. "Oh. It's you."

Without further response, she walked away, disappearing into the crowd of people milling around in the living room. Nice.

The house looked and smelled exactly the same, like Lemon Pledge and gun oil. How could so much about my life have changed but this place remain the same? The crowd parted as I walked through the living room, like Moses walking through a particularly gossipy sea. I could hear murmurs, snatches of conversation, "no blood missing," "so torn up Marge wasn't allowed to identify him."

I also heard hissing whispers of "Who does she think she is?" and "How could she?" from the other mourners. My memory flashed back to the days before Rob's funeral, in this very room, being comforted by some of the same people. I'd sat on Marge's couch, hands clenched together so tightly my knuckles felt bruised, desperately trying not to have some reaction, some moment of weakness that could be criticized later. Now these people were staring at me like I was something they wanted to scrape off the bottom of their shoes. And I could not give less of a damn. There was a real freedom in simply not caring.

I smiled at the lot of them, as sweet as pie, but without showing fang, because there were limits to what I could get away with in a group this trigger-happy. From what I understood, bullets couldn't kill me, but they stung like hell.

Marge was sitting at the kitchen table, a cup of coffee clutched between her hands. She looked older, tired, and shrunken, as if she'd lost twenty "flu pounds" since the last time I saw her. She was wearing an old denim gardening shirt and no makeup, and her hair was slicked back into a bun instead of in its usual feathery helmet. Several of her friends from church sat with her, patting her arms and murmuring comforting platitudes, but she didn't seem to hear them. She was staring straight ahead.

I put the funeral potatoes on the counter with all of the other dishes and approached her slowly. Her best friend, Joyce Mayhew, shot to her feet, vibrating with righteous indignation. "How dare you show your face in here, Libby Stratton? Rob would be so ashamed of you—"

"Don't," Marge said softly. "Give us a minute."

"Marge, honey, you're not strong enough to make good decisions right now," Joyce told her, patting Marge's hair.

Marge clearly didn't like being told she wasn't "strong enough" for anything, despite the fact that she'd told me the same thing almost every day while I was on chemo. "It's fine, Joyce," Marge insisted. "There are things we need to talk about."

"I will be right over there," Joyce said, glaring at me. "I'm watching you."

I slid into the chair abandoned by Joyce. Marge stared down at her full coffee mug, rubbing her thumb along the handle.

"I'm so sorry, Marge."

"I don't even know how to respond to that anymore. I've heard it so many times today," she said, shaking her head. She looked up at me, eyes shimmering with tears. "Is this how it felt for you?"

"Yes," I said. "But at least Rob's death was an accident. Knowing that someone hurt Les, that's got to be so much worse."

"I just don't understand how this happened. I keep asking, who would want to hurt Les? And the police were here, and they asked so many questions. I didn't know how to answer so many of them. He was behaving so strangely, ranting about you, making phone calls that he didn't want me to hear. I just don't know what happened to him in the last few months. I feel like the man I married died a long time ago."

Tentatively, I reached out and patted her cool, dry hand. She didn't take mine, but she didn't flinch, either. I considered that progress. "I don't know what the police told you, but I didn't have anything to do with this, Marge. I am sorry about what happened to Les," I told her. "I was angry with him, toward the end, but I would never wish that on him."

"I know that," she assured me. "I know I said some things right after you were turned—things I regret. But deep down, I know that you couldn't hurt Danny or Les or me. We just needed time to adjust. If we'd just had more time, maybe Les would have . . ." Marge's voice trailed off as twin tears rolled down her cheeks. "It's going to have to be a closed-casket funeral. Did the police tell you that? There was so much damage. Even so, I don't think it would be a good idea for

Danny to be there. That's just too much to ask of a little boy. Have you talked to him yet?"

I shook my head. "I didn't know how to explain to him."

"I could help you with that," she offered. "Maybe it would help, coming from both of us."

"I think so, too," I said. "We can tell him tomorrow night. You could come over, maybe help him with bathtime and bedtime stories. That might help both of you."

Marge's thin, unpainted lips trembled into something that resembled a smile. "I would really appreciate that."

14

Confrontations with other parents are going to happen—
at your child's school, at the ball field, at the mall. The
important thing to remember is that thanks to the
prevalence of security cameras and smartphones, you're
probably being recorded. So footage of your retribution
will be held against you in a court of law.

—*My Mommy Has Fangs: A Guide to Post-Vampiric Parenting*

Jane told me to lie low, to let the Council investiga-
tors look into Les's murder.

And I intended to follow her instructions, at least in
spirit. She was already a smidge displeased with me
for doing a mourner's run over to my mother-in-law's
without talking to her. But since she hadn't specifically
told me not to condole with Marge, she couldn't exactly
get mad at me. Well, she could, but she chose not to.

Finn called, offering—hell, pleading—to help me
manage this new crisis, but I sent his calls straight to
voice mail. I had decided, for once, that I would listen to Jane's advice about Finn and keep my distance.
Finn's charming little fibs had grown to a tsunami of

lies I just couldn't ignore. And while I wanted to believe that he felt something for me, everything he'd ever said or done seemed too carefully calculated, an orchestra of manipulation that left my head reeling and my heart sore.

Telling Danny that evening that his papa was gone had not been easy, even with the added consolation of his mamaw coming over to make his favorite dinner—spaghetti and cut-up hot dogs. Danny had been too young to understand when Rob died, and my resurrection hadn't exactly helped him comprehend a grave one couldn't escape. He didn't quite grasp where his papa had gone and why he wouldn't be back.

"But who's going to take me camping and fishing?" he'd asked. "Papa said he had to make a man of me."

"Mamaw will take you fishing," Marge promised. "And camping."

"But it won't be the same," Danny insisted.

"No, honey, it won't be the same. But our lives weren't the same after Mom became a vampire, right?" I asked. He shook his head, wiping at his nose with his sleeve. "It was different. But it was good. We've made the best of it. And we still have fun together, right?"

Danny nodded again.

"Your mamaw and your mom love you so much, Danny," Marge said, pulling him into her lap. Despite recent protests that he was not a baby and too big for our laps, he snuggled into Marge's neck and let her hug him. "We can't bring your papa back. We can't make things the way they were, but we can make the best of it."

"OK," Danny said, wiping at his nose again—on Marge's sweater. "Does this mean Mamaw is going to be visiting me more, Mom?"

I gave Marge a small smile. "Yeah, buddy, Mamaw is going to come see you more."

Marge ruffled his hair. "Which is a good thing, because Mamaw's tablet crashed a month ago, and your mom is the only one I trust to fix it. Mamaw hasn't played her Sudoku in weeks!"

I gaped at my mother-in-law, who was actually telling a joke in a time of crisis. It seemed that parts of my personality were rubbing off on her after all.

"Poor Mamaw," Danny said, sighing and sitting up to pat her hair. "Mom will take care of it."

Marge reached over and squeezed my arm. "Mom always takes care of the things that are important."

Of course, my chilly reception from my former friends and neighbors at Marge's was just the tip of the "so you're a suspected murderer in a small town" iceberg. I couldn't go to Walmart without other shoppers clearing the aisles to get away from me. I heard whispers behind my back whenever I ventured out of the house. I was hoping to get some sort of official notice not to attend PTA meetings, but apparently, being suspected of murder was not enough to get me out of parent volunteerism.

Eager to distract me from potential legal troubles, Wade made regular visits with Harley. He and the boys would eat dinner—rowdy, lively meals filled with knock-knock jokes and burp chastisement—while

I added commentary from the living room. (I loved them all, but there was a definite limit to my food-smell tolerance. And that limit was burgeroni.)

Despite the olfactory offenses, it was nice to have Wade and Harley with us. They fit into our lives, not just as a convenience or assistance but in the way Wade seemed to understand what I needed, in the way he took the path of least resistance just because it was there. It was in the way Wade treated me as a vital, desired part of the unit instead of support staff. It was in the way the boys played so easily together, settling their own squabbles and building their own little worlds together. It was in how Harley sought me out as much as Danny did and how Danny thought Wade was the fixer of all broken things. That strange, unbalanced, half-empty feeling that had plagued our family even before Rob's death seemed to be tilting back to rights.

And because I was a parent, a master multitasker, I could lie low *and* help nudge the investigation along. I made lists of Les's friends for Jane and Dick to speak to about the last weeks of his life. I made lists of character witnesses who would testify that I was not an insane murderer. I made lists of the arrangements I would need to make for Danny if I was sent to vampire prison.

What I could not prepare for was my father's arrival on my front porch.

It was the Thursday after the Pumpkin Patch debacle. Les would be buried the following morning, and Marge had asked for Danny to stay at her house that night, to give her some company and comfort as she got used to a quieter home.

The ease with which I packed Danny's overnight bag surprised me. The old anxiety about letting my son spend time at his grandparents' house without me was practically nonexistent. Marge and I had unofficially agreed to a ceasefire, trying to make this new transition easier for Danny. I hoped I wasn't making a mistake. I hoped that without Les's intense all-or-nothing approach, we could find some happy balance that would keep both of us in Danny's life. Frankly, I was tired of the competition. I didn't have the energy to scheme and spin myself as the ideal single vampire mom anymore. I just wanted some sort of peace.

I was slipping Danny's stuffed monkey—the one he insisted he didn't need to sleep with anymore, though Banana Bob always seemed to find his way into the bed—into his sleepover bag when I heard the doorbell ring downstairs.

"I'll get it!" Danny yelled, abandoning his LEGO kingdom to run toward the foyer. Lightning-quick, I hopped over the bannister and landed between my son and the front door. Danny, now accustomed to his mother zipping around the house at vampire speed, merely skidded to a halt before we collided. Through the front-door glass, I could see a strange man standing on my stoop.

"Sweetheart, what have we said about opening the door without an adult?" I asked, glancing over my shoulder at the stranger. Should I even answer the door? I wondered. What if it was more bad news? What if he was from the Council or, worse, the family court? What if he was some friend of Les's looking for a confrontation?

Danny chewed his lip and considered. "Not to do it."

I glanced pointedly at the door and back to him, and realization seemed to dawn on his face. "Oh."

"Yeah, oh," I deadpanned. "Hey, the moon is supposed to be full tonight. Why don't you go to the kitchen and see if you can spot Sasquatch in the backyard."

"You're just trying to keep me from seeing who's at the front door, aren't you?"

"Yes, I am," I told him.

"Fiiiine." He sighed mightily and slumped toward the kitchen.

I stepped closer to the door, considering the man on the other side of the glass.

He smiled, a wide, friendly, not at all hostile expression, like we were old friends reunited. He had wavy blond hair, a long nose, high cheekbones, and light blue-green eyes. Now that I could get a closer look, I could see the telltale pearlescent perfection of vampire skin. The stranger had been turned in his late thirties, and he was handsome, in that same "devil in a Sunday suit" manner as Finn. You could tell from the twinkle in his eyes that he was a charmer, the kind of guy who could talk you into a used car, a timeshare, *and* Amway and have you thanking him for the opportunity.

I unlocked and opened the door, careful to keep my foot propped against it so he couldn't push in on me. "Yes?"

His grin seemed to broaden even further but in a sincere way. He was beaming so brilliantly I was going to need sunglasses soon. "Liberty." There was no question in his tone. He knew that I was Liberty Stratton, which was odd, considering how few people knew my embarrassing birth name.

"Can I help you?"

Behind him, a sedan careened into my driveway, practically on two wheels. The driver, Finn, slid to a stop and hopped out.

"The hell?" I muttered, making the stranger snort.

"Max, this is not what we talked about! She's still pissed at both of us! She's not going to appreciate you—"

"Max?" I asked.

"Max Kitteridge," he said. "You look so much like your mom. Her hair and her nose, that stubborn little chin. I saw enough of that whenever I tried to tell her what to do. You've got my eyes, though."

I glanced down and back at my son, who was peering around the kitchen doorway at the stranger. He seemed to be evaluating the man for potential bad-guy beardness, staring him down with my eyes. Danny's eyes. Max's eyes. The same shade of blue-green with the ring of navy around the pupil.

When I whipped my head back toward the door, Max smiled at me, and those eyes almost disappeared into crinkly laugh lines. It pissed me off. That after all these years, my father could smile like that at me and act like he was happy to see me, when he hadn't bothered with a visit in thirty years.

"I thought vampires couldn't have kids," I said, shaking my head.

"I was with your mom, and then I was turned. I came back. I tried to contact her after you were born."

I stared at him as if he were speaking a foreign language. How was it possible that after all these years, I was looking at my father? And where in the everloving hell had he been since the day I was born?

"She was a smart girl, your mom, always picked up on the little cues that no one else got," Max said. "And when she realized what I was, she didn't want me around. She was scared, and I couldn't blame her. Nobody knew about vampires then, and who would want one around their baby girl? She told me to leave, that it was safer for you if I was nowhere near you. She made me promise to stay away from you. And if nothing else, I kept my promise to her."

Finn huffed behind him. "Max, she's not ready."

Max still pointedly ignored his old friend. "I followed your life over the years. I hadn't spent a lot of time here, but I still had contacts in town. They'd take pictures for me, let me know when you had something big coming up—graduations, your wedding. If it was at night, I'd slip into the crowd so I could feel like I was part of it, too."

The words were spilling out of him, like he'd been rehearsing them for years, patient and slow, but now they were running away with him. I thought back to any of the "big events" in my life and realized how pitifully few crowds he'd had to slip into—my high school graduation, my community-college graduation, my wedding; that was pretty much it. I felt sort of bad for his bored spies.

"Danny, I was there at the hospital on the night you were born." Max peered around me, trying to get a better look at my son.

"Really?" Danny asked, stepping closer.

Max grinned. "Yeah. I waited in the lobby at the hospital until I heard you crying from all the way down the hall. You were a loud little thing." He turned to me. "It's not easy for us to be in hospitals, you know. Too many smells, the least of which is blood. And I think the nurses mistook me for a baby snatcher. But I got to hear my grandson's first cries. It meant a lot to me, knowing that you had a good life, a nice, safe life. It was more than I could offer you."

I stared at him for a long time, silent, as all of the questions I wanted to ask, the demands, the insults, everything I'd ever wanted to say to my father in all those years alone, ran through my head.

"I don't think you can be my grandpa. You're not old enough," Danny said softly. I had to wonder what was going on in his little head. He'd only just lost his papa, and now some young guy shows up claiming to be his grandfather? I mentally added a higher total goal for Danny's potential therapy fund.

Max winked at him. "You'd be surprised, kiddo. And at least I don't have a bad-guy beard."

Finn made a displeased noise in his throat.

I straightened my shoulders and asked, "So you're my father?"

Max looked oddly proud as he said, "I am indeed."

"OK." Quick as a snake, I raised my fist and punched him in his handsome, stupid face. He was clearly not expecting the blow and tottered back on his heels, clutching his bleeding nose as he crashed into the door.

"Mom!" Danny cried. "You hit him! You said hitting isn't OK ever!"

"Well, sometimes it is, under special circumstances," I told him.

"You should say you're sorry!" Danny said.

Feeling a pang of hypocritical-mother guilt, I sighed. "I will, later. I promise."

"Feel better now?" Finn asked as Max groaned and I rubbed my healing knuckles.

I nodded. "Oddly enough, yes. Get any closer, and you're next."

Finn seemed disappointed but accepted the threat. "Look, I've known your dad since we were both human. We were turned by the same sire around the same time for a—"

"If you say 'misunderstanding,' I will poke you in the eye," I told him. "Why didn't you come see me before, Max? Why did you wait until now? Do you have any idea how different my life could have been, how different *Mom* could have been, if you'd just shown up every once in a while?"

"I was trying to respect her wishes. And frankly, she was right. The way I was living my life, it wasn't safe for you. I did send her money every month, but she just sent it back."

"And when she died, you didn't think maybe you

should send a note?" I demanded, thinking back to meeting Rob at the loneliest time in my life. Knowing my father might have changed the decisions I'd made. Then again, I might not have had Danny. I cleared my throat. "I really—I could have used a friend then."

"I was scared," he admitted. "I didn't know what your mom had told you about me. And the thought of you rejecting me, I couldn't stand it. Sure, it was tough seeing you live your life from far away. But at least I could keep up the illusion of being involved. Knowing for sure that you wanted nothing to do with me? It was terrifying. Every time I'd almost talked myself into coming to you, I'd talk myself out of it all over again."

"And after you and Finn decided that he would turn me into a vampire?" I asked, glaring at my sire.

Finn touched my arm, and I pulled loose from his grasp. "I was afraid that if he approached you right away, you would bolt, so I told him to keep his distance. And his patience ran out, officially, this week when he heard about your father-in-law. He was supposed to give me time to let you get used to the idea. But he jumped the gun."

"But you knew he was in the Hollow, and you didn't tell me."

"You know, I am standing right here," Max pointed out.

We both whipped our heads toward him, glaring.

Max raised his hands. "Carry on."

"I'm sorry," Finn said. "I know that I misled you—"

"Misled?"

"Misinformed," he amended.

"Really?" My eyes narrowed at him.

"But I hope that we can still try to make things work between us. So much of what I did was because I was trying to get more time with you. And not because of your ability but because I want you for you."

"I know I'm new to this parenting thing, but I am certain I am not supposed to be hearing this," Max muttered. "Danny, let's go into the kitchen, or maybe the backyard, out of earshot."

"We have a Sasquatch in the backyard!" Danny told him proudly as they retreated toward the back door.

"You don't say!" Max said. "You know, I was in Canada once, and I swear I saw one in the parking lot of a Tim Horton's."

"No way!" Danny cried as the door closed behind him.

"I will always be grateful to you for turning me," I told Finn. "And I appreciate the way you've tried to help me, easing my transition into being a vampire. But—"

"Uh-oh."

I started again. "But—"

He shook his head again. "Don't say the thing."

"I think we're going to be better off as friends," I told him as he bounced his head against the porch railing.

"You said the thing." He groaned.

"It's not that I don't find you attractive, which I do. And it's not that I don't think we have chemistry, which we do. It's that I can't trust you."

"You know I would never hurt you or Danny!" he exclaimed.

"Physically, yes, I know you would never hurt me or Danny," I agreed. "And you seem to feel some sort of protective loyalty to me, because of Max and your friendship with him. But I can't trust you to tell me the truth. Not some variation of the truth. Not some version of the truth. Not a *hint* of the truth. The whole truth. You've lied to me too many times, Finn."

"To protect you!"

"From what? From information you didn't think I was ready to know? Why do you get to be the one who makes that decision? And let's not forget the part where you neglected to tell me that you broke the Council's embargo on spending time with me to help you mute your gift and save your own ass."

"OK, yeah, that's a bad example," he admitted.

"I spent most of my life lying. I let my mom think that I was perfectly fine growing up with basically no parenting. I let my husband think I loved him, that I was happy with our life, because I didn't know how to ask for what I needed. I can't build a relationship with you when I can't trust anything you say. I would be like an alcoholic dating a bartender. Not completely dysfunctional but not an awesome idea."

Finn sighed, his expression sad and contemplative. "I knew that when you met Max it would probably be the end of whatever we'd started."

"I'm sorry. I'm not saying I don't want to see you anymore. It just won't be in a romantic way."

"I don't think I can accept that."

"Well, it's not up to you to accept it. This is the way it is."

"I get it." He sighed. "I don't like it, but I get it."

After much more discussion with my wayward sire and my long-lost father, I worked out a delicate agreement with Max. One evening, every other week, he would come over for a visit. No more, no less, unless there was a specific invitation. He would not interfere with my life. He would not spy on me. He would not disappoint Danny or break promises. And if he did, all bets were off, and we would go back to life as if he'd never showed up on our porch. Max agreed to all of these stipulations, which spoke to either his guilt at abandoning me or his desperation to connect with the only family he had left.

Finn, on the other hand, was on strict probation and was only to contact me if I contacted him first. He was pretty graceful about accepting the end of any sort of romantic connection between us, something I suspected would change when he sensed my anger ebbing.

I thought that maybe simplifying my romantic life would help me focus. But it just narrowed my worries to a constant loop about Les's murder. Who would want to kill him? He'd had no contact with the vampire world until I was turned. What was he doing at the Cellar? Was he meeting with a vampire? Had he been going to the Cellar for long? Was he buying some sort of antivampire defense weapons? A poison? Was that why he'd looked so smug and self-assured the night he died? Because he was going to get rid of me? Was it possible he was El Chupacabra? I thought the man in the mask was a vampire, but maybe Les had found some way to mask his heartbeat. What the hell had Les done differently in the last few weeks that had led to his death?

Then, one morning, the idea bubbled up to the surface of my brain as I was drifting off to sleep. I did take care of things that were important, like Les and Marge's bank account, which I'd managed since I married Rob. If Les was up to something, maybe some strange activity would show up in their bank statements.

My father-in-law did not understand how online banking or e-mail worked. So Rob had insisted that we help his parents out by paying their bills online, since I was a bookkeeper. Years before, I'd set up their online bank account and taken care of the utilities, mortgage payments, insurance payments. Marge still had the checkbook, and since she hadn't brought it up, I assumed she'd taken over her own bills, but since her e-mail password was "1234danny," I guessed she hadn't taken the time to change the password for her bank account, either.

So at the crack of sundown the next evening, I sat down at my laptop. If my in-laws hadn't changed their account password and I technically hadn't been barred from accessing the account, it wasn't a crime to log in, right? I could call and ask her permission, but I wasn't so sure I wanted her to know that I suspected Les of chicanery. That would definitely upset the fragile truce we'd reached.

I typed in Marge's user name. My fingers hovered over the keyboard as I tried to rationalize my snooping.

"Seriously? Of all the things I've done so far, this is the least ethically offensive," I muttered, typing in the password.

Marge and Lester's bank account opened up, showing a meticulous list of payments and credits. I scanned the list, finding the usual debits at the grocery store, the quilt shop, Marge's hairdresser. They weren't actual debits, of course, because Les didn't trust debit cards. But I could see scans of the checks Marge had written. She seemed to have taken on the task of paying her own bills handily, though she hadn't logged into the online system at all. I suspected my mother-in-law was a lot more capable than she let on.

There were a few odd line items—the payment to the funeral parlor for Les's service and a payment to a landscaper with the note "weekly mowing service" in the memo line. I shuddered, imagining how Les would react to another man mowing his lawn so soon after his death. I thought he would have preferred that Marge immediately start taking lovers. I scrolled back a couple of pages, to before Les's death, looking for other unusual vendors.

I noticed that Les had transferred about twenty thousand dollars out of their retirement account and moved it into checking. That was unusual. Les considered their retirement account sacrosanct. He'd toiled at the feed mill for almost fifty years to secure their golden years. He wouldn't have touched it, unless maybe he was planning to use it to fund their legal fees to obtain custody

of Danny? I scanned the vendors for names of law offices and found a two-thousand-dollar retainer paid to
Freeman, Newton, and Lahey, a local firm. I also noted
that it was paid about a month before I was turned,
meaning that Les had been planning on taking custody
of Danny while I was still clinging to life. Lovely.

So what was the rest of the money for? I scrolled
back to the date of my turning. About a month after I
"came out of the coffin" to my in-laws, Les had paid
ten thousand dollars to "Argentum Investment Advisers." My eyes went wide. Les didn't believe in investing
in anything beyond a savings account. When the mill
switched over to a 401(k) system, he ranted for days
about the instability of the market and the untrustwor-
thiness of stockbrokers. He threatened to withdraw his
retirement plan and bury his money in mayo jars in
the backyard. I think the only thing that stopped him
was that Marge refused to save the jars because they
were "germy."

I'd heard the word "Argentum" before but couldn't
remember where. Somewhere in my new-vampire
reading, maybe? I opened my copy of *The Guide for
the Newly Undead* and checked the index. Silver. "Argentum" was the Latin word for silver. That seemed
significant, considering what silver represented to
vampires. Itchy, blistery potential death.

I opened my browser window and Googled "Argentum Investment Advisers."

Nothing.

No Internet presence whatsoever. That seemed impossible. My father-in-law wouldn't have given ten

thousand dollars to a firm unless it had a solid reputation. And a friendly cartoon animal mascot. And commercials during the Super Bowl.

My late father-in-law *had* been up to something super-shady right before he died. But what? Could he be cheating on Marge? Maybe he had a second family over in Murphy and was sending them money. No, I wasn't thinking big enough. Les had been killed just a few weeks after this payment had been made. That had to be significant, too.

I rubbed my hands over my eyes. Maybe I was just seeing what I wanted to see.

I stared at the screen and tried to will all of the pieces of this puzzle to come together. Unfortunately, I was not a psychic. I was not a private investigator. I was an accountant, and this was beyond my skill level. I needed someone with know-how when it came to this sort of thing. Someone with shady connections. So I went to the shadiest person I knew. I went to Dick Cheney.

Leaving Danny sleeping at home under Kerrianne's watch, I drove downtown to Specialty Books and parked outside the warm glow of the store's front windows. Despite her status with the Council, Jane had insisted on continuing to work from her shop. She tried to split her hours, but Andrea had to pick up a lot of slack.

To my surprise, Finn was sitting at one of the coffee tables with Jane and Dick. All three of them wore grave expressions, so I could only guess that they were talking about me. Gabriel and Andrea were behind the bar, cleaning the coffee equipment, pretending not to be listening.

Finn's face lit up with a grin when he saw me, though Jane and Dick looked concerned.

Before any of them could speak, I approached the table and announced, "I have a question for you, and it will involve discretion and shady connections. Finn, this doesn't change anything, but it's probably a good thing that you're here."

Finn looked affronted. "That's . . . No, OK, that's fair. Frankly, I'm a little insulted you came here before looking for me," he said. "At least my shady connections are current."

"Hey, just because I haven't been in the game for a few years, that doesn't mean I've been forgotten," Dick protested.

Jane covered her face with her hands. "I can't believe you two are having this argument. Libby, please explain before I lash out and say something I'll regret."

I explained my ethical-gray-area investigation of Les and Marge's bank accounts and its implication of Les's potential criminal activity. To my surprise, Jane and Dick weren't all that upset, and they informed me that thanks to some heavy-handed negotiations with the nation's legal branch, Council representatives didn't have to put up with pesky details like search warrants or just cause. So technically, I hadn't broken any laws.

Dick was not, however, thrilled with my plan to drive to Louisville and scope out the address of the mysterious payee.

"Why not just let us send a local Council rep to the address to check it out?" Jane asked. "Less risk. Less chance of tipping off this hit person that you're aware of them."

"Because I might see some link to Les that you wouldn't recognize. Also, I won't give you the address unless you let me go."

Dick stared pointedly at Finn. "I blame your influence for this."

Finn shrugged.

Jane sighed. "Well, we're going with you. As a member of the Council, I feel an obligation to protect my constituents. Plus, I'm afraid you'll never come back."

"Your faith in my fighting skills is a comfort, really," I told her.

"Yeah, well, my faith in my own fighting skills means we're taking backup with us," she said, pulling out her cell phone. "You know the great thing about being a Council official? You have a SWAT team on call."

The almost four-hour drive to Louisville was awkward, to say the least. Finn gamely tried to start polite conversations, but I was too uncomfortable around him to reply, and Jane tended to be cagey around people she didn't quite trust. Dick tried to bridge the gap between the two, but it mostly ended in fizzled "getting to know you" prompts, like "Finn, didn't you live in Tibet once? Jane has an amazing collection of Tibetan prayer bowls at the shop." And it turned out that neither one of them was that interested in talking about prayer bowls.

I couldn't sleep in the car, because I was mulling over what this confrontation could mean. Yes, finding out that Les was up to some nefarious activities would exonerate me and take a lot off my plate, legally speaking. But it would taint my father-in-law's memory within the community. People wouldn't remember him as Les Stratton, the Sunday-school teacher who loved University of Kentucky basketball and bass fishing. He would be that guy who got tangled up in vampire politics and got his throat ripped out for his trouble. Poor Marge. How was she going to deal with this?

We drove into an industrial section of town, poorly lit and barely occupied. The address put us at what looked like an abandoned bulk-dry-cleaning facility. Most of the windows were broken out, save for a small section on the top floor. From the gate, we could see a light in the window, which winked out the moment we pulled into the parking lot.

Jane pulled to a stop just as a van marked "UERT" (undead emergency response team—vampires needed to learn how to make acronyms that spelled actual words) rolled to a silent halt beside us. Jane unbuckled her seatbelt and turned to me.

"Right; you are going to wait in the car where it's safe, because after all this, I'm not going home to Danny to tell him that his mom survived cancer and getting turned only to be killed by vampire friendly fire." She turned to Finn. "And you are going to stay here, too, because you walking into the line of said friendly fire would mean a lot of paperwork for me."

And with that, Dick and Jane closed the doors, leaving me in the least comfortable car in the world. After several long, silent minutes, Finn said, "You know, when I pictured the two of us in the backseat of a car, it was a bit more romantic than this."

I glared at him.

He tugged at his collar. "You're right. Not appropriate. It's just that it's strange to be around you now without saying that sort of thing."

"If you want to see me at all, you're going to have to figure it out," I told him. "I don't want to make things awkward for you and Max. I know you two are kind of a package deal. And don't go blaming Wade for us not being together, because you did this yourself. If you do anything to hurt him, I will not forgive you."

"I know that I—" Finn stopped talking as we watched the UERT team's lights sweep around in the windows like Danny's class was inside playing flashlight tag. Silhouetted against that light, a shape emerged from a dark window one floor below and shimmied down the fire escape ladder.

"What?" I turned the door handle and stepped out of the car.

"Wait, Libby, no!" Finn grabbed for my arm, but I was already on the pavement, walking toward the building. Even my keen eyesight strained to make out the movements of the person climbing down the building.

I heard Finn behind me, quietly creeping out of the car. My nostrils flared as the familiar scent of old burnt coffee hit me with full force. My fangs dropped as I hissed quietly. The figure above dropped to the asphalt with no noise at all, a considerable feat for someone his size.

He stepped into the moonlight, and it was Bob—coffee-hogging Crybaby Bob. The same Bob who sat at those damn meetings and whined about not being understood by his family. The same Bob I'd felt sorry for, despite the coffee hogging.

And me without my rake.

"You!" He growled.

I growled back. "You."

"Libby!" Finn called out in warning, but I'd already ducked under Bob's swing. I'd learned from our first encounter. I dropped so far down my ass nearly smacked against the pavement, but then I sprang up, fist at the ready, and caught Bob underneath his chin. I put all of my strength into the blow, knocking Bob back off his feet and onto the ground.

"Stay back!" I yelled at Finn.

"Libby!" Finn barked.

"Just let me do this." I grunted as my boot connected with Bob's ribs. He caught my leg and rolled, dragging me to the ground. I landed on my back with an *oof* but jammed my heel into his sternum—hard. I scrambled to a sitting position, straddling his massive chest and punching him in the face.

"Stay back!" I yelled at Finn again as he prepared to spring into the fray. "Let me handle this!"

"This is very emasculating!" Finn yelled.

Bob threw up his hips, tossing me aside like a rag doll. I rolled to my hands and knees, hopping to my feet as he was already charging at me.

"Why won't you just die?" he yelled as I sidestepped him and shoved him into the wall.

"Force of habit!" I yelled back as he shoved me. My head smacked against the bricks behind me. Ow. "Also, you tried to kill me! I take that personally!"

"I only tried to kill you because your father-in-law paid me to," he said, swinging his massive fist at me. I ducked again but stumbled over some garbage and ended up taking a kick to the ribs.

So that was it. Les *had* hired someone to kill me. In the back of my mind, I had known it was a possibility, but it still hurt my feelings that our relationship had deteriorated to the point of murder for hire.

Bob backhanded me across the face. Ow. I would take time to contemplate my hurt feelings later.

"It's never personal when I take a job. But then you went and humiliated me with that spectacle at the school, resisting, throwing me off my game, blocking my talent. Do you know how long it's been since I lost a fight?"

"The spectacle . . . that was witnessed by no one!"

"*I* witnessed it!" he roared, swinging at me. I dropped under the swing but popped back up and gave him a sound uppercut to his stomach. He wheezed a bit but shoved me aside, still venting his frustrated rage. "Do you know what it's like, knowing that I've been beaten by a neophyte? By some suburban soccer mom who drives a minivan?"

"Why does everybody assume I'm a soccer mom? My son has very limited foot-eye coordination!" I exclaimed.

I head-butted him right in the hollow of his throat, making it hard for him to talk for the next few seconds. Then I clapped my hands over his ears, palms cupped. He dropped to his knees while I nursed my aching ribs.

"OK, now it's a little more personal." He groaned, his voice froggish and hoarse. "Look, if this is about my killing him, I did you a favor."

Behind us, I heard the clomping of multiple boots on the ground. Jane and her miniature army had arrived, moving stealthily in formation. Jane did not look pleased with me.

"Apparently, we need to go over the importance of following instructions," Jane said as the UERT guys surrounded Bob, stakes drawn. "Did you learn nothing from my tales of parking-lot fisticuffs gone wrong?"

"He was getting away," I said, shrugging.

Jane glared at Finn. He threw up his hands. "I have a problem childe."

Dick was standing behind Jane, smirking, but said nothing.

"Now," Jane said, clearing her throat and nudging Bob with her boot. "I believe you were doing your bad-guy murder-confession thing? Please continue so we know exactly what to charge you with."

"Do you have any idea what a pain in the ass it was trying to kill you?" Bob seethed at me. "You always had someone around you. If it wasn't one of the damn Council leaders, it was some other vampire or that shifter or your human friends. It was hard enough trying to get you alone. And then, when I finally do, you pull that rake-in-the-face bullshit on me. That's just not sporting. Honestly, a little decorum."

"Yes, how rude of me to defend myself from your attempted murder," I deadpanned.

"I couldn't figure out why you gave me so much trouble. Normally, I just go in for the kill, easy-peasy, in and out. I'm not used to having to fight so hard. I lull my victims into a false sense of security, make them feel like they're sliding into a warm bath with Mum's pot roast in their bellies. They're so relaxed they barely even feel it when I kill them. But you, I couldn't get a fix on you."

"Yeah, well, my power trumps your power, so suck it."

I did feel a little less proud of my above-average fighting skills now, though, knowing that I'd basically taken out Bob's main method of offense.

Bob huffed. "Les Stratton wasn't going to stop at me. When we met up the night of your school carnival, after our little tussle in the yard, he was supposed to make the final payment of what he owed me. He got pissed when I didn't get you on the first try and said he was going to offer the contract to someone else. He would have kept hiring people until he got the result he wanted. Bastard said he wouldn't pay, though our contract clearly stated that he owed me the money even without proof of death," he said. "He said he was going to need the money to hire someone else, since I had trouble closing the deal. It was an insult to my integrity as a professional."

"So instead of killing me, you killed the guy who hurt your feelings and had me framed for his murder," I muttered. "Kind of a dick move."

"And you dominated my NEV meetings with your childish weeping just so you could pump us for information about your target, also a dick move," Jane said, shaking her head.

"Framing you was more of a convenient coincidence than anything else," he said. "I didn't have any interest in what happened to you after the contract was, er, terminated. And I was being genuine at the NEV meetings, by the way. I'm not newly emerged, but those emotions were real. I have a lot of repressed pain."

"If you start to cry, I will smack you in the face with that Dumpster," I told him.

"Oh, the paperwork on this is going to suck so very much." Jane sighed. "OK, Crybaby Bob, by the authority vested in me by the World Council for the Equal Treatment of the Undead, I hereby place you under arrest for murder, conspiracy to commit murder, assault, and generally behaving like a jerk. You don't have the right to remain silent, because I'm going to need you to repeat this story to the human authorities so Libby here isn't charged for your crime. Everything you've said has already been held against you, because you've already spilled your guts."

The UERT guys clapped very sturdy-looking cuffs on him.

"Well, young Libby, I hope you feel better having watched justice being served," Dick drawled.

"Not just yet," I said. Before the UERT guy closest to me could react, I grabbed the extendable stake from his holster and stabbed the blunt end into Bob's chest, right where he'd jabbed me with the rake handle. It wouldn't enter his heart, but, as I knew all too well, it would hurt like a bitch.

Bob howled, only letting up when he realized I had not, in fact, killed him. "You're crazy!"

"OK, now I feel better."

"You can't really do that when we already have him in custody," Jane said.

"Well, then, charge me with abuse of a contract killer."

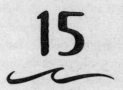

**Parenting is a lot of work, but whether you're living or
dead or somewhere in between, there are plenty of
moments that make all that effort worthwhile.**

—*My Mommy Has Fangs: A Guide to Post-Vampiric Parenting*

I was using my vampire speed to whipstitch my son's
best friend into a sumo costume—which seemed like a
misappropriation of vampire superpowers.

"Mom, hurry up, we're next!" Danny hissed, smoothing his fingers over his upper lip to make sure his adhesive matador's mustache was still in place.

Honestly, this was the strangest school Christmas
play I'd ever seen.

Well, technically, it was a winter *holiday* play, because we weren't allowed to call it a Christmas play.
Even in Half-Moon Hollow, the schools had to give at
least the appearance of separation of church and state.

The theme of the first grade's presentation was
"Peace on Earth," and all of the kids were dressed
like people from other world cultures. Well, stereo-
types of people from other world cultures. Harley

was a sumo wrestler. Danny was a matador. Other cast members included a chubby Italian chef, a mime, and, for some reason, a mummy. I found that offensive on behalf of living Egyptian people, but I also knew that Parker McHune's mother couldn't sew, so wrapping her son in Ace bandages was the best she could do.

I glanced around the painted globe backdrop and spotted Marge. She was smiling to beat the band, anxiously shifting in her seat, trying to get a glimpse of Danny backstage. He wanted his costume to be a surprise for his mamaw, and she could hardly wait to see her tiny bullfighter.

Danny and Marge had been spending more time together after school and had regular sleepovers with all the popcorn and extra-smelly treats he could reasonably consume. I couldn't say there was *no* tension in our relationship now, but Marge was much more respectful of boundaries. When I said no to something, she actually agreed instead of trying to renegotiate. When I asked her to have Danny back home at a certain time, she brought him back at that time. She was his grandmother again, instead of a surrogate mother, and I'd like to think we were both more comfortable with it. I had hope for us both.

In other grandparental news, Max was sitting in the back row, next to Finn, recording the play on a very expensive-looking video camera. I could make out his huge, blinding-white smile even in the darkened auditorium. I was less open to letting Danny spend time with my father unaccompanied, but since Max seemed intent on quality time with both of us, that bothered him not at all. We'd had family movie nights and family park outings, which I would admit were a little strange after dark. But Danny loved having the swings all to himself, and it was . . . nice spending time with Max. He filled in holes in my history I didn't even know existed, telling me stories about my mother, how they met, their courtship. While I didn't quite trust him, I wanted to, and that was progress.

Wade was sitting in the front row, dutifully holding up his cell phone in preparation for Harley to walk out onstage and sing his line from "We Are the World." He caught my eye and winked. I smiled, shaking my head. I finished stitching the torn sleeve of Harley's fat suit and ran the thread across my extended fang, severing it.

"OK, sweetie," I said, straightening the fake topknot on Harley's head. "Go knock 'em dead." I kissed his forehead. He tolerated the kiss in a manly fashion and had the good grace not to wipe it off in front of me.

"Me, too," Danny muttered quietly as Harley waddled out onto the stage. I chuckled and kissed his forehead.

"Go out there and belt out some ridiculously outdated nostalgic tripe."

Danny screwed up his face in confusion. "What?"

"Never mind."

"Emma's mom isn't this weird," he grumbled.

I clucked my tongue, adjusting Danny's matador cape. "Well, sweetheart, your mom's always going to be just a little bit weird compared with the other kids' moms."

"Eh, that's OK," Danny said. "You're pretty cool."

"I love you more than anything," I told him.

"Love you, too, Mom."

I pushed the matador hat over his ears. "You ready for your big moment?"

"Yep."

I watched Danny walk out onstage, sweeping his cape as he sang, "We are the ones who make a brighter day, so let's start giving!" He stood next to Harley, wrapping his arm around his friend's heavily padded shoulders. He was so happy. Happy and safe and secure.

I'd made the right choice, getting turned. If I hadn't taken the sketchy route to immortality, I would have missed this moment, and so many moments to come. All of the trouble I'd had—the heartbreak, the confusion, the murder charges—was worth it.

Out of the corner of my eye, I noticed movement backstage. Jane was lurking in the wings. Considering that she was neither a parent nor a staff member, this was unusual. She waved to me, pressing a finger to her lips. Dick appeared from behind her, waving, along with Andrea.

Chelsea Harbaker, who was watching her child perform from backstage for entirely different reasons, shrank away from Jane and retreated deeper into the shadows. She was having a rough month, having just been ousted as PTA president. After the success of the Pumpkin Patch, Chelsea—flush with new power—had taken to wearing a lapel microphone during PTA meetings. She wanted to be sure that *everybody* could hear *everything* she had to say. And they did. Especially when she neglected to turn off said lapel mic after the November meeting. And went into the teachers' lounge to complain to her cronies about the "hillbilly idiots" she had to deal with in the parent volunteer pool and how she wanted to tell all of them what she thought of their "little brats." And started naming names.

Casey Sparks dove for the amp that was carrying Chelsea's remarks into the meeting room, but Kerrianne grabbed her by the arms and prevented her from turning it off. Casey's rant was delivered at full volume for every member present.

She was Half-Moon Hollow Elementary's first PTA president ever to be impeached. Kerrianne was running to replace her in the emergency election in January.

Seeing Jane, I moved carefully through the veritable maze of stacked cafeteria tables and old play props— backward, because I didn't want to miss a moment of Danny's performance.

"You know you don't actually have to show up at all of the school events now," I told Jane. "I have my bloodthirst well under control."

"We're not here because we don't trust you," Jane whispered. "We're here because we enjoy musical performances by elementary-school children . . . That sounded less creepy in my head."

"I should hope so," Andrea muttered.

"Just tell her the truth," Dick said, rolling his eyes. "We are here on actual Council business."

"Nice shirt, by the way," I told him, nodding toward the T-shirt that read "Don't look *up* for the mistletoe" with an arrow pointing toward his waistband. "Do I have to remind you that you are at an elementary school?"

"I didn't know we were going to an elementary school when I left the house," he grumbled.

I frowned, shaking my head. "Still."

"So I can't help but notice that Finn is sitting in the audience, with your dad, which is sort of weird," Andrea noted, nodding toward the vampire in question.

I shushed her. "Yes, Finn is here as a friend," I told her. "We're trying this new thing where we spend time together, and we're cordial, but we don't make out. Considering that my dad is with us most of that time, it's working out better than I expected."

"And Finn's OK with this?"

"Well, he's not thrilled, but he's not pouting about it, which I appreciate," I said.

"But I want you and Finn to be together." Andrea groaned. "He's all scheme-y and redeemable. Like Loki but with better clothes."

"Your fangirl shipping issues are not my problem."

"But what about Finn's daywalking tendencies?" Jane asked.

"Actually, Gigi's boyfriend, Nik, thinks he might be able to help him with that," I said. "Some of the post-curse techniques he's learning specifically target keeping control of your emotional head space. It's been very helpful for him."

Jane sighed. "Well, in other news . . ." she said, glaring at Andrea. "The news we actually came to deliver is that you have been awarded a substantial reward for aiding in the capture of one of the Council's most-wanted criminals."

With a flourish, Dick handed me a slender envelope marked with the Council's insignia.

"Really?"

"It turns out that Crybaby Bob was a hit man of some repute," Jane said. "And while the Council generally tolerates murder, it finds murder for hire distasteful. Particularly when it causes trouble between the human and vampire authorities. Bob has been on the Council radar for the past ten years. He changed his appearance frequently to put us off. We were looking for someone with a dirty-blond bowl cut and a goatee, which, honestly, should have tipped us off. What sort of vampire has a bowl cut? The international office was very pleased to have him off the streets. And because you did technically defeat him in battle, they added a little something extra to your check. Like a tip that says, 'Thank you for prompt and polite service in catching our pesky murderer.'"

"I thought the 'defeat in battle' clause only came into play in cases where one vampire kills another," I said as I opened the envelope.

"They were that happy to have Bob in custody," Jane said.

I damn near dropped the slim slip of paper when I saw all of the zeros. "This is the price on Bob's head?"

"Plus tip," Jane reminded me.

"That's a heck of a tip," I marveled. "This is . . . this is insane. I didn't know you could fit that many digits in an amount box."

"I had to have the accounting department process it twice," Dick said with a hint of childlike glee.

I just stared at the check. I didn't have to worry about Danny's college tuition. I could buy us the biggest house in Half-Moon Hollow. I didn't have to worry about depending on anyone. I was completely independent. I didn't have to worry about money. And thanks to the delicate peace I'd started with Marge, the specter of my in-laws and their threat to custody of my son was gone. And I didn't have to worry about my position in the community, because my community had changed.

It was going to be a merry freaking Christmas indeed.

Dick bussed my cheek. "Enjoy your spoils of war, sweetie."

"See you at Christmas dinner at my house?" Jane asked.

"Danny can't wait," I said.

Grinning, I peeked around the backdrop, watching Danny take his big bow. I clapped loudly, whistling through my teeth. In the back of the auditorium, I saw Finn sitting in the last row. He saw me and grinned, pointing to Max's camera. *Got it*, he mouthed.

I waved back and whispered, "Thanks."

A good bullfighter didn't back down from aggressive livestock or cheek kisses. Especially when those kisses came from his mamaw.

"You were such a good matador!" Marge cooed, smooching Danny's cheeks. He was a man about it and accepted it without wiping them off.

"Thanks, Mamaw," he said, holding up his accessories. "Did you see my cape?"

"I did," Marge said, nodding. "Mom did a wonderful job sewing it for you."

"Thanks."

"My sister is having Christmas Eve dinner at her house, and she would love it if you would both be able to join us," Marge said.

"Christmas isn't at your house this year?"

"I'm not up for hosting this year. I'm actually looking forward to being a guest for once," Marge said.

I smiled at her, a little sad. I'd put a lot of thought into our holiday schedule this year. I didn't want Marge to be alone for her first Les-less Christmas season. But I wanted to try to make Danny's holiday as normal as possible. He'd agreed readily to waking up in the wee hours so we could have Christmas morning early enough for me. (Honestly, it was only an adjustment of an hour or so from his normal Christmas-morning wake-up call.)

"Actually, while I'm sure Danny would enjoy it, I don't think Christmas dinner would work for me, what with the smells of the food," I said. The *also, your relatives drive me insane* was silent but implied. "But we've been thinking about Christmas, and we were wondering, what would you think of coming over first thing Christmas morning, after I go to sleep for the day, so you can have all day with him and his new toys?"

"Yes!" Danny crowed. "Santa's going to bring me all kinds of toys, Mamaw. A castle with real shooting cannons and a remote-controlled fire truck with a real siren!"

"Sirens *and* cannons, hmm?" Marge asked.

I grinned and nodded. "Lots of battery-powered noise."

"This is payback for that percussion set we got him when he was three, isn't it?"

"A little bit," I agreed.

"It's going to be the best Christmas ever!" Danny cried, raising his hands and hopping up and down.

"You say that every year," Marge reminded him.

"And I'm always right!"

"Hey, Danny!" Harley came barreling toward us, practically clotheslining my son.

Marge's eyes went wide as the boys struggled to right themselves, hindered by their costumes. Wade and I had agreed to take the sumo and the matador out for cheeseburgers and milkshakes at the Coffee Spot. And we'd agreed to let them wear their costumes, because we didn't get nearly enough stares when we went out together.

Wade was shrugging into his coat, watching the kids with amusement. "Hi, Mrs. Stratton."

"Wade," Marge said, clearing her throat. "Harley, you did a lovely job playing a sumo wrestler."

"Thank you!" Harley exclaimed. "We're gonna go get milkshakes. Except for Miss Libby, because eating people food makes her throw up. Like buckets and buckets of throw-up."

"Thanks for the visual, sweetie," I said, patting his sumo topknot.

"Buckets," Harley said again.

Wade grinned and gave me a quick kiss on the cheek.

I caught the slightest frown flitting across Marge's features, but she was graceful enough to school her face into a neutral expression. "Thanks for the sumo save," Wade said. "I have a lot of skills, but sewing my kid into a fat suit isn't one of them."

"It's a limited area of expertise," I said, kissing him back.

"Mamaw, are you going to come with us for milkshakes?" Danny asked. "You can have Mom's burger, since she won't eat it."

Marge threw me an uncomfortable glance. "Oh, well, I'm sure your parents didn't plan on me—"

"Actually, we'd really love it if you came with us," I told her. "Danny's told Harley all about you."

"I have questions," Harley told her.

"Well, that's very sweet of you. In that case, I accept," Marge said, taking both boys' hands.

"Danny, I can't remember a more riveting rendition of a Lionel Ritchie song." I turned to find Max and Finn standing behind us. Max was grinning full-bore and held out his hand for a big high five from his grandson. Finn was smiling but somehow also staring Wade down, as if he was calculating the best way to get rid of his body without tipping off the Council. And while Wade's grip around my waist tightened slightly, his expression didn't change.

This was awkward.

"Er, Wade Tucker, this is my sire, Finn Palmeroy. Finn, this is Wade. And my, uh, Danny's grandmother, Marge Stratton. Marge, this is Finn Palmeroy and my father, uh, Max Kitteridge."

"Your father?" Marge exclaimed. "I didn't know you knew who your—" She stopped herself and cleared her throat. "I didn't know you'd met your father, Libby."

"Charmed," Max said, raising her hand gently and kissing her knuckles. I lifted an eyebrow at the gesture and prayed Max was just trying to be polite. But he winked at her, so . . . that was not making me comfortable.

"Yeah, isn't it cool, Mamaw?" Danny chirped. "I have a vampire mom *and* a vampire grandpa."

"Well, that certainly explains why you're so young," Marge said.

"Age is just a number, Marge," Max said smoothly. "Or could I call you Marjorie? You don't strike me as a Marge."

Marge tittered. I'd never heard someone titter, but she did it, brushing her fingers through her hair. And Max, well, he didn't look insincere in the admiring stare he was giving her. I glanced back and forth between the two of them with growing alarm while Finn and Wade seemed to be locked in a death-grip handshake-athon.

"Yes, I've heard so much about you," Finn purred, his knuckles tightening around Wade's.

"Really?" Wade asked through gritted teeth. "Because Libby hasn't mentioned *you* all that much."

And yet more awkward.

And it was always going to be this way, because I'd chosen Wade. Finn was always going to be a little bit tense, but he would have to adjust. And Wade . . . well, Wade seemed to be holding his own, because based on his descriptions of some of his crazy redneck relatives, I could see how Finn wouldn't seem so threatening. I cleared my throat and caught Finn's eye, giving their clenched hands a pointed look. He huffed, but he loosened his grip on Wade's hand. Wade tried—quite manfully—to cover up the fact that he was wringing the blood back into his fingers.

"Well, boys, I don't think I've ever seen better theater," Finn said, dropping to the boys' level to give them both high fives. "Moving and heartfelt."

Danny hooted. "You're so weird, Mr. Finn."

"Says the guy wearing a matador costume in western Kentucky," Finn said, tickling Danny's sides. Danny giggled while Harley retreated to Wade's side.

"And you still have a bad-guy beard, so there," Danny squealed.

I smiled at Finn and Max, who was still giving Marge what I can only describe as middle-aged vampire Blue Steel. "We're going to the Coffee Spot for milkshakes and burgers. The diner also happens to stock Faux Type O. Would you like to join us?"

"Yes," Max said immediately.

Finn nodded. "I would enjoy that."

And Marge was staring at Max. Hard.

Oh, boy.

"OK, we'll meet you there," I told Marge. "Could you get us a table? A *big* table? It's going to take us a while to load the sumo into my van."

"We'll meet you there," Finn said, winking at me before walking off.

"Can I walk you to your car, Marjorie?" Max asked, offering her his arm.

"Oh, well, thank you," she said, fluffing her hair again.

I stared at the unlikely pair crossing the parking lot. Nothing good came out of Half-Moon Hollow parking lots.

I took a deep, unnecessary breath. I would find the positive in this. I had friends. Scratch that. I had *family*, the large extended family I never thought I needed growing up. People who loved me for me, not for what I could do for them or what I represented but for me. Now I just had to figure out how to blend them with the people I was actually related to.

Wade sidled up to me and wrapped his arm around my shoulder. In the distance, I could see Danny shoving Harley into my van, throwing his whole weight against the back of his friend's fat suit. "So your dad is flirting with Marge. I didn't see that comin'."

"No one could have seen that coming," I told him, shaking my head.

"That is not somethin' you can control," he reminded me.

"I wasn't going to try to control it," I told him. "I was going to see if *Jane* could control it."

"Yeah, because that's normal."

I tilted my head as Danny took a running start at shoving Harley into the van. "Should we really be debating normal when my son is using football techniques to shove your son's inflatable body into my minivan?"

"Probably not," he admitted. "But I like our not normal." He snorted, kissing my temple.

With a smile, I leaned into him. "I like it, too."

Keep reading for a peek at the next hilarious
Half-Moon Hollow romance from

MOLLY HARPER

Where the Wild Things Bite

Coming Summer 2016 from Pocket Books!

1

Before you find yourself stranded in the woods with a cranky apex predator, ask yourself—do I really *want* to go on a camping trip with a vampire?

—*Outdoor Underworld: A Survival Guide*
for Camping with the Undead

Some evil transportation-hating monster had devoured my plane.

And in its place, the monster had left behind a little bite-sized plane crumb.

I stood on the tarmac of the Louisville airport, staring in horror at the plane crumb as my brown leather carry-on bag dangled from my fingers. This was not a momentous beginning to my trip to Half-Moon Hollow.

Despite the fact that I could see crowds of people milling around the airport through the windows, I felt oddly alone, vulnerable. A handful of planes were parked at nearby gates, but there were no luggage handlers, no flight staff. I'd never boarded a plane from the tarmac before, and the short, rickety mobile staircase being pushed up against the side of the plane like a ladder used for gutter-cleaning didn't make me feel more confident in the climb.

When I'd booked my flight to westernmost Kentucky, I knew small planes were the only models capable of flying into Half-Moon Hollow's one-gate airport. But I'd thought the plane would at least seat thirty or so people. The vessel in front of me would maybe seat a baker's dozen, if someone sat on the pilot's lap. There were only three rows of windows besides the windshield, for God's sake.

"This is the right plane, in case you're wondering," said a gruff voice that was accompanied by a considerable whiff of wet tobacco.

I turned to find a florid, heavyset man in a pilot's uniform standing behind me. His wavy black hair was counterbalanced by a pitted sallow complexion and under-eye bags so heavy they should have been stored on the nearby luggage cart. A lifetime of drinking had thickened his features and left a network of tiny broken capillaries across his broad nose. Given the sweat stains on his uniform, I might have doubted his current sobriety, but I supposed it took considerable motor control to keep that large unlit cigar clamped between his teeth. His name tag read "Ernie."

"That is not a plane," I told Ernie. "That is what happens when planes have babies with go-carts."

Snorting, he pushed past me toward the plane, his shoulder bumping into mine. The olfactory combination of old sweat and wet cigar made me take a step back from him.

"Well, if you don't want to fly, there's always a rental car," the pilot snarked, climbing the stairs into the plane. "It's about a four-hour drive, until you hit the gravel roads."

I frowned at Ernie the Pilot's broad back. If there was anything I hated more than flying, it was driving alone at night on unfamiliar, treacherous roads. Besides, there were too many things that could happen to the package on a car ride between here and the Hollow. I could spill coffee on it while trying to stay awake. It could be stolen while I was stopped at a gas station. A window malfunction could result in the package being sucked out of the car on the highway. I needed to get it back to Jane as soon as humanly (or vampire-ly) possible. So driving was a nonstarter.

I gritted my teeth and breathed deeply through my nose, watching the way the sickly fluorescent outdoor lights played on the dimpled metal of the wings. The tiny, tiny wings.

The pilot stuck his head out of the plane door. "Plane's not gonna get any bigger," he growled at me around the cigar.

"Good point," I muttered as I took the metal stairs. "I really hope that's not some sort of euphemism, Mr. Creepy Late-Night Pilot."

Even though my cargo was completely legal, I still felt the need to look over my shoulder as I boarded. My superspy skills were supremely lacking. It was bad enough, the looks that security gave me as I visibly twitched when sending my bag through the X-ray machine. But I'd never hand-delivered an item to a customer before, especially an item of such high value. My bonding and insurance couldn't possibly cover an item that was considered priceless to the supernatural community at large. I just wanted to get it out of my hands and into those of my client, Jane Jameson-Nightengale, as quickly as possible.

The plane was not at all TARDIS-like. It was not bigger on the inside. And besides Ernie the Portly Pilot, it was completely empty. This was, after all, the last flight from Louisville to Half-Moon Hollow for the night, which made it a risky proposition, layover-wise. From what Jane told me, most Hollow residents didn't want to risk being stuck overnight in Louisville, so they planned their connections earlier in the day. But I'd had a client meeting that kept me in Atlanta until the last minute and had booked a late flight. It worked better for me to land late anyway, since Jane, an oddly informal vampire who insisted on a first-name basis, would be picking me up from the airport. Pre-sundown pickup times didn't work for her.

Though minuscule, the interior of the plane was comfortable enough, with its oatmeal-colored plastic walls, the stale, recently disinfected smell, and its closely arranged seats. I clearly had my choice of spots, but I took the time to find my assigned seat in the second row. I declined putting my carry-on bag in the tiny storage compartment in the front of the plane. I was not comfortable with the idea of not being able to see my bag at all times. I turned, checking the distance from my seat to the door-slash-emergency-exit. Studies showed that passengers were five times more likely to survive a crash if they sat close to the emergency exits.

I knew I was being silly. The flight would only take an hour or so. What were the chances of the plane crashing when it was only in the air for sixty minutes?

I was thankful that my brain had not absorbed and catalogued that particular bit of information. Just then, the pilot belched loudly.

OK, maybe my chances of crashing were better than average if this guy was at the controls.

And for some reason, as I boarded, the cruel, ironic bits of my brain were running through the list of famous people who had died in small plane crashes. Ritchie Valens, John Denver, Aaliyah.

My brain could be a real jerk when it was under stress.

I flopped my head forward, smacking my forehead against the seat in front of me. I was too tired for this. I'd spent almost two hours in Atlanta traffic just to get to the airport in time for the flight to Louisville. I'd braved lengthy and multistepped security checks. I missed my cozy little restored home in Dahlonega. I missed my home office and my thinking couch and my shelves of carefully preserved first-edition books. I promised myself that when I survived this trip, I would reward myself by retreating to my apartment for a week, bingeing on delivered Thai food and Netflix.

I heard footsteps on the metal ladder but did not move my head from the seat back. I heard whoever it was move down the aisle and slide into the row of seats across from me.

"Fear of flying?"

I ceased my forehead abuse long enough to look up at him. The other passenger smiled and quirked his eyebrows, the sort of "we're in this together for the next hour or so, so we might as well be polite" gesture most people appreciated in a fellow traveler.

I, on the other hand, drew back in my seat. Oh, he was handsome, in that polished, self-aware manner that made women either melt in their seats or shrink into themselves in immediate distrust. Unfortunately for him, I fell into the second category.

I did not dissolve at the sight of his high cheekbones. I didn't coo over his dark chocolate eyes or the dark goatee that defined his wide, sensual mouth. The collar of his blue V-neck T-shirt showed a downright lickable collarbone and the beginnings of well-defined pectoral muscles, and I did not liquefy. In fact, my initial reaction was to trust him far less than I trusted Ernie. So I might have been a bit more snappish than polite when I responded, "No, fear of awkward conversations before crashing."

But it seemed my curt tone only made him grin. It was a sincere grin, without an ounce of condescension, which made him even more handsome. Some tiny nerve inside of me twinged, and I wished, just for once, that I could be the kind of woman who could start a conversation with a handsome stranger, approach some new experience—hell, try a new brand of detergent—without analyzing all of the possible ways it could go wrong.

While my mother had made it clear on more than one occasion that I was not "conventionally pretty," I knew I wasn't completely unfortunate-looking. My DNA had provided me with my father's fine-boned features and my mother's wide, full lips, though mine weren't twisted into unhappy lines as often as hers were. My skin was clear and soft with warm peach undertones. My eyes were large, the amber color of old whiskey, with a slight, undeserved mischievous tilt. Taken all together, my slightly mismatched features made for a pleasant face. And yet, thanks to my wounded ego, men like this, completely at ease with themselves, sent me into a spiraling tizzy.

The handsome man's smooth voice interrupted my mental self-flagellation yet again. "It's too bad the flight is so short. They don't even have a beverage service. You might have been able to take the edge off."

"I'm not much of a drinker," I told him, giving him a quick, jerky smile that felt more like a cheek tremor than an expression. I nodded my head toward the back of the plane. "Besides, where would they put the beverage cart?"

"Oh, well, maybe I'll be able to distract you," he offered, the corner of his mouth lifting again.

The intimate way he'd said it, the way he was smiling at me, eyes lingering on my jean-clad legs, sent a little shiver down my spine, despite the simultaneous warning Klaxons sounding in my head.

"And how are you going to do that?" I asked him, holding up my well-worn paperback. "You've got some very serious competition."

Thank you, conversational gods, for not letting the phrase "stiff competition" leave my lips.

"Oh, I'm sure I could come up with a way to entertain you."

And his smile was so full of naughty promise that the only response I could come up with was "Guh."

The conversational gods had abandoned me more quickly than I had hoped.

I blushed to the tips of my ears, but he seemed

amused by it, so maybe a red face was considered charming on the planet of the narrow-torsoed.

Given that I was from a very different planet—home of the ladies built like lanky twelve-year-old boys—I doubted very much that our definitions of "fun" matched up. He looked like the sort of guy for whom bottle service was invented. My idea of a good time was a movie marathon with my friend and assistant, Rachel, featuring at least five different actors playing Sherlock Holmes, and then a debate over who did the best job.

That's right. Anna Whitfield, one-woman party.

"Do you consider Dante's *Inferno* a little light travel reading?"

"It's an old favorite," I said.

"Well, you've successfully intimidated me, so congratulations."

I laughed, but before I could answer, the door slammed behind us and the plane started to taxi. A small overhead speaker began to play pre-recorded safety instructions and I relaxed back into the seat. I pulled the safety instruction card from the seat pocket in front of me and began reading along.

"Really?" the stranger asked. I nodded without looking at him, checking the emergency exit door for opening instructions. It looked like a case of "Turn the big red handle upward and left while trying to contain your terror." Excellent.

I followed along, checking the location of the air masks (there weren't any) and running lights toward the emergency exit (also no). They really needed to make safety cards specific to tiny planes.

"You have flown before, yes?" the stranger asked.

Although he was distressingly attractive, I ignored him. I would not die in a fiery plane crash because I had neglected the safety card for a pair of beautiful blue eyes. I tucked it away in the seat pouch in front of me, tightened my seatbelt, and clenched my eyes shut while the plane struggled to lift off from the runway. I pressed my head back against the seat rest, as if holding a rigid posture would somehow get the plane in the air safely.

I prayed the only way I knew how, visualizing the exact opposite of all the horrible potential outcomes running through my head. I pictured the plane lifting off, maintaining a nice straight path through the air, and landing in Half-Moon Hollow with my suitcase intact. Oh, and I pictured the antianxiety meds releasing into my system exactly as I'd timed them, so I wouldn't climb the walls of the plane from the moment it took off.

And when I opened my eyes, my purse was open on my lap and my hands were swimming through the contents, searching for the package I was bringing to Jane. Across the aisle, the stranger's head was bent over a magazine. I felt faint, as if I were falling inside of myself, separated from my own body as my arm started to lift. I could see myself yanking the package out of my purse, as if I were watching it happen on a movie screen.

This was wrong. What was I doing? I hadn't pulled the package from my bag since getting through security; why would I show it to this person I barely knew?

As suddenly as it began, the spell was over and I

practically sagged against my seat. My long, sweater-clad arm was still raised and my hand still stretched as I shook off the strange dizzy sensation. I'd never felt anything like that before. Was I coming down with something? Had I had some sort of stroke? I didn't feel tingling or numbness in my extremities. I wasn't confused, beyond wondering what the hell had just happened to me. Maybe it was an inner ear problem? Or the veggie wrap I'd eaten at the airport sandwich shop? I should have known better than to trust airport cuisine. I probably had some sort of dirt-borne E. coli from unwashed lettuce.

I glanced across the aisle to the stranger, still poring through his magazine, completely unaware of my inner turmoil. I sighed. I was a very special sort of weird. I turned my attention back to my book. While the takeoff was fairly smooth, the rocking of the plane and the dark, quiet space actually made me a little dizzy again, and I wondered if I really was coming down with some strain of E. coli that affected the inner ear. Stupid airport lettuce.

With the stranger distracted by magazine articles about abdominal workouts that would change his life, I traveled through Dante's rings of hell with the aid of the weak overhead light. After twenty minutes or so, I got tired of the weird, dizzy sensation intermittently flashing through my head and set my book aside.

"Not quite the beach-read romp you were promised?" the stranger asked.

I looked up to find him staring at me again, intently, on the border of attempted smoldering. Frankly, I found this to be unnerving. Either the stranger was the world's chattiest traveler, or he was one of those skeevy men you saw on *Dateline* who targeted women who travel alone and tried to lure them into a human trafficking scheme. Forgetting every lesson my mother had ever drilled into my head about good manners, I gave him my full-on "disapproving professor" face I'd learned as a teaching assistant.

He was not fazed.

He did, however, get distracted by a child's truck, a toy left over from a previous flight, rolling down the aisle toward the cockpit. The plane's nose seemed to be tipping downward. I checked my watch. We were only twenty-five minutes into the flight, which was way too early to be starting our descent into the Hollow. I exchanged a glance with my handsome seatmate, who was frowning. Hard.

A metallic crunching noise sounded from the front of the plane, catching our attention. After flipping a few switches and hitting some buttons, Ernie the Pilot yanked what looked like an important lever from the control panel and stuck it in his shirt pocket. And then he took a large hard plastic mallet from his laptop bag and began swinging it wildly at the panel. He got up from his seat, snagging what looked like a backpack from the copilot's chair. The stranger and I sat completely still as the pilot eyed him warily.

"What the hell are you doing?" I demanded as the pilot slipped the backpack on and clipped the straps over his thick middle. Some instinct had me reaching for the strap of my tote bag, winding it around my wrist. The plane continued to descend at a smooth, steady pace. "Get back to the controls!"

"I don't want to hurt you. I just want the package you're carrying. I know it's not in your suitcase; I checked at the baggage screening," Ernie told me, raising his hands and reaching toward my lap. The invasion of space had me grabbing at my bag to feel for the little canister of pepper spray I usually kept clipped to the strap. Of course, that little canister was not currently clipped in place because that's the sort of chemical agent the FAA frowns on bringing through security. If I got through this, I was going to write them a long letter.

I clutched the bag to my chest. Why was Ernie doing this? How did he know what I had in my bag? Hell, how did he manage to get into my suitcase? Did someone send him after me? And what sort of person could bribe a pilot to commandeer a (admittedly underpopulated) commercial flight?

Another wave of dizziness hit me, full force this time, and I had to fight to keep my attention on my mind-numbing terror. This was it. This was the worst-case scenario. The pilot was abandoning the airplane while trying to mug me. I ran through all of the transportation studies I'd read on flight safety and crisis management to try to come up with some sort of solution to this problem . . . and nothing. I had nothing. None of them covered purse-snatching, plane-jacking pilots.

Shrugging off the heavy, sleepy weight that dragged at the corners of my brain, I took a deep breath. OK. I would handle this one problem at a time.

Problem one, no one was flying the plane. And Ernie—who I was absolutely correct in not trusting, yay for me—appeared to have broken off something important from the control panel, which probably rendered the plane unflyable. So, I could draw the conclusion that Ernie was a horrible person and that he had no plans to land the plane. So I seemed to be screwed on that front.

Problem two, Ernie was trying to snatch my bag. All of the personal safety guides I'd read said you should hand over your purse if you're being mugged. Nothing in your wallet could be worth dying for. It would be easier just to hand him my bag. *I might as well let him have it*, a soft voice that didn't sound entirely like mine whispered inside my head. *It isn't worth dying for.*

I could feel my arms lifting, my hands unwinding the strap from my wrist. Suddenly, a loud, shrill warning beep sounded from the cockpit. I whipped my head toward it just as the plane dropped suddenly, throwing me against the seat in front of me. I hissed as Ernie bent and tried to yank the bag away, dragging my strap-ringed arm with him.

I was going to die. Whether I handed over the bag or not, the plane was going to crash with me on it.

A heretofore unknown spark of anger fired in my belly. I'd been entrusted to take care of Jane Jameson's package. Jane was a high-ranking member of the local World Council for the Equal Treatment of the Undead. She'd trusted me with Council business. She expected me to take care of the package for her, to deliver it safely. She was paying me a handsome sum to do so. And this pilot was trying to take it from me, to kill me for it. He'd put me in a terrifying, no-win situation to intimidate me into handing it over.

This was *bullshit*.

That little spark burned into a full-blown stubborn flame and I wrapped the leather bag strap around my wrist even tighter.

I wasn't going to give it up. I couldn't do anything about the plane crashing, but I could keep Jane's package from falling into clearly unscrupulous hands. As much as we both loved books, I was sure Jane would rather see it destroyed than dropped in the hands of people willing to kill for it.